P

HOW TO

'A clever debut from Joanna Jenkins who uses her experience as a lawyer to create a powerful mystery that looks at the dark side of the legal profession. Shocking and highly addictive, this is a very impressive novel from a talented new author.' *Canberra Weekly*

'A cracker of a mystery where every character has motive, means and opportunity and the victim is so loathsome that your sympathies lie with the suspects at almost every turn. Joanna Jenkins has penned a truly captivating debut that will grab you by the heartstrings and play you like a harp! Rich with relatable characters, ethical dilemmas and soul-searching truths about the human condition—*How to Kill a Client* should be top of the pile for holiday reading!' Nina Campbell, author of *Daughters of Eve*

'I read this in two sittings! Totally unputdownable tale by Joanna Jenkins. Her background in big law firms is put to deft use as she guides us effortlessly through the intense legal drama where not only don't the big men win, sometimes, they die. Love the strong female characters who have more than a few tricks up their sleeves.' Vikki Petraitis, author of *The Unbelieved*

'Stylishly written, and keeps you gripped—as well as full of outrage—to the end. The perfect tonic for anyone who has had a difficult client.' Richard Beasley SC

'A complex and compelling corporate noir full of intrigue, betrayals and explosive revelations, *How to Kill a Client* masterfully smashes through the façade of Big Law in the guise of a murder mystery. With its delightfully sinister Agatha Christie-esque style . . . the untimely death, a large cast of possible suspects, a multitude of motives, and, best of all, a strong female sleuth . . . this is a novel that hums with energy, delivers a tight storyline, and keeps you guessing right to the final pages.' Lyn Yeowart, author of *The Silent Listener*

'Nobody knows how to play dirty like a lawyer; Joanna Jenkins gives John Grisham a run for his money.' Candice Fox, author of *The Chase*

'A fabulous page turner . . . A terrifically written novel about vengeance, dominance and politics in a major law firm. I am anxiously looking forward to Jenkins' next book.' *Sydney Arts Guide*

'Jenkins delivers a brilliant debut novel which satisfies on many levels.' *Country Style Magazine*

'*How to Kill a Client* combines deft characterisation and symbolism with a long hard look at law firm partnerships at their most challenging . . . All readers of *How to Kill a Client* will probably be looking forward eagerly to Jenkins' next novel.' *Law Society Journal*

'Set in the cold atmosphere of the corporate world and the competitive homes of the rich, *How to Kill a Client* skewers the greed, misogyny and malfeasance in the corner offices of capitalism in a satisfying and twisting thriller.' *Books + Publishing*

'Jenkins' own experience in a Brisbane office of Big Law infuses the thrilling whodunnit with close-to-the-bone believability . . . Eminently readable, *How to Kill a Client* is an uncomfortable depiction of Big Law (minus the murder, of course). A strong debut, and hopefully more to come.' *The Justinian*

Joanna Jenkins grew up on a small farm in country Queensland. After graduating from the University of Queensland with degrees in English Literature and Law, she practised as a solicitor, including for many years as a partner of an international law firm. She now writes full-time. Married with three sons, Joanna lives in Brisbane. Her debut novel, *How to Kill a Client,* was published in 2023. *The Bluff* is her second novel.

THE BLUFF

JOANNA JENKINS

ALLEN&UNWIN
SYDNEY • MELBOURNE • AUCKLAND • LONDON

First published in 2025

Allen & Unwin
Cammeraygal Country
83 Alexander Street
Crows Nest NSW 2065
Australia
Phone: (61 2) 8425 0100
Email: info@allenandunwin.com
Web: www.allenandunwin.com

Allen & Unwin acknowledges the Traditional Owners of the Country on which we live and work. We pay our respects to all Aboriginal and Torres Strait Islander Elders, past and present.

NATIONAL LIBRARY OF AUSTRALIA
A catalogue record for this book is available from the National Library of Australia

ISBN 978 1 76147 064 6

Set in 13/16.5 pt Adobe Jenson Pro by Bookhouse, Sydney
Printed and bound in Australia by the Opus Group

10 9 8 7 6 5 4 3 2 1

FSC www.fsc.org MIX Paper | Supporting responsible forestry FSC® C001695

The paper in this book is FSC® certified. FSC® promotes environmentally responsible, socially beneficial and economically viable management of the world's forests.

For Andrew and Judith

AUTHOR'S NOTE

THIS BOOK WAS WRITTEN ON MEANJIN. I PAY MY RESPECTS TO THE traditional custodians of this land, the Yuggera and Turrbal people.

I made Myddle up, not just its name and its inhabitants but also its geography. The rough setting is the exquisite hinterland of the mid-north and north coast of New South Wales. I also pay my respects to the custodians of that area, the Gumbaynggirr, Bundgalung and Yaegl people.

The characters are fictitious. Similar events in a particular scene may have happened, but to different people, and in different circumstances. For example, my mother cleared a shelf once in a pharmacy, but she was holding a two-year-old at the time, was in the throes of grief from the death of my brother, and—despite her sometimes problematic behaviour—was very happily married to my father. So if you think you recognise in this book an event or a facet of a person, you can't extrapolate from that to think I'm describing a real person. Because I'm not.

This book includes some racist dialogue and depiction of sexual assault.

1

BEA

A Wednesday night in June

THE NIGHT'S A THICK BLACK; THE MOON A SLIVER OF SILVER.

Bea Baulderstone moves away from the house, across the lawn, her eyes adjusting to the dark. The roar of the football crowd from the TV fades, subsumed by the rustles and hoots of the bush. She heads for the shed, its hulk silhouetted against the Milky Way.

A wet nose on the back of her knee. She stops to pat the kelpie on the head. 'Go back, Bryan,' she whispers. 'Back to the house. I'll be okay.' He sits. When she moves again, he stays with her.

The shed smells of hay and diesel. She feels her way along the wall beside the ute, past the saddles and bridles hanging over rails.

Well inside now, it should be safe to turn on her phone light for a moment. She needs it to choose a bike. Mountain bike. Heavy but sturdy.

Phone light off, she walks the bike out of the shed.

That's right. They keep a rifle in a locked box on the back of the ute. Better she has it than them.

She lays the bike on the gravel farm track, carefully so there's no clatter, opens the driver's door, feels in the centre console, pulls out some keys. Phone torch back on, the third key opens the metal gun box behind the cabin.

Is the rifle loaded? Probably not. She feels around and finds the bullet box, unlocks it, puts some in her pocket, and slings the rifle over her shoulder.

A yell and a roar of 'Yesss!' from the house. The Blues must have scored a try. Great. They'll be watching the replays for a good five minutes and yelling at the TV and the video ref. If she makes some noise as she rides past, they won't hear her.

She mounts the bike and takes off with a wobble, past the LandCruiser parked outside the house. In the dark, she can just make out the difference between the grass and the track. Bryan trots beside her.

At this pace, the cattle grid at the fence by the road is at least five minutes away. Downhill, so she doesn't have to pedal much.

Dark shapes mill ahead on the track. Are they cows or bulls? The bike won't be fast enough to outrun a pissed-off bull. She calls out, as loud as she dares, 'Scat.'

With an ungainly bound and a low moo, they jump out of the way. Cows.

A shout from the verandah, 'Bea, Bea, where are you?'

She pedals, her breath loud and uneven.

A roar as a four-wheel-drive diesel starts and heads down the track towards her. The paddock lights up. Spotlights, one on each side of the vehicle.

The cattle grid is only a few metres ahead. She stands on the pedals as the vibrations reverberate through her, then brakes to a stop on the other side, dumps the bike in the ditch, and lies down in the long grass. The rifle is hard against her hip. She unstraps it, places it beside her, puts her arm over Bryan who has lain, tensed, against her other side and whispers, 'Shhh'.

The vehicle drives past slowly, blaring light.

She stays still, in case they turn back.

Her hands shake as she yanks her phone from her pocket so hard it flies from her grasp before she can check whether the bars on the phone indicate she has coverage.

She spots it in the grass, the screen lit, Bryan's red face and tongue illuminated as he looks to her for reassurance.

The car approaches again, slow, spotlights shining over the side of the road.

2

RUTH

June, the following Monday

RUTH WAS JIGGLING A TEABAG IN A CHIPPED MUG IN THE LINO- AND laminex-encrusted space that passed for a kitchen when the bell jangled on the old cedar door. Someone had just entered the office from Myddle's main street.

She ran her fingers through her hair. She was still getting used to the wavy layers after years of a sharply delineated bob. Shaggy dog. That's how she felt, too: like an unkempt dog looking for a home.

Deb on reception didn't stop the person. Whoever it was would be in front of Ruth in a moment, unvetted. Could be anyone. Wanting anything. With some wacky idea of what lawyers do. Ruth had only been filling in for the local lawyer for two months but she'd already refused some weird requests (kidnap a labrador from an ex-spouse; clean out a hoarder's home).

She made a dash for her office so she could shut the door before they saw her.

Too late. In the hall, Ruth found a woman, wispy, like a frayed scrap of beige cotton.

The woman looked familiar. Ruth struggled to place her.

'Can I help you?' she said.

'I'm here to report a missing person.'

'Who's missing?' said Ruth.

'My daughter.'

'I'm so sorry to hear that.' Ruth softened her tone. 'But you should go to the police.'

'I've tried that,' the woman snapped. 'He won't listen.'

'How old is your daughter?' Ruth asked.

'Seventeen.'

Ruth had met a lot of people since she'd first arrived in Myddle six months ago and their faces had blurred together in her mind: a conga line of fleeting acquaintances. She held out her hand. 'Sorry. I should have introduced myself. I'm Ruth Dawson. I've taken over Harry Dunstan's office while he's on sabbatical.'

'Victoria,' said the woman, proffering limp fingers. Her accent jarred as it didn't correlate with the shabby person in front of Ruth. It was affluent, redolent of black-tie dinners in designer frocks. This was rural Myddle—a tiny town in the verdant hinterland of the Northern Rivers of New South Wales, not Sydney's Bellevue Hill.

'And your daughter's name?' Ruth asked.

It was a long, romantic name: the first syllables a languorous 'Bayart'; the second a clipped 'riss'.

'Beatrice?' Not a name Ruth had heard in Myddle. 'How were you thinking I could help?' Ruth asked. She kept her voice distant, to repel any idea that she was capable of conducting a search for a missing girl.

'You're a lawyer. You could talk to the police about their obligations.'

'Did they say why they wouldn't look for her?'

'He thinks she's run away from me,' Victoria said.

'How long has she been gone?'

'I last saw her on Wednesday morning.'

Today was Monday. So five days.

A seventeen-year-old girl had been gone for nearly a week and the police were doing nothing about it? Why would that be?

'What do you think happened to her?' asked Ruth.

'I don't know.' Victoria's eyes darted sideways. 'She did hang around with some bad people. Shouldn't someone be asking questions?' The woman's anger was rising and she was struggling to control the shape of her mouth.

Victoria was right. If it was Ruth's son Jack, there would be more than questions.

Ruth made a decision she hoped she wouldn't regret. 'Let's have a chat in my office,' she said, pointing to her door.

'Deb, can you get Victoria a cup of tea?' Ruth called out. She moved closer to the receptionist and whispered, 'And can you ask Troy to come into my office?'

Deb's eyebrows shot up. But she slowly stood and walked down the hall in the direction of the kitchen.

'What did the police say exactly?' Ruth asked when Victoria sat down.

'He told me she'd turn up. To stop worrying.' Her rage seemed to rear up again, like a stallion, lashing out.

Ruth was sure she had met this woman before.

Victoria paused. She seemed to understand that if she wanted something from Ruth, she should assuage her fury. 'I waited for her to turn up. She'd been gone longer than usual. One of the reasons why I waited so long to go to the police in the first place.'

'What's the other reason?'

Her foot was jiggling. 'He doesn't like us.'

'The policeman? Why do you say that?'

Victoria waved the question away.

Ruth tried another tack. 'Does your daughter have a job?'

'She works in the chemist.'

Then it struck her. 'Not Bea?' Ruth said. 'From the pharmacy.'

Finally, she realised why Victoria looked familiar. Ruth had seen her at the chemist when she'd first arrived in Myddle, just before Christmas.

'I told her to get a better job, but she won't.'

Poor Bea. It must be hard work having to handle this barrage of negativity.

'And the pharmacist hasn't seen her?'

'She didn't turn up to work.'

'Who was the policeman you spoke to about her?'

'Constable Parker,' said Victoria.

'Gazza?'

'Yes.'

'I've met them both,' said Ruth. She'd seen Bea and Gazza at a party together, and not in a good way. She kept that to herself.

'You don't need a lawyer, Victoria, but I'd be happy to talk to the police if you think that would help.'

'Thank you.' Victoria looked down at her writhing hands. 'I appreciate it,' she added, almost surprised.

'There'll be no charge. You're not my client. I'm not opening a file. There's not much I can do apart from mention it to him.' This was a community service to help a distressed woman whose anger made it hard for her to communicate with the world. Ruth stood, to make it clear to Victoria that their meeting was over, and escorted Victoria to the door to make sure she left.

It would be a simple matter to sort this out. Surely if Bea was actually missing, someone other than her mother would notice.

'Where's Troy?' Ruth asked Deb.

'Dunno,' said Deb. 'Gone walkabout probably.'

Deb could be depended on to drop a snide remark.

Ruth walked back to her office. She'd taken Troy on to get some work experience but, as he liked to say himself, he had a tendency to smoke-bomb. Like a magician in a disappearing act.

Ruth had seen Troy with Bea several times. He might know where the girl had gone.

Winter days in Myddle were clear and bright, the warmth of the midday sun tempered by the corrugated iron roof that curved over the footpath. The street had barely changed since it was built a century and a half ago. Ruth passed the pub—a few stolid drinkers at the bar—and the courthouse, gabled red brick set among the silver trunks of the gums, which were full of rosellas having a raucous argument. She smiled. The flashes of red and blue, and the cacophony, delighted her.

The low-set sandstone police station was by the river, a verandah separating it from the street.

Constable Parker—Gazza to his mates—was leaning on the front desk in his navy-blue uniform, every breath through his ravaged nose a gusty effort.

'Hello,' she said with friendly cheer.

'What can I do for ya?'

'I thought we should get to know each other a bit better, especially as we may be appearing opposite one another in court.'

Usually, at this point there'd be an offer of a cup of tea. Ruth waited. He looked at her benignly. The next person to speak would have to be Ruth.

'Actually, Victoria—' she paused, forgetting Victoria's full name. 'Bea's mum,' she finished.

'Victoria Baulderstone.' He said it with the smug certainty of a man who had all the facts. His eyes strayed to some paper on the desk beneath him as if he needed to attend to more important things.

'She's upset,' said Ruth.

'Well,' he said, 'she's usually upset about something.'

The office was festooned with signs explaining how visitors should interact with the police, how far from the counter glass they should stand, how to report a theft. One just behind Gazza's head said: *Thank you for your patience and courtesy.*

'She's worried that she hasn't seen Bea for nearly a week.'

'If the kid has shot through, she'd have a good reason.'

'It's worthwhile making some inquiries, isn't it?'

'Is Victoria Baulderstone your client?'

'No.'

'Then I'm not going to tell you how to do your job, if you don't tell me how to do mine.' There was an impasse while they stared at one another.

Ruth wanted to exclaim, 'Do you know who I am?' but that would be folly. Not least because, in this town, who was she? A middle-aged sheila who had taken over the lawyer's office for a few months. All the locals were interested in was her marital status, and Constable Parker wasn't much interested even in that.

'You know Bea,' said Ruth.

Gazza raised an eyebrow.

'I saw you with her at the New Year's Eve party. At Dash Rogers' place.'

Gazza just stared at her.

'Not with her,' Ruth said. 'But you clearly knew her. And you seemed to want to know her better.'

Gazza's face turned a deeper shade of purple. He sneered at her but said nothing.

The landline rang, loud. Gazza's hand reached for it.

'Thank you, Constable Parker,' she said. Ruth dredged up what she hoped looked like a disdainful smile.

'See ya later,' said Constable Parker, as he picked up the handset.

Ruth shuddered as she walked down the front steps. What a creep.

Back at the office, Troy was at his desk.

'You know Bea Baulderstone.' It was a statement of fact not a question.

Troy kept his eyes on his computer screen, his fingers on the mouse. 'Yeah.'

'Did you hear she's missing?'

Troy concentrated on the screen while he typed in a few words, then he slowly turned to look at her, almost wary. 'I heard her mum's worried about her,' he said, and turned back to the computer.

'But you're not?'

'Not what?'

She was speaking to the back of his head. 'Worried about her?'

He turned again, sighing as he did so. 'Why would I be worried about her?'

'I don't know. I just thought you might know the scuttlebutt about town.'

'Scuttlebutt?' He had the same ironic expression Jack had when she said something he thought stupid or boomerish, even though, as Ruth pointed out to him, she wasn't a boomer. She was Gen X. She'd looked it up. Several times.

'Is there talk around town that she's missing?' Ruth asked.

'Not that I've heard. Except from her mum.'

'And what do people think about that?'

'They think her mum is nuts.'

'Do you think she's nuts?'

'I think she's'—he paused to search for a word and found one he didn't use much—'nasty. I stay away from her.'

'That why you smoke-bombed?' Ruth asked. 'When she came here before?'

'She's not a nice lady.'

He was stonewalling so Ruth thought she'd try a new tack. 'Are you on Instagram?'

'Sometimes.'

'Do you follow Bea?'

'Probably. Went to school with her.'

'Can you see if she's posted lately?' Ruth indicated to his phone, which he picked up reluctantly and then put his thumb on the app icon with a well-practised movement.

There were pictures of Troy horsing around with his mates: swinging from a rope into a river; surfing; sitting around a fire on the beach at night; a group of young men in their footy kit after the game, holding beers, laughing.

'Can we go to Bea's page? Is that what you call it? A page?'

Ruth expected a series of pouting selfies, but all that popped up were photos of women at the local yoga studio.

'When was her last post?' Ruth asked, noting Bea's username.

A week ago. At one of the yoga events.

'How often does she post? Normally?'

Troy scrolled back. Bea posted every two or three days, but for the last week, nothing.

'You're friends with her?' Ruth had seen them hanging out together a few times.

'Nah. Not really.' Troy was concentrating on the screen.

'You seemed pretty friendly with her at the New Year's Eve party.'

Troy spun the chair around to face her, his arms crossed. 'Are you trying to accuse me of something?'

'No, of course not.' She was annoyed now. 'But your responses are not filling me with delight.'

'You don't seem to understand what it's like being someone like me in a country town in Australia,' he said. 'If a crime has been committed, or even if it hasn't, I'll be accused of it. Or my cousin will.'

Ruth's hackles rose. 'I'd hoped you would realise I was better than that,' she said. 'You shouldn't assume that everyone who looks like me is the same.'

Troy laughed.

'What?' she said, affronted.

'Couldn't have said it better myself.'

'Oh.' She smiled. He had a point.

'Can we have a sensible discussion about Bea now?' she said.

'What do you want to know?'

'Where do you think she is?'

Troy shrugged. 'Bea has a few issues.' He turned back to his computer with a sense of purpose, as if he wasn't going to be moved from it.

Troy hadn't answered the question. He hadn't answered any of her questions. Instead, he'd started an argument with her, and when that had been defused, he'd deflected.

She considered taking him on. Challenging him. But he was withholding for a reason. And she knew from long experience there was no point in trying to forcibly extract information from a teenage boy.

Better to lure the information out of him. Make him feel comfortable enough to let it go. Stay calm, and gently persist. She walked back to her office.

Outside, in Myddle's main street, the police siren went off. Probably another car accident on the road to the beach at Azuri.

For a moment she felt almost sorry for Gazza.

⁂

Ruth went onto Bea's Instagram page and scrolled down. She was surprised. Most of the photos were landscapes: mist rising off the river at dawn; a leggy heron; a contented bull staring down the lens in a green paddock with some kangaroos in the background. Even the photos taken at Chandra's yoga meetings were quirky. Bea had captured Chandra as she led a yoga class: head back, laughing; long fingers spanning out as she made a point.

Bea was a bit of an artist.

The only selfies were a couple taken at the New Year's Eve party—even those featuring not her but a reflection of the campfire in the river behind—and another of her in the iconic Rolling Stones lips and tongue T-shirt, which swamped her tiny frame. Bea smiled uncertainly into the camera seeking some affirmation.

Why was nobody looking for her? Why was it only her mother who cared?

⁂

Ruth spent an hour googling how to bypass local police to report a missing child, and in doing so went down a rabbit hole on the missing persons register, which featured a lot of teenage girls who'd been missing for decades.

She shook herself. This was getting her nowhere. She pulled her laptop out of the docking station so she could put it in her backpack.

Her phone lit up with a tinny version of 'Satisfaction'.

Roscoe. Her long-time friend and former colleague. Mentor, even.

'Have you heard?' he said as soon as she answered.

'About Bea?' said Ruth, because that was at the top of her mind.

'What?' Roscoe sounded confused.

'Oh . . . No, I clearly haven't heard. What?'

'Dash Rogers.'

'What about him?'

'He's dead.'

Sharp intake of breath. An image of Dash jumped into her mind: his shiny smile, laughing eyes. People like Dash didn't die. He was only what? Mid-thirties? Well off. Adored. By some anyway. World at his feet. Well, Myddle at his feet, which was his world.

And another image: Dash lying prone on her floor, even then flashing his gorgeous smile at her.

'What happened?' she asked Roscoe.

'Gunshot wound. And he was hit by something big and hard . . .' Roscoe paused.

Dread, hot and heavy, hit her gut. 'Where?' she said.

'Must have happened somewhere near their farm gate. On Clive Road.'

'Did you find the gun?'

'We found a rifle nearby.'

'We?'

'Gazza. Constable Parker.'

The police siren. The call on the landline while she was standing in front of Gazza at the police station.

'Oh God. Poor Dash. How's Evie?'

'She's still away. We're trying to contact her.'

'Who found him then?'

'I did. Two of their dogs turned up at our place covered in blood and sniffing for food. I was driving them back to their house when I found him.'

'Horrible,' said Ruth.

'Not great,' Roscoe agreed. 'He'd been there a while.'

'Anything I can do?'

'I just thought you ought to know.' Roscoe turning to Ruth in a crisis, as it had always been.

'I'll come over,' she said. 'Be there at six?'

She checked her watch. Three pm. She had a bit to do before then. She had to visit Victoria. And she wanted to check in with her son Jack in London. It was early morning there.

'No need to come over,' said Roscoe unconvincingly. He liked to give the impression of inviolability.

Ruth insisted. 'See you in a few hours. I'll bring some pasta.'

WhatsApp

Ruth
You awake?

Jack
Yep

Ruth
Bit of action here

Jack
?

Ruth
Missing girl and a dead man

Jack
In Myddle? Who?

Ruth
Girl from chemist. Dash Rogers.

Jack
What happened to Dash?

Ruth
Shot

Jack
Did the same person do both? Or did the girl shoot him and scoot?

Ruth
Don't know

Jack
Is there a gunman on the loose?

Ruth
Don't think so. They found the gun.

Jack
Must be awful there

Ruth
Surreal. Still processing.

Jack
And you went to Myddle for some peace and quiet

Ruth
Maybe it's me. Maybe chaos follows me 🙄

Jack
Well, you're the woman for the job

Ruth
😱

3

RUTH

23 December, six months before

IT WAS ROSCOE WHO FIRST LURED RUTH TO MYDDLE.

'I'm worried about Dad,' Ruth's god-daughter Patch said on the phone. 'He'll invite you for Christmas. Can you come?'

'What's the problem?' Ruth said.

'He's been a bit lost since the firm collapsed,' said Patch. 'He's usually so focused. And now it's like he's searching for something.' She paused before she added, 'I'm worried it makes him vulnerable.'

Roscoe? Vulnerable? Ruth scoffed. He'd been Chairman of Partners of their huge law firm. The vibe he gave off was more that, thanks to his charm and intellect, the world bent to his will.

Although it hadn't bent to his will, had it? The firm had collapsed under his watch because of his failure to detect a psychopath among the partners; a man so bad he'd murdered a client.

Ruth was struggling in the void the firm's collapse had made in her life. Made sense that Roscoe would be, too.

He would probably never work as a lawyer again, but as he was nearly sixty—respectable retirement age—Ruth doubted he'd care much about that. He didn't need more money. It just would have been better to go out on a high rather than a spectacular low.

'And there's Chandra . . .' Patch trailed off.

Roscoe's new girlfriend. Patch was upset that her mother had been usurped by a younger woman. The wound was fresh. It had only happened six months ago. Ruth was upset about it, too. Susan had been the epitome of calm, tolerant mother and wife, prepared to put up with Roscoe's vagaries and absences.

But it wasn't up to Ruth to police Roscoe's romantic life. If that was on the agenda, she would avoid it by not going.

Then Roscoe rang, his voice resonant with that familiar warmth. 'Come for Christmas,' he said. 'The place will be awash with small children. You can get up at five am and watch them open their presents. And you'll be miserable without Bill.'

Roscoe had always known what would appeal to Ruth. They'd worked together since she'd started at the firm as a graduate nearly thirty years ago, when he'd been her supervising partner. He knew there was something life-affirming about people under the age of ten squealing with delight at the sight of a wrapped present. And he was right about another Christmas rattling about in the house in Sydney which was so empty without Bill. She would drink too much champagne and cry. It was nearly two years and she still hadn't recovered from Bill's death. There was the aloneness—even cleaning her teeth was a different experience now—and there was the trauma. (The accident happened in front of her: Bill on a bicycle; a gravel truck.) And their twenty-one-year-old son Jack was in London studying for a year. She'd be completely alone if she stayed in Sydney.

Ruth decided to go. Roscoe wasn't the type to wallow, and she could do with the company and the cheer.

Just before Christmas, Ruth, with a *brrrr,* drove over the cattle grid outside Roscoe's new house, and along the rutted farm track.

As she pulled up outside the house—a concrete and glass architectural marvel cantilevered over the river—a man emerged in a green caftan. He had grey hair, short back and sides. He looked like a corporate lawyer in a flowing maxi dress. Roscoe.

Patch appeared behind him, her wide-open face glowing with the smile that was always either on display or simmering in her eyes. Four tiny red-headed children bounced around her, and beside her was a tall red-headed man, the only person in the whole menagerie who exuded calm. Shane, Patch's husband. Patch had come to Myddle as a young teacher ten years ago, met Shane, and now had a farm and four kids.

'Ruth!' said Roscoe with theatrical affection as she emerged from the car, and they exchanged a hug and double-cheek kiss. 'Have you taken up running or something? You've faded away.'

'A bit. It's mostly not having half a packet of Monte Carlos from the tearoom at three pm because I was so busy I missed lunch.' Then she added, 'Is that a nice way of telling me I used to be fat?'

Roscoe shook his head as he smiled at her. 'I'd forgotten how hard it is to give you a compliment.'

She was about to say, 'What's with the frock?' when Shane stepped forward. 'How's it going?' he said, his hand—the shape of a Christmas ham—gripping Ruth's.

Ruth enveloped Patch in a hug and whispered in her ear, 'So good to see you. How's your mum?'

And Patch whispered back, 'She's okay. Just sad.'

The children leapt about. The little one, Milly, was two and they went up in increments of two years. Patch had pumped them out with mathematical precision. Two boys, two girls.

'Who are these people?' said Ruth of and to the children.

'Roscoe calls us the Wildlings,' explained a four-year-old with wide-eyed solemnity.

'Does he?' She turned to Roscoe. 'They call you Roscoe, not Pops? You in denial?'

'No way anyone will ever call me Pops,' said Roscoe. 'And it's easier to give them a collective noun. Four is an enormous number of children.'

Ruth couldn't disagree with that. 'They look so sweet.'

'Sweet is one thing they're not. Feral is the word Shane uses. Frank,' said Patch, swiping at the corgi whose nose was wedged into Ruth's crotch—no mean feat given its extremely short legs. 'Stop it.'

Frank trotted off, his ears erect, a smile on his face. The Wildlings went with him, playing a game where they each held an imaginary sword.

Stepping over a half-finished path, they headed into the house. It was vast, filled with light; ripples from the river reflecting on the ceiling. The furniture was shades of white, with the occasional hot orange and blue cushion. A woman floated towards Ruth, arms outstretched. Her wild long silver hair was tamed with a loose curl of white muslin; her dress, a white silky shift, wafted over her lanky body, touching the right curves, and finished just above the silver toe rings on her bare feet.

Roscoe beamed, as if she was a new painting he had acquired.

Ruth couldn't tell how old the woman was. Her face glowed, with a hint of laugh lines around her eyes. She looked like she'd been embalmed at forty and mounted on the prow of a boat in full sail.

'Ruth!' Chandra exclaimed. 'I'm so glad to meet you. Roscoe talks about you all the time. I feel like we've met in a previous life.' She enveloped Ruth in a hug which smelt of incense.

Roscoe's collection of abstract art, displayed so prominently in his house in Sydney, was nowhere to be seen. Instead, on the wall was a huge mandala, an intricate pattern of vivid colour. Ruth examined it up close. Grains of coloured sand had been glued to a board.

Roscoe stood beside her. 'Picked it up in Nepal,' he said. 'Done by Tibetan monks. Usually when they finish the mandala, they destroy it. They scatter the grains of sand in the wind to signify the transient nature of life.'

It was indeed beautiful. Mesmerising. But wouldn't gluing the sand to the board destroy the meaning? It was like Roscoe was trying to capture and pin down the ephemeral.

She and Roscoe had both changed. They'd worked together for decades, been mutual sounding boards for the problems that popped up like ducks in a shooting game in sideshow alley: difficult questions of law; tricky clients; greedy fuckers in the partnership who bullied their way to higher status and riches.

She wondered if they would struggle to find things to talk about now all that had disappeared. Did Roscoe have the same twinge of loss?

Roscoe laid a meal out on the table, a series of salads comprising mostly lettuce and kale. Delicious, but Ruth waited for some carbs and protein. None came.

The bottle of wine Ruth had brought had disappeared and been replaced with homemade kombucha. Ruth supposed it was a good thing for her liver.

Shane had an esky he'd placed in the corner, from which he quietly retrieved a beer every now and then.

Roscoe wanted to introduce Ruth to his neighbours, from whom he'd bought his block of land. They'd carved a couple of hectares from their cattle property and sold it to him three years before.

'You'll have to come to their New Year's Eve party,' he said. 'It's always a hoot.'

'They're lovely people, even if they do produce cattle,' Chandra added.

'Bit like Shane,' said Patch of her husband. 'He's a lovely person, even though he produces cattle.'

Shane shuffled in his chair.

'I think you might be living in the wrong neighbourhood, darling,' said Roscoe to Chandra with clipped benignity, 'if you are ideologically opposed to the raising of beef cattle.'

Chandra waved a hand. 'I think it's cruel, though,' she said. 'And if we are going to solve humanity's problems, we are going to have to solve the biological and ethical difficulty that we have of exploitation.' Her voice carried no hint of hostility, or outrage.

Ruth glanced at Shane, who winked at her over the top of his beer.

Roscoe turned to Ruth. 'Chandra can be a little intense, can't you, darling?'

'Sorry, Shane,' said Chandra. Her smile was beatific. 'My passion for ethics makes me a bit tactless sometimes. Occupational hazard.'

'Chandra's a yoga teacher, aren't you?' Roscoe continued. 'Although that sells her a bit short. She's a philosopher, looking to come to a new understanding of an ethical world.'

Patch rolled her eyes. Time for Ruth to change the subject. 'Do you think you'll ever go back to the law, Roscoe?' Ruth asked.

'I dabble on boards. But back to practise full-time? No, I don't think so.'

'Are you working, Ruth?' asked Chandra.

She nodded. 'Three days a week. Project for a client who wants me to fix an intractable problem.'

'And?' Roscoe said.

'A wall of passive resistance. Watching minutes pass in meetings while people think up reasons why they can't do what I suggest. My soul is slowly dissolving.'

'Are you sure it's not just relevance deprivation syndrome?' said Patch. 'Now that you're no longer in charge?'

Ruth laughed. 'Probably. I used to change the way things were done by issuing a directive and cheerily waving away complaints.'

'They were too scared of you to say no.' Roscoe smiled at her.

'Good thing, too,' said Ruth.

Roscoe replenished the kombucha. Shane got himself a beer from the esky.

'I don't know much about lawyers,' said Chandra. 'But I don't understand why they all wear black in court. Even judges. They cloak themselves in it. Surely they know that black absorbs bad energy.'

Patch's yoghurt-covered spoon was suspended in mid-air, her mouth open waiting to receive it.

'So they're in court listening to all this bad stuff,' Chandra continued, 'and absorbing the'—she paused to find the right word, her hands working in a circle—'like, the terrible vibes of it. The negativity they hear goes right into them. How must the judges feel afterwards?'

Patch's spoon went into her mouth.

There's a particular discomfort to a puzzled silence. Ruth felt she should break it. 'I've always wondered why judges are so grumpy,' she said. 'I thought it was the stress.'

'It's why I wear white,' said Chandra. 'To reflect bad energy away from me.'

Everyone nodded slowly while staring at their plate.

'Well,' said Shane, 'time for these kids to go to bed.'

For Ruth, Roscoe had hired his neighbour's restored stone farmhouse, which they let on Airbnb; wood floors, white linen, Nespresso machine. It was less than a kilometre from Roscoe's house.

Ruth settled in after dinner. While she was getting ready for bed, a text pinged in from Patch. 'See? We'd kill her except we wouldn't know how to dispose of her body. Because plastic won't decompose.'

Bit unfair, Ruth thought. Chandra seemed to be uncomplicated with a charming bent towards idealism: a person dreaming of a better world, one yoga pose at a time, with great taste in frocks and soft furnishings. And some wacky ideas.

Patch was reeling at the eviction of Susan, her mother, from Roscoe's bed. Stood to reason she'd be annoyed about it.

Ruth didn't want to get embroiled in family politics.

One of the great things about emojis, Ruth found, is that you can give a neutral response without expressing a view. After some consideration she sent back an open-mouthed emoji to denote nothing in particular, except mild shock, which Patch could interpret as she wished.

Ruth needed to fill some scripts and replenish her supply of Panadol.

In Myddle, the pharmacy was called the chemist, but a more appropriate title might have been apothecary. The bell on the door clanged as Ruth was admitted into a lair of cedar shelves piled with potions, and a wall of tiny drawers promising treasures within. It must have been built in the 1860s.

Only a fluorescent-lit display of makeup covering the back wall jolted the shop into modernity.

The girl behind the counter was young—late teens, Ruth guessed. Her eyes were kohled, her lips crimsoned.

She had a name tag on her left breast: *Bea*.

'Can I help you?' said Bea.

'I just need this script filled.'

Bea put Ruth's script in a little plastic box and placed it on the shelf behind her. A middle-aged man in a short white coat behind the shelves took it. Name badge: *Chris*.

'It'll be a few minutes,' said Bea. 'Do you need anything else?' She surveyed Ruth's face. 'Perhaps some lipstick?'

'You're right,' said Ruth. 'I could probably do with some lipstick.'

The girl's face fell. 'Oh, I'm sorry. I didn't mean to . . . It's just that I always like some lipstick if I'm feeling a bit . . . you know.' She searched for the right thing to say. 'Lipstick always cheers me up,' she said with a note of victory.

Ruth smiled. 'I could do with some cheering up,' she said. 'What've you got?' She turned to examine the garish vertical array of makeup.

The doorbell jangled again. A woman came into the shop.

'I'm just looking after this lady,' said Bea.

'I only need a moment,' said the newcomer, her voice small, tight and slightly nasal, as if it had come from a constricted zone at the top of her throat.

'I'm helping this lady, Mum,' said Bea. 'Won't be a sec.'

Bea stooped to open a lipstick up, and made a pink dash on the back of Ruth's hand. 'There are some new colours that are just lovely.'

'I only need a moment,' the woman repeated. Her voice was loud and high. Combative. 'You never take any notice of me.'

The note of conflict in the woman's tone made Ruth turn.

The woman's mouth was quivering into a rolling curve, like an ocean swell. She struggled to suppress some powerful emotion, grief perhaps, or anger. Ruth instinctively reached out to calm her. That small movement was enough to trigger her.

'Don't you touch me.'

The woman turned to Bea and shouted, 'You can't just walk out like that!'

Bea backed away. 'Sorry, Mum, but I had to go to work.'

'You always say that when I need you.'

Chris, the pharmacist, stepped between Bea and her mother. 'Come on, Victoria. Calm down,' he said.

'Don't you speak to me like that!' Spit flew from Victoria's mouth. 'I've had enough of all of you!'

Bea shielded herself, one hand over her forehead, the other across her chest.

Ruth wondered if she should step in. But how?

Victoria emitted a stream of vitriol: Bea hadn't cleaned up her breakfast plates or swept the floor.

'Victoria,' said Chris firmly, 'chill.'

'Don't you patronise me!' Victoria screamed. 'Your shop with all this'—she halted, searching for a word—'rubbish.' Victoria held out her right hand and swept it along the shelf beside Ruth.

The myriad little bottles of foundation, moisturiser and clarifier smashed on the floor. Beige goop oozed out of broken bottles.

'Oh, Mum,' said Bea.

Victoria flounced out of the shop.

'I'm sorry, Chris,' said Bea. 'I'm so sorry. I'll pay for it.'

Chris held out his arms and hugged her. 'It's not your fault, love. And don't worry, it's covered by insurance.'

'I don't know why she does it,' Bea sniffed.

Not the first time then. How did the town coalesce around this kid? Or was Chris giving her a job the extent of the support she got?

'Come on,' Chris said. 'Let's clean it up.'

Bea and Chris remembered then that they had a customer in the shop.

'Sorry about that,' said Chris to Ruth. 'I'll get your script filled. I'm nearly done. And have a lipstick on the house. Bea, help the lady choose a lipstick.'

'Are you all right, Bea?' said Ruth once Chris had headed back behind the counter. 'You don't need to give me a lipstick, I'll pay for it.'

Bea tried to focus on the pinks and the reds and the relative merits of each. She scraped samples on the back of Ruth's hand, her own hand trembling. Ruth restrained an urge to wrap an arm around the girl's shoulders.

'I'm so sorry,' Bea said. 'Mum gets angry sometimes.'

Angry didn't seem like a strong enough word to describe what Ruth had just witnessed. Incandescent fury. She wondered if Bea understood how extreme her mother's rage was, and how irrational.

That poor child.

Ruth bought two lipsticks—one pink, one red. It wouldn't have mattered if they'd been blue.

WhatsApp

Jack
Update?

Ruth
In Myddle with Roscoe

Jack
How is the old boy?

Ruth
He's wearing a caftan. And has a new girlfriend.

Jack
?

Ruth
[picture of Roscoe, Patch, Chandra and the children]

Jack
OMFG. Where did he find her?

Ruth
Yoga class

Jack
I'm taking up yoga

Ruth
Commendable. It's very good for core strength.

Jack
Patch's kids look cute

Ruth
Adorable. Noisy. Patch thinks the yoga teacher is evil.

Jack
?

Ruth
If she is, she's very good at hiding it under
a facade of idealistic waftiness.
What's happening with you?

Jack
[Screenshot of Strava showing time for 5 k run. PB]

Ruth
Impressive.
Uni okay?

Jack
Great. Can you read my assignment?

Ruth
What's it about?

Jack
The Euro. Impact of Brexit.

Ruth
Out of my league. I'll only be able to look for typos.

Jack
And grammar. And sense.

Ruth
Send it over.
You're lucky I'm sane btw.

Jack
Are you sane? You hide it well.

Ruth
Ha ha.
Terrible scene in chemist today. Woman cleared a shelf of
makeup while screaming at her daughter who works there.

Jack
Wow. Poor girl.

Ruth
Awful

Jack
Are you going to fix it?

Ruth
Sure. I'll knock on her door and say: I know nothing of medicine and I've not even met you but you seem nuts. Go and see a psychiatrist.

Jack
Good point

Ruth
Nighty night, little dude

Jack
👍

Ruth smiled as she plugged her phone into the charger.

Jack was well over six foot but the little dude that she and Bill spawned and adored was still in there.

Bill would be so proud. She wiped away a tear and got into bed.

The wiping didn't help. She sobbed until she fell asleep.

4

RUTH

31 December, six months before

STRANGE TO MEET THE HOSTS FOR THE FIRST TIME WHEN YOU WALK INTO their party. Evie and Dash Rogers had the hallmarks of landed gentry. Their vast cattle property, which abutted Clive River, had been in the family for more than a century.

They had transformed their garden with fairy lights, and in the centre was a campfire, over which a pig was roasting on a spit.

Ruth had been apprehensive, concerned that Evie's vowels might be rounded, her neck pearled, her conversation imperious. Ruth had even dug out a frock for the occasion. She still carried the scars from school: sneered at for being the daggy girl from a country town; the brainy one, whose parents couldn't afford a new dress for the formal. Thirty years later—a corporate lawyer so good she featured in legal rankings—she still quivered at the idea of talking to a posh girl at a party. Laughable really.

She needn't have worried. Evie—mid-thirties, lanky, wiry—looked like she had just hopped off her horse. In jeans and elastic-sided riding boots, her only concession to the party seemed to be a clean white shirt.

They were quite a couple. Dash was so good-looking he was almost pretty. With impending middle age, the beauty he'd evidently held in youth had faded a little—his girth had softened, a vertical furrow had replaced a dimple in each cheek—but it only added to the allure, giving him the gravitas of a retired athlete.

He was all largesse, plenty of spare beers in the eskies and some white wine for 'youse sheilas' as he called them, with a self-deprecating exaggeration of his Australian accent.

Notwithstanding the cheer, Ruth felt very alone. Roscoe was working the room or, in this case, the home paddock. Chandra was absorbed into a gaggle of women who raptured about yoga. Ruth stood on the edge of a cluster of people she'd just met as they spoke about people she didn't know.

Bea, the girl from the pharmacy, teetered into the party on heels that sank into the grass, wearing little more than a fabric swatch. The girl spent several minutes taking selfies in front of the river, checking behind her before she pouted side-on to the phone, her improbably lush eyelashes at half-mast. Photoshoot complete, she looked around, then walked nervously up to a crowd of kids her age. They ignored her at first, but she persisted, leaning in every now and then to make a comment, her fingers agitating the hem of her dress.

Dash Rogers approached. 'G'day, Ruth is it?' He flashed a shiny white smile.

'Yes, I'm in your lovely Airbnb farmhouse. Thank you.'

'No worries,' he said.

He was good at small talk. In a few minutes, he extracted from Ruth the fact that Jack existed but was in London; that she was Patch's godmother; and that she had known Roscoe for a couple of decades.

'And you still like him,' said Dash. 'Huh!'

Ruth laughed. 'No accounting for taste.'

The girl, Bea, joined them with another girl, each exuding a glow like a ripe peach.

'Hey, Dash,' said Bea's companion.

'Yeah, g'day,' said Dash, flashing his smile. He turned to Bea and held out his hand. 'Dash Rogers.'

Bea's eyelashes dropped then flicked back up again. 'I'm Bea,' she said. She paused, looking for something to say, and eventually decided on, 'Great party.'

'Yeah, thanks,' said Dash. 'Haven't I seen you at the chemist?'

Bea's eyelashes went into overdrive. 'Yeah. I work there.'

It wasn't just Ruth then. Dash's allure transcended generations.

Dash turned back to Ruth, wanting to introduce her to a mate of his called Gazza, whom he called over. 'You'll like Gazza,' said Dash. 'He's in the law, arncha, Gazza?' He laughed as if he'd said something funny. 'Gazza, Ruth here is a big-time lawyer from Sydney.'

Gazza was underwhelmed by this news. He fixed a wary eye on Ruth. 'Defence, is it?' he said.

'Pardon?' said Ruth.

'Are ya a defence lawyer?' said Gazza, slowly and loudly, as one would do for the hard of hearing.

'Oh! No,' said Ruth. 'I work in corporate law. You know, fights between big companies.'

What little interest Gazza might have had in Ruth fizzled when she told him that. He turned to Dash and made a remark about an upcoming footy game. Ruth stayed on the edge of the conversation, wondering if she should sidle off. Gazza had once played rugby, evident from his nose, which was splayed across his face, and his calves, which looked like they had each swallowed a tennis ball. Time had not been kind to the policeman, but it was clear he'd had fun while it ravaged him. In his forty-something years, he had consumed so much beer, his face was a vivid hue of purple.

After Ruth edged away, Gazza stayed in a corner, nursing a beer, surrounded by men who looked similar to him, leaning back frequently to roar with laughter.

Ruth moved to the periphery of a circle of women which centred around Evie Rogers. They were talking about their children, except Evie, who delivered occasional quiet compliments: 'But Jess is so clever'; 'I saw Tim in the hundred metres. Amazing'. Patch had explained that Evie had no children. Ruth watched her face, impassive as the conversation wafted around her. Was she bored by this talk of children? Or was her expression a facade she pulled over a well of grief for the child that never came?

There was a group of boys—young men really—engaging in a bit of horseplay. One of them was doing backflips from a standing position, and then from upside-down off a low-hanging branch of a poinciana tree, while the rest of them cheered.

'Troy, mate,' one of the boys yelled. 'Show us the thing you did when you scored that try in the final.'

Troy refrained, perhaps out of modesty, perhaps because he realised it wasn't a good idea after the few beers he'd had.

'Nah,' he said. 'I'll land on me head. Then what?'

They all laughed and speculated about the injuries that could be caused by a poorly executed triple backflip while they engaged in some performative wrestling, displaying the easy muscularity of youth.

Troy reminded Ruth of Jack. During the years Jack had spent perfecting his standing backflip, she had tried to hide her anxiety.

The music was turned up, the campfire flickered.

Ruth noticed Bea nearby, dancing unsteadily, holding a can of a sugary vodka drink aloft, and shouting out the words to 'Creep'.

Just past her, in the shadows, lurked Gazza. He had withdrawn from the group of men to ogle at Bea.

As Ruth watched with growing dismay, Gazza moved forward out of the shadows, beer in hand. He had the swaying gait of a man whose knees had seized up, and his gut hung over his waistband, causing considerable stress to the straining buttons of his shirt.

He danced slowly near the campfire, edging closer to Bea. There was a sense of intention about him—of menace.

At law firm parties Ruth had had enough authority to stop bad behaviour with nothing more than a raised eyebrow. This was different. Gazza clearly held Ruth in small regard and she did not know who here had enough gravitas to step in. She could hardly say to Dash Rogers, 'I think that girl over there is at risk of being sexually assaulted by your friend Gazza.' Could she? Maybe she'd have to. Or maybe she could approach Gazza and say, 'Gazza, mate, you need to leave that girl alone.' Gazza looked like an argumentative type, very clear about his entitlement to do what he liked.

Ruth edged towards the campfire, to try to engage the girl in conversation and draw her away. In her inebriated state, Bea was oblivious, shuffling from side to side, moving her arms around as she concentrated on the ground in front of her.

As Ruth drew closer, she noticed Troy nearby. He was holding a beer and talking to his mates, but he was also watching Bea.

Then Troy noticed Ruth. There was a calm intelligence about him. Without moving his head, his eyes moved sideways towards Gazza and back to Ruth. She nodded, just slightly.

Troy stepped forward towards Bea. 'Hey, Bea!' he shouted.

Bea looked up from her dancing. She took a few moments to focus on Troy. She held her arms out. 'Troy, baby,' she slurred.

'Mate,' he said. 'Come and have a hamburger with me.'

'Okay,' she said, pliant. She slumped against him.

He put one arm around her, holding her up while he led her away.

'You're my mate, Troy,' Ruth could hear her saying. 'You know that? I think you're amazing.'

'Good on ya, Bea. You're my mate, too.'

Ruth shadowed him as he found a log and sat Bea down on it.

'I'll be back in a sec,' he told Ruth. 'She needs some food.'

Ruth nodded. 'I'll stay here 'til you get back.'

Bea was slumped on the log, her hands on her knees.

Gazza sidled nearer. As a middle-aged woman, Ruth was invisible to him, even though she was maybe only six years Gazza's senior.

'Bea,' Gazza said, 'how yer going?'

'Yeah, pretty good, Gazza,' Bea slurred.

'Fancy a dance?' he said. 'Got ya another drink.' He proffered a vodka cooler.

She was just taking it when Troy sauntered back with supplies.

Ignoring Gazza, he sat down beside Bea, gave her a burger and a bottle of water, and moved the vodka cooler to one side.

Crisis averted. Ruth was about to sidle away to get a burger herself when Gazza approached again, standing over the pair, his hips forward, his knees curved back. 'What you up to, son?' he said to Troy.

'Nothin'.'

'Why don't you go and do nothin' over there?' Gazza tipped his head back in the direction of Troy's mates.

'Nah. I'm right here.'

'Might be better for ya if ya went over there,' said Gazza.

Bea watched Gazza through her drunken haze. 'What are you doing to Troy, Gazza?'

Gazza didn't answer her.

'Leave him alone,' she slurred. She squared her shoulders and steadied herself to deliver her next line. 'You're just a racist, Gazza. You're a disgrace.'

Ruth tensed, holding on to her glass of wine tighter. Troy said nothing, just looked up at Gazza, his shoulders relaxed.

Bea was warming up. 'You coppers,' she said, 'you're supposed to treat everyone equal, but you treat Troy like shit. Even though he's the best footy player you've got. Just because he's a Blakfella.' She spat out the word, and took a breath as though preparing to embark on a soliloquy.

Troy put a hand on hers to quell her.

Gazza held Bea's gaze, then looked around. Ruth turned away, pretending she hadn't heard. Gazza would react better if his humiliation by this scrap of a girl was limited to a party of three.

He clenched his fist by his side and then stretched out his hand two or three times, while he went through his options. He turned his head to look at the other revellers, all with their backs turned, oblivious.

Finally, Gazza shook his head and walked off.

Ruth waited until Gazza had gone then stepped up to Bea and Troy. 'You all right?' she said.

'Yeah, we're okay,' said Troy.

'I saw all of that,' Ruth was addressing Troy, 'and I'm impressed with how you handled it.'

'Yep. Thanks.' Troy was a master of monosyllabic conversation—the universal language of teenage boys. Ruth had learnt from parenting Jack that the short answers and grunts were a not-quite-impervious cover for a raging sea of love, hate, pride and fear which swelled and fell beneath.

'Anything I can do?' Ruth said.

'Nah,' said Troy. 'We'll be right.'

Bea said, 'I think I'm going to be sick.'

WhatsApp

Ruth
HNY

Jack
HNY

Ruth
How's London?

Jack
Cold. Wet. [Picture of red bus on wet street.] Fun. Ange is kicking goals. [Picture taken from nosebleed seats in a football stadium with tiny white figures running in the misty rain below.]

Ruth
Your father would be horrified you're not following Arsenal

Jack
It's Ange Postecoglou. He'd understand.

Ruth
Fair

Jack
What did you do for New Year's?

Ruth
Met grand lady and gent who own most of the land around Myddle. And saved a drunk girl from a sleazy copper.

Jack
?

Ruth
The girl from the chemist. I had an accomplice. In the rescue.

Jack
?

Ruth
Lovely boy. Reminded me of you.

Jack
You mean devastatingly handsome?

Ruth
Wise beyond his years. And can do a standing backflip.

Jack
Gifted then.
What are the grand lady and gent like? Scary?

Ruth
Lovely. Normal. Lady seems sad. Gent
lights up a room. Or a paddock.

Jack
Sad because?

Ruth
Not sure. No babies maybe.

Jack
Even though she must be rich as fuck if
they own the land around Myddle

Ruth
Land rich maybe. They sold some land
to Roscoe. Might need cash.

5

EVIE

1 January, nearly six months before

EVIE ROGERS DIDN'T LIKE PARTIES. BUT IT WAS EASIER TO AGREE. Especially the New Year's party. It was a Myddle institution. If she said no, the town would speculate about the reasons.

But still, she had to admit, after all the work—tidying the lawn, setting up the tables and chairs, preparing the food, packing multitudes of eskies with ice—the party turned out okay. There was a crowd of more than a hundred, everyone having a good time. There were the usual niggles, chief among them the endless chat about children.

She loved other people's kids. Literally, in the case of her friend Patch's brood. It's just that there was a gaping chasm within her that should by rights be filled with her own children. And sometimes, when the conversation got stuck on family, like a wheel stuck in a rut that it seemed impossible to steer out of, she was engulfed in panic and despair. Evie was thirty-eight now. The years ticked by quicker and quicker. There wasn't much time left.

It had been so long. Every month she hoped. And every month she was disappointed.

It was looking like IVF was the only option. They'd have to plan it: the long trips to the clinic; the disruption to the farm. Next year, Dash said. But he said that last year. And the year before. She needed to set a deadline. Give an ultimatum. He acted like they had forever.

Evie watched Dash's joy as people gathered around him, the light to which the moths were attracted. All those women. Even the young ones were drawn to him. They'd probably have no trouble conceiving. They had the opposite problem: fear of overabundant fertility. The knot in her stomach tightened.

When people reached the point where they were too drunk to notice her absence, she withdrew, tidied up as much as she could, dumped empty bottles and disposable plates in the bins.

When she'd done enough of that, she went to the horse paddock. Even in the dead of night, Jasper ambled up to her and shoved his long muzzle in her neck, as if he'd been waiting there for her. Evie sank her nose into his black mane, inhaled his earthy scent, of grass and horse sweat. He snorted and snuffled softly.

She wept a bit. It must have been the conversations about children. What would happen to Clive Downs if no baby ever came? Who would keep the property going?

Perhaps she'd talk to Chandra about it. She'd been offering. Dash described her yoga schtick as some wacky shit, but it couldn't hurt. It might even make her feel better.

Above Jasper's rump shone Venus, tucked just outside the curl of the vivid new moon. The silhouette of a big kangaroo bounded away, into a grove of eucalypts.

Evie snuck into the house through the verandah screen door, tried to sleep through the noise—the cheering, the yelling, the throb of music roaring into the night. Cold Chisel yearned for a man lost to the Vietnam War. 'Eagle Rock' came on, and she heard the cheers as all the blokes dropped their dacks—something they did together at the end of every party.

Dash rolled in at three am, snuggled into her, beery fumes through the room, mumbled 'kitten' and 'possum' as he nuzzled her, settled immediately into roaring snores.

She shuffled back so her body curved against his. They fitted together: his exuberant joy complementing the curmudgeon in her. 'I love you, Dash,' Evie whispered as he slept.

Tomorrow, she'd ring Troy. There was some fencing she wanted him to look at. Now that he had finished school, he'd have more time. She hoped.

6

BEA

1 January, nearly six months before

THE MORNING AFTER THE NEW YEAR'S PARTY AT CLIVE DOWNS, BEA FELT sick. Her head ached. She had a vague idea she may have said something terrible to that dickhead cop Gazza but couldn't remember what it was. She put the sheet over her head, curled up and tried to go back to sleep.

She recalled dancing by herself near the campfire. Nobody else was dancing. She must have looked like a dork, dressed in that stupid short dress and heels she'd only worn to look like the other girls.

Had Dash noticed? He'd spoken to her. He was older, sure, but he would understand her more than the boys in her class. He must have seen her dancing by herself, though. Drunk. Her hand went up over her eyes.

She heard her mother leave the house, so she snuck into the kitchen to guzzle some Panadol, fired up the computer and checked out the socials, to find out what people were saying.

They weren't talking about her, thank goodness.

She flicked at her phone, found the selfies she'd taken early in the night. There was one with a great background: orange firelight shining off the river. She edited it, posted it, then flicked over her other selfies on Instagram. Her face was almost completely obscured in all of them. She liked it that way. She only put herself in the photos because that seemed obligatory when posting to Instagram. She'd rather just take photos of landscapes; experiment with rustling light.

Troy had invited Bea to the New Year's Eve party at Clive Downs. Sort of. Bea had seen him in his front yard when she walked past and said to him, 'What are you doing on New Year's?' and Troy had said, 'I'll probably go to the Rogers'.'

Bea was never invited to parties. Not much anyway. When Troy mentioned the party, Bea had looked away, trying to think of a way to get him to invite her. The silence hung between them, until finally Troy had said, 'You should come,' and she'd said, 'Do you think they'll mind?' and Troy had said, 'Probably not—there are a lot of people coming,' by which he seemed to mean they would mind ordinarily but if the party was crowded they wouldn't notice that she was there.

So she went. She spent a long time thinking about the right outfit and things to say in conversation. She could take selfies and put them on Instagram and it would look like she went to parties all the time.

She knew nearly everyone there. That was unavoidable in Myddle. The kids in her class who were waiting to find out which uni they were going to were there. They asked her what she was doing now school was finished and she said, 'I'm working in the pharmacy,' and their faces went blank before they turned to someone else to talk about how great uni was going to be. Even though she was at a party, she still felt like a loser.

So she drank. It loosened her tongue and then it provided oblivion.

But it induced her to dance. By herself.

She winced again.

Bea surfed from one page to another, flicking from TikTok to Instagram to a news page to a blog; a blur of funny dances, pets cavorting, otters swimming, people doing stuff so stupid it looked like they must have suffered some terrible injury.

She flicked back to Instagram every couple of minutes. No likes. Something inside her shrivelled each time she looked, until it was hard and wrinkled as a walnut, right in her gut.

They were all online. Annabelle, who was going to be a flight attendant, had posted a photo twenty minutes ago and already twenty-six people had liked it. 'You look so beautiful,' someone had commented, and 'So great to see you Annabelle'. The photo was curated: fixed smile, one leg curved out in front of the other. Nobody stands like that in real life.

They ignored Bea's posts. It was like she didn't exist.

She'd had limited success with selfies. The selfie that got the most likes was her in a T-shirt she found in the op shop. It was pink with big red lips and a tongue on it. Even her mum liked it.

'Where did you get that?' her mum had asked. 'I had that album.'

'What album?'

'Rolling Stones.' And her mum had looked happy for a few minutes.

Bea had YouTubed Rolling Stones and listened to the album and heard a song called 'Wild Horses'. She liked it. There was a yearning in it: the guitar; the voice. She played that song over and over. And the likes of the photo of Bea in the T-shirt proliferated. She got fifty-four, some from people she'd never heard of.

That was her greatest social-media moment, and that was six months ago.

Bea longed to leave Myddle, to do something amazing. But where would she go, and what would she do? The future was completely obscured, like the river on a foggy morning.

It was as if there was a giant hole inside her that she couldn't work out how to fill. There had to be some way she could make the world better. But how can you do something important if nobody even notices you are alive?

In a science class in Year Ten, the teacher had talked about potential energy: an arrow pulled back on the bow, quivering. That's how she felt. Buzzing with energy. Just waiting for the catalyst that might release it.

What could she be? How could she make an impact?

Bea was looking for a cause, one that got a lot of likes. She experimented with a few by posting links to articles on Instagram—some people in China who were being persecuted; climate change. Lately, she had fixed on racehorses, because it was terrible what happened to them after they stopped racing.

Maybe she should start riding horses. Troy was friends with Evie out at Clive Downs. They had a lot of horses. Maybe Troy would take her. Maybe she would see Dash while she was there.

7

GAZZA

1 January, nearly six months before

GAZZA WOKE UP WITH A SORE HEAD. HE COULDN'T REMEMBER HOW he'd made it home. The police LandCruiser was out the front so he must have driven.

He hoped no one saw him. He was already on a warning because someone saw him weaving up the road in the police vehicle a few months ago.

He did remember that kid Troy being a smart arse. About that chick Bea.

And some lawyer woman looking at him like he was the Elephant Man.

Dawn was touching the sky pink. He'd had hardly any sleep. He sighed and got up to boil the jug. He'd left the lid off the International Roast so it was a bit lumpy.

That lawyer was a bit of a looker. Out of his league, though, which was the story of his life. Probably just as well but. She'd be at him all the time to smarten up: stop drinking; stop swearing.

Bloody women.

His phone rang. A triple zero call for an MVA on the Azuri Road. He sighed. Single car. Corner. Tree.

Worst part of a shit job.

'Ambos there?' he said.

'On their way. Looks like a fatality. Firies, too. Jaws of life.'

He put on his uniform even though his head was on fire.

It took seven minutes to get there, siren on. The boys from Broughton were already at the scene. He was a good driver. They should give him credit for that at least.

Hyundai hatchback. P-plater driving his mates home from a party. Kids and car mashed together. One kid not wearing a seatbelt had been flung out over a bush, legs and arms at terrible angles, eyes wide open, frozen in terror. Forever.

He used to vomit when he saw this stuff. Now he just took a breath and walked over while adjusting his trousers.

But he knew he'd be seeing this one for months in his head.

Beer helped blot it out a bit. Made it a bit fuzzy. And vodka.

But nothing eradicated it. Not completely.

By the time the accident was sorted it was nearly lunchtime. He was on duty for the public holiday, New Year's Day.

He went back to the station and continued with the list of break and enters he was collating.

He knew who'd done them. Plain as day. But he couldn't do anything about it.

When he got out of the police academy, life was simple. There was footy, there was beer, and there was Barb. And when you knew who'd done the break and enters, there were ways you could get an arrest. Just get them to confess.

Now. Jesus. All these bloody rules. They were always changing them, too. Protecting this person, and that. All the suspects had a protection blanket over them. Made the job impossible.

He was tempted to tell the higher-ups to shove their job. But what would he do? There were no security jobs in Myddle. He could move to Broughton, but who'd have him? It hadn't exactly been a stellar career.

He had no money saved. Barb had cleaned him out. So he was stuck here.

God, his head hurt.

He shuffled to the first aid cabinet and pulled out the aspirin.

Gazza looked at his watch.

Nearly two. This arvo, he'd take a few beers to Dash's.

Life was pretty simple for Dash. Handsome, sporty. Got the rich wife. Evie wasn't Gazza's cup of tea, though. Hard enough to work out what women were thinking at the best of times, never mind one that is rich and handles a gun and a horse better than a bloke.

But Dash didn't seem to mind. Almost liked it.

Gazza supposed it made life easy for Dash.

He knew Dash dabbled. That was his weakness. When he cast that grin around, the women melted and he couldn't help himself.

One day Evie would catch him at it and all hell would break loose.

Although Gazza knew from bitter experience that Dash would get a big chunk of Clive Downs if Evie kicked him out. That was the feature of no-fault divorce. One of the many things Barb had taught him. Wasn't enough for her to run off with his mate in the force. She took his house as well.

Dash had it made, no matter what he did.

8

RUTH

Early January, five and a half months before

A WEEK AFTER NEW YEAR'S, RUTH WAS LAZING ON THE VERANDAH OF the farmhouse watching the river ooze past. The house was old and pretty: square granite blocks with white shutters. Except it was odd that the shutters opened on the inside of the house instead of outside.

One more week in this beautiful place and then she'd be back in Sydney with the passive-resistant client.

Her future seemed bleak—and lonely. A year after Bill's death, she'd fallen into an affair with Charlie—one of Bill's doctor mates. It hadn't survived her visit to Charlie's home in Baltimore, where it became apparent that she wasn't his only girlfriend. The failure of that relationship only reinforced her fear that Bill was all there would ever be for her.

'Don't mind me,' said a voice.

Ruth startled and stood. She was still in her pyjamas: an old T-shirt and long faded paisley pants. No bra. Creased face. Unbrushed hair.

Chandra drifted in. Wrapped around her wild silver hair was that white scarf again—a riff on a turban—giving her an air of mystic charm.

'I brought you some falafels I just made,' Chandra said. 'And hommus.'

Ruth loved falafels. But she viewed them with trepidation because they always caused an outbreak of farting. She couldn't imagine that happening to Chandra. She looked to be a fart-free being.

'That's so kind,' Ruth said. 'Sorry I look so awful. Hadn't got round to getting dressed. Got absorbed with the currawongs.'

Chandra emitted a beatific smile. 'I should have warned you that I was coming.'

'Would you like a drink?' Ruth asked.

'That would be lovely.' Chandra scrabbled about in the big woven bag she had over her shoulder. 'I have my own supply of teabags. Just in case.' She held them out. 'Would you like one, too?'

Ruth was taken aback. Roscoe had always been in control of every interaction he had with another human, but this was on another level.

Ruth put the kettle on, hurried into the bedroom to chuck on a baggy linen dress, thanking the heavenly being who had ordained that ironing linen was no longer compulsory, then dangled Chandra's teabags into some boiling water, and took them out again.

'You know Roscoe is very worried about you,' Chandra said.

'Is he?' Ruth's stomach tightened. What was coming?

'He thought I might be able to help you.'

Ruth took a sip of tea and stared at the river. Out of politeness, she ought to say something, so she settled on 'Oh?'

'It must be so distressing to lose your husband, and then your job.'

Here we go.

'You must be wondering about the future.' Chandra had very beautiful skin, very green eyes and a very warm smile that lit up her face. Ruth almost wanted to confide in her, but if she let go—if she told the truth—she'd cry. And once she started, she might not be able to stop. 'I'm just working out what I'll do next. While I stare into the middle distance.'

'I have always found meditation helps.'

Ruth felt like she'd been in a permanent state of meditation lately. But maybe she was depressed. Maybe Chandra was just being kind.

'You might want to come to one of the yoga sessions I host,' Chandra said gently. 'It might help to talk to like-minded people. And you'll get some cake and a cup of tea.' She laughed, a resonant tinkle, like stream water over a rock.

Chandra stood to leave but then stopped at the door. 'Almost forgot. We've organised a goodbye picnic for you on Wednesday at Dash and Evie's campsite. We'll drive to Evie's and they'll take us there in a ute.'

'Sounds great,' said Ruth.

'And Roscoe said to tell you he'll drop by to pick you up at six for dinner at Patch's,' said Chandra. 'I'm so sorry I can't be there tonight.'

Ruth closed the door behind Chandra and resumed her position on the verandah.

She couldn't settle. It was like Chandra had managed to find a way into Ruth's soul and scratched a hole in the protective covering she had carefully built up.

She was beginning to wonder if she was suffering from a touch of PTSD. Not surprising, she supposed. The image of Bill on the bitumen flashed into her head, as it did several times a day.

An hour later, Patch rang to ask her what she thought about Chandra.

'Dad's completely infatuated with her. Mum's convinced it's tantric sex.'

Ruth let that one go.

'She seems okay to me. And one of the many things your father prides himself on is that he's a great judge of character.'

'Dunno about that,' said Patch. 'When it comes to his penis, his judgement turns to mush.'

Ruth skirted around talk of Roscoe's penis.

'I think you should give her a chance,' said Ruth. 'She might be a wonderful, selfless person.'

'She keeps telling everyone that she's a wonderful, selfless person. That's usually a sure sign the person saying it is an arsehole.'

Ruth laughed. 'You are my favourite godchild.'

'I'm not wrong, though,' said Patch.

Ruth thought it was still too early to say.

They agreed to go to Chandra's yoga session the next day. Ruth thought it would be good to see Chandra in her natural habitat. She could see what all the fuss was about: Roscoe's ardour and Patch's concern.

It was a fifteen-minute walk from the Airbnb to Roscoe's house. Ruth met Patch near the front door.

The yoga was held in what had been designed as a rumpus room under the main level. The vast room was milling with people, most of them, like Chandra, with a white muslin scarf wrapped around their heads in a loose turban.

Ruth and Patch rolled out their mats at the back.

Chandra, dressed in white fisherman's pants, sat cross-legged on a raised platform. A brass gong, as tall as her back, hung beside her. Roscoe tapped it, sending a long low note into the room.

Her spine straight and still, Chandra's hands moved rhythmically, as if drifting in a gentle current that encircled her. Her voice was mellifluous, like warm honey. 'Welcome. It's so great to have you all here ready to make your body a better place after all the drinking and eating over Christmas.'

Soft laughter around them.

'This year we are going on an ethical journey, where we align our bodies and our minds to make good decisions. The world's in a bad place and we're going to look for solutions from inside ourselves, where we will find calm and strength.'

Ruth opened an eye to look around. The congregation sat in rows on the floor, each arm outstretched in a V, rapture on their faces. Roscoe caught her eye and sent her his little secret smile. In the past she and Roscoe had exchanged looks like that in meetings where someone was making an arse of themselves, but she knew that wasn't what Roscoe was thinking now. He thought he'd given Ruth a gift by bringing her here.

Ruth closed her eyes.

'When we find our ethical core,' Chandra said, 'we become complete. We can direct our life path with confidence that we are doing the right thing, by ourselves and by Mother Earth.'

It was soothing. Reassuring. Ruth exhaled.

'Ask yourself this question: if in the next moment your actions would affect all of humanity forever, what would you do? That's the question you should ask yourself every moment of your life; every step you take, every lift of your hand, every morsel you eat.' She raised both index fingers to emphasise the next point.

'Every time you buy something, you must ask, is this going to save humanity?'

Ruth opened her eyes again. That seemed like a big responsibility.

'That's a lot, right? Well, to make it easier, we have ethically sourced products for sale here to help you in your journey.'

Ah. Pose a problem, then solve it with a product. Chandra was saving the earth with capitalism. Maybe she and Roscoe were perfectly suited after all.

'Let's centre ourselves. Legs crossed. Hold the tummy. Hands gently over knees. Breathe in for three,' she instructed, drawing a noisy breath. 'Breathe out for six.'

The window behind her framed a lush garden of ferns and pink bromeliads.

'Imagine,' Chandra said, in a voice that flowed and glowed, 'light from above is flooding into your body. We are constructing a space where clarity can invade. When you reach that place, your pineal gland will illuminate and your spirit will be visible to those around you.'

Ruth could feel Patch twitching beside her. She wasn't game to look at her. What the actual fuck was Chandra talking about?

Ruth found it difficult to contort her body into shapes it was too tight for. And she didn't have the strength to hold the poses. When Chandra offered a lesser choice for the weak and uncoordinated, Ruth had to take it. But there was something about the stretching which made her feel pure and vigorous.

At the end, when they lay on their mats for a few minutes, her mind felt more at rest than it had for a while.

When the session concluded, the audience rose to have some refreshments and check out the books, ethical food and boho fashions for sale at the back of the room.

Ruth bought two kombuchas for the suggested ten-dollar donation, and she and Patch stood side by side watching the crowd hug one another. Everyone looked like they'd had a transcendental experience, as if Chandra had reached down into their souls, found the aching heart which made them vulnerable, and caressed it.

Ruth's body tingled. She was calm but full of possibility. 'That wasn't so bad, was it?' she said to Patch. 'I feel fantastic. A bit glowy even.'

'Don't you think the sales pitch is a bit off?'

Ruth shrugged. 'We've all got to make a living.'

Patch screwed up her nose. 'What's a pineal gland?'

'Buggered if I know. I've never seen a glow emitted from someone's head either.'

Patch took a sip of a kombucha. 'Mum reckons she must go off like a cracker in the sack.'

Roscoe sidled up to Ruth and whispered so Patch couldn't hear, 'Isn't she wonderful?'

Before Ruth could respond, Chandra made an announcement. 'Just one thing before you leave. We are looking at building a retreat so that we can share these beautiful practices to help others. To do that we need to raise quite a bit of money. I would ask you to consider making a donation to help us help others and welcome people into our community. We take credit cards. And of course we are a registered charity. So any contribution you are kind enough to make is tax deductible.'

A tax-deductible charity. That smelt of Roscoe.

Ruth wondered if Chandra's congregation had any idea how rich Roscoe was.

'I'll drive you back to your house,' said Patch firmly.

'How did they meet?' Ruth asked. 'Roscoe and Chandra, I mean.'

'That's the worst part. Chandra was Mum's yoga teacher when they came up here to visit me a while ago. She convinced Mum to bring Dad along to a class at Azuri. Once she met him she was like a heat-guided missile. Only took a couple of months. Poor Mum was back in Sydney while Dad was finishing the new house with Chandra.'

'That's not good.' Poor Susan.

'I feel bad because the only reason Mum and Dad fixed on Myddle to build their retirement dream home was because of Shane and me.'

'Not your fault,' said Ruth as Patch pulled up outside the Airbnb.

'I s'pose I should be grateful I get to see him, and the kids know him. We hardly saw him while we were growing up.'

Ruth was familiar with that issue in men of Roscoe's age. Work–life balance for them was working while their wives ran their lives. When they reached retirement most of them realised they barely knew their kids.

'We've got the picnic tomorrow. Did Roscoe tell you?'

'Chandra did.'

'That'd be right. She always makes it look like she's responsible for happy things. Evie and I organised it, just so you know.'

Ruth didn't respond. She didn't want to feed Patch's intense dislike of Chandra.

'Thanks for the lift. And see you tomorrow,' she said as she got out of the car.

'You'll love the campsite,' said Patch from the open car window. 'It's spectacular.'

Ruth rang Susan. Partly to check in, and partly to check Patch's story.

'How are you?' said Susan.

'Great! And you?'

Susan didn't answer that. 'How's Myddle?'

That was a loaded question.

'Charming,' said Ruth. 'Bucolic.'

'How long are you there for, you poor thing? I adore my grandchildren, but living there all the time would do my head in. I never signed up to be a farmer's wife. Who'd have thought that's where Roscoe would end up.'

Roscoe wasn't exactly a farmer, but Ruth let that go.

'How's Chandra?' said Susan.

'Wafty,' said Ruth, which was as neutral an expression as she could muster at short notice.

'She was my yoga teacher,' said Susan. 'Did Patch tell you? Treacherous bitch. Watch out.'

There was a pause, which Susan eventually broke by adding, 'Still, she saved me from the farm. That's something, I suppose.'

WhatsApp

Ruth
I've taken up yoga

Jack
Send me a picture of you standing on your head

Ruth
I can barely sit cross-legged.
But I see why people rave about it.

Jack
And Chandra?

Ruth
Higher moral plane. A few wacky thoughts. But underneath it a mind directed towards commerce. And I like the yoga. She's a very good teacher.

Jack
Are you coming to London? You said you'd visit.

Ruth
March?

Jack
Ok

Ruth put her phone down.

Was it Chandra's yoga session that had given her the clarity?

She was leaving Myddle in a few days. She'd go back to the passive-resistant client for a fortnight, produce a report telling them what changes they should make, knowing they'd probably never do any of the things she recommended. Then she'd bugger off to London.

She missed Jack.

Dreadfully.

9

RUTH

January, five months before

IT WAS THE DAY OF THE GOODBYE PICNIC.

From Ruth's Airbnb, the road was a steady climb that narrowed until it was just a strip of bitumen between two gravel shoulders edged by a deep ditch, thick with grass. The hill was steep near the farm gate. She turned in, over a cattle grid. The driveway was two kilometres of further climbing until she reached the house: white weatherboard surrounded by a wide verandah, a huge deck high above the river.

Evie emerged from the house to welcome Ruth. Her thin face culminated in a Gallic, aquiline nose; a high ridge of mountain above the tree line.

It was a hot day. Evie was in a T-shirt, shorts and an ancient pair of elastic-sided boots with thick black tread. Ruth eyed her pink sandals: flat but flimsy with soles meant for a brief excursion on a city footpath. Had she misjudged? Surely not. It wasn't like they were going for a walk.

A peacock and six peahens were pecking in the garden.

'Peacocks?' Ruth said.

'Dash's brain snap,' said Evie. 'Noisy as fuck and they crap everywhere.'

'Elegant, though,' said Ruth.

Evie grunted.

They piled into Dash's ute. 'Sorry, Ruth,' said Dash. 'Just clear a space in the back.' He swept a pair of footy boots, an oily rag and a drill to the floor.

They headed back out to the road, then travelled three kilometres further up until the narrow strip of bitumen petered out into a gravel track.

'Is that the national park?' Ruth pointed to a sign.

'Yeah,' said Dash. 'It's an entrance nobody uses much. The main entrance is off the Dongo Highway west over the range.'

They turned into a gate, then drove past grazing auburn cows for twenty minutes over a bumpy farm track, pausing to open and close gates.

Dash pulled up at a eucalypt glade overlooking a broad bend in the rushing river, a steep granite escarpment looming over it. Big grey kangaroos, camouflaged by the dappled light and shade, were outed only when they hopped away in slow motion.

A campsite which Dash and Evie rented out to tourists was just downstream, a dozen campervans and tents, orange and khaki spread along the bank.

Patch and Shane and the kids were already there with Roscoe and Chandra.

'No cows in here?' said Ruth.

'It's a carbon project,' said Evie. 'Been registered for five years. The grass was degraded from grazing and it's so steep it wasn't great for cattle anyway, so we fenced it off.'

'We should take Ruth up the Bluff,' said Patch, pointing at the escarpment. 'You'll love the view.'

The walk was five hundred metres up a gravel track, which culminated in a slippery rock face so steep that Ruth had to crawl up with hands and feet. Everyone else skipped up in their clumpy Blundstone boots, even two-year-old Milly.

Ruth had definitely misjudged the fashion requirements for a country picnic.

At the peak were a few square metres of flattish granite.

'Wow,' said Ruth. It was a grand vista. The river wound through dark green forest and emerald green cane farms. On the horizon an inch of navy sea met the vast dome of cerulean sky.

Evie pointed at the saplings and vines and bush growing into forest below. 'That growth generates carbon credits, but it's also good for the land. See that erosion?' Evie pointed to a deep red gully below, like a scar. 'Half the topsoil was disappearing down the river when we had rain. That will stop with the regrowth.'

Ruth peered sideways over the edge. Fifteen metres below, the river rushed through a gorge, rapids skipping through boulders, the water clear and bright. The sheer drop made her nervous. She stepped away.

A pink sandal slipped on the smooth rock. Her leg shot out in front of her and she landed with a thud, right on the lip of rock. She leaned back to stop herself sliding over the cliff.

'You all right?' said Dash.

'Just a sore bum.' Ruth got up quickly. She'd banged her coccyx. It hurt. A lot. But her pride hurt more.

'Better a sore bum than a sore head. Wouldn't have been good if you'd gone over the edge,' said Shane.

'We should've told you to wear non-slip shoes,' said Evie. 'Bare feet would be safer than those.' She frowned at the sandals. 'But, you know, snakes.'

Patch laughed. 'Those sandals wouldn't offer much protection from a tiger snake.'

'You can take the girl out of the city . . .' said Roscoe.

'What a view,' Ruth said, to change the subject. Teasing city-dwellers for their incompetence could go on all afternoon. 'And so tranquil.'

But Ruth had spoken too soon. The peace was shattered by a revving engine. Two jet skis fired up at the riverbank down at the campsite.

'Who's that?' Ruth asked.

'Grey nomads. Our biggest customers.'

'Jet-skiing?' Ruth was surprised. The noise was a violent invasion of her head—the aqua version of a Harley Davidson.

'We rent them out. Mostly it's the local boys from town who use them.'

'Can't you make them stop, Dash?' said Evie. 'It's deafening.'

Dash glared at Evie and shook his head.

Ruth took her sandals off to get down the rock face, waiting for the others to go first in the hope that the snakes would have slithered away from the commotion.

Back at the bottom, Shane lit the fire under a cast-iron grill placed over some rocks.

A silver ute pulled up and disgorged four adults.

'You know Harry Dunstan, don't you?' said Dash.

'Of course,' said Ruth.

Harry had been a year ahead of her at uni, a dissolute young fellow. She'd seen him more at the rec club than the law library, more often drunk than sober. But drunk in the nicest possible way. Slurry. Affectionate. Now he looked like the responsible local lawyer and Rotarian that he was, although greying around the edges.

'Heard you were coming,' said Harry. 'We've been at the beach so we missed the New Year's party.'

Harry introduced his wife Marge and his children Julia and Sam: mid-twenties, wholesome, handsome, square white teeth. In the awkward way of the barely acquainted, Harry and Ruth filled in the twenty-five years since they'd last seen one another with a few short sentences, which stalled completely after Ruth laid out the rudimentary facts associated with Bill's sudden death.

To fill the uncomfortable silence, Ruth turned to Dash. 'Such a lovely property. How long has it been in your family?'

'It's my family's,' said Evie. 'My great-great-great-grandfather settled here a hundred and seventy years ago now. He came to log it. When the cedar trees were gone, he brought in the cows.'

Ruth felt like an idiot for assuming the property had come down the male line. She had to stop herself saying sorry, which would only make her gaffe worse.

Good to hear that a girl had inherited the farm. Especially as, even in these enlightened times, it was still not the norm. Or maybe there were no sons in Evie's family.

'It must have been hard for him,' Ruth said. 'Settling here.'

'He was a hard man,' Evie said. 'His own father was a convict. Sheep stealing.'

'First settlers in the district,' said Marge.

'First white people,' Evie corrected her. Her tone was terse, dismissive, like she wanted to shut the conversation down.

Marge didn't notice. 'It's interesting actually. The shutters in Evie's old farmhouse open inwards, so they could close them when the Aborigines attacked.'

'I wondered about those shutters,' said Ruth. 'Horrible truth. I'll be awake all night thinking about it.'

'Time to get the sausages on,' said Evie to Dash.

Mentioning the frontier war which white Australians deny ever happened was always guaranteed to stop a conversation dead.

10

RUTH

January, five months before

WHILE SHANE AND DASH MANNED THE BARBIE, RUTH AND EVIE PICKED their way down to the river where green water tumbled over the rocks. A small, bloodied, furry animal lay in the mud by the water, a flat brown beak lying separate to the body.

'What's that?' said Ruth.

Evie crouched down to examine it. 'Platypus,' she said. 'Dismembered.' She shook her head. 'A camper had a cat that had a litter of kittens here a couple of years ago. They left them here and the native wildlife's been under attack ever since.'

'That's horrible.'

'Worst part is cats kill for fun. It would be less offensive if they only killed for food, but it's a sport for them. And they leave the carcasses around for us to find. This little fella was killed last night I reckon.'

Evie kicked some mud over the body. 'The kids don't need to see that.'

Poor little platypus, Ruth thought. *Left under the mud.*

'Bloody campers, eh,' said Ruth.

'Too lazy to find the cats a home and too gutless to kill them. Does my head in.'

'Those sausages ready yet?' Evie asked Shane as they wandered back to the barbie.

'Yep.'

They lined up for the great Australian dish: a sausage on white bread with fried onion and tomato sauce. Cooked over an open fire, it tasted of smoke and vast blue skies.

'How's the campsite business going?' Harry asked Evie.

She grimaced. 'Better ask Dash. The punters drive me nuts. Leaving a litter of kittens was the worst thing they've done. But they also leave the gate open, then complain when the cows go through it. They complain about everything actually: the dunnies, the snakes, the lack of phone coverage.'

The jet skis roared again.

'Come on, Evie,' said Dash. 'They're not that bad.'

'How hard is it to close a bloody gate?' said Evie.

'Evie doesn't understand the need people have for being connected by phone.' Patch gave Evie a soft punch on her arm.

'Why bother taking it with you everywhere?' said Evie. 'I don't get it. There's no coverage on the farm because we're in the shadow of the Bluff, so there's no point. Even in the house we have to use wi-fi.'

'But what if someone needs to talk to you?'

Evie shrugged. 'If they really want to talk to me, they'll leave a message.'

'So you just have a landline?' Ruth was in disbelief.

'Nup. The only people who ever called it were scammers and Dash's mother. We just use our mobiles and wi-fi.'

Ruth wiped some tomato sauce from her chin, and tried to imagine a world where she couldn't google gaps in her knowledge whenever and wherever they occurred to her.

'What about social media?' said Ruth.

'I have Instagram and Facebook to post photos of the cattle. Otherwise, I stay away.'

'Quite right,' said Roscoe. 'It's a hell-scape: half banality, half abuse.'

Chandra changed the subject. 'It's such a beautiful spot here. Almost spiritual. Have you thought that maybe it's wasted as a campsite?'

Dash leaned forward. 'You read my mind, Chandra. I've been thinking about building some cottages here and putting them on Airbnb.'

'That's a thought,' said Chandra in the tone of a person who had a better one.

Roscoe said, 'What about a wellness retreat? A luxury getaway. Spa. Yoga. Meditation. People would pay a fortune to come.'

'How much?' Dash asked.

'There's one near the Gold Coast that charges five grand a week.'

'For a couple?' asked Evie.

'Each person,' said Chandra. 'It's all inclusive. Food. Yoga. Wellness lectures. It's beautiful. But your river bend is just as beautiful. And it's more remote but close enough to the airport at Broughton.'

Harry's son Sam whistled. 'Jeez. The booze must be good.'

'There'd be no alcohol,' said Chandra, as if that were obvious. 'It's a wellness retreat, about healing. No caffeine either.'

Dash and Sam scoffed at the idea of a couple who'd pay ten grand to do yoga for a week with no coffee and no booze.

'It's something to think about anyway,' said Roscoe.

'Are you offering to run it?' Ruth said to Roscoe.

'I'd be happy to help,' Chandra said. 'I was involved in one in Azuri. If you need any advice, or any contacts, I can point you in the right direction.'

'It's where I met Chandra,' Roscoe said, with proprietorial pride.

'Their eyes met under the downward dog,' Ruth added.

Patch snorted. Roscoe ignored the remark.

She probably had gone too far. She drifted away from the conversation to Harry and Marge who were sitting on a log under a eucalypt watching the Wildlings play a game of touch footy with Evie.

She gingerly lowered her bottom onto a large rock facing them, jiggling to find a spot that didn't have a sharp edge.

'I hear you're out of work,' said Harry.

'Voluntary,' said Ruth. 'Doing contract stints.'

That embarrassed him. He stuttered. 'I wasn't suggesting . . . Sorry. I just see it as an opportunity. For Marge and me.'

'Why's that?' asked Ruth.

'We wondered if you could take over the practice for a few months, as a locum, so we could have a holiday.'

He shifted uncomfortably. She realised that she was probably delivering what Jack and Bill had called 'the death stare'.

'Sorry, Harry. I can't get past the fact that I don't have a clue what you do. Family? Wills? Conveyancing? Never done any of it. Ever.'

'It's not hard. You're the smart one. You'll pick it up in no time.'

Roscoe sauntered up. 'Of course you could do it, Ruth. On your ear.'

Ruth decided she'd say no. She was so removed from the type of work that Harry did, he may as well have been suggesting she take over the local medical practice.

Milly squealed in delight as Dash and Sam and Julia joined the touch footy game.

'I can't find anyone to take it over for me,' Harry pleaded. 'Six months. That's all I need. I'm at the end of my tether. Haven't had a proper break for thirty years.'

Some onion slipped out from the end of Ruth's sausage. She caught it with her fingers and licked them clean.

'C'mon. It'd be fun having you in town,' said Roscoe.

'It's not that hard, really,' said Harry. He was desperate, eyes narrowed into a plea for help.

Maybe it would be all right. After she got back from London, a stint in the country doing yoga would salve her damaged soul while she figured out what to do next.

Her lack of expertise in country legal matters could be overcome. She could always use Google to point her in the right direction or phone one of the myriad barristers, judges and solicitors in her long list of friends. 'What's your internet like?' she asked.

'It works, most of the time.'

'What about your staff?'

'It's me and Marge and Deb, who is part secretary, part receptionist and part paralegal. She's all over it. Been with me for years.' He corrected himself. 'Decades.'

'Let me think about it,' Ruth said.

A squeal from two-year-old Milly distracted them. Sam and Julia were pretending to tackle her.

Evie ran in. 'Pass me the ball, Milly,' she said, taking it and sprinting to the imaginary line. She was fast, but Sam took off after her, grabbed her and pulled her to the ground. 'We're playing touch, Sam!' Evie objected, laughing. 'Not grab.'

The Wildlings piled on top of Evie and Sam, who lay side by side on the ground.

Evie would make a great mum, Ruth thought as she watched them.

Patch came over. 'Has Harry spoken to you about the locum, Ruth?'

Ruth wondered if it was her idea, a way to keep Ruth in Myddle to observe Roscoe and Chandra.

'It would be so great, Ruth,' continued Patch. 'We'd love to have you around.'

'Is this a set-up?' said Ruth.

Chandra joined them, using a paper napkin to wipe her fingers. 'Imagine how great you'd be at yoga in six months.' She laughed.

That did sound appealing. She'd be strong and thin, and blissed out.

'Okay,' said Ruth. 'I'm going to London in March to see Jack. I suppose I could come back at the beginning of April. But no longer than six months.'

Marge clapped. 'Terrific,' she said. 'You can have our house.'

Later Ruth realised it was the fact that she was wanted which clinched it. Belonging somewhere. Being needed.

Replete with sausage and onion, the adults lay on the grass in the shade, white cockatoos squawking in the eucalypt canopy above. The children went off in a posse to have adventures. Shane, with a beer, propped himself up on an elbow to keep an eye on them.

'Hey, Dad,' one of the children yelled out from under a spreading gum. 'There's an animal in a hole. It's hissing at us.'

'Don't disturb it,' yelled Patch.

'Does it have fur or scales?' yelled Evie.

'Fur.'

Evie headed over and peered down. She turned and stomped towards the ute. 'Did you bring the rifle, Dash? It's a cat.'

'Yep. It's in the lock box. Keys are in the console.'

Evie unlocked a long metal box attached to the tray of the ute and pulled out a rifle.

The children ran beside her. 'Can I shoot it?' asked Patch's eight-year-old.

'No,' said Shane. 'Stay back here with me.'

'They bring a gun to a picnic?' Roscoe whispered to Ruth.

'You should see the platypus the cat mutilated,' Ruth whispered back.

Evie walked back to the hole, pointed the rifle down and pulled the trigger.

A cacophony of squawks, and the trees cleared of birds. Further down the hill, campers emerged from their caravans.

Evie locked the gun away.

Dash got a hessian bag and pulled the bloodied carcass of a cat out of the hole. It extended down to his knees.

'It's huge,' said Patch.

Dash dropped the bag in the cabin of the ute and closed the door.

'Have to keep it away from the dogs,' said Evie. 'Sorry, Ruth. You might want to get a lift with Shane back to the house.'

'I want to shoot the gun,' said Patch's six-year-old, prompting a clamour of demands from the four children.

Shane closed down the buts with a raised eyebrow and a shake of his head.

'Sorry about that, everyone,' said Evie. 'We've been looking for those cats for over a year.'

Chandra hovered behind everyone, her arms crossed, her jaw taut. 'You shot a living creature,' she said.

The sinews in Evie's neck tightened as she restrained herself.

What would you do, Chandra? Ruth wanted to ask. *What would be the ethical choice?*

Instead, Evie slowly nodded. 'If we leave out baits, we kill everything.'

'What about catching it and taming it?'

'If you want a feral cat in your home,' said Evie, 'feel free to come and catch one. There are more here. Just let me know what equipment you need and I'll do what I can to help.'

Chandra turned away.

'C'mon,' said Evie. 'Let's pack up before the campers come and ask us what we're doing.'

WhatsApp

Jack
How's Myddle?

Ruth
Went to a picnic on Dash and Evie's property. Very weird.

Jack
?

Ruth
It's exquisitely beautiful by the river. But Dash has turned it into a campsite. With jet skis.

Jack
Ruthie wouldn't like that

Ruth

And then in the middle of the picnic, Evie pulled out a gun and killed a cat

Jack

Woah

Ruth

To be fair, it was a feral cat.
Which had mutilated a platypus.

Jack

A gun at a picnic?

Ruth

They keep it in a lock box in the back of the ute. Farmers need them I guess.
Chandra was outraged.

Jack

Not really in keeping with wafty idealism

Ruth

Evie and Chandra don't speak the same language.
I've bought my air tickets. 2 March.

Jack

👍

Ruth

I've booked a hotel in Kensington

Jack

[Photo of a very small and very messy sitting room]
Just as well

11

EVIE

January, five months before

WHEN THEY GOT BACK FROM THE PICNIC, DASH DIDN'T SPEAK TO EVIE. She made scrambled eggs for tea, and he gulped them down silently, took his plate to the dishwasher, then wiped down the kitchen bench with such vigour, he knocked one of her mum's flying ducks off the wall and it broke.

She'd upset him. Evie thought back over the conversation that day, trying to pinpoint what it was. 'What's up?' she said from the sink where she was washing the saucepans.

Dash was engaged in silent, angry sweeping, cleaning up the duck.

She tried again. 'I'm sorry, Dash, if I offended you.'

He stopped sweeping and shook his head. 'You never support anything I do.'

Evie knew then what it was. She had criticised the campground and jet skis. He took it as a personal affront. 'That's not true.'

'I'm just trying to make the Bluff work for us, as a money spinner, and all you do is chip away at it. All those people think I'm hopeless.'

'I'm sorry, Dash. I think you're wonderful, you know that. The farm wouldn't work without you.'

He put down the broom and got the dustpan from the pantry.

'Imagine if it was just me,' she said, 'shooting cats at picnics. Myddle would talk about the mad lady up at the Bluff.'

'A bit of support. That's all I'm asking for.'

She put a wet, soapy hand on his shoulder. He was still but didn't shrug it off.

Sex would always heal a rift with Dash. She squeezed his upper arm. 'Nice guns,' she said.

He shook his head, but he smiled.

'Come on,' she said. 'Let's go to bed.'

That's how they did their marriage: a waxing and waning of affection and hostility, like waves at the beach—sometimes rough, sometimes smooth, but always there, a constant energy.

12

BEA

March, three months before

BEA WAS IN THE KITCHEN AT TWO AM GETTING A DRINK OF WATER WHEN her mum's bedroom door opened and someone—not her mum—softly closed it and shuffled out in bare feet.

It was too late to go back to her room and close the door. The man was in the hall between the kitchen and her bedroom. Bea stood, the glass to her lips, waiting. These encounters were never good. It was just a question of how bad they would be, and how much Bea's mum would blame her when things turned sour.

'G'day, Bea,' said Gazza.

Beer fumes wafted over her. Gazza was naked. He realised that at the same moment she did and made a half-hearted attempt to cover his crotch with his hand. At least she hadn't turned on the light. Bea had on a T-shirt and pyjama pants. She didn't walk around the house nude because she never knew who she might run into.

'Sorry,' said Gazza. He pointed in the direction of her mum's bedroom door. 'Your mum and I . . .' His voice drifted as he got to the part of the sentence where he would have to explain why he was in her house.

Bea crossed her arms over her chest. She wanted to return to her room but she would have to brush past Gazza to get there, so for now she was stuck, leaning against the sink.

Victoria's bedroom door opened and her mum came out, wiping her eyes. She'd put on a dressing gown, at least. 'What are you doing up?' she said.

Bea concentrated on being as small a target as possible. 'Just getting a glass of water.'

'Go back to bed,' said Victoria. 'Come on, Gazza. We should go back to bed, too.'

'Nah,' said Gazza. 'I should be off.'

'Come back to bed,' Victoria wheedled. Her mother's default persona in these situations was desperate with a veneer of coquettish.

'Nah. Best get going,' said Gazza.

'You'd better get some clothes on,' said Bea. 'Or you'll be arrested for exposure.'

'Beatrice!' said Victoria. 'Don't be rude. And go back to bed.'

'I'm not the one with no clothes on,' said Bea. 'In someone else's house.'

'He's my guest,' said Victoria. 'And I expect you to be polite.'

Gazza expelled some air through his ravaged nasal passages, and turned to go back to Victoria's room.

Victoria hissed at Bea, 'Go back to bed! We'll talk about your behaviour in the morning,' then turned to hurry after Gazza, who had closed the door behind him.

Bea noisily dumped some books and the fan behind her bedroom door. She'd asked her mother to install a lock on the door, but Victoria had told her to stop undermining her, so Bea had to provide her own security against any incursions as best she could.

She crawled back into bed and pulled the doona over her head.

Could she leave?

If she knew who her father was, she could ask him for help. But that topic was a no-go zone. She wondered sometimes if Victoria even knew who he was. Her mother had been working as a nurse in Sydney when she got pregnant, at nineteen. Maybe Bea's father was a big-deal doctor. She dreamt sometimes of tracking him down. She'd show up at the hospital where he'd just got out of theatre and she'd tell him who she was and his eyes would light up. She would be the daughter he'd always longed for.

He'd invite her out to dinner. They'd go to an Italian restaurant with great pasta. 'How's your mum?' he would ask with a tone of ironic regret and she would say, 'Well, you know?' and roll her eyes. And he would say, 'I'm so sorry. If I'd known you existed, I'd have come for you.'

As if.

She could hear her mother's high-pitched murmuring on the other side of the wall, then the rhythmic banging of the bedhead. Gazza grunted, and it stopped.

There were thumps and footsteps as he moved around Victoria's bedroom.

The bedroom door opened and he thudded away. 'Will you call me?' Victoria yelled after him, and Gazza muttered as he closed the front door.

Bea lay in bed, her eyes open. She shuddered.

Her mum's taste in men was shocking. She was always banging on about how she came from Bellevue Hill and went to some posh boarding school. As if it still mattered. Now she hung out with blokes who had never heard of Bellevue Hill.

Victoria had thrown way too many violent tantrums at family Christmases to ever be invited back. Mind you, she wasn't the only one. Being a dickhead was hereditary in that family. Victoria's father was some big-time lawyer. A judge or something.

Victoria's mother—Bea's granny—rang up every six months or so wanting to speak to Bea. Victoria always refused, shouting down the phone that she didn't want them interfering in her life anymore. Then she'd go to the fridge and pour herself a glass of wine from the large cardboard box in there.

When Bea was about ten, and Victoria's father had kicked them out of the last family Christmas, Victoria had moved to Myddle where the grass was green and the houses were cheap. She'd bought the house with money she inherited from a childless great aunt and lived on the dole because she couldn't hold down a job. Her mother had given up on herself. Bellevue Hill was a distant dream.

At least Gazza had a job. That was a big plus. Pity he was such a sleaze.

The afternoon after the Gazza incident, Bea dawdled home from work. She found it was best to expect Bad Victoria to meet you at the door, because then you wouldn't be disappointed.

'Hello, darling,' said Victoria. 'How was work?'

This was as close to an apology as Bea would get.

'Pretty good.' She smiled. Bad Victoria was awful, but Good Victoria could be fun.

'I've made boeuf bourguignon and I thought we'd watch *Fleabag* tonight.'

It was Bea's favourite dish, and the show she and Good Victoria watched together.

'I'll make risotto,' said Bea.

Victoria pulled her homemade chicken stock out of the freezer and defrosted it in the microwave while Bea cut up some golden shallots and blanched them in olive oil.

'My best girl,' said Victoria, hugging Bea while she stood at the stove. 'You've got a gift when it comes to risotto.'

'That's me,' said Bea. 'Gifted.'

They ate in front of *Fleabag*. They'd watched it so often they could recite some of the lines. 'Love isn't something weak people do,' they shouted together, and Victoria laughed and kissed Bea on the forehead.

13

GAZZA

March, three months before

HE KNEW VICTORIA WAS A DANGEROUS CHOICE, BUT HE WAS PISSED AT the pub and one thing led to another. He was desperate. He accepted that.

Then he ran into the kid at two am, starkers.

He tried to be embarrassed but, actually, it turned him on a bit. Helped with the brewer's droop when Victoria made him perform again soon after.

Victoria was better than nothing, which was the only alternative Gazza had right now. But she could turn from flirt to banshee in an instant. A bloke would get whiplash trying to work out what had happened.

Bea was a good kid. He felt a bit sorry for her, having to put up with Victoria all the time.

She reminded him of Barb when they first met while still at high school. The before times, he called it, when Barb still laughed at his jokes.

14

EVIE

March, three months before

SATURDAY AFTERNOON. DASH WAS AT THE FOOTY. EVIE LOOKED DOWN at her bloodied undies with numb dismay. It always made such a mess. A big crimson chunk fell into the bowl. She leaned forward, but it didn't ease the relentless gnawing in her abdomen: like someone had grabbed her uterus with both fists and was twisting it until the lining gushed out in big, red, slimy dollops.

God, it hurt. She was pretty sure she had used the last of the Naprogesic. She'd have to go to the chemist. Until then she'd have to put up with it. Nausea engulfed her.

Fibroids, the doctor said. He could fix it so it didn't hurt anymore—poke a wand up her vagina and irradiate her uterus, kind of burn it out—but that would mean her uterus couldn't ever hold a baby. So she was stuck with the fibroids and the pain.

Still sitting on the loo, she leaned over and put her head in her hands.

Just after Patch had Milly, she'd complained about the post-birth gushing of blood that went on and on. Patch had said the midwives asked, 'How's your loss, love?' Patch had let out a sarcastic guffaw. 'Massacre more like! They think up the worst euphemisms.'

But for Evie it *was* a loss. Every month. And it wasn't tempered by the sweet joy of a fresh baby nuzzling.

She sat, delaying the moment when she'd put the stopper in, a finger bloodied as she poked that wad of cotton right up, striving to find the right spot so that she couldn't feel it in there. God, she hated it. So messy. So dark red.

Her phone dinged with a message. Still sitting on the toilet seat, she reached for it. An unknown number. Evie tapped on it. There were two messages, sent in quick succession.

Just thought you ought to know, the first one said, *Dash and I have been seeing one another for six months.*

The small room, still and heavy, closed in around Evie.

The second message said, *We fuck every Wednesday night when you think he's still at footy training.*

Evie read it again, struggling to process it.

It finished with a name: *Deirdre*. Did she know a Deirdre? She couldn't think of any.

She read it a third time.

Could it be true?

The phone pinged again. This time a photo.

She recognised the pubic hair.

The feelings came in then, more tsunami than wave. She stood, and then sat again as blood rushed down her leg. Her body was letting her know she had to prioritise. She had to sort out the mess between her legs before she turned her thoughts to her marriage.

She made herself insert the tampon, and she lay on the bed in the foetal position. The pain that radiated from her uterus consumed her, destructive, sucking back then surging forward to strike her again.

First there was fury, a guttural scream of rage. Then a maelstrom: fear, denial, rechecking the photo, blame, asking what she could have done to make him do that. She stuck her fingernails into her thigh.

And then there was the pain. Not the pain in her uterus, but a deep, melancholic howl spreading up through her throat.

Who was this Deirdre? Why was she so cruel? Why would she take Dash when she knew he was married? The tsunami turned red with hatred.

Was Dash even the person she thought she had married? That person loved her, adored her. His smile lit up his face when he saw her. He wouldn't do this.

She tried not to picture Dash having sex with someone else, but again and again it appeared in her mind.

She sobbed, in anger and sorrow, for the death of the life she thought she had.

At last she heard the screen door bang. He was home. Dusk had fallen and the house was dark and cold.

'Evie?' he called out. His footsteps came up the hall. 'Evie?' he said again. 'What's wrong?'

She couldn't speak so she unlocked her phone and handed it over. She watched him read it, disbelief and dismay registering in his face. He stared at it.

And then he said, 'That spiteful little slag.'

He sat beside her on the bed and tried to hold her. She shrank away.

He said, 'She chased me Evie. She's mad. She only sent this because I told her I couldn't do it anymore.'

'You're saying she made you do it?' Evie almost laughed. How stupid.

'No.' His arms were jerking. 'It's been so hard—trying to conceive. I guess I just wanted to see what sex would be like without the planning. And she was offering. Like, more than offering.'

Oh, so it was Evie's fault then.

'You prick,' she shouted. 'Get out. Just go.'

Dash left the room but stayed in the house, making enough noise for her to know he was in the second bedroom.

She didn't sleep. The house was heavy with tension.

The next morning he made her coffee. She didn't speak to him. He disgusted her.

'I'm so sorry, Evie,' he said. 'I told her I couldn't do it anymore. It was only a couple of times anyway. It didn't mean anything. It was just sex. I don't want to hurt you. It was stupid. It'll never happen again.'

For a week, Deirdre texted her every day.

Just so you know, said one text, *I had an abortion.*

Evie's hatred became a kind of madness that overwhelmed her. She stoked it every day. She wished she could stop, but she kept going over it in her mind.

She found out Deirdre was the receptionist of a real estate agency in Broughton. Evie hung outside, peering in. Deirdre couldn't have been more than twenty-five. She had a bony face, not unlike Evie's, although where Evie's nose was like a mountain, Deirdre's was pert and upturned.

Evie walked inside. Deirdre stared at her, slack-jawed.

Evie put her hands on the reception desk and leaned over until her face was level with Deirdre's. 'Keep away from me,' Evie snarled through gritted teeth. 'It will be better for you if you do.'

Deirdre's eyes widened further.

'Understand?'

Deirdre swallowed as she nodded.

Evie had an urge to destroy something: push a lamp, kick over a chair, slap Deirdre on the face. She squared her shoulders, and made herself turn away and walk out.

The rage, it frightened her.

She told him to leave. He didn't.

He promised that he would never do it again. He promised with flowers, champagne, meals he made himself. Charm; always the charm.

If there was any leaving to do, it had to be him. She couldn't go. It was her farm.

Evie made an appointment with Harry Dunstan.

'How can I help?' said Harry.

She couldn't say it so she handed her phone to him, opened to Deirdre's texts.

His face went white. Harry had probably never seen a dick pic before. Or perhaps he had. Lawyers see the dark side of human nature.

'Oh, Evie,' was all he said.

'I want him to leave. I can't live with him.'

The edges of Harry's mouth turned down. In slow motion, he clasped his hands and placed them on his desk. 'Here's the thing about divorce and family properties,' he said.

If the marriage ended, he told her, there'd be a fight about money. And Dash would likely get a good chunk of the farm.

She could pay him out instead. But that was impossible when you calculated the land value, farm income and interest rates.

'But it's my family's farm,' she said.

'Doesn't matter.'

'What about Mum?'

'Your mother only has a life interest. You own the farm but you can't sell it while your mum is alive. Not unless she agrees. Or you use the power of attorney.'

'So I'm stuck with him.'

Harry shrugged. 'No. You just need to understand the consequences.'

How was this knowledge right here at the front of Harry's mind? He must have answered these questions before. A hundred times.

'What do other people do?' she asked.

He shifted in his seat. He didn't want to answer.

She reached back into her mind.

'Is that why Shane Dwyer got the farm while his parents were fairly young? His parents split up straight after the succession went through.'

Harry shrugged and raised his eyebrows. Of course he couldn't say anything.

But that's what it was about. Succession. Give it to the son or daughter, and then split up. After the land has been secured.

She couldn't even do that. There was nobody to give it to.

She left Harry's office. Got in the ute. Drove home. Saddled Jasper. Went for a ride up to the Bluff.

The haze over the eucalypts in the valley below calmed her.

She sat on the escarpment. Lay back.

There were no clouds. Not one.

A hawk hovered above. It seemed to be watching her. Its mate flew near. They were a partnership, suspended together over the world.

A roar. The fucking jet skis.

The hawks tilted their wings, and disappeared.

She sat up. Two jet skis were doing doughnuts. Morons.

One of the campervans had a burnt orange tent, garish under a eucalypt.

She hated the campground. Everything about it reeked of Dash: his get-rich-quick schemes that never worked out because, in his mind, all he had to do was come up with the idea, and Evie would execute it.

She slid down from the Bluff, retrieved Jasper, mounted.

It was either farm and Dash, or . . . nothing? She had no qualifications to be anything but a farmer. She'd given that up to have the farm. Half a farm would be barely viable.

Her future had to include him.

Jasper's body, huge and muscled, ambled beneath her. With a twitch of the reins she could release his power. He would gallop, jump.

She had to build a life with Dash, with this truth festering within it. When she framed it like that, she could think about him differently.

He said he loved her. She didn't doubt it. The core truth to Dash was that he believed every whim he had should be satisfied, and there would be no consequences. So if he saw a woman, a Deirdre, his face would light up with that world-changing smile, and off he'd go. Dash thought his superpower was that he could charm his way out of any sticky situation.

She made herself list the good things about Dash.

Number one: who else could she go through the pain of conceiving with?

Number two: she didn't have the time to find someone else before the chances of conception expired.

Number three: she loved him. And Dash was all the love she had now. She had to take what he offered. Everyone else was dead, except for her mother. And her mother, whose mind was already drifting away, would soon be gone in body as well.

⁂

'Are you eating, Mum?' Evie stroked her mother's hand. Every time Evie saw her mother, she was thinner. Her nose, like the hooked beak of the sea hawks at Azuri, dominated her face. Mrs Clive was hunched over in the large, beige, vinyl chair the nursing home provided, dwarfed by it, as if her spine had given up the struggle to keep her erect. Evie hated the smell of this place: urine, gravy, disinfectant, and the musty pong of old flesh.

Evie searched her mother's cloudy eyes. She wasn't blind; she could discern shapes and colours. If she got up to walk to the next room, she skirted around chairs and coffee tables. But her eyes could not observe or interpret; they could not connect the things she was looking at now with things she had seen in the past.

She didn't recognise Evie anymore, although she pretended she did. She was aware that Evie was a good person in her life. She just had no idea of Evie's name, or how she knew her.

Her mother drifted further into the past every time Evie visited. Last time she had wondered fretfully where Dad was. This time it was Joof.

'Is Joof coming?' Her voice quavered.

Evie put her hand over her mother's. Squeezed it. 'No, Mum, he's not coming today.'

'Perhaps tomorrow,' she said.

When her mother had first asked this question, Evie had told her he was never coming because he was dead, and her mother had grieved again. So Evie had started pretending that Joof was alive and might saunter through the door to give his mother a kiss on the cheek, say, 'How are you, old duck?' and sit down and talk about his horses.

Oh, how wonderful that would be.

Evie sat, stroking her mother's hand, listening to her stories of Joof falling off the horse and landing head-first into a show jump, or starting school and pleading with her to let him stay home and play with the bulls instead.

When her mother died, the event she both dreaded and wished for, Evie would be alone.

Except for Dash.

When Evie Clive was in her first year at uni (back when she was going to be a physiotherapist), her flatmate Amy came to her bed, shook her awake and said, 'Evie. Your brother's been in an accident.'

'What's he done this time?' Evie said through the fog of sleep. Because Joof was always getting into scrapes: a broken arm from falling out of a tree when he was five; several concussions after being thrown off his horse; a broken leg from parachuting. He always bounced back.

But this accident was different. Amy sat beside the bed, her face flat and sad.

Joof had been in a car crash. On the Azuri Road.

Evie's body rose from the bed, pushed up by some primal force. There was an urge within her, a call to action, to fix whatever was wrong with Joof.

Joof was on life support. That's what her mother said when she rang, her voice so tight Evie barely recognised it.

Evie needed to be with Joof. She shouldn't drive, people said, and home was eight hours of driving away. She had to wait for her mother's brother to take her.

It was almost lunchtime before her uncle picked her up. He didn't say much—he was crying—so Evie stared out the window, looking at cows chewing their cud in the paddocks, life continuing while hers had been torn apart. Already, she could feel the absence of Joof, an absence of the larrikin, the boy who would climb up on the roof to clean out the gutters during a thunderstorm and lean over the edge, three storeys up, and ask her how she was doing while she urged him to come down.

By the time she got to the hospital, her mother had told the doctor to turn the life support off. 'He was a fine young man,' her mother had said to the doctor. 'He can't spend the rest of his life like this.'

She'd been a nurse, her mother. She knew.

Her father said nothing. He stood in the corner, hunched in misery.

It's for the best, people said. How could the death of a twenty-one-year-old be for the best? People meant his injuries were too awful to live with. As if those were the choices: a life with brain damage, or death. Wasn't there a third choice? Wasn't there the choice that he didn't get into the car at two am, that his mate didn't drive too fast round that bend?

Joof was supposed to inherit the farm. That was his destiny. He was the instrument by which the farm would be held in the family for another sixty or eighty years. Evie was going to be a physiotherapist and bring her kids to the farm on holidays from the city to learn how to ride a horse.

How could Joof, indestructible Joof, be dead?

Evie walked into the house. There were no Joof sounds, but there was still a Joofness. His wet towel was still on the floor of the bathroom, his dirty clothes hung out of the laundry basket and in a trail from the bathroom to his bedroom. She buried her nose in one of his shirts, clinging onto his musky smell. Then she sobbed, and she couldn't stop.

There was a hole in the wall, which her father had punched when he had heard the news about his only son.

Her mother always cooked when she needed a distraction, so now she was constructing a mountain of cakes. The women of the district were in the kitchen helping.

Truckloads of flowers arrived. They ran out of vases and shoved them into saucepans.

All Evie remembered of Joof's funeral was the coffin, right in front of her, with a large bunch of white lilies and roses on it. She stared at it, willing Joof to come out of it, laughing at them for falling for his practical joke.

After Joof's funeral, the house stank of rotting flower water and pollen, which fell from the lilies all over the rugs.

The local builder turned up and said, 'I'm just going to patch up that wall,' and removed the physical reminder of the family's grief.

When the cakes were all eaten or thrown away, and her mother had discarded the dead flowers, the visitors stopped coming, because that's when life was supposed to return to the normal rhythms.

It never did. Evie watched her parents hollow out, as if the animal within them had vacated the shell. Her father kept working the farm, but in a desultory way, as if he was in a dream. The fences weren't properly maintained. The cows escaped. Neighbours brought them back.

Joof's horse faded and died. So did her father. He wasted away. Cancer they said. But Evie knew it was grief.

Once Joof died, Evie knew she had to stay in Myddle and be the farmer.

She never went back to university.

A few years later, Dash came calling. He brought joy back into her life, with his easy athleticism and his abandon. He made her laugh. He rescued her.

Now she was living Joof's life, trying to be as Joofy as she could be—mending the fences, breeding the bulls, tending the cows, getting the yearlings ready for sale each year. They left in the B double and she listened all night to the cows' long moan of grief.

She wondered what Joof would have thought of her prize bull Horace; of her skills with the cattle gene pool.

Dash was making his breakfast by dousing his muesli in milk.

'I'm prepared to give it another go,' said Evie. 'Us, I mean.'

'Oh, love,' he said, putting the milk down and coming around the island bench to envelop her. 'You won't regret it. I'm so sorry.'

'We have to get serious about IVF, though,' she said.

'Of course,' he said.

'I've got the name of a doctor in Brisbane. She's the best.'

He held her face in his hands.

'Tell you what, let me make the appointment. I'm sorry I've been so slack.'

She'd believe it when she saw it. Doctor's appointments were one of the many things he left to her. She'd give him two days, then do it herself.

But that afternoon he said, 'I've made the appointment.'

'Really?' she said.

'She's booked up, though. Couldn't get in until July.'

Four months away. That was okay. It would give her enough time to arrange things so she could be away from the farm.

'Did they say what we need to take?'

'What you'd expect. Those test results we got last year.'

'Nothing else?'

'Nup.'

He stepped forward to hug her. 'I'm so excited,' he said.

She hugged him back. 'Me too,' she said with a conviction she did not feel.

She could live with him if there was a baby.

And he'd make a great dad.

That would have to do for now.

15

RUTH

April, two months before

THREE MONTHS AFTER THE PICNIC THAT HAD SEALED HER FATE FOR THE rest of the year, and after a glorious sojourn with Jack in London and a lonely trip around Europe, Ruth arrived at Harry and Marge's rambling house on twenty emerald hectares on the riverbank.

The place was drowning in clutter: dog-eared artworks from semi-talented small children, side tables piled with framed photographs of long-ago weddings.

'Just put the photos away if it gets too much,' Marge said. She pointed to a huge sea chest which doubled as a coffee table. 'Wedge them in there if you like.'

In the morning, currawongs sang their throaty chorus from the gum trees as mist rose from the river.

Ruth took a video and WhatsApped it to Jack.

He sent back a video of a red bus obscured by misty rain.

A cedar doorway on the main street opened into the musty reception area for Harry's office: threadbare carpet, an ancient sofa and a cedar desk piled high with files.

A woman with short brown hair in a voluminous floral dress was peering at a telephone—dark cream, nine square brown buttons—as if it might reveal the clues to the universe.

'This is Deb,' said Harry.

Deb looked up and scowled. 'Pleased to meet you.'

'Deb will sort things out for you, won't you, Deb? She's been here since the beginning of time.'

Deb rolled her eyes and returned to her close scrutiny of the telephone.

'That's where the secure documents are kept,' Harry said, pointing to a long ancient cedar cupboard along the wall of a vast hall. He unlocked one of the doors with a cast iron key.

'Very Dickensian,' said Ruth.

'Dad had it built,' Harry said. 'Still has some of the old documents in it.'

A grid of pigeonholes was crammed full of manila folders.

Ruth pulled out a few at random: a couple of wills, a power of attorney, some title deeds. 'This must hold the secrets to the land titles for the whole town.'

'Yep,' said Harry, with quiet pride.

He moved down the hall. 'We never seem to get around to archiving files.' He opened a door to reveal a sagging chair at a chipped table surrounded by rickety piles of manila files tied up with pink tape. A filing cabinet, drawers open, was stuffed with paper, some ancient stapling equipment and an accumulation of dust so impacted they could plant a citrus grove.

It was very old fashioned to have paper files. Even more old fashioned to have this higgledy-piggledy, dust-laden chaos.

'I know it looks messy,' said Harry apologetically. 'But Deb knows where everything is. If you need a file, she'll find it in a jiffy. You probably won't need to look at these files anyway. All of the active ones are in my office.'

He led her back down the hall to his room, which was standard lawyer fare: vast cedar desk; iconic print of two lads playing cricket on a dusty red street; metal filing cabinets with Harry's active files, neat and in alphabetical order.

'Tell me about the files that keep you awake at night,' said Ruth. 'So I know what to look out for.'

'I've done you up a list.' Harry pushed over a neat document describing each file and a paragraph on where it was at. Harry had a very organised mind. It never ceased to astonish Ruth how her impressions of people from university turned out to be so wrong. He'd seemed so shambolic then, but now he quietly put the Myddle problems in order.

'Pretty sure the other files will be asleep until I get back,' said Harry.

Famous last words, Ruth thought, remembering ruined holidays from her past. Still, the thing about surprises is that you have no idea they'll happen. Until they do.

The next day, in the dawn's pink light, Harry disappeared with Marge down the highway in the LandCruiser, the campervan bouncing behind, off to the Kimberley. 'We'll be back for the start of the bowls season,' said Harry.

Ruth laughed, then stopped. Perhaps he was serious. Was his life really ruled by bowls? Was that how old she had become?

She meandered through breakfast, and drove through the peak-hour traffic to work which, in the ten-minute drive to the wooden bridge at the edge of town, comprised four white utes coming the other way.

Excellent.

Ruth spent her first week immersed in areas of law she'd never had to deal with before: conveyancing, family law, drugs charges. She'd forgotten how exhausting it was to work outside your comfort zone.

Harry didn't realise how much he knew. Ruth had to start from scratch every time someone asked a question. At her own big firm, she'd had an army of bright young people to look things up for her when she didn't know what the answer was.

She needed that here or she'd never have time to sleep. There wouldn't be any law graduates in Myddle dying to work for her, so she was going to have to think outside the square. A research clerk didn't need to be a law student, just a bright, curious kid she could point in a general direction.

Harry rang in. 'How's it going?'

'I'm struggling a bit. So many different areas of law. You know so much.'

'Well I s'pose if you asked me about company litigation I wouldn't have a clue.'

'I know a lot about what I'm realising is a tiny little area of the law, none of which is the slightest bit of use in Myddle. You know a lot about a lot.'

'You're selling yourself a bit short there, Ruth,' said Harry.

'I might need some help. Someone to do the legwork, filling out forms, finding legislation. Would you mind if I got a kid in to help?'

'Got anyone in mind?'

'No. I thought I'd ask Patch. One of her ex-students might be toying with the idea of being a lawyer.'

'Sounds good to me,' said Harry.

'Do you want me to run it past you if we come up with a name?'

'I trust you and Patch to find the right person.'

'You're staying for lunch?' Chandra said to Ruth at yoga the first weekend back in Myddle. 'You go and talk to Roscoe. I'll be there in a few minutes.'

Ruth wandered into the kitchen where Roscoe was reading his phone at the marble countertop.

'Hello, darling,' said Ruth, kissing Roscoe on the cheek. 'What doing?' Patch had used that expression when she was two, and it had been adopted into their lexicon ever since.

'Doomscrolling,' he said, putting his phone down. 'How did we fuck up the world so badly?'

Through the vast window overlooking the river, light dappled through the leaves of the silver gum. The fucked-up world was far away.

Ruth pointed at his phone. 'That thing is a portal into a nightmare.'

Roscoe pushed it away. 'I wish I could be like Evie and not bother carrying it around. How's Harry's practice?'

'I've got no idea what I'm doing. But apart from that it's fine.' She rolled her eyes. 'I wish I was back in my comfort zone.'

They resumed their never-ending conversation about the demise of their law firm, picking over the things that went wrong, the people who were suffering, the people to blame. It felt good in the moment but—like scratching an itch—it only made the wound worse. It was a relief when Chandra wafted in with her easy smile.

'Have you made Ruth a cup of tea, Roscoe?'

'Do you want one?' Roscoe asked Ruth in surprise.

'I would actually,' said Ruth.

'How's the yoga business going?' said Ruth. 'The classes are wildly popular.'

'Pretty good,' said Chandra. 'As far as it goes.' She picked up a dirty cup and opened the dishwasher, looked inside it, sighed, put down the cup and started to unload the clean plates from the dishwasher. 'It's hard to earn enough to live on, though.'

So you're not sponging off Roscoe? Ruth thought. She and Patch had quickly jumped to a pretty nasty judgement about Chandra.

'I think she should charge more for the yoga sessions,' said Roscoe.

'I don't want to,' said Chandra. 'It's how I gather people together.'

'Man cannot live by spirituality alone,' said Ruth.

'Not true,' said Chandra. 'People have made a living providing enlightenment to people since the beginning of time. It's a basic human need. Once we have food and water and shelter, we need to understand the other dimension to life.'

'I don't think I've ever got to the search for enlightenment,' said Ruth. 'My definition of food and water and shelter has expanded the more I've earned: bigger house, better wine, more elaborate holidays.'

'But has it made you happier?' Chandra opened a drawer, heaved out another sigh, and rearranged the contents to fit in a clean salad bowl.

'I had some pretty good holidays,' said Ruth.

'I guess buying stuff is a kind of religion,' said Chandra. 'You think you can fill the hole inside you with more and more of it.'

Ruth looked around the vast room.

'She's looking at my expensive new house, Chandra,' said Roscoe. 'She thinks you're a hypocrite.'

Chandra smiled. 'Don't get me wrong. It's much nicer to live in a place like this than the house I was brought up in. Beauty and comfort are great but they will never fill the gap. You'll always be looking for answers. It's the basic human condition.' Chandra stopped on the other side of the bench, a plate in her hand. 'What's the best holiday you ever went on? Not the most expensive one. The first one that jumps into your head.'

Ruth considered it. On those criteria, the best holiday had been with Jack when he was five, and she and Bill took him on a road trip with two other families that involved a farm stay in a shed. Cheap as chips, and a multitude of belly laughs.

There was a note of triumph in Chandra's nod.

'What about you, Chandra? What's the best holiday you've been on?' Roscoe was diverting attention from himself, Ruth guessed, to avoid a conversation about his annual ski holiday in Aspen.

Chandra didn't answer at first, just continued to unload the dishwasher.

The silence expanded, and Chandra stood with a saucepan in her hand.

'It was more a quest than a holiday. I'd been on a ten-year bender and went to a sun festival in Arizona. I was supposed to be drying out but ended up having a transcendental experience. Changed my life.'

'Ten-year bender?' Ruth repeated. A startling admission for a person who never touched alcohol.

Chandra had her back to Ruth when she spoke. 'I had a few issues when I was younger.' She turned and leaned towards Ruth over the kitchen bench. 'What picture comes into your mind when you think about that farm holiday?'

Chandra had a knack of transfixing you with her green gaze.

'The look on Jack's face when the farmer said he'd take him for a ride on a tractor. And the scarlet bottlebrush in bloom around a billabong shaped like a boomerang.'

Chandra slapped the bench. 'I want my retreat to be for people like you and Roscoe, who have been sucked into the corporate vortex but have a gaping hole in their soul. I can fill that hole; show them what life means.'

Did Ruth have a gaping hole in her soul? What an odd accusation.

'You can make a difference, darling,' said Roscoe. 'Can't she, Ruth?'

'Are you going to work in a law firm again, Ruth?' Chandra asked.

'Probably. An inexorable force is drawing me back.'

Chandra opened the fridge, pulled out some vegetables, brought them to the counter and started chopping. She handed Roscoe a knife and an avocado. 'Here. Give your life some meaning with food preparation.'

Roscoe cheerfully took it and grabbed a cutting board.

'What's the force?' said Chandra. 'What do you miss about it?'

'Problem-solving. The people.'

Chandra pointed a chopping knife at her. 'The status?'

Ruth nodded. 'I suppose so, although it feels dirty to admit it. Sounds self-obsessed and selfish.'

Chandra put her long fingers into the salad to toss it. 'Māori have this great word to describe it: *mana*. It means a combination of status and authority and has a spiritual dimension—regard from the community that's earned with wisdom and good deeds.

And it's not individual glory. The *mana* of a chief spreads over the people in the *iwi*.'

'Huh,' said Ruth.

Chandra nodded. 'There's power in language. Once you give a concept its own word, it changes the way people think about it.'

Salad ready, Chandra handed Roscoe some plates and cutlery, and he laid the table.

'Napkins and glasses,' she said, and he obeyed. Chandra was capable of working miracles. Ruth nearly said so, but stopped herself. Roscoe was content and oblivious.

When they sat, Frank, with a little grunt, positioned himself on the floor under the table, his four legs sploofed out in a star.

Ruth took a bite. Here was another miracle: Chandra had managed to make kale taste good.

It wasn't until they'd mowed their way through most of the salad that Chandra said, 'Ruth, you asked about my ten-year bender.'

Ruth was about to say, 'I didn't mean to pry,' when Roscoe reached out and put his hand over Chandra's.

Chandra was still and straight, facing the window overlooking the river. She'd prepared herself to share something awful. Ruth shut up and let her speak.

'It was the day I graduated from college,' said Chandra.

She'd had lunch with her family ('it involved a few wines') and was meeting some friends at a bar for a drink before dinner. She was half an hour early, a little drunk, and the bar was almost empty.

A man sat alone at the bar. He seemed old to her—older than her dad anyway, and when you're twenty that's how you measure the age of men and work out whether you can trust them. He struck up a conversation, she told him she'd graduated that morning, and he bought her a tequila shot. She slung it back, as she'd seen it done in the movies, and he bought her another.

'I realised more shots would be a bad idea,' she said. 'He was getting a bit creepy and I needed to do a wee.'

She did what women do the world over to escape from a man they don't want to talk to, and went to the bathroom, which was tucked behind the bar.

The cubicle door didn't close properly, but she was the only person in there, and had been the only woman in the bar, so she wasn't worried about it.

As she peed, she heard footsteps. Before she could react, the man was there, in the cubicle.

Chandra hadn't moved while she told this story, and hadn't diverted her gaze from the river out the picture window. It was Frank who offered some respite, by exhaling, heaving himself to an upright position, waddling over to the middle of the Persian rug in the sitting room, and splaying out. Ruth wanted to go there with him, and cover her ears so she wouldn't have to hear what was coming next.

Chandra was matter of fact. 'He closed the cubicle door behind him. I didn't know what to do. I kept going as if everything was normal in the hope that it was. I finished the pee, stood, and pulled up my underpants. He opened the cubicle door and let me pass. For a moment I thought it would be okay. I stood at the basin and washed my hands.'

For the first time she looked at Ruth, her big green eyes awash. 'That's when he raped me. From behind while I washed my hands.'

Ruth felt like she'd been punched in the gut. Nothing feels adequate in those moments. 'Oh, Chandra,' she said, reaching over the table and squeezing her hand.

Roscoe stood, brought a box of tissues to the table, and stayed beside Chandra, a hand rubbing her shoulders.

'Sorry,' said Chandra. 'I've told this story thousands of times, to police and courts, but it gets worse, not better.'

'So you made a complaint?'

'I tried carrying on as normal. But a friend got the story out of me, and kind of made me go to the police.'

Ruth was almost afraid to ask. 'Is he in gaol?'

Roscoe answered. 'He was convicted by a jury, but won on appeal. They said that the trial judge hadn't let the defence counsel cross-examine Chandra about consent. The old story, not whether she consented, but whether he thought she did.'

'Christ,' said Ruth. 'What a travesty.'

'I couldn't face another trial,' said Chandra. 'It was worse than the rape. I couldn't do it again.'

'I was pretty fucked up for a while. Booze and drugs. Then about ten years later I went to the sun festival in Arizona. Had a bit of an epiphany.'

'And here we are,' said Roscoe.

Sometimes, it was hard to define the rule of law. Sometimes, it was best not to try. 'Chandra, I'm so sorry. That you were let down. By society and then by the legal system.' Ruth added, 'It's totally fucked.'

Chandra smiled. 'I realised later he must have watched himself in the mirror.'

WhatsApp

Jack
Update?

Ruth
Back in Myddle

Jack
And?

Ruth
Am terrified that I know nothing. Petty local matters sound easy until you have to think about the range of laws Harry must know. How to sell a farm. Divorce. How to get someone out on bail. Scary.

Jack
You'll figure it out

Ruth
Steep learning curve

Jack
Can't Roscoe help?

Ruth
He stopped doing any legal work twenty years ago. I did it while he went around the town slapping people on the back and telling them how wonderful they are.

Jack
How did he get away with that?

Ruth
Worked well for both of us. I hate slapping people on the back.
Spent tonight talking about consent laws in rape cases with him.

Jack
?

Ruth
About a rape more than thirty years ago

Jack
Cheery conversation. What sparked that?

Ruth
Someone Roscoe knows

16

EVIE

April, two months before

YOGA WASN'T EVIE'S THING, BUT SHE WAS PREPARED TO GIVE IT A GO.

Chandra had been pressing her to come. And Evie wanted to be in the best place possible when she saw the IVF doctor. Deep down, she harboured the hope that this would be it: the magical ingredient to pregnancy. People said it might be stress. It was worth a try.

Chandra welcomed her with a scented hug. 'So glad you came.'

The room was filled with middle-aged women and a low hum of anticipation. Evie rolled out her yoga mat at the back.

Chandra sat on a platform beside a large brass gong. 'Welcome,' she said, her smile beatific.

The ferns and pink bromeliads were framed by the window behind her.

'Who wants to change their life?' Chandra's husky voice was both commanding and ironic, as if there was a funny secret she was about to disclose.

The yoga was simple enough. When Evie had studied physiotherapy years ago, she had learnt about the importance of the core muscles, and that yoga was about strengthening them. A lifetime of riding horses and moving cattle had ensured she was strong and fit. The other women in the room huffed and puffed and struggled with the poses, but for Evie, it was effortless.

Afterwards, Chandra took Evie to her office, a separate building attached to the garage, decorated with crystals and paintings with intricate colour.

'You have an aura of indomitable power,' said Chandra, 'but I sense you're in pain.'

Chandra's eyes were light green with a dark blue rim, like a cat's. Her hands over Evie's were very warm. Evie felt her reserve melting. 'I want a baby,' she said.

'I can help you,' Chandra whispered. 'I want to look at the ethics of decision-making. You have a great asset: the spirituality of your land. You can use your intentions to make a positive contribution to the wellbeing of the planet. I think we can work with you to transform your life.'

Chandra's sentences had the portent of meaning, but when you examined them, they didn't seem to say anything.

And what did the land have to do with a baby?

Back in the yoga studio, Evie went to the table laden with Chandra's books and ethical products. There were packets of individually packed spices and lentils, books and wafty white frocks that reflected Chandra's boho elegance.

Evie bought a recipe book and Chandra's magnum opus, *Speaking to the Soul*.

When she got home, Dash was still at footy training. She lay prone on the sofa and picked up the recipe book, called *The Ethical Diet*.

She opened it to the Foreword. The essence of an ethical diet, it said, was eradicating the evils of farming. The first to be targeted was the exploitation of animals for the production of meat. It was cruel, inhumane. There was a gruesome picture of dismembered cows in an abattoir, and the fearful face of a live cow in front of a gun. Any animal subjugated to a human should be freed. There was a picture of a woman riding a horse. The horse would be let loose to live a life of spiritual freedom.

As the light faded, Evie turned the pages with growing dismay.

The land given over to the exploitation of animals should be transformed to spiritual places. That was step one. Then they would set their sights on factory farming of plants so that each plant would be ethically raised, with the intention of nourishing it so that it would nourish mankind. The evils of the world would be righted, creating a society of spiritually aware people. In the meantime, it was important to eat only plants, each seed to be ethically sourced. That, together with incantations and yoga, would transform the adherent to a higher plane in the matrix—whatever that was.

The good news, according to the book, was that Chandra had done the work. Food stuffs bought from her satisfied the requirements of ethical eating and the clothes she had handmade satisfied the requirements for ethical clothing. If you sourced your food and clothes through Chandra, you were well on your way to living an ethical life.

Evie put the book down.

It didn't matter how deep Chandra's voice was, how graceful her intentions. Chandra life purpose was to undo everything that Evie was.

Was Evie evil? Was her family evil?
She didn't think so.
Chandra couldn't help her.
Evie resolved never to return.

17

BEA

April, two months before

BEA WAS IN HER PYJAMAS ON THE SOFA WATCHING TELLY WHEN GAZZA wandered in from Victoria's bedroom and sat on one of Victoria's faded chintz armchairs.

He wanted to converse.

Bea said, 'Hey,' because it would be rude not to. At least he had some clothes on this time. His feet were bare and his toenails were long and dirty. She folded her legs beneath her and crossed her arms.

'How's it going?' said Gazza.

'Yeah. All right.' Bea kept her eyes on the telly. It was a reality TV series about people who hadn't met before getting married. It was dumb and a bit shit, but she didn't want to be drawn into an even shitter conversation with Gazza.

'Watcha been up to?' said Gazza. Bea guessed he'd had some beers but not enough to be completely drunk. Figured. He'd need some sort of lubrication to hang out with Victoria.

'Not much.'

'Going to the show?' Gazza was obviously struggling for things to talk about. The show wasn't for another month, but it was the biggest Myddle event of the year.

'Dunno,' said Bea. 'Probably.'

A blonde chick on the telly was complaining that the bloke she'd married didn't like dogs and she thought that meant there was something wrong with him. The bloke said he'd been bitten by a dog when he was a kid. There was some sad dramatic music. The bloke wiped his eyes. Was he wiping his eyes about being bitten by a dog? He pulled up his trouser leg and showed the scars. It was pretty bad. Hard to believe a dog could cause that much damage.

'Must have been a big dog,' scoffed Gazza.

Bea smiled and nodded but kept her eyes on the screen.

The blonde chick cried, too, and they had a big hug. Now they were being asked what they'd learnt from that, and they agreed that they needed to talk more.

What a pile of crap. Time to go to bed.

'Show should be good this year,' said Gazza.

'Yep,' said Bea.

Victoria appeared in a dressing gown with a towel wrapped around her head. She walked to Gazza and draped herself over him.

'What're you two talking about?' she said.

'Nothing,' said Bea. She concentrated on keeping her eyes on the TV screen, hoping to signal to both Gazza and Victoria that she had no interest in talking to Gazza.

'I was asking Bea if she was going to the show,' said Gazza.

He was relaxed in the armchair. He didn't realise he'd made a mistake.

Victoria undraped herself from Gazza and said, 'You didn't ask me.'

It dawned on him then. 'It was just something to say, Victoria. I wasn't asking her on a date.'

'What a disgusting thought.' Her mum's posh accent just got worse. She stood and stepped away from him.

Here we go, thought Bea. 'Got to get ready for work tomorrow,' she said, getting up.

As she left the room, she could hear her mother saying, 'Were you going to ask me?'

'I'll be on duty, Victoria. I can't go on a date.'

'Well, why did you ask her?' Her voice was rising.

'It was just something to say.'

Bea got into bed and put the doona over her head as Victoria's voice got louder and higher.

It was at this point in Victoria's relationships that the men got confused but convinced themselves it was just a misunderstanding. Gazza would be in Bea's life for a few more weeks.

The screaming abated, the wheedling started, and then the bed bumped and Gazza grunted and the dark silence thickened.

Gazza was gone when Bea emerged—cautiously—for breakfast.

Victoria sidled up to Bea and put her arms around her. 'How is my darling girl this morning? Ready for a beautiful day?'

Bea looked down on Victoria's hair, each strand so slight it wrapped flat against her skull. Was it going to be a *Fleabag* and boeuf bourguignon day? Best not to hold any hope.

18

GAZZA

April, two months before

GAZZA DIDN'T KNOW WHAT WAS WORSE: THE TANTRUMS OR THE uncertainty. Victoria was fucking nuts.

There would come a point, and it wasn't far off, where the sex wouldn't be enough to negate the tantrums.

Then it would be him and the vodka again.

There hadn't been an MVA since New Year's, so he was left with the last one flashing up in his mind, and it was gruesome. He wondered if he should see the police counsellor about it, but worried that it would be the excuse the force needed to get rid of him. Admitting to a big fucking problem in your head was never a good idea, and once he opened up the tap, who knew what would come gushing out of him.

There was a howl inside him, and it was all he could do every day to keep it contained.

Nah. Gazza's counsellor was Dash. He was always happy to have a beer and a chat. Just keep the conversation light, about the footy and stuff, and the howl would stay locked up inside.

19

BEA

April, Saturday, ten weeks before

TROY LIVED AROUND THE CORNER FROM BEA. SHE DAWDLED AS SHE went past for work in the mornings but no luck. Finally, close to Easter, he was in the front yard, about to get into his car.

'Hey,' she said.

'Hey.'

'Watcha doing?'

'Nothing much.'

'Going out?'

'Work.'

'Where do you work?'

'Clive Downs.'

'Doing what?'

'Ride the horses 'n' shit.'

'Cool.' This might be her chance. It came out before she could analyse it to make sure it wouldn't piss anyone off. 'I've never ridden a horse. Do ya reckon they'd let me ride one?'

'I'll ask.'

She asked again the following week. The third week, he said, 'Yeah, Evie said it's okay.' He drove her out on Saturday afternoon.

First he had to feed the heifers.

The shed was laid out with the precision of a bookshop: two matching silver utes, tools, bikes, saddles and bridles hanging on hooks along the walls.

Troy jumped into a ute and turned it on.

'Is the key in the ignition all the time?' she said.

'Who's going to steal it out here?'

He backed the ute to a big square pile of hay in one of the sheds. She stood on the tray and he tossed the bales on. She pushed them with her foot, arranging them symmetrically as best she could. They were heavy.

She pushed at a big metal toolbox to move it out of the way. It didn't budge. She looked underneath. It was screwed onto the tray of the ute.

'What's that?' she said.

'Lock box. For the rifle.'

'Do you shoot it?'

'Nah. Dash uses it for feral pigs.'

She'd never seen a rifle up close before. 'Can I have a look?'

Troy went to the cabin of the ute. She watched through the back window as he got the key out of the centre console, came around and opened it.

The gun lay in black foam, long and straight.

She picked it up and looked through the sight at Troy. 'Hands in the air,' she said.

He snatched it from her. 'Don't be so fucking dumb,' he said. 'Never point a gun at anyone or anything unless you want to shoot it.'

'Sorry,' she said. She felt small and stupid.

'Never mess around with guns,' said Troy. 'Ever.'

'Sorry,' she said again. She had to concentrate not to cry.

'It's okay,' he said. 'I shouldn't have called you dumb.'

They got in the ute and drove over a farm track to a paddock. Troy didn't talk much to Bea. Instead, he chatted with the heifers about their meal—'You like that don't ya'—and the dogs—'Get out of that Bryan.'

Back at the shed, Troy looked at her Nikes. 'You'll need riding boots. They have a leather sole so you slip out of the stirrups if anything goes wrong, so you don't get dragged. Back in a sec.' He went off to the house. 'Here you go,' he said when he returned with some elastic-sided boots, the brown leather cracked and misshapen. 'An old pair of Evie's.'

They were the right size.

He lured the horses over with a carrot, put on the bridles and brought them over near the shed to saddle them. The docile pony, the fat one, Old Girl, was for Bea while Troy had Evie's horse Jasper: a black thoroughbred, skittish, elegant long legs.

'Just stay there for a sec. I need to get the beans out of him.' Troy mounted Jasper and took him to the other side of the paddock under the poinciana tree. Jasper bounced forward a couple of times, planted his front feet and kicked his back feet up, jumped forward and did it again. Troy giggled, patted him on the neck and returned.

'My horse won't do that, will she?' said Bea.

'Nah. Jaspy does that for fun. Old Girl doesn't have it in her.'

Troy dismounted then shoved Bea into the saddle by pushing her bum up from below. They set off at an amble.

A crowd of black crows cawed from a tree as they passed under it. 'I wonder what they're saying about us,' Bea said.

'You know what they call a mob of crows?' Troy said.

'Nah. What?'

'A murder,' he said. He looked at her, waiting for her delight.

'Hah,' Bea said. 'I don't think crows are murderers. Look at them. They're gossiping about us. I bet they're saying, "Look at her. She can't even ride a horse."'

Troy let that slide, even though she was looking for reassurance. It turned out even Old Girl wanted to launch into a trot, which was brutal on Bea's crotch.

'Get the rhythm,' said Troy. 'Rise up and down with it.'

She had to concentrate hard to make her body do it.

When they slowed to a walk, Troy smiled. She didn't see it much, that smile. Mostly, he had no expression on his face. You could never tell what he was thinking.

'You ever wonder about your dad?' she asked.

'Nuh.'

'I think about mine a lot.'

He didn't say anything.

'Does your mum talk about him?'

'Nuh.'

'Nor does mine,' said Bea. 'Maybe we're half brother and sister.' She laughed.

He smiled, but kept looking straight ahead.

'That's a lie isn't it. You must think about him.'

'Yeah, sometimes,' he said.

'Is he alive?'

'Nuh.'

'Do you remember him?'

'Nuh.' He touched the horse with his heels and lifted the reins. Jasper took off. She had to trot to catch up.

They stopped in a glade by a creek. Troy stripped down to his jocks. 'Coming in?'

'Nah. Bit cold for me,' she said, but actually she hadn't brought any bathers and she wasn't going to undress in front of Troy. She didn't want him to get the wrong idea.

At the beginning of Year Ten one of the boys had approached her in the quad at school and asked her if she wanted to go down to the creek. The others had sniggered, elbowing one another. She'd gone and they'd done the thing. It became a pattern with different boys asking her. One of them used cling wrap from his Vegemite sandwich because he didn't have a condom. After, the boy would rejoin his mates, and not talk to her, until the next time. She used to hope it would change, until she realised it wouldn't. For the last six months of Year Twelve, she'd just said nah, she was busy.

Bea didn't want Troy to think of her like that. She knew she was out of Troy's league. He was everything she wasn't: smart, good-looking, good at sport. And she didn't want to settle for the interest she knew she could provoke in him: a quick shag when there was nobody else.

He immersed himself in the water and lay spread out, face up, legs and arms akimbo. Bea walked away rather than ogle at the eight muscles lined up on his stomach. She lay on her back on the grass. The horses stood under a tree. They ripped off a mouthful of grass and then chewed on it, desultory, rhythmic.

Troy got out of the water, then said softly, 'Hey, Bea, come and look at this.'

She went over to the riverbank and he pointed at a fat little thing that was brown and furry.

'What is it?' Bea asked.

'Platypus.'

It nuzzled along the surface of the water, wiggling sideways to propel itself forward—flat rectangular tail swaying.

An engine revved, harsh, out of sight. The platypus ducked and disappeared.

'What's that?' Bea asked.

Troy rolled his eyes. 'Jet skis.'

They got back on the horses and ambled up the creek a few hundred metres to the confluence where it joined the Clive River, then they rode up a steep hill. They dismounted, attached the reins to a sapling, and climbed up the last granite outcrop to the top. Bea kept slipping.

'That's the riding boots,' said Troy, giving her a hand up. 'Not great for rock climbing.'

Bea sat on her bum and gingerly shimmied to the edge. The Bluff, Troy called it. Bea stepped back from the edge.

They descended back to the horses and walked them down the steep hill. At the campsite they stopped between a campervan and the riverbank to watch the jet skis. *If there was a collective noun for them, it would be an outrage of jet skis,* Bea thought.

A woman—old, Bea thought, at least fifty—was sitting nearby in a chair under a tree with a cup of tea, listening to the horseracing on a radio. She stood and glared at Troy and Bea, hands on her hips, then darted into a campervan.

A man in a blue singlet with a beer gut and skinny legs emerged. 'What are you doing, son?' he shouted at Troy.

Troy shrugged. 'Just watching the jet skis.'

'You shouldn't be here. It's a private campground,' the man yelled.

Troy walked off, not fast, just ambling, Jasper's reins loose in his hand. Bea followed with the pony. What was this man's problem? Bea wanted to tell him to fuck off, but Troy was avoiding a fight.

'If I see you back here I'll tell the management.'

Was it always like this for Troy? He didn't look back, didn't change pace, just kept walking slowly. Another couple emerged from a campervan, and watched but didn't say anything.

As they approached the gate, Evie drove up in a silver ute. She got out and smiled at Troy. 'Hey,' she said.

The man yelled from his position in the campsite thirty or so metres away, 'I let him know he's not welcome here!'

'It's my property,' said Evie. 'He can come here whenever he wants.'

The observers disappeared back into their camper, but Bea could see them at the window.

'Makes my wife nervous.'

'Why?' said Evie.

The man didn't say anything just harrumphed and stomped off.

'Sorry you have to put up with that.' Evie moved towards Troy. For a moment Bea thought Evie was going to hug him.

Troy must have thought so, too, because he stepped backward. 'Yeah, well, see ya.'

'Want some arvo tea?' called Evie, walking fast after Troy. 'Drop in after you take the horses back.'

'Nah, thanks. We've got to get back to town.'

As they reached the gate, Evie jumped in the ute and drove into the campground towards the old guy's camper, her face promising thunder.

Troy rode back to the house, his back stiff. Bea tried to make small talk, asking about the platypus and horses, but received only grunts in response. He was seething, his jaw and his mind set so hard, he couldn't let anything in or out.

'Don't you want arvo tea?' she said.

Troy glared at her, then turned away again. 'I didn't want to hear her excuses and her gushing and her "We're not all like that". Fucking whitefellas.'

Bea didn't know what to say except, 'Yeah.'

'If she meant it, she should kick him out of the campground. But she won't.'

They rode back to the homestead and put the horses in the paddock. Troy brushed them down.

'Are you sure you don't want a cup of tea? I'm kind of hungry.' Bea knew Evie wanted to smooth it over, and she hoped Dash would be there.

Troy didn't say anything, but after he fed the horses, he strode towards the house. He knew Evie so well he just walked up to the back door and let himself in. Bea followed him.

Evie and Dash were at the kitchen bench. Evie was cutting up an apple, and Dash had cracked open a beer.

'Hey,' said Troy.

'Oh, hey,' said Evie, and straight away she filled the jug and turned it on. 'Bea, isn't it?' she added.

'Yeah,' said Bea. 'Hey.' She didn't know where to put her arms so she wrapped them around her torso. She loosened her hand to give a jerky wave to Evie and turned to Dash, who winked at her.

20

EVIE

April, Saturday, ten weeks before

EVIE PULLED THE UTE UP JUST OUTSIDE THE CAMPERVAN DOOR, GOT out, and waited.

The net curtain inside twitched, there was a pause, then the man came out of the campervan.

'So what's the problem?' Evie said.

'Those kids just turned up. Close to our camper.'

Half a dozen white cockatoos flew above, screeching. The man shifted from one foot to the other. Eventually, he said, 'Theft's a big problem in campgrounds.'

'He works for me,' said Evie. 'As a stockman.'

'I didn't know that.' The tone was defensive, but also somehow accusatory. As if she was obliged to provide a list of her employees.

'He's entitled to be here.'

'Yeah. Well. He didn't look like he was working.'

He waited for her to say something. She didn't.

'My wife gets a bit nervous. There's been stuff on the news.'

What am I waiting for? Evie wondered. *An apology?* That wasn't going to happen. She turned to go.

'You just can't tell,' he yelled after her, 'if it's a good one or a bad one.'

Evie stopped, then walked back towards him. 'I think it'd be better if you packed up and left.'

He spluttered an expletive and yelled after her, but by that time she'd turned the engine on and roared away.

She drove home, going straight to Dash, who was tinkering with an engine in the shed.

'What's up?' said Dash.

'Those fucking racists you've got in the camp.'

Dash laughed. 'What've they done now?'

He got out his spanner and wound something in the engine block, listening while she spat out the encounter at the campsite.

'Troy just walked off?' Dash said. He put down the spanner, held his closed fists up in a sparring position and asked, 'He didn't have a crack?' delight in his face.

'Of course he didn't.'

'Don't worry about it,' Dash said. 'Troy'll be fine. He's learnt to withdraw. He could slot 'em if he wanted to but he knows the coppers'd be onto him.'

'I told them to leave.'

Dash looked up, dismayed. 'You can't do that,' he said. 'Word'll spread.'

'Good,' Evie said. 'Do we want people here who think it's acceptable to speak to people like that?'

'Like what?' said Dash. 'He only asked whether Troy was an authorised visitor. Did you tell him that Troy was authorised?'

It always ended up like this. Somehow it was Evie's fault, every time.

'Love,' said Dash, wiping his hands on a dirty towel. 'Come here.' He opened his arms.

Bryan sat in front of Evie, and she patted him. 'Imagine how horrible it must be for Troy. People telling him he doesn't belong.'

'It's not a ridiculous assumption for the bloke to make,' said Dash. 'How many Blakfellas own land?' He paused and looked out towards the paddock. 'Natural that he'd question it. And you know how paranoid people get. He was probably standing too close to their rig. They worry they might get robbed or something.'

Evie shook her head.

She needed to be better prepared to have a conversation about it with Dash. It would turn into an argument.

She turned and walked to the house.

Dash followed her. 'You're obsessed with him,' he said.

Evie didn't trust herself to respond; instead, she grabbed an apple and a knife.

Dash let out a gush of exasperated air, went to the fridge, took out a can of beer, cracked it, and pretended to be looking at a magazine on the kitchen bench.

'By the way,' he said, 'Chandra is coming over.'

'What for?'

Dash examined the can in his hand. He was about to say something, but changed his mind and said, 'Not sure.'

Then Troy arrived after all. That girl was with him again. Evie struggled to remember her name. Funny kid. That's right: Bea. He'd asked if she could ride the pony. Troy never asked for anything, so she could hardly say no.

'Sorry about that,' Evie said to Troy. 'I told that guy he had to leave.'

Troy nodded, briefly met her gaze, then looked away.

21

RUTH

April, Saturday, ten weeks before

ON SATURDAY, RUTH RECONNOITRED THE NATIONAL PARK WHICH overlooked Myddle: rainforest canopy, water gushing over lichen-encrusted boulders. She walked for hours; basked in it.

On the way home, there was a *thunk thunk thunk*. The steering wheel stiffened. The car slowed.

Ruth pulled over. The tyre on the back passenger side was completely flat.

The implications of this dawned on her slowly. Ruth's patchy understanding of the mechanics of changing a tyre were that you needed a ratchetty thing that held up the car while you took off the wheel with a spannery thing. Which involved jumping on it or something to get sufficient leverage to undo the nuts. She opened the boot and lifted the base. Which device was the ratchet? She picked out a black tool and turned it around. Where would she put it?

Did the NRMA exist this far out of Sydney?

There was Shane. He would sort it in a jiffy, in his customary benevolent silence.

Nope. There were no bars on her phone. No coverage. The NRMA would never arrive. And neither would Shane.

A car approached. She had a frisson of fear—a woman alone by the side of a deserted road. But it was Myddle, and she was approaching fifty, a bit lumpy in the middle regions and well past the age when vulnerability in a woman was alluring. She leaned against the boot, feigning a nonchalance she did not feel.

The small white hatchback was coming fast. It slowed, and came to a halt beside her. A woman in her sixties leaned out the open window, her elbow on the sill.

'You all right?' said the woman.

'Flat tyre,' said Ruth, embarrassed. 'Don't think I've ever changed a tyre on my own.'

The woman gave a half chuckle, not in contempt but in solidarity. 'The shoulder's a bit soft here. Why don't you jump in? I'm on my way to my son's house. He should be able to sort it for you.'

'Oh, really?' said Ruth, relief flooding over her. It was a sensible solution but also very generous. People who lived in the country were so much nicer than city people, more prepared to share what they had.

'No drama,' said the woman. 'Hop in.'

Ruth folded herself into the front seat.

'We met at the New Year's Eve party. I'm Diane,' said the woman as her foot sprang off the clutch. The car jolted forward.

Ruth had met a lot of people at the New Year's Eve party, a blur of faces. 'Ruth,' she said.

Diane embarked on a monologue about a person called Wayne, whom Diane loved and admired with a fervour only possible for a mother. Wayne was blessed. Right from the get-go, he had gifts other children did not have: first basketball hoop at four; first try at six.

Diane slammed her foot on the clutch and crunched the gearstick from second direct to fourth. The engine wailed in distress.

Wayne's more recent ventures featured a tourism development. Ruth worried that she should know who Wayne was so she remained silent except for the occasional 'Wow' and 'Really? That's amazing'.

What must it have been like to be Wayne, his ego bathed in adulation as he grew? Did it result in an absence of self-doubt? Would that be freeing, to not have that voice on one's shoulder, whispering in one's ear even as you were enjoying your biggest triumph?

That's the problem with telling your kid he's a genius. He might believe it, and think that's all he needed to succeed; that he didn't have to work.

Diane slammed on the brakes and turned left onto Clive Road.

There was only one farm up that road.

It was only then that Ruth twigged that the amazing Wayne must be Dash; that Diane was Dash's mum. Ruth had been determined to despise Wayne but that wasn't possible with Dash, thanks to his broad smile and his easy friendliness.

Diane pulled up on the teardrop driveway set on the emerald green lawn overlooking the river. A peacock strutted around in full blue and green display. The drab peahens pecked at the ground, indifferent.

Dash came out of the house to welcome them. 'Mum,' he said to Diane, giving her a stiff hug. He turned a dazzling smile onto Ruth. 'Great to see you, Ruth,' as if it was perfectly normal for her to turn up at his house with his mother.

Evie emerged from the back of the house in dirty jeans, a dusty shirt and socks.

It occurred to Ruth that, during her monologue, Diane had barely mentioned Evie.

'We're just having a cup of tea,' Evie said, leading them out to a deck. The house was light and open, a breeze coming off the river.

The handsome young fellow from New Year's Eve was sitting at the long wood table on the deck—what was his name? Troy. He was with the girl Bea from the pharmacy. Perhaps she and Troy were an item.

Diane was suddenly quiet. Troy's silence bordered on sullen.

Ruth was scratching around in her head for something to say when a large white BMW pulled up. Out wafted Chandra. 'Helloo,' she crooned. 'Sorry I'm a bit late.' She made her way around the table and gave each person a long, perfumed hug, looking into their eyes after she did so as if the one thing she had longed to do all week was see them again.

'So wonderful to be here with all of you,' Chandra said as she sat down. 'What have you been doing?'

Ruth explained her flat tyre, Diane described a brush with death while doing the ironing (in a gloomy cupboard, a snake mistaken for an electrical cord), and Ruth said she'd always suspected ironing was dangerous, which was why she never did it.

It caused a confused hiatus in the conversation, until Bea said she and Troy had just been up the Bluff.

Chandra leaned forward and said in breathy wonder, 'The Bluff is so beautiful. I take our little boat up the river and just sit there, absorbing it. One day a pair of king parrots swooped over me. It has a spiritual significance, I'm sure.'

'That must be right,' said Bea. Her voice had a touch of rapture about it. 'It's so peaceful, except for the kookaburras.' She smiled and her face opened.

Dash responded with cheerful enthusiasm. Ruth wondered, as that dialogue continued, whether it was the campsite Bea was rapt in, or Dash. They held one another's gaze. Dash invited Bea to ride the horses on the property whenever she liked, which Bea accepted with a flutter of her eyelashes.

'So what did you think of our proposal?' Chandra asked Evie.

'Proposal?' said Evie.

Chandra looked at Dash, who squirmed. 'Sorry, love, I didn't get a chance to show you.'

'It's to develop the Bluff,' said Chandra, 'into an eco-health resort. Roscoe and I would arrange investors and help you operate it. Sorry, I assumed you'd already read it and had Ruth here for legal advice.'

Ruth put her hands up. 'I'm here by accident,' she said. 'Don't know anything about it.'

'We've got a bit on in the next year or so,' said Evie. 'Property development isn't on the list, is it, Dash?'

Dash shrugged.

'It's just that it's an exceptional property.' Chandra persisted. 'And there are huge opportunities in the eco-health space right now. I've got the concept plans, if you're interested.'

Concept plans? They'd spent some money on it then. Chandra's language had morphed from spiritual guru to property developer. And she sounded like a pro. Ruth had rolled her eyes through a lot of meetings where the words 'space' and 'opportunity' and 'concept' had been dropped.

'You should see the drawings, Evie,' said Diane. 'They're amazing.'

Now Ruth understood why Diane had been banging on about tourism development in the car.

'We're not thinking about it for at least a year.' Evie stood, firmly bringing an end to the discussion. 'Anyone want another cup of tea?'

Another silence hung.

Evie obviously knew nothing about the development proposal. But it seemed Dash did, and had told his mum. Weird.

This time, Diane stepped in to change the subject. 'You taking on Harry's practice?' she asked Ruth.

'Roscoe and I are so looking forward to having you around,' said Chandra. 'Your wisdom,' she added.

'Not sure about wisdom,' said Ruth. 'I'm a newbie at a lot of the stuff Harry does.'

'Troy, you were thinking about being a lawyer, weren't you?' Dash said.

Troy nodded more at the ground than at Ruth. 'Dunno what it's about but.'

Why was he so monosyllabic? He seemed upset about something. Angry. Ruth tried to draw him out.

'That'd be good,' she said. 'We need fellas like you in the profession.'

She stopped then, embarrassed, wondering if she had caused offence. It was true, though. The profession needed to dilute the preponderance of whiteness. Change the group think.

Evie looked at Troy. 'I thought you were thinking about ag science. Farming.'

'Yeah. Not sure yet.'

'Why don't you drop in to the office?' Ruth said. 'We'll have a chat. You can see what we do.'

Troy's eyes lit up. 'That'd be great. Thanks.'

There were murmurings of 'good idea' and 'kind of you' when Diane casually dropped a dead cat into the conversation: 'It'll be a problem if you have a criminal record, though. Being a lawyer, I mean.'

The comment hung there in all its profane glory for a good thirty seconds. The gathering examined their mugs of tea, fiddled with their Tim Tams. Dash said, 'Mum.'

'I'm just being practical,' said Diane, doubling down. 'You need to think about these things. No point in doing all that work if you can never be a lawyer.' She finished the sentence with an air of satisfied belligerence.

Ruth said, looking Diane in the eye, 'Doesn't necessarily mean you can't be a lawyer. Or shouldn't get a law degree. There are lots of options.'

'Oh,' said Diane. 'I thought they wouldn't accept people like that as lawyers.'

Ruth was tempted to have a crack at Diane but decided instead to ignore her. Whatever Troy's problems, however they might affect his future, were none of Diane's business. She turned to Troy. 'Come to the office and we'll have a chat.'

'Thanks,' he said. His face was hard. Impenetrable.

Troy picked up his mug of half-drunk tea and leaned over to pick up Bea's. 'Better go,' he said.

'Thanks for today, Troy,' said Evie. 'How were the heifers?'

'Yeah, good,' said Troy.

'I'll put the money in your account.'

Ruth had been wondering why Troy was there. He must work for Evie.

'Yeah,' said Dash. 'Great job, mate.'

Ruth said, 'See you in the office on Monday.'

Troy nodded. 'Thanks,' he said.

Diane's nose crunched down and her lips lifted up in a sneer.

Ruth wanted to go but was stuck until someone offered to drive her.

Dash stood. 'C'mon, Ruth. I'll fix that flat tyre for you.'

WhatsApp

Ruth
Ended up at an arvo tea at Dash and Evie's farm

Jack
Good?

Ruth
A lot of tension. Something to do with an eco-health resort. And something else with Troy.

Jack
Eco-health resort???

Ruth
😱
Chandra wants to build a yoga retreat on Evie's land by the river

Jack
So Troy was there?

Ruth
Yep. He barely said a word. Sat in the corner. Seething about something. Dash's mother referred to his criminal record.

Jack
What's he done?

Ruth
Dunno. But she's very nice to me and really nasty to Troy. Seems racist to me.

Jack
?

Ruth
Troy's a local Koori kid

Jack
Right

Ruth
Thinking about offering him a job actually

Jack
Why?

Ruth
Because I need someone smart to help me in the practice. And to stick it to Diane.

Jack
Hah. Who else was there?

Ruth
That girl from the chemist. She came with Troy, but spent the whole time fluttering her eyelids at Dash.

Jack
Time to talk?

Ruth pressed the telephone button.

'I've been invited to the parents' place of a Pom for the weekend. I need to take a present, don't I?' Jack said.

'Yes.'

'What should I take?'

They whiled away ten minutes discussing the relative merits of chocolate or Australian wine.

'Is the friend female?'

'I share information with you on a strictly need-to-know basis and, at this time, you don't need to know.'

'Fair enough.' Ruth yawned. 'Time for bed, I think. Nighty night, little dude.'

'Yep,' said Jack and hung up.

22

EVIE

April, Saturday, ten weeks before

EVIE WAS BRUSHING JASPER DOWN IN THE HORSE PADDOCK JUST OUTSIDE the shed when Dash returned from fixing Ruth's flat tyre.

'What proposal?' she said.

'Yeah, sorry, love. I didn't get a chance to raise it with you.'

'But you invited Chandra over to talk about it.'

'She invited herself.'

Evie didn't realise she'd stopped brushing until Jasper moved away from her. She pulled on the halter to bring him back and resumed the vigorous strokes over his withers. Was that true? Or was Dash hoping that Chandra would launch the idea so he didn't have to?

'What is it exactly?'

'She gave me some plans. I've got them somewhere.' He shuffled around in the cabin of his ute, produced a cardboard tube, extracted some paper from the tube and unrolled it on the bonnet.

The drawings were in colour; an artist's rendering of a series of buildings nestling among trees by the river, carefully landscaped.

'It's huge,' said Evie. 'And it goes halfway up the Bluff.' She pointed at the plans. 'What's that?'

'Like a cross between a lift and a cable car. Goes up the hill at an angle.'

Evie scoffed. 'They're going to raze my regrowth. And it'll cost millions. Tens of millions.'

'Chandra says they have investors.'

Evie took Jasper's halter off and gave him a slap on the rump harder than she'd intended. He jumped. She whispered sorry in his ear and, still with her back to Dash, stomped off.

'What's for dinner?' Dash said to her back.

'Mince.'

That night, after eating in sullen silence, Evie went to bed with her book. Dash came in twenty minutes later, cleaned his teeth, put on his T-shirt and jocks. When he got into bed, he leaned over and touched her arm.

'Sorry, love,' he said. 'Chandra got a bit carried away. I thought it would be better if she explained it herself rather than me trying to.'

'I just want a baby and a farm. I don't want to run a hotel.'

'Whatever you want, love,' he said, stroking her leg.

Now her strange conversation with Chandra after yoga made sense. Chandra wanted the Bluff so she could develop it into a resort, and was using Dash to get at Evie.

'You don't want people and builders and hotel operators crawling all over the Bluff do you? We'd lose control of the farm.'

'Nah, you're right. It'd be terrible.'

She melted, first her leg draping over his then her hand over his chest. She was always a sucker for him.

Now that they had the doctor's appointment and she wasn't so worried about IVF, if they had sex, her body would be relaxed enough to allow conception. It happened, people said, when you stopped worrying about it.

She woke at three and couldn't go back to sleep.

She sensed Dash was awake, too, by his stillness. In the dark, she said, 'They must have got an architect to draw those plans.'

'Oh, yeah,' said Dash. 'They came out to the campsite a few weeks ago. You weren't around.'

What the fuck? He'd kept it from her for weeks.

23

BEA

April, Saturday, ten weeks before

WHEN BEA CAME HOME FROM EVIE AND DASH'S, VICTORIA WAS IN A flurry cleaning the house, which involved rearranging the books and magazines about the royal family into marginally neater piles, and then shoving the vacuum cleaner around what she could see of the floor.

Cleaning always put Victoria in an even worse mood. Soon she would scream at Bea for causing the mess. Bea sighed. She was tired. She just wanted to go vegetate on the internet for a bit. She liked the yoga lady she'd met at Dash's and had looked up the website for her yoga studio, which was called Mandala. It looked cool. Kind of peaceful.

'Where have you been?' Victoria said.

'Riding horses,' said Bea. It seemed safe to tell her. It should tick all the boxes for Victoria: posh people who went to boarding school; wholesome activity in fresh air. Very Enid Blyton.

'Where?' said Victoria, her lips pursed into that faded rose button.

'Dash Rogers' place.'

Victoria looked like someone had put some sour milk under her nose. 'Isn't that where you spent New Year's? You spend more time with them than you do with me.'

Jesus, thought Bea. *Nothing I do is right.*

She was hungry. She went into the kitchen to make toast. Victoria interrupted her tussle with the vacuum cleaner to make a cup of tea. Bea braced. Victoria never had a cup of tea after lunch. Boiling the jug must be an excuse to be in the kitchen while Bea was there. What had she done now?

'Don't worry. I'll tidy up after I finish,' Bea said, to pre-empt the tantrum.

'Did you have a nice day, darling?' Victoria asked, using her syrupy high-pitched voice.

'Yeah, okay,' said Bea. When the syrupy voice came out, it was because Victoria knew that whatever she was about to ask for was unreasonable.

'I was just wondering,' said Victoria, fiddling with a teabag, 'if you could be out tonight.'

'For how long?'

'Well,' said Victoria, considering it, 'I suppose it would be all right if you came back after midnight. If you were quiet.'

This from a woman who threw a tantrum and questioned Bea's morals if she came home after ten without ringing her.

'Why?' said Bea.

Victoria pursed her lips to indicate how invasive that question was. 'Someone's coming over for dinner.'

'Who?' Bea asked. But it must be Gazza. Who else would it be? Pickings were slight in Myddle.

'None of your business.'

'It is my business if there's going to be a man with his dick hanging out in the kitchen at two am.'

Victoria's face turned puce. She was always on the edge of rage. The smallest trigger could send her over it. Bea was usually careful to avoid anything that might set her off, but the naked man incident was fresh in her mind, and Bea was still on the edge of rage about it herself.

Victoria's hand drew back and she slapped Bea on the cheek. 'How dare you!' she spat. Her vowels rounded when she lost control, and her language became imperious when she felt that her dignity had been impugned.

Bea rubbed her cheek to soothe it.

'You are so vulgar!' Victoria shouted.

Bea walked away down the hall to her bedroom. Victoria followed her to scream in Bea's face. 'I didn't bring you up to be so common!'

Bea slammed her bedroom door shut. She pulled out a backpack. Her nose was running. There were no tissues in the house, and to get some toilet paper she'd have to go back into the hall.

'I'm so ashamed of you!' Victoria screamed.

Victoria shook the door and banged on it. Bea held on to the knob so that Victoria couldn't come in.

'Even in this dead-end town, people think you're a slattern.' That was Victoria's closing sortie. She stomped away.

Bea jammed her bed up against the door. The anger and outrage at her mother's hypocrisy boiled over, and she shouted as she shoved her phone and a hoodie into the backpack, 'Takes a slut to know one!'

Victoria's stomping stopped. Bea opened the window, climbed out onto the louvred-in verandah, let herself out the lattice front door and ran down the front steps.

Victoria shrieked after her, 'You're so coarse. You're the reason I can't get a partner. You can stay away!'

Bea jogged to the end of the street until she was sure her mother hadn't followed her. There was nobody about except a red dog snuffling in the gutter.

Where would she go? Her only friend was Troy, and she didn't want him to know how bad her mum was.

Also, if she asked to stay the night he might get the wrong idea.

She wished she had a female friend.

She wished she had a dad. He wouldn't let this happen.

She could just hang out down by the river until later. Her bedroom window was open, so she could sneak back in and her mum wouldn't know.

On the main street, she went to the riverbank and sat on a bench near the playground. Dusk was falling. A fish flew through the air and landed back in the water with a slap.

She had nearly four hundred dollars saved. Would that be enough to move out? Her mum charged her a hundred bucks a week board, but it would be a lot more than that to get her own place. Also, she had no furniture.

She wandered back past the end of the street. After twenty minutes, the police LandCruiser pulled up three doors from her house, Gazza got out, adjusting his trousers under his gut, looked around furtively, then disappeared into her house.

She went to the pub. Some old fellas were holding up the bar. 'Can I have a burger, Twister?' she asked the barman.

'Sure, love. Are ya gonna eat it here?' His eyes darted sideways, an indication Twister was suffering some dilemma, probably to do with her being seventeen and in a bar.

'It's all right,' said Bea. 'Gazza is at Mum's. No chance of him turning up here to crack down on underage drinking.' She rolled her eyes.

Twister smiled and leaned over the bar. 'At ya mum's, is he?' he said, leaving a space for her to elaborate. She didn't.

The hamburger was awful. The patty had been pulled out of the freezer and chucked in the microwave, the grill marks tattooed into it before it was frozen. Twister's latest employee had shoved some sad lettuce, a slice of wet tomato and a slice of bright yellow cheese into a stale bun before reinserting it into the microwave in the hope that it would melt the plastic cheese and freshen up the bun.

She watched the horseracing on the telly behind the bar for a bit until one of the old fellas with a gap-toothed leer offered to buy her a beer. She left and went back to the park.

It was cold. There was going to be a frost by the feel of it. Her jeans and hoodie wouldn't be enough.

She went back to the house and checked the kitchen window. Victoria was sitting on Gazza's knee. There was an empty bottle of wine and another one nearly empty, candles and dirty plates.

She climbed in through her bedroom window but knocked over a candle on the bookcase. It clattered and banged.

Victoria hissed through the door. 'It's only eight o'clock. You agreed to stay out longer. You scared the living daylights out of him.'

'Shouldn't a policeman be braver than that?'

'Get out!' Victoria hissed.

Bea got her doona and climbed through the window and went back to the park. She tried to sleep in the picnic shelter but something was scratching in the bins. Possums maybe. Or rats.

The flying foxes screeched and flapped, their bat profiles in silhouette when they flew from tree to tree.

She pulled the doona up to her chin. She couldn't close her eyes. Christ knew what would scamper over her.

24

RUTH

April, nine weeks before

RUTH LIKED HER SUNDAY YOGA CLASS WITH CHANDRA. SHE WAS stronger now and could hold the poses. Chandra still did the schtick about the light in the head, but Ruth just zoned out. It was strangely comforting to be in a different world where peace and love reigned.

She had a herbal tea with Roscoe afterwards.

'What's with the eco-health resort?' she asked.

'Oh, I heard that you were there.' He was bashful. 'Bit of a fiasco.'

'How so?'

'Chandra said Dash denied all knowledge. Awkward.'

'So it's his thing, too?'

'Of course it is. He walked over the site with us and the architect. I was under the impression that Evie was all over it. Turns out, not. Pity. It would be a great thing for Myddle. We're hoping we can convince her.'

'How are you going to raise the money?'

'We're talking to some people,' said Roscoe vaguely.

This thing was big, Ruth thought. And clearly a much more concrete idea than what had been discussed at the afternoon tea.

In the afterglow of her yoga session, Ruth took Harry and Marge's labrador Buster for a long meander along the river, listening to the birds.

Back at home, she showered and scrabbled together some food. Then she had a few hours to kill before going over to Patch's for dinner.

She read. She'd never watched much television, but Harry and Marge had invested in all the streaming services so she binged a bit of telly.

Empty time stretched before her.

She opened Facebook. Someone she hadn't seen for the thirty years since she'd left school had posted a picture of a champagne glass superimposed in front of a beach. Ruth shivered and hit the cross in the top right-hand corner of the screen.

Her Facebook page gave her the heebie-jeebies: the conspiracy theories; the commiseration posts she got when Bill died from people she barely knew offering love, prayers and weird advice; the creepy ads she was bombarded with about belly fat, menopause and schemes for getting rich; people listed as friends curating their best lives with holiday snaps that all looked the same. She squirmed with discomfort every time she ventured on there.

A friend suggestion popped up for Evie. Ruth clicked the page, which Evie had said was her one concession to social media. It comprised many pictures of cattle at shows, with ribbons around their torsos: rectangular prisms of sleek bovine contentment.

Evie's hand rested on the withers of a bull. The caption read: *Horace from Clive Downs. Best in show.*

Evie's post said, *The judges described Horace as good weight, proud, with a good set of testicles. Be still my beating heart.*

Ruth pressed like. Evie was a funny woman.

There was a friend request from Dash. Ruth accepted it out of equal parts politeness and curiosity. His profile picture was a beaming Dash, shirtless, holding a large fish, standing beside a jet ski.

He took a good photo, Dash—a dazzling wide smile, white teeth, pectorals glistening golden. The burgeoning flab of beer and impending middle age was nowhere in evidence.

He was a prolific poster: Dash at the footy club; Dash in front of vehicles (jet ski, motorbike, boat, large ute); Dash with a beer aloft and an arm cast over the pretty girl or boy next to him.

He and Evie were very different people, but they complemented each other she supposed: Dash gregarious; Evie curmudgeonly and very focused on the farm.

'Tell me about Troy,' Ruth said to Patch that evening, over Milly's sleeping head. 'I'm thinking about offering him a casual job. Helping out in the office.'

'Oh, that would be great. He's very bright.' She looked out into the garden as she searched for a way to articulate something. 'He understands how people tick. What's it called? Emotional intelligence.'

Ruth told Patch about the incident on New Year's Eve where Troy rescued Bea from the lascivious Gazza.

'Yeah, doesn't surprise me,' said Patch. 'He has the ability to bore through people and extract their essence. A lot of the teachers thought he was a bit sullen, even arrogant. But my theory is it's his coping mechanism.'

'What is he coping with?'

'Their low expectations of him,' said Patch. 'It's like he pulls over a titanium shell, sits inside it and watches.'

'Sounds forbidding,' said Ruth.

'He has a biting wit when the armour plating is lifted. It would be good if you showed him how the law works. And I think he'd be good at it if you could spark his interest.'

Ruth paused. She needed to know. 'Has he had any problems with the police? Criminal record?'

Patch looked surprised and a little affronted. 'Not that I know of. He's a good kid. Why would you say that?'

The last sentence was almost an accusation. Fair enough, too. By asking the question, she was propagating Diane's toxicity.

Still, it was important to know if he was going to work in the office, with the secrets of Myddle sitting in the files.

On Monday morning, Deb's head appeared around Ruth's office door. 'Young Troy Matheson is here. Says you're expecting him?'

There was doubt, even hostility, in her scowl. Ruth wondered, not for the first time, what Harry saw in Deb. She was the most unenthusiastic employee Ruth had ever encountered.

Ruth rose to greet Troy in reception. The unruly wave in his wiry hair had been subjugated with a wet comb, but now that it had dried, clumps of it were making a bid for freedom.

'G'day.' Troy frowned as he said it, and after a small hesitation held out his hand to shake Ruth's.

Ruth took Troy into her office. 'What do you want to know? About the law?' she said.

Troy arranged his body in a simulacrum of cool, sitting back in the chair, his right foot suspended in the air over his left knee. He had an athlete's confidence that his body would do whatever he asked, and a stranger's uncertainty about where he should put the gangly bits (legs, arms, hands).

'Wouldn't mind knowing what a lawyer does,' he said. 'How it works.'

What could she say? That the external manifestation of lawyering looked sedentary, involving as it did reading, tapping away at a keyboard, talking on the phone and sitting in meetings, and, for some, talking in court. The high-octane stuff—the tension, the conflict, the effusive joy of winning a case—happened inside your head. You had to contain it. Public displays of distress or glee were unseemly. How do you describe that to a kid fresh out of school who was used to celebrating a try with a standing backflip?

'I could make a speech about the importance of the rule of law. And about how society functions because of the scaffolding provided by it. People need lawyers to work out how the rules apply to them. Lawyers have to understand how it all fits together and be able to interpret it for people.'

Troy nodded slowly, in an unconvincing attempt to appear interested, as if he was trying to humour a Martian who was attempting to explain why Mars was the planet essential for making the universe function.

'You know what?' said Ruth. 'Best way to work that out would be to help me for a bit. It will give you a better idea.'

His eyebrows sprang up. 'Really?' The word came out uncensored, an expression of disbelief. He hadn't expected a job offer.

'I need help from someone smart who can organise information and solve problems.'

The chair creaked as Troy rearranged his legs.

'Do you think you fit the description?' she asked.

'Yeah.'

She told him how much she'd pay him. He looked surprised. Then he asked a question she hadn't expected: 'Why are you doing this?'

'I need someone in the office who will laugh at my jokes,' she said.

He nodded slowly without moving his gaze. 'You need to pay someone to do that?'

'Helps,' she said.

'Okay,' said Troy. 'I can do that.'

'Good. Well, you can start next Monday if you like.'

'Thanks,' he said.

She said to his back as he left: 'Also, Patch, your maths teacher—she's my god-daughter—told me you're smart.'

Troy lifted a hand in acknowledgement, then turned at the door. 'Smart as fuck,' he said and grinned.

'Just one thing,' she said. 'I'll need to do a criminal record check.'

He paused. His brows dropped, hooding his eyes.

'Sorry. It's routine. Because'—she faltered—'you know, secrets on files.'

That sounded so lame, and so contrived. She wanted to tell him about 'the protect your arse' principle. One of the first things Roscoe had taught her. Have a paper trail, just in case.

She held out the piece of paper. He signed it. But the joy had been sucked out of the room.

The criminal record check came up empty.

It occurred to Ruth that, as he was only just eighteen, any crimes he'd been convicted of while a child might not have made it onto a formal record. The courts were cautious about tarring a kid with the criminal brush, because it could ruin a life before it had properly begun.

But Patch was the best kind of reference: his teacher, who'd known him for ten years, and had every reason to be candid. She'd been genuinely surprised and annoyed by the suggestion.

Troy turned up on Monday morning in the same outfit he'd worn to the interview, except that he hadn't bothered with the wet comb. He put something wrapped in a tea towel on Ruth's desk. 'Mum made you some scones,' he said. He put down a jar. 'And some jam.'

'Oh my goodness,' said Ruth, eagerly opening the tea towel.

They were huge, they were fluffy, and they were still warm.

'Deb,' Ruth yelled, 'second breakfast.'

Deb looked uncharacteristically enthusiastic when she stuck her head around the door, saw the scones and said, without prompting, 'I'll make us some tea.'

'I honestly think,' Ruth mumbled through a full mouth a few moments later, 'these are the best scones I've ever tasted.'

'Yeah, she's pretty good, my mum,' said Troy.

Even Deb looked contented.

First things first: Ruth gave Troy a lecture about confidentiality. 'People trust lawyers with their secrets. You can't tell anyone about stuff you learn on the files, even if it's something other people know. And if you know the client, or the person on the other side of a file, like really well, you have to tell me, and not look at it.'

She explained the concept of the vault, the locked cabinet in her mind. 'Stuff goes in there, and it never comes out. Telling someone their client's secrets is the worst thing a lawyer can do.'

He nodded. 'Fair enough,' he said. 'Although stealing their money would be worse, wouldn't it?'

She shook her head. 'Sometimes the secret is worth more than money. Sometimes it means their freedom, or their reputation.'

After checking he didn't know the clients, Ruth handed Troy three files that would give him an insight into the sort of stuff Harry's practice did. They were very different. There was a sale of land, a divorce, and a fight in a family about a contested will. 'Have a look at them, then come and have a chat, and we'll work out what needs to happen next,' she said.

By mid-morning he was in her office. 'What do you think?' she asked.

'They're all about property rights,' Troy said.

'Not really,' Ruth said. 'They're very different areas of law. Family. Succession, which is who gets what when someone dies. And conveyancing, which is about land.'

'Yeah,' said Troy. 'They're all about who owns the land.' He held up three fingers and folded them one by one as he went through the list. 'Who gets the land when there's a divorce, who gets the land when there's a death, and how to sell it.'

Ruth's head drifted to the side as she considered that. 'I suppose that's right,' she said. 'But the law treats them all very differently.'

Troy's face hooded into a frown as he looked at her. He didn't contradict her again. He brought a completely different perspective to it. Ruth had been trained from university to look at it in three different silos, completely unrelated.

'Funny, isn't it,' Troy said as he left her room. 'If Evie Rogers divorced Dash, she'd have to give him half the property, even though neither of them did anything to acquire it.'

'I'm going out for a sandwich,' Ruth said to Troy as she walked past. 'Want to come? It's on me.' Lunches for the staff in the firm in the city involved either a pile of sandwiches and cakes on platters, or an excursion to a fancy restaurant. Here they had to venture out to the local caff.

They both ordered egg and lettuce, which reminded Ruth of the tuckshop at primary school. They ate the sandwiches at a table between the river and the footpath. The April day was balmy, a cloudless azure sky, the light so clear it danced off the leaves of the gums up on the main street.

A woman jogged past in a baggy T-shirt, baggy shorts and running shoes, her hair pulled back in a ponytail. She had the legs of an athlete.

The woman smiled when she saw Troy and stopped in front of him. 'Hey, bub.'

'Hey,' Troy said.

The woman looked pointedly at Ruth, who smiled back.

'Ruth.' Troy shuffled his feet. 'This is my mum, Rita.'

Ruth had to consciously close her mouth. This woman was way too young to have an eighteen-year-old child. She looked to be mid-thirties. At most. And spectacular. The T-shirt hung from her and had some holes in it, but Rita would look fantastic in a hessian sack.

The woman nodded. 'Just going for a run,' as if she needed to explain. 'We've got a hockey final in a fortnight. Only time I get to exercise is on my day off.'

Ruth must have looked mystified. 'My other kids are in preschool and primary school,' she added. 'I work at the nursing home in Broughton. Shift work.'

'Thanks for the scones. Best I've ever had. I'm so glad to have Troy helping out in the office,' Ruth said.

'Thanks for having him.'

'I'm hoping to convince Troy to go to uni,' said Ruth. 'He'd make a great lawyer.'

'Do you reckon?' said Rita.

'He's very bright. And there's something about him. He has a quiet judgement. He seems to get people.'

'I'm right here,' said Troy.

Rita ignored him. 'He'd be all right, you reckon?'

'More than all right. Uni is a lot of fun. And it's like a key that unlocks a lot of stuff.'

'I was going to go to uni,' said Rita. 'Didn't get there. Had Troy instead.'

Troy scrunched up his sandwich wrapping, stood and said, 'Better get back.'

Ruth was dying to hear Rita's life story. She wondered how she could nudge her into revealing it. 'He's very like you,' Ruth said, nodding in the direction of Troy's back.

'Yeah,' Rita said. 'He has his dad in him as well.'

Nobody had mentioned Troy's dad.

Ruth smiled and nodded, hoping that Rita would tell a story. She didn't.

Harry rang on the landline every few days and had a chat to Deb before she put him through to Ruth.

He and Ruth talked through the files, and the grand time Harry and Marge were having, exploring gorges in the middle of the Western Australian desert.

'Oh, by the way,' she said. 'Patch recommended young Troy Matheson to help out.'

Harry didn't respond.

'Is there a problem?' Ruth asked.

Harry took a few seconds to answer. 'I s'pose it'll be okay.' His voice was filled with doubt. 'He knows a few of the people on the files.'

'I've spoken to him about that. And I'm keeping him away from files where he knows them well.'

'Right,' said Harry, his voice indicating it was far from right. 'Need to be extra careful about that.'

Irritation rose up within Ruth. 'Anyone in particular you're worried about?'

Harry breathed into the phone. 'None of the active files, I guess.'

'Anything I need to watch out for?'

Long pause.

'No, I guess not.'

This town was incorrigible. She was trying to think of something to say that didn't sound like a retort, when Harry changed the subject.

At dusk Ruth went up to the pub to get some wine for dinner. Troy was in the main street with a bunch of his mates. Constable Gazza Parker had a tight grip of the arm of one of the lads, who was not more than sixteen, with that awkward scrawniness of teenage boys and bum fluff on the chin.

Ruth's hackles rose. She strolled over, feigning insouciance. 'Everything all right, Troy?' she asked.

'Yeah. Don't worry about it,' Troy said.

'What's going on?' she asked.

Troy's eyes narrowed as he watched Gazza. The other boys looked at their feet, scuffing the dirt with their old sneakers.

Gazza gave the boy's arm a final twitch upward. The boy winced but didn't say anything.

'Don't let me see ya misbehaving again.' Gazza put his hand on his holster and swaggered off.

'What was that all about?' Ruth asked.

'Gazza Parker asked the boys if they were going in the witchetty grub competition at the show.'

The racial slur made her wince.

'Then—well—you know how there's a race in the show where a bunch of kids try to catch a greasy pig?'

She knew the Australian tradition at country shows.

'Billy here asked if Gazza Parker was gonna be the greasy pig.'

Ruth snorted with laughter. 'What did he do?'

'You saw. He was about to arrest Billy.'

'For what?'

'Language.'

Ruth raised her eyebrows.

'He might have said fucking greasy pig.'

'Christ,' said Ruth. 'Does that happen a lot?'

Troy looked at her in disbelief. 'Yes,' he said, in the tone Jack used to say 'der' to her. 'Except it's usually followed by a charge of resisting arrest. Didn't happen this time because you rolled up.'

'How do you avoid it?' Ruth asked.

'My mum has a rule: never make a joke funnier than the cops.'

Ruth's laughter spurted out unbidden. 'Your mum is a very wise woman,' she said.

⁂

WhatsApp

Ruth
I just saw Troy and his mates being harassed
by Gazza, the local copper

Jack
What were they doing?

Ruth

Being teenage boys. Smart-arse jokes.
Hilarious in a teenage boy way.
I didn't realise how much of a bubble it is in the inner city.

Jack

My mum. Who lives in a bubble.

Ruth

It's like we dust over the top of it and
pretend it's not happening

Jack

Are you going to fix it?

Ruth

How?

Jack

I dunno. Make a complaint to the anti-discrimination tribunal or something.

Ruth

I could spend my every waking hour in the anti-discrimination tribunal. But I have to do paying work for paying clients. Also, what would that achieve, apart from alienating me from the town?

Jack

[The top of the screen said 'online'. He had read it but he didn't respond.]

25

BEA

April, eight weeks before

BEA WAS REARRANGING THE MAKEUP DISPLAY WHEN CHANDRA THE beautiful yoga lady came into the pharmacy.

'I've seen your photos on Instagram, haven't I?' she asked.

Bea nodded.

'You've got a great way with a camera. I love the visual stories you tell, the heart in them.'

'Thanks,' said Bea. She acted cool by arranging the display on the counter as if she received compliments like that every day.

'I'd love it if you joined us at Mandala.'

That Saturday afternoon, Bea ventured out to Chandra's on her bike. She was nervous—she always was with a new group of people.

Chandra told everyone to close their eyes and then they did what Chandra called 'meditation practice'. It took a long time. Bea was supposed to empty her mind but lots of random thoughts jumped in, like whether she'd cleaned up breakfast properly and what would happen if her mum found out she was coming here, and whether that would be a screaming-level problem or just a snarky-remark-type problem?

But after the meditation and the yoga, her head was filled with light, as if a star was shining in her brain, just like Chandra said.

Afterwards, Chandra hugged her and said to everyone, 'This amazing woman is the most talented photographer I know. Why don't you bring your camera and practise photographing us?'

Bea didn't have a camera. She used her phone to take photos. But she had some savings and looked up second-hand cameras on the internet. She bought a Canon and spent the next three days figuring out how it worked.

She uploaded five photos of the next Mandala meeting onto her Instagram page and got more likes than she'd ever received before.

'Wow, Bea, you're so great at documenting us,' said Chandra, leaning forward so that her nose was very close to Bea's. Her eyes were an intense green, pale but full of light, with a dark rim. 'We're building something special here at Mandala. I'm so honoured you're a part of it.'

'Oh, by the way,' Victoria said when Bea got home from Mandala, 'Gazza's coming over tonight so you'll have to be out again.'

The idea of Bea spending the night away from the house had turned from a saccharine request to a foregone conclusion. Victoria was like that. Requests that she knew at first were unreasonable soon became an expectation.

'Where will I go?'

'I don't know,' said Victoria, irritated that she had to consider it. 'To a friend's place. Same place you went last time.'

Bea went to her room and sat on her bed. She had work in the morning. She needed to sleep. She had planned to watch a bit of TV and go to bed early.

Then it occurred to her. She did have a place to go this time.

She rang Chandra. 'Do you mind?' she began. 'Would it be possible?' That was better. 'It's just that I need a place to sleep tonight and wondered if maybe . . .' The end of the sentence drifted away, unsaid.

'Right,' said Chandra. 'I suppose you could stay on a blow-up mattress in the yoga studio.'

Bea put some clothes in her backpack and rode her bike out to Chandra's. It was only five k.

She knocked on the door of the house.

'Have you eaten?' said Chandra.

Bea nodded, even though she hadn't had anything to eat.

'Sit down,' said Chandra. 'I've got some leftover dhal. I'll heat it up for you.'

The mandala on Chandra's wall was vibrant and intricate. It was made of sand. Someone coloured those grains of sand and then arranged them with crisp lines between them, no bleeding of one colour into another. Must have taken ages.

'Do you like working in the chemist's?' said Chandra. 'Are you thinking of going away to uni?'

'I'm too dumb to go to uni.'

Chandra leaned forward and touched Bea's hand. 'Why would you say that, Bea?'

That was the truth she'd been brought up with; it had been drummed into her by her mother, every day.

'Everyone thinks I'm dumb.'

'Do they, though?' asked Chandra. 'I don't think your boss thinks that. What's his name?'

'Chris. No, that's probably right.'

'And I don't think it.'

'My mum told me I'm too dumb to go to uni.'

'Why would your mum say that?'

Bea had never thought to ask that question. 'I don't know.'

'If you go to uni, you'd have to leave town and go to Sydney or Brisbane?'

Bea nodded.

'How would your mum cope without you?'

Bea shrugged.

'Does she have anyone else?'

'No.' She didn't count Gazza. He'd be gone in a few weeks.

'If you go she'd be completely alone. You might never come home. That would scare her.'

It would, too. All Victoria's tantrums were directed at keeping people in her life. She threw a tantrum when Bea got a new friend. She threw a tantrum when she wanted Bea out of the way—temporarily—so she could entertain a new boyfriend. She'd throw a tantrum if Bea tried to leave.

Ironic, really, that the only way Victoria could interact with people was a display of rage, which she used to manipulate people into staying. The only person it worked on was Bea. Because the rest of them could escape.

Chandra made her think of the world differently.

26

EVIE

April, eight weeks before

EVIE LEANED OVER THE SATURDAY PAPER ON THE KITCHEN BENCH.

A mobile buzzed and vibrated underneath. It wouldn't be hers because, as usual, hers was flat.

Evie lifted the paper. The name on the screen said, 'Chandra'.

Dash was in the bathroom.

'Dash,' Evie yelled, 'your mobile is ringing!'

Dash stumbled out doing up his fly. By the time he swiped the green dot, the call had gone to voicemail. He called her back.

Evie could only hear the Dash half of the conversation, which went like this:

'How big?'

'That's pretty big.'

'Sure, I'll be over in ten.'

He walked out the back door and put on his boots.

Holding her coffee, Evie followed him to the door. 'What does she want?'

'She saw a snake in the house.'

'Why do you have to go?'

'Roscoe's not there.'

Evie turned back to the newspaper.

She was suspicious now of every interaction Dash had with women. Something in their marriage had died. She no longer trusted him. She hated that in herself, in her marriage.

Would a baby make it better? Or worse?

That night, Dash hovered as he always did when he had something he wanted to ask of her. He leaned on the bench, making small talk and a series of fulsome remarks: 'I love it when you cook mince like that'; 'You look so beautiful in that shirt.' It made her feel greasy, like he'd sprayed her with olive oil. She could feel something brewing, so she took her time making dinner.

He poured her a glass of wine, waited until she drank it, then poured her another.

'I've been thinking about it,' he said. 'I reckon we should consider Chandra's proposal. At least look at it.'

Oh. She'd hoped she'd deflected the scheme, but obviously not.

Evie needed to tread carefully. Dash was sensitive to any slight about his capacity to be a tourism entrepreneur, and it was simpler to keep up the fiction than deal with the injured pride.

'What did Chandra call it? An eco-health resort?' she said. 'Sounds like a hotel with a lot of yoga and kale instead of booze.' Evie took a mouthful of pasta. 'Did you kill the snake?' She tried to change the subject.

'By the time I got there, it had gone.'

'Right.'

'She's got investors,' said Dash. 'It wouldn't cost us anything.'

'It's a big building,' said Evie. 'A lot of concrete.'

'No point starting smaller,' said Dash. 'We'll need scale if we're going to make any money.'

She poked at the pasta and slowly twisted her fork to wrap together a mouthful. 'It's a very different business to a grazing property.'

'Chandra says we'd build an access road right on the boundary to keep the resort separate and, anyway, the punters would like seeing an operating farm, especially if they can see the regenerative farming you do.'

That was strange. Chandra's philosophy expressed in her book was about eradicating cattle farms.

'This huge building would be on the land we've set aside for regeneration.'

Dash shrugged. 'More money than carbon credits,' he said.

A surge of irritation put some acid in her tone. 'More risk.'

Dash's shoulders slumped. 'You're always so negative about everything I do.'

The peacock let out a mournful caw. A peahen answered. The noise reverberated inside her body, the low vibrations releasing a river of melancholy. Or maybe her hatred of the peacock family and its showy invasion brought it out.

'I'll have to think about it. And we have to ask Mum.'

'You don't have to ask her,' Dash said. 'You've got power of attorney. She won't understand it anyway.'

'We still need to ask her.'

Dash shook his head. 'You're in denial about her.'

She knew Dash thought she used her mother as an excuse to stick a spanner in the spokes whenever he showed a bit of initiative.

'I don't care what the lawyers say,' she said. 'My mother needs to agree.'

'But she's incapable of agreeing to anything.'

That was true. But Evie still needed to have a conversation with her. And that only complicated the whole thing more. What was the hurry anyway?

He pushed his chair out. It made a roar as it scraped across the wooden floor. He stomped to the bedroom and slammed the door.

She got up and stood outside it. 'Come on, Dash. Let me think about it,' she said. 'Let me see how it would all work, what they want to build and who'd run it.'

'We'll run it,' said Dash, as if that was obvious. Dash, who'd never meditated or been to a yoga class in his life. A man who had an aversion to greens of all kinds: green vegetables; the Greens party.

'We have no idea how to run a hotel. Or anything to do with wellness retreats. We've never even been to one.'

He opened the door. His face was contorted into rage. It made him ugly, his pretty face blighted.

'You never support me. I just want what's best for us. See us right for our kids.' His voice was getting louder as he spoke so that the word 'kids' was shouted, with little balls of spit. She stiffened, as she always did when he mentioned children.

She needed to lower the noise; meet him halfway. 'Same, darls,' she said. 'I just need to think about it a bit.'

It set him back. His voice lowered. 'A bit of support,' he said. 'That's all I'm asking for.'

No, she thought. *You are asking me to surrender myself, to subjugate my family's land, give up my life's work. And take a chance that somehow you will finally succeed at something. When it fails, we'll be left with a huge debt and a scarred landscape.*

Chandra must be a powerful persuader. What were her techniques for convincing Dash? How far did it go?

⁂

That Sunday she visited her mother at the aged care facility. Troy's mum Rita was on shift and came in, fussing around her mother's bed. 'It's nice your mum gets another visitor now,' she said.

'She does?'

'That yoga chick,' said Rita. 'What's her name? Chandra.'

'That's weird.'

Rita shrugged. 'They were neighbours, weren't they? Your mum was still at home with you when Chandra moved in with Roscoe?'

'Only for a few weeks.'

'She runs a yoga class here and visits a few of them afterwards. I think she feels like she's delivering pastoral care, like a priest.'

Evie wanted to warn Chandra off. Was that being too paranoid? All this attention from her was giving Evie the creeps.

'Did Chandra come to see you?' Evie asked her mum.

Her mother's clouded eyes searched for Evie's. 'Did she?' her mother asked. 'That's nice.'

⁂

Evie got her chance the next day when she ran into Chandra in the pasta aisle of the IGA, rolling her ancient trolley over the undulating linoleum floor. The yoga teacher had a sublime expression on her face even while working out whether to buy the penne or the farfalle.

'You've been visiting Mum.'

'Evie, how are you?' Chandra enveloped her in a scented hug. 'It's the least I could do. I know how difficult it is when parents get sick. And your mum is so young to have dementia. What is she? Seventy?'

Evie had meant it as an accusation, but Chandra had interpreted it as thanks.

'Seventy-two.'

Chandra's eyes were a strong shade of green. 'It must be such a worry for you, having her so sick,' she breathed.

'She's physically strong,' said Evie. All those years working on the farm. 'She just has an addled mind.'

Chandra smiled and frowned at the same time.

It turned out Chandra was right. Within a week, Rita rang.

'Evie, it's your mum,' she said. 'You'd better get over here.'

Evie's mum had died during her afternoon nap.

Her mother had been happy, Rita told her. Chandra had visited in the afternoon then her mum had laid down for a snooze.

And poof.

Gone. Just like that.

Evie held her mother's cold hand. She was pale, gaunt, eyes closed.

Rita's arm lay over Evie's shoulders.

'Is it weird that she died so suddenly?' Evie asked.

'A bit,' said Rita. 'But the really progressed dementia patients can't tell you if they're feeling bad. She might have been having a heart attack over breakfast for all we knew.'

Evie had to be more blunt. 'Chandra was the last person to see her.'

'Yep,' said Rita.

Evie stroked the back of her mother's hand. 'Is there any way she could have . . .' Evie trailed off.

Rita reached out and covered Evie's hand. 'Look at her, love. There's no sign of a struggle.'

True. Her mother's face was blank, as if she had left her shell.

She had maroon bruises on her papery arms, but they had come and gone over the last few years.

'Why would there be a struggle?' said Evie.

'Pillow over the head. Even the weakest of them fights for life when it's ebbing away. It's a basic human instinct.'

Evie turned back to her mother and lifted the sheet a little to reveal her mother's wasted chest. 'What if she was asleep, or she straddled her; held her under the sheet?'

'Why are you torturing yourself with this?' Rita said.

'I told Dash I needed my mother's consent before he and Chandra build an eco-health resort on the land. Next thing, she's dead. Before I even got a chance to speak to her about it.'

'Aw, darl.'

'You talk about the pillow as if it happens all the time.'

'Well,' said Rita, 'it's cheap, effective and untraceable.'

'Are you saying it happens a lot?'

'Dunno. It's untraceable. But there are people in here who are old and sick and unhappy and dying. Euthanasia the legal way is complicated. A lot of bureaucracy.'

'What do the police do?'

'Never called,' said Rita.

'I think I should report it,' said Evie.

'The doctor will be here in a minute, to certify the death and ascertain the cause. Why don't you talk to her?'

Evie gathered her mother's things. The clothes could go to the Salvation Army. She put her mother's favourite cushions in a garbage bag to take home, with the photos of her dad and Joof, and Evie when she was young. A couple of paintings. She put the weddings rings on her own right hand. At the end of her mother's life, the possessions had been whittled down to the essentials.

The doctor was gentle with her mother's body and with Evie.

'Why do you think she died?' said Evie.

'I would say heart failure. Euphemism for old age.' The doctor's voice softened. 'It was time for her to go.'

'Any sign of suffocation?'

The doctor didn't register surprise. She sat with Evie on the bed, asked her what worried her, listened, and said she'd arrange an autopsy.

Evie said nothing to Dash about her concern.

He could interpret her lack of communication as grief, and he did.

Two days later, the doctor rang and softly told her that the cause of death on the death certificate would be heart failure.

'No signs of a suspicious death?' said Evie.

'There were burst blood vessels, but your mum was old and sick, and bumped into things. I wouldn't last two minutes in a witness box if I tried to say in a court that she'd been murdered.'

'So inconclusive then?' said Evie.

'I've reached a conclusion,' said the doctor, firmly but gently.

27

RUTH

April, eight weeks before

'MRS CLIVE DIED,' RUTH SAID TO HARRY WHEN HE PHONED IN.

'Gee,' said Harry. 'That's tough for Evie.'

'I dug her will out of your Dickensian cupboard,' said Ruth. 'Looks straightforward.'

'Yeah. She didn't own much herself. Just a life tenancy in the farm. Evie gets it outright now.'

'I might go and see Evie.'

'Give her our regards,' said Harry. 'We're in the Pilbara. I don't think we'll make it back for the funeral. Would you mind if Sam stayed with you at the house? I'll make sure he can go.'

'Sure,' said Ruth. 'Of course.'

'Evie's gone for a ride,' Dash told Ruth when she arrived at Clive Downs.

There was a *clumpety clump* of hooves and Evie rode up. Ruth wasn't a horse person, but she knew enough to know Evie was an expert. She rode with her thighs, her hands low, the reins loose.

Evie dismounted and heaved the saddle off the horse. 'Come on, then. We'll go and have a chat to the girls.' She whistled for the kelpies, who leapt onto the back seat of the ute. The dogs were excited, mouths open, tongues lolling out.

Evie's ute had a thick coating of dust and dog hair. Ruth's black dress would be festooned with red volcanic soil and rust-red kelpie hair.

'Sorry,' said Evie, giving the seat an ineffectual wipe with her hand, which caused the dust to swirl and resettle. 'Should have suggested you wear jeans.'

'Sorry about your mum,' said Ruth as the ute thumped over the farm track. Evie drove fast, trailed by a train of dust. 'You okay?'

'Yeah. Just sad.'

Four big grey kangaroos hopped languorously away before stopping to rest on their tails to watch the ute pass.

'Have to get used to being an orphan,' said Evie. 'I'm the only one left.'

Ruth had Jack at least, the one thing Evie didn't have.

A kelpie licked Ruth's cheek, then stuck his tongue in her ear.

'Bryan,' said Evie, 'leave poor Ruth alone.'

'Good for my immune system,' said Ruth. The smell from Bryan's mouth was appalling. 'Have you been chewing on a bone, Bryan?'

The dog reinserted his tongue in her ear, a wet snuffling. She patted him on the head.

'Here they are,' said Evie. 'The girls.'

About a hundred cows were spread out in the next paddock, grazing.

The cows cheered up when they saw Evie and the ute. Those in the distance trotted over. There were now a hundred cows packed on the other side of the gate, big and clumsy.

'You okay to open the gate?' said Evie. 'They won't hurt you. They're friendly.'

Cows scared the bejesus out of Ruth. They were curious animals, eager to have a closer look. If they didn't like what they saw, they'd put their heads down and give it a bump, which from an animal which weighs more than half a tonne can have a suboptimal outcome for a human who weighs sixty kilos, especially a human in a frock and boots with slippery soles.

But it was a matter of pride.

'I had a look at your mum's will,' said Ruth when she got back into the cab unscathed.

'Should I be worried about it?'

'It's straightforward. Especially for the farm.' Ruth explained the process, which would be quick.

Evie slowed for another gate.

Another herd: auburn, sleek. 'My heifers,' said Evie.

She stopped the ute then got on the tray and untied a bale of hay. She kicked it off.

'They don't seem to be fazed by us,' said Ruth.

'Most days I come and have a chat,' said Evie. 'So they get used to me and the dogs being around. I give them a pretty good life and it pays to have contented cattle. They get on the truck easier.' She smiled. 'And they're worth more.'

There was a disturbance on the far side of the herd. The cattle shuffled away from something in the grass.

A dog barked, with staccato, high-pitched, ear-shattering constancy. The heifers snorted and jumped with alarm.

'That bloody corgi,' Evie said. 'Get, Frank!' she shouted. 'Get out of here!'

Ruth jumped into the cab of the ute. She didn't want to get in the path of half a tonne of panicking cow.

Roscoe and Chandra's corgi trotted into sight, with smug short-legged self-satisfaction. He stopped right under the nose of a cow to bark again. The heifer leapt and tried to headbutt the dog. Frank scooted out of the way, and barked at the nose of another cow.

The disquiet infected the herd, which scattered as fast as their bulk would allow.

Evie chased Frank. He tried to evade her but she tackled him. He yelped. She picked him up and chucked him into the cabin at Ruth's feet. She whistled for the kelpies to get onto the tray of the ute.

'Sorry,' said Evie. 'I have to separate them, or I'd have to return Frank with bite marks. Which is tempting, but not worth the blowback I'll get from that stupid fucking woman.'

Ruth surmised that the stupid woman was Chandra, who shared with Frank an ideological disdain for cows. So Evie's relationship with Chandra wasn't rosy then. She wasn't surprised. They had very different beliefs and values.

Frank wagged his ample bottom.

'Terrible dog,' Evie said. 'Needs to be in a city, not out here upsetting the animals. She won't lock him up. Keeps banging on about the stupid little fucker's rights to roam. If my father was still alive he would have shot it months ago.'

Frank smirked, oblivious to the mortal insult directed at him, his huge ears at attention. He moved onto Ruth's feet, arranging his body for a more comfortable sleep.

Half a dozen emus strutted by, necks rolling forward. Ruth was about to point them out but thought better of it. Evie must see them all the time.

'Beautiful property,' said Ruth as Evie headed at speed back to the house.

'I do love it,' she said. 'But it's hard running it on our own. Hard to get help. And I can't afford to employ someone full-time.'

'Looks to me like you're made to be a farmer.'

Evie shrugged. 'What else could I be? I dropped out of uni when I was nineteen. I have no qualifications.'

'So you're not thinking about the eco-health resort idea?'

'Nah. I'm more Basil Fawlty than Conrad Hilton.'

Ruth laughed. 'You and me both, sister,' she said. 'The punters would drive me nuts.'

'I just wish I could find someone to help with the farm, that's all.'

Evie drove to the yards, which were a couple of hundred metres from the house—close enough to walk, far enough away to avoid the dust and smell. They comprised fifty square metres of interlocking pens: fences and gates made from galvanised steel pipes. On one side was pasture, on the other the home paddock full of hazards for a cow or a horse: large machinery, the shed, tools.

'Leave that corgi in the ute,' said Evie. 'He'll cause pandemonium if he yaps at the bulls. They can't get away from him here, so they'll panic.'

Sixteen young bulls were in one of the pens. They were mucking about: locking horns, pushing one another back and forth, snorting, shaking their heads.

'Nice bulls,' said Ruth. They reminded her of the young men at the New Year's Eve party with Troy, laughing, wrestling, revelling in their strength.

'Yeah. We do all right.' Evie pointed out the biggest of them, called him over for a pat. He stuck his nose in her hand for a carrot. She wrapped her arms round the bull's neck and kissed him on the nose. 'My beautiful boy, aren't you, Horace,' she said.

She ran her hand across his spine as she walked down his torso and slapped him on the rump. 'See that magnificent arse?'

It was capacious and muscular, but Ruth was more worried about whether his hind leg would jab out with a quick, well-targeted kick.

Evie ran her hand across the top of his tail. 'A bum like an apple.'

'That's a good thing?'

'The best kind of bum to have.'

'If you're a bovine,' said Ruth.

Horace shook his huge head and gave a contented snuffle.

'He's very docile,' said Ruth. In her childhood, large animals with testicles—bulls, stallions—were cause for caution and a wide berth.

'A lot of hours have gone into Horace,' said Evie. 'He's still a bull, though. Don't turn your back on him. Especially if you're not me.'

A piercing mournful caw sounded behind them. A dozen big peahens and a huge peacock, his long blue and green tail dragging behind him, were eating the grain in a feeding trough that lined one edge of the bulls' yard.

'Piss off,' said Evie to the peacocks. 'Get.'

With a squawk and a flap, the peacocks moved to the rung up on the fence, then back down again.

'Dash bought them for the campers, but they never go near the campsite. Easier pickings here. I hate them. They shit in the bull's feed.'

Ruth and Evie jumped in the ute for the last short journey to the house.

'Thanks for coming out,' said Evie.

'Love the cows,' said Ruth. 'Love Horace. See you at the funeral.'

She gave Evie a hug and was surprised when Evie squeezed back.

WhatsApp

Ruth
Evie's mum died

Jack
Sad

Ruth
She's the only one left in her family

Jack
What happened?

Ruth
Dementia. But sudden.

Jack
[online]

Ruth
Evie has a prize-winning bull she kisses on the snout

Jack
So there's a warm and friendly person inside the woman who shoots cats at picnics

Ruth
She's a gifted cattle breeder

Jack
Huh

Ruth
I get the impression Dash doesn't do much actual farming. Or anything much. He seems to spend his life tinkering in the shed.

Jack
[online]

Ruth

Evie doesn't like interlopers. Chandra's corgi really pisses her off.

Jack

The corgi better watch out he doesn't meet the same fate as the cat

28

EVIE

April, eight weeks before

EVIE'S GREAT FAULT, SHE KNEW, WAS HOW SHE REACTED WHEN SHE WAS furious. And she was furious about that dog of Chandra's, and the chaos it caused on her farm. Stupid, yapping, useless lapdog.

Evie drove over to Chandra and Roscoe's house, picked Frank out of the ute, dragged him by the collar into the house. Chandra was home alone. Roscoe was on one of his Sydney trips.

'You need to keep this dog locked up,' she said.

'Oh, did Frank disturb you again?' breathed Chandra. 'I'm so sorry. You bad boy, Frank.'

Frank trotted to his water bowl.

'I was so sorry to hear about your mum,' said Chandra. 'Are you all right?'

'Thanks,' said Evie. She wanted to talk about Frank, not her mum. She couldn't get the pillow out of her head.

'You need to keep Frank at the house. He upsets the animals. He barks at them incessantly. One day, it's going to cause an injury.'

'Well, I try, but you know we only have a barbed wire fence around the house. He has to get out. You know, to do his business. And he does enjoy a walk.'

'He's not going to enjoy it much if he gets a hoof in his face.'

'Oh, Evie,' Chandra said. 'I feel your frustration. It must have made you so angry.' Chandra's voice was like silk waving in the breeze. 'Would you like a lemon myrtle tea? That always calms me down.'

At that moment Frank sauntered back in, bouncing from one leg to the next, his ears alert, his mouth drawn back in a smile. He spread out into a sploof, tummy on the ground, legs splayed out.

'Frank, you bad boy,' said Chandra. 'You really mustn't go anywhere near the cows.'

'Or the bulls,' Evie said, her anger already dissipating.

'Or the bulls, of course,' Chandra repeated.

Evie was pretty sure that Chandra couldn't tell the difference between a cow and a bull. Livestock made her shudder, as if every time she saw one, she associated it with the violence that was necessarily interposed between the animal in the paddock and the product in the supermarket.

'I'm so sorry,' Chandra said. 'I'm glad you came over, Evie. I'll see you at the funeral. Roscoe and I will be there.'

Evie walked back to the ute, paused, then backtracked to the house. 'Chandra!' she yelled through the door.

Chandra wafted out again.

'Thank you for visiting Mum. At the nursing home.'

'It was the least I could do. Your poor mum. I'm so sorry.'

Maybe it was innocent, and the doctor was right.

Evie nodded, her eyes wet. 'Thanks,' she said, turning back to the ute, sobbing. First time she'd cried since her mum died.

The whole district turned out a week later for Evie's mum's funeral. Several hundred people spilled out of the Anglican church, and the proceedings had to be beamed onto a screen outside for the overflow. Evie was aware very few of these people had come to see her mother when she was in the nursing home. The ceremonial part of finishing a life attracts even those who only exchanged a nod in the main street.

Evie was grateful they'd made the effort. Town solidarity; a display of kindness.

Evie sat in the front pew with Dash and stared at the lilies on the coffin. Just like Joof's. She couldn't cry. It was as if there was a layer of black foam—a shock absorber—around the part of her that felt things.

Then came an array of faces and sensations, in vivid colour and slow motion.

Bea came and hugged Dash instead of Evie in the line of mourners.

Chandra whispered in Evie's ear, 'I'm here to help. There are techniques for the grieving process. Just let me know.'

Because Dash organised it, the wake turned into a festival of beers, just what her mother would have hated.

A dozen women including Rita and Patch helped her with the food, then to dispose of the paper cups and plates, and wash the serving dishes.

Evie slunk away as dusk descended. That was the trouble with having the wake at your own home. You couldn't call the proceedings to a halt by leaving. And death was exhausting. She felt like she could sleep for a week. She went to the horse paddock to say goodnight to Jasper, then went to bed.

It was after the funeral, after the hullaballoo had died down, when Dash's life resumed its natural rhythms of camping ground, footy and pub, that the loneliness—a life stretching out with no family—loomed like a big dark storm cloud. No mother. No father. No brother.

No child.

So much hung on the trip to the IVF clinic three months away.

29

RUTH

April, seven weeks before

HARRY'S SON SAM ARRIVED THE EVENING BEFORE MRS CLIVE'S FUNERAL, in a blue shirt which matched his eyes.

Ruth cooked him a steak, and they shared a bottle of red.

The only topic of conversation was Evie: how good a farmer she was, how fit she was, what a natural she was with animals. He spoke of nothing else. It was like he had a crush on her.

What was he? Twenty-six? Thirty at the outside. Evie was mid-thirties.

Sam and Ruth went to the funeral together.

The whole town was there, including Troy, his mum Rita and Bea.

Gazza turned up in his dress uniform, his hair plastered down with a spray of water.

Sam disappeared into a scrum of people his own age.

Ruth sat with Roscoe and Chandra, near Patch and Shane and the Wildlings.

Chandra was in a pearl-white long shift. 'I don't know why people wear black,' said Chandra. 'It absorbs all the sad vibes at a funeral.'

Patch caught Ruth's eye and rolled her eyes.

Ruth wished she could share Chandra's terrible back story, but it wasn't her call.

Roscoe was wearing a suit; the corporate lawyer who lurked beneath the caftan.

Evie was washed out, wan, her cheeks gaunt. She seemed so alone, detached, while Dash played host.

He was very attentive to young Bea, who directed her condolences to Dash rather than Evie. It involved a very long hug, and Bea stuck to him throughout the party. Blatant flirting at a funeral. Unseemly. And Bea so young. And so—how to put it—lacking in life's opportunities. *Except for youth,* thought Ruth. Bea had that. And allure. She glowed like a ripe peach. And vulnerability. She had that in spades. To some men, that would make her irresistible.

A lot of beer was consumed. As the conversation increased in volume, Ruth withdrew.

Sam arrived home at midnight, banging through the unlocked door.

⟡

The morning after the funeral, as he poured some milk into his muesli, Sam said, 'Sad about Evie's mum.'

Finally, a discussion about the person he'd come to Myddle to bid farewell.

'Yes. Still. Dementia is a sad end.' Ruth paused. 'Better than the alternative, though.'

Sam looked confused.

'If you don't die old, you die young,' said Ruth.

Sam nodded as he took a mouthful of muesli. 'Like Joof.'

Joof was mentioned a lot at the funeral, but nobody ever said how he died.

'What happened?'

'Car accident,' Sam said. 'He was in his early twenties. I don't remember much about it because I was in Year One at the time but it rocked the town.'

'What was he like?'

'A bit of a larrikin. Good at footy. Sort of a golden boy really.'

Ruth thought, but did not say, *Like yourself. And like Dash.*

Sam continued his thought. 'I mean he was set, wasn't he? He was going to inherit that farm.'

'Yes, beautiful property.'

Sam, elbows on the table, chewed, swallowed and looked into his bowl to fill his spoon. 'I think Dash is going to trash it.'

Ruth raised an eyebrow, because she wanted him to continue but didn't want to participate in a conversation denigrating someone she knew.

'I don't think he gets it,' said Sam. 'What makes it so special.'

Ruth poured more orange juice into her glass.

'Tranquillity and black cockatoos over the Bluff on a bright day,' he added.

Sam was a bit of a poet then.

'Is everyone in town worried what Dash will do to the farm?'

Sam shrugged. 'Dunno. Nobody talks about it. Not to me anyway.' He sloughed through some more muesli. 'I worry about Evie.' He swallowed another mouthful. 'I mean, you see Dash with the girls. He doesn't even bother to hide it.'

Ruth let that remark float by, even though she agreed, except that she only saw one girl holding Dash's interest.

Ruth needed one of Harry's files for a client who wanted to reactivate some drama he was having with a new tractor; something about the lifting thingy not going up or down when it should. The file wasn't in Harry's room.

Ruth went to the room out the back and its haphazard dusty piles of files. It could take all morning to sort through them.

'Deb,' Ruth said, 'any idea where the Bevan file is?'

'No idea,' Deb said. 'Must be somewhere.' She glowered at Troy, as if it was his fault.

'Would you mind having a look in the file room?' said Ruth.

'I'm a bit busy at the moment,' said Deb.

Ruth was tempted to say, 'What, surfing YouTube?' Deb always made sure the screen was pointed at a wall so nobody could see what she was doing. But Ruth couldn't sack her, or even discipline her. Deb was one of the things Ruth had to tolerate while she was in Myddle.

'I can have a look for you,' said Troy.

'Thanks. That would be fantastic.'

After lunch, Ruth returned to the spare office to check on Troy's progress and to offer moral support. Troy stood proud, looking at his handiwork: twenty clean, neat piles. The dust from the files had transferred to his clothes, his hands, his face and an old towel he'd found. 'Bevan, was that it?' he said, handing her a fat pile of paper wrapped in pink ribbon.

'Mate,' said Ruth, 'you're amazing.'

He waved his hand over the room. 'Alphabetical order,' he said. 'By client.'

'Come and see what Troy's done, Deb!' she yelled.

Now that the job was complete, Deb could spare the time to offer advice. But she just grunted when she saw what Troy had done. No word, not so much as a thank you.

WhatsApp

Jack
How was the funeral?

Ruth
Lot of people. The whole town turned out.

Jack
How's the office going?

Ruth
Troy is a gem.
He tidied up the files in the dead file room.

Jack
Stands to reason. He can do a backflip.
He must be able to do anything.
🙄

Ruth
Exactly

30

RUTH

May, five weeks before

MORNING. A FROST. RUTH STAYED UNDER THE DOONA. THE DUST DANCED slowly in the beams of light through the window.

She heard 'Satisfaction' and eyed her phone suspiciously. Far too early for someone to ring. Then she saw the name. 'Charlie.' From his Australian sim card.

She toyed with not answering it, but that would just mean she'd spend the morning wondering why he was ringing, and where he was. She touched the green dot.

'What,' she said.

'Where are you?' Charlie asked.

'In bed.'

'Alone?'

'None of your business.'

'Where's the bed?'

'Myddle.'

'The small town near Broughton?' Incredulity. 'What are you doing there?'

'Remember Harry? From college?'

'Harry Dunstan?'

'I'm doing a locum for him.'

A snort of laughter. 'You? Doing conveyancing in a country town?'

She tried to be offended, but he knew her so well.

'Can I come to visit?'

'I don't think that's a very good idea,' she said.

'It's an excellent idea. Why don't I book myself into the local hotel and take you out to dinner to apologise.'

It was a ruse. He wouldn't stay in the hotel. Unless she made him. There was a shaft of schadenfreude as she pictured Charlie in one of the rundown rooms that Twister—who owned the pub—kept in a desultory way for drunks who couldn't drive home.

He didn't say what the apology was for. He didn't have to. The last time she'd seen him was at his apartment in Baltimore. Alerted by a roar of female rage from the street below, they'd gone out on his balcony to see a woman throw some clothes and a toiletry bag out of her car. Ruth had said, 'Yours?'; he had nodded, sheepish; Ruth had said, 'I didn't sign up for this,' and left to traipse around the United States on her own for a few weeks before returning to Sydney.

Should she let him come to Myddle? It hadn't been a great way to end an affair.

'All right,' she said.

'How do I get there?'

'Fly to Broughton. I'll pick you up.'

She could hear clicking. 'There's a flight on Friday. Gets in at ten.'

'Okay. See you then.'

As she pressed the red dot to hang up she wanted to feel foreboding, but she had to admit she was a little bit excited.

✦

Ruth had to leave home at eight forty. At least it was too early to have sex, and just to be sure, she put on a pair of undies with saggy elastic. They had once been ivory but had gone through a dark colour cycle so were a dull blue-grey.

She cursed Bill. If he'd still been alive, she wouldn't have to think about what undies she put on. In that moment, of all the things she loved about Bill, she loved most his indifference to her undies. Although now that she thought of it, he used to buy her new undies when the old ones got too bad.

Lucky she was wearing jeans. That would hold them aloft.

Charlie walked across the tarmac, curls tumbling to the bottom of his neck and his face still cyclist gaunt. Alluring. But she would resist. The man was a womanising arsehole. He would have put curl-inducing French conditioner in his hair and worn that olive corduroy jacket knowing the effect they would have on her.

'Ruth! So good to see you!' He hugged her.

They walked to the car, exchanging information about Jack, and Charlie's kids, mother and sister. Five minutes into the drive, the conversation ran dry. The silver trunks and khaki canopies of the vast gums rushed past.

He said in a small voice, 'I'm really sorry about Baltimore.'

'Are you?'

Ruth moved the car onto the gravel shoulder to share the thin strip of bitumen with an oncoming ute. She and the driver of the ute each raised an index finger.

Charlie's response was carefully curated. 'Bethany was a bit possessive. I didn't realise how much.'

'Is your excuse to say the woman you were sleeping with is mad? Because that's not an excuse that will work with me.'

Charlie took some time to answer. 'She was a bit mad, though.'

'And you were sleeping with her,' said Ruth.

'To be fair, I was sleeping with her before you and I . . . sort of, you know . . . teamed up.'

'And then again afterwards,' said Ruth.

'Also, I thought you were being very careful about our acquaintance being casual,' said Charlie.

Ruth resisted the urge to point out a rust-coloured eagle that soared ahead.

'I'm sorry,' he proffered.

Charlie was right—Ruth had made it clear that she wanted no long-term emotional entanglement with him. But she didn't want to be the cause of another person's pain. She thought less of Charlie for having hurt Bethany, wittingly or unwittingly.

Ruth and Charlie were never going to resolve the rights and wrongs of her disastrous trip to Baltimore. Maybe it was best to just move on.

'That's enough of that,' said Ruth. 'Why are you in Australia?'

'Moira duties.' Charlie's mother, the indomitable, indefatigable Moira. 'And I have to go back to Brisbane to finish off a paper.'

There was a rhythmic *clunkety clunk* as they crossed a wooden bridge. The river was wide and docile, gleaming in the morning light. Three emus picked their way across a paddock, beaks moving forward and back. 'It is beautiful here,' he said. 'Although I never pictured you as a herding cows type of gal.'

She waved her hand at the paddock out the window. 'The ambience delights. And so do the people.'

'I'm thinking about coming home,' he said. 'For good.'

'Really?'

'America is a bit of a shit show at the moment.'

'Guns, God and Trump?' said Ruth.

'That. And the unresolved race thing. Does my head in that they're so rich and they do that to the poor.'

'Don't speak too soon,' said Ruth. 'Myddle isn't exactly an oasis of racial equity.'

They pulled into the sleepy main street.

'Time for lunch,' said Charlie.

'Egg and lettuce sandwich?' asked Ruth.

'Seriously?'

'We could go up-market and have a countery at the pub.'

'What's on offer?'

'An overcooked steak, a soggy hamburger, a chicken parmy, or a limp pie. Washed down with a beer.'

'Sounds fantastic.'

After lunch, they checked Charlie into the room at the pub, paint peeling off the walls, and faded yellow and brown floral sheets, presumably to disguise the stains.

Ruth sat on the bed and bounced. It squeaked.

Charlie sat beside her. He put his hand on her head. 'I'm sorry,' he said. 'I've missed talking to you.'

She leaned into him. Kissing, then fumbling: bumbling first then urgent.

'Oh my God,' said Charlie. 'What are these undies?'

'They're arsehole repellents.'

'Well, I find them rather attractive,' said Charlie. 'Does that mean I'm not an arsehole?'

'It means you are a liar. Anyway, the principle was not that you would be stopped in your tracks, but that I would be too embarrassed to let you see them.'

'Complicated. And also somehow flawed,' said Charlie.

Twenty minutes later, as they were studying the ceiling, Charlie said, 'This bed is very lumpy.'

'Oh, all right,' said Ruth. 'You can stay at mine.'

'They don't call you curmudgeonly for nothing,' said Charlie.

⁂

Ruth hadn't been to a country show since she was a kid. Charlie—brought up in the eastern suburbs of Sydney—had never been.

'Let's go and look at the cows,' she told him. 'And the woodchop. And then we could take the Wildlings on the teacup ride and buy them some fairy floss.'

It was a sparkly day, halcyon blue sky. A light westerly made the dust eddy just above the ground.

Horace was munching on some hay. He had a fat blue ribbon draped over the top of his stall. Evie sat beside him in a director's chair.

'Best in show,' Charlie read the certificate. 'Impressive.'

'That's my boy,' said Evie, kissing Horace on the snout.

'Was it his testicles that won the day?' asked Ruth, recalling Evie's Facebook post.

Charlie leaned over to have a look underneath. 'Good God,' he said. 'I'm surprised he doesn't get a sore back lugging that around.'

'More his solid good looks and piercing intelligence,' said Evie. 'We're meeting for beers and hamburgers at the Cattleman's Bar at six. I'll take Horace home and come back.'

⁂

Roscoe had discarded his caftan in favour of the cattleman's uniform of moleskins, a tweed jacket, a blue collared shirt and brown elastic-sided boots.

'Hello, darl,' said Ruth. 'Do we order hamburgers up at the bar?'

'I think so,' said Roscoe.

'We're not eating,' said Chandra. 'Obviously,' she added with a light tinkle of laughter. The Cattleman's Bar was not known for its vegetarian food.

Dash already had a table with Evie, Patch and Shane. Ruth introduced Charlie.

'Gazza!' yelled Dash. 'Come and have a hamburger, mate.' Gazza had obviously just had a shower and washed his hair as it was plastered, wet, around his purple face.

'C'mon, mate,' said Dash, proffering the jug. 'Have a beer.'

'Yeah, best not.' Gazza adjusted the waist band of his trousers, which had slipped below his overhanging stomach. 'I'm meant to be on duty. Just got here from an accident on the Azuri Road early this morning. Took all day to clean up and do the paperwork.'

'Fatality?' said Evie.

Gazza held out a hand and put it on her shoulder. 'Yeah, Evie. One of the black kids.'

Evie's eyes welled up. 'Which one?'

'Young Wayne Grierson.'

Evie's distress eased slightly. 'I don't know him,' she said. 'How old was he?'

'Nineteen.' Gazza shrugged as if to shake it away. 'Maybe I do need a beer.'

'Don't envy you that work,' said Charlie. 'It must be difficult.'

'It's not great.'

Ruth felt for the poor guy. Must be horrific. 'Are there a lot of car accidents?' she asked.

'Not as bad as it used to be. Azuri Road was notorious. Young blokes driving back late at night too fast with a few beers on board.'

Evie sloped off abruptly, hand at her mouth. Patch, busy with her kids, hadn't noticed so Ruth followed.

Evie was slumped over the basin when Ruth entered the bathroom.

'You okay?' she asked.

Evie waved her hand in front of her face, as if she was trying to swat away a fly. 'Oh, don't mind me. My brother was killed on the Azuri Road. It was years ago, but still catches me out. And with my mum . . .' She trailed off.

Ruth knew that you could never tell what grief people were carrying. When Bill died, people Ruth had known for years shared past trauma she'd had no clue of: dead mothers, sisters, brothers, fathers. Brain damage. Cancer. Fiery crashes. Wars. A secret river of mourning.

'I heard about your brother. Joof?' she said.

'Geoffrey. I couldn't pronounce it when I was little so the name Joof stuck.'

'My partner was killed in an accident,' Ruth said, almost apologetic.

'I think you mentioned it at the picnic. I'm so sorry.'

Ruth gave a rueful laugh as she wiped her cheeks.

A hug, a splash of water, and they went back to the table.

Diane, Dash's mother, had arrived and was already halfway through an enormous glass of sav blanc.

Dash gave Evie a secret smile, as if he was laying a warm blanket over her from the other side of the table.

Gazza's face was soft with dismay. 'Sorry, Evie. I didn't think.'

'No worries, Gazza,' said Evie. 'I should be better at it.'

'I should get my head in gear before I open my mouth,' said Gazza.

It was the first time Ruth had spotted a soft side to the police officer. She smiled at him.

'Did you know that policeman from Bathurst, Gazza?' said Diane. 'The one who was convicted for killing his ex-wife?'

Ruth saw Dash's hand on Evie's knee as the conversation was diverted. Evie entwined her fingers with his.

'Nah,' said Gazza, relieved that the subject had changed. 'But what a dickhead getting arrested.'

'What choice did he have?' said Diane.

'If it was me,' said Gazza. 'I'd disappear.'

'How would you sustain that?' said Ruth. 'Couldn't get medical care, couldn't have a credit card.'

'Do you know what happens to coppers in the lockup?' said Gazza. 'Better off-grid.'

'Not much of a choice,' said Charlie. 'If he hadn't killed her, the problem wouldn't arise.'

The talk petered out, and there was a lull, a moment of awkwardness.

'How are your plans going with the Bluff, love?' said Diane to Dash.

Evie looked away.

'Still working it out,' said Dash.

'If you're gonna build anything up at the Bluff,' said Gazza, 'you need to get the bulldozers in there right now. Otherwise if they find any "Aboriginal artefacts"'—he used two fingers on each hand to denote the quotation marks—'construction will be held up for months.'

Ruth was stunned by this remark: an exhortation by the local copper to commit a serious offence. But it was greeted with nods of assent around the table.

'The new sports oval was held up for months just over some rock,' Diane said.

Charlie's eyebrows were raised in astonishment.

'I feel I need to say it's not a great idea, though,' said Ruth, thinking if she made it sound like a joke they wouldn't mind her interjection. 'I think it's an offence under some act.'

There was an awkward silence, which Roscoe tried to defuse. 'You lawyers, always sticking a spanner in the works,' he said, and everyone laughed.

'Funny, isn't it, how artefacts turn up on the most valuable bits of land?' Diane was a double-down poker player.

So was Ruth when her hackles were up. 'Perhaps,' she said, 'we all think those pieces of land are important for similar reasons. I've heard people say the Bluff is a spiritual place.'

'Who's for another beer?' said Dash.

Ruth noticed Bea wandering by with a self-conscious sway of the hips. Her eyes slid sideways towards their table. She wanted to be noticed.

And she was.

'Hey, Bea!' Dash yelled.

Her face opened up with delight. 'Hey, Dash.' Her hand went up in a tight little wave.

Evie scowled and rolled her eyes at Patch, who rolled hers back.

'Grab a chair,' said Dash, hauling one from a neighbouring table and placing it between his and Gazza's.

'Thanks, I've got a chair over here,' said Bea, as she sat down opposite Dash and Evie with a smile so small it indicated more shame and fear than joy or greeting.

Evie turned away, not bothering to hide her disdain. The list of women she held in obvious contempt was growing: Chandra, and now Bea.

'I'm off for a round of beers,' said Dash. 'Who's in?' There were grunts of assent, including from Gazza who'd obviously succumbed in his battle to remain sober.

'May as well get a jug then. Charlie, you in? What do you ladies want?'

Ruth detested being called a lady. Made her feel sixty.

'Not for me thanks, Dash,' said Charlie and Ruth at the same time. One of them had to drive home. Although judging by the way Gazza was settling in, caution may not have been warranted.

'Looks like I'm driving then,' said Evie, cold with irritation.

It seemed Chandra was determined to turn the conversation back to her eco-health resort. 'I realise that the energy which drives the idea for the eco-health resort is a long way from what you do, Evie, but if you'd like me to sit down and try to explain it . . .'

In the yoga class, Chandra's wafting voice added to the vibe. Here, in the Cattleman's Bar at the show, amid the roar of drunken chatter of a crowd dressed in rabbit fur hats and riding boots, it sounded like she was from a different planet.

'Explain what exactly?' said Evie. There was a tart edge to her voice that Ruth noticed but Chandra missed.

'An eco-health resort is a long way from cattle farming. I realise that you might not get what we're about. Or why the Bluff could mean so much to so many people.'

'You mean the land that my family has looked after for five generations.'

Dash moved uncomfortably in his seat.

Evie leaned forward in hers. 'You seem to think that somehow your new understanding of energy and light, or some fucking thing, gives you a deeper appreciation than we could ever have. Is that it?'

Chandra's jaw slackened. 'I didn't mean . . .'

'You people keep telling me that I have no idea what the Bluff is. But you want to desecrate the place by clearing all the vegetation, drilling holes in it and putting a fucking cable car up it, for Christ's sake. Then, when it fails, the land will be left with the scars. Because there won't be any money to fix it up.' She stood. 'You can stick your energy zones up your arse.'

She walked out.

The next morning, Ruth dropped Charlie at Broughton airport.

'What now?' he whispered during the parting embrace.

'I'll come to Brisbane while you're there if you like.'

'I would like.'

She drove over to Roscoe's. She'd been enjoying her weekly yoga class since she'd started living in Myddle, but she didn't much feel like going today. She stopped off in Roscoe's kitchen so he could make her a cup of tea and she could avoid the class for a few more minutes.

Chandra walked in, less of the usual waft about her. There was a slump in her centre where she normally held herself erect.

'Hello, Ruth,' she said. 'Have you heard from Evie?'

Ruth shook her head.

'I've upset her.'

Ruth crossed her arms.

'I didn't mean to,' said Chandra.

'Her mother just died,' Ruth said. 'She's the last person in her family. And she's feeling it.' Ruth wondered whether she should go on, and then thought if she didn't tell Chandra nobody else would. She softened her tone, to say it as gently as she could. 'And she probably doesn't need people telling her she doesn't understand how beautiful her land is.'

'She never talks about it,' said Chandra. 'I'm sure she isn't aware of the intrinsic nature of it.'

Ruth shook her head. 'I'm pretty sure she's aware, Chandra.'

A parcel was delivered to Ruth's office. She shook it. No noise, just a quiet shuffle. No sender identified.

She opened it cautiously.

Out fell a note, and eight pairs of undies: lacy, but practical in the sense that they provided full coverage where it was needed.

Thought you might need to update your wardrobe, said the note. Then C.

Ruth put a pair on and sent a picture to Charlie.

WhatsApp

Ruth
Evie's bull won best in show

Jack
Nice. How does a bull win best in show?

Ruth
Ginormous testicles. Bum shaped like apple. Pliant personality.

Jack
Remember when I had large testicles, and it turned out to be a cyst?

Ruth
My role as the mother of someone over twenty means
I no longer have to discuss those things with you

Jack
What if I ever have a serious problem with my testicles?

Ruth
You can mention it then.
We had vegans at the cattleman's bar at the show.
And Charlie went on a teacup ride with Milly.

Jack
Charlie?

Ruth
Sic

Jack
?

Ruth
Strictly need to know basis

Jack
Touche

Ruth
I forgot to ask how the weekend in the country went

Jack
Poms like red wine but think Oz wine is too
strong. 🙄 And they have a way of saying so
which makes you feel like a cretin.

Ruth
It's an art the Poms refined over centuries. Ignore it. It's
built on hubris. Remember: they fucked up the world
with colonisation, and hubris was a key reason.

Jack
Ha

Ruth
So the romance was short-lived?

Jack
Need to know, Ruthie. Need to know. Can you send me the recipe for that chocolate cake made with beetroot? I'm trying to convince some people I know how to bake a cake.

31

GAZZA

May, five weeks before

THE MVA ON SHOW DAY WAS THE WORST HE'D SEEN. HEAD-ON CRASH on the Azuri Road.

Called out at five am. Took most of the day to clean up. It was awful. Bits of kid everywhere.

That bird Ruth got it. She looked at him, her eyes full of sympathy. Like she actually saw him as a human being.

Then he said something stupid to Evie and upset her. Then he said something really stupid about the blacks and the Ruth bird reverted to hating him. Her default position.

She had some boyfriend with her. A doctor or something. Of course.

Gazza drank a lot of beer that night.

If the higher-ups found out how drunk he was on duty, he'd be fucked.

Especially if they knew he drove home.

He was having a couple of vodkas before bed when Victoria rang him up and abused him because he'd seen Bea at the show or some bullshit.

'I can't do this anymore, Victoria,' he said. 'I'm sorry.'

She screamed down the phone. 'What do you mean?'

He held the phone away from his ear. 'I just don't think we're very good for one another,' he said and hung up. Then blocked her number when she rang twelve times in an hour.

At least he'd taken some decisive action for once. He pulled out a bottle of Scotch to celebrate.

32

EVIE

May, four weeks before

EVIE WATCHED DASH WITH BEA AT THE CATTLEMAN'S BAR, HIS FACE lighting up, the scrabbling for a chair, the unashamed flirting. Bea's simpering made her want to vomit.

This girl was less than half Dash's age, little more than a child. She could have been his daughter.

Could she spend the rest of her life like this, wondering about every female who wandered into his orbit?

And Chandra's persistence about the fucking eco-health resort was really pissing her off. The spirit-splaining about the significance of the land made it worse. And the pillow theory was still worming its way around the back of her mind. She was glad she'd only raised it with Rita and the doctor: accusing someone of murder would make her sound mad. But her mother's death was convenient for Dash and Chandra, obviating as it did the complications of getting her mother's consent to develop the land or using the power of attorney.

She was trapped. Two choices: keep the farm, stick with Dash and the hope of a baby, and a strong possibility of the hotel at the Bluff; or no Dash, no farm, no baby, and a strong possibility of the hotel at the Bluff.

Evie needed to get away. Replace the rage with drunken joy. Just for a few days. With any luck, it might be her last chance for years.

She decided to go to Sydney for a weekend, to a concert with songs of female rage.

She wanted Rita to come. Because Rita would make her laugh. And for her sharp cynicism.

Rita's face lit up when Evie suggested it. 'Deadly,' she said.

It took longer to convince Patch. ('Shane's too busy to look after four kids as well as bale the hay,' she said. So Evie mentioned it to Shane. 'You should go, Patch,' he said. 'I'm capable of looking after the kids you know.')

They arrived on Friday afternoon at the tiny apartment Evie booked in Darlinghurst. They were in Oxford Street on their fourth glass of chardy, as Rita called it, when Sam Dunstan turned up, all short back and sides and square white teeth.

'Hey,' he said.

Evie hugged him and whispered, 'You came.' She clung on a bit longer than she should have.

'You three seem to be a bit pissed,' said Sam.

'He was always very observant,' said Patch. 'My favourite student.'

'What are you celebrating?' Sam asked.

'Well,' said Evie, 'Patch is celebrating escaping from her four children for two nights, Rita is celebrating escaping from her three children for two nights.' Evie paused. The other three were looking at her in open-mouthed dismay, terrified that she was going to mention the thing they never spoke of—her infertility.

'And I'm celebrating Horace winning a prize at the show.'

She lifted her glass as if proposing a toast.

They exhaled.

'Quite right, too,' said Rita. 'Best-looking bull I've ever met.'

Someone—it might have been Sam—bought a third bottle of chardy.

The band started playing. The four of them were dancing; Sam had his arm over Evie's shoulders.

That wasn't what she'd meant when she'd told him they'd be in Sydney.

Was it?

Sam disappeared to buy another bottle of wine.

Patch stumbled towards her. 'Are you sure this is a good idea, Evie?'

'What?' said Evie.

'Sam.'

'What about him?'

'Sis,' Rita remonstrated.

Evie dug her phone out of her bag, pulled up the text messages from Deirdre, and handed it over.

'Oh, sis,' said Rita.

'What an arsehole,' said Patch.

'What's the worst that can happen?' Evie asked them. 'Sam is a very nice young man who seems keen for a one-night stand. And if Dash finds out? Well, fuck him.'

Rita grimaced.

'Anyway,' Evie said over her shoulder as she walked away, 'Dash told me it's just sex.'

Evie sashayed over to Sam and whispered in his ear, 'What say we go to your place?'

Sam's eyes lit up. 'Really?' he said.

Evie snuck into the Airbnb apartment as dawn was breaking.

She could see the light on in Rita's room so crept in and lay down beside her.

'How was the revenge fuck?'

'Okay,' said Evie. 'Sam is a bit of a spunk, isn't he?'

They giggled. 'It's like we're fifteen,' said Rita.

'Sam's lovely,' Evie said, 'but there's a lot to be said for familiarity.'

'Maybe Dash is just a cracker in the sack,' said Rita, doubtful.

'Poor Sam. Pretend I didn't say that.'

'Are you going to see him again?'

'I don't think so.' Evie moved her back away from a hard lump in the middle of the bed. 'Do you think it's going to be awkward when he comes to Myddle?'

'Yes,' said Rita.

They cackled, way more than the joke warranted.

'What are you going to do about Dash?' Rita asked.

'Dunno,' said Evie. 'I'd like to kick the bastard out but I'm not sure I have it in me. He got me out of the hole I was in after Joof. After my dad died. He's my family. He's it.'

Rita reached over and held Evie's hand.

'We're about to start IVF,' said Evie. 'What if it doesn't work?' She sniffed. 'I'm scared I'll die a lonely old woman. No husband. No kids. No Mum. No Dad.'

'Oh, sis,' said Rita. 'You've got me.'

With her spare hand, Evie wiped her eyes.

'If Dash and I split up I might even lose the farm. He'd get half and build a hotel on it. I don't think I could stay.'

They held hands in silence. The ceiling was so dirty it was grey with dust.

'That girl, Bea,' said Evie. 'I don't know what to do.'

Rita got up on an elbow to get a view of Evie's face. 'She's seventeen,' she said.

'I know,' said Evie at last. 'He can't resist her. It's creepy.'

'Let's think about something else.' Rita squeezed Evie's hand again. 'Let's talk about ceilings we like.'

'Rita?' Evie said.

'Yeah?'

'I love you.'

Evie turned to Rita and opened her mouth to ask a question just as Patch emerged from the bedroom opposite. She had a pink dressing gown on.

'Have you two been crying?' she asked as she came in and stretched out on the bed, wedging Evie in the middle.

'Nothing like a good cry when you wake up,' Rita said. 'Helps you face the day with vigour and resolve.'

'When did you get back, Evie?'

'Twenty minutes ago.'

'Oh my lord.'

'It's okay. It was just sex,' said Rita.

They laughed.

The ceiling seemed to lower. Perhaps it was the hangover.

'Dash is an arsehole,' Patch said after a while.

'How did you manage to marry a saint, Patch?' Evie asked.

'Don't know,' said Patch. 'Luck?'

'Shane is such a saint,' said Rita, 'I bet you don't even have to bother waxing your pubic hair.'

'Why would I do that?' said Patch. 'Think of the pain. And the scratching when it grows back.'

'You must do a little tidy up, though,' said Evie. 'Surely.'

'Nope. It makes the ends sharp and stabby.'

'If I didn't take some measures,' said Rita, 'there'd be a flock of parrots nesting in there.'

They chuckled.

Evie pointed. 'There's a spider web in the corner of the ceiling.'

They considered it in silence for a minute or two. Then Evie said, 'What kind of parrots, Rita?'

'A pair of king parrots, those big red and green ones. And ten or fifteen blue and green budgies, I reckon.'

'Lots of vivid colour,' said Patch.

'Noisy but,' said Rita.

They laughed, with loose abandon.

Later that day, Sam texted her. *I had a great night last night.*

She texted back, *Same,* because she was aiming for a monosyllabic response that wasn't a bald rejection.

He replied straight away. *Coffee this morning?*

Can't, sorry.

Oh God, this was going to be awkward.

I'll be home in a few weeks. We could catch up then. He named a date a month and a half away. She didn't respond, at first because she couldn't think of anything to say, and then because she still couldn't think of anything to say. She just wanted to pretend the whole incident hadn't happened.

He wouldn't tell his parents, would he? Of course he wouldn't. No normal grown-up man would tell his parents whom he'd had a one-night stand with, especially if the parents knew her. Would he? Besides, his parents were away, somewhere on the death march, as Rita called the apparently compulsory trip white people in their sixties and seventies made around Australia.

But their absence meant the only reason Sam was planning to come to Myddle was to see her.

33

BEA

May, two weeks before

BEA'S LIFE WAS LOOKING UP. GAZZA HAD SPLIT UP WITH HER MUM, AS predicted. And Bea had really got into the yoga at Mandala, so didn't have to spend much time at home with brooding, bitching Victoria.

She was getting quite good at taking photos and posting them on Chandra's Instagram. She also did some videos and posted them on TikTok. It was harder as it took a lot of editing. One of them, where Frank, Chandra's corgi, looked like he was doing yoga, went viral.

'You're so good at this, Bea,' said Chandra. 'We're very lucky to have you.'

She started talking to some of the regulars. The lawyer lady Ruth came to yoga every week. She usually went up the back and she wasn't into all the stuff: when Chandra talked about the pineal gland lighting up, or the ethical decision-making, Ruth's face went completely blank, like she'd moved her thoughts into another place.

She disengaged when she didn't want to engage, and extracted what she wanted without losing her cool or saying anything awful. Bea wondered if she could ever be like that.

Sometimes Mrs Dwyer, the teacher from school, came with her. Ruth called her Patch. Mrs Dwyer wasn't as good at hiding stuff. She didn't like Chandra and rolled her eyes when Chandra said things she thought were dumb. Chandra pretended not to notice, but Bea could tell she was hurt by it.

Last week, Patch was telling Ruth about the weekend she'd had in Sydney with Rita and Evie.

'Sounds fun,' Ruth said. 'Evie probably needed a bit of a break. Let her hair down.'

'Poor Sam Dunstan didn't realise a teacher could get so pissed,' said Patch.

Ruth looked confused.

'We ran into him at the pub,' said Patch, and blushed. She looked away, as if she wished she hadn't said it.

Chandra was just behind her. 'Sam Dunstan was with you on your weekend away?' she asked.

'Just at the pub,' said Patch. 'Complete coincidence. We sort of ran into him.' She blushed again and ran her fingers through her hair. 'Anyway, the concert was great.'

Ruth and Chandra both took a sip from their glasses at the same time, watching Patch. They had the same expression on their face: like they were solving a complicated problem. Bea took a photo of the three of them: Patch talking and Ruth and Chandra studying her over the tops of their cups.

It was a funny photo. They were concentrating so much they didn't realise that she'd taken it.

34

EVIE

June, eleven days before

EVIE FELT SICK AND ACHEY—THE BURGEONING STORM OF ANOTHER period about to descend.

Horace and fifteen other young bulls were in the yards. She flushed out the troughs, and poured more feed in. The fifteen were off to the sales at the end of the week. Because of Horace's expanding fame, she would get a good price this year for all of them. She'd be sad to see them go, even though they were a lot of work.

She'd still have Horace. She wasn't going to sell him. Ever.

Over at the horse paddock, Troy gave Bea a leg-up onto the pony. Bea yelled out to Dash in the shed. Something about a stirrup. She was luring Dash over to touch her leg.

In the few weeks since the show, Bea had stayed away, so Evie hadn't bothered having the difficult chat with Troy, the one where she told him to leave Bea in town where she belonged. She'd do it tomorrow.

With penetrating squawks, six peacocks descended on the bulls' feed.

'Get!' she shouted.

The young bulls were skittish, their massive foreheads locked into a pushing competition, feigning the fights they would have in earnest if they were ever out in a paddock with some cows and another bull. Evie was glad there was a solid fence between them and her. They could knock her down by accident, and then trample her in panic.

Horace, a year older than the others and much bigger, chewed his cud in quiet disdain. He kept his distance from them, in the corner near the gate.

Evie heard the corgi before she saw him. He was in the yards, right under the nose of the bulls, and he barked that staccato high-pitched yapping.

The bulls bellowed and jostled.

Frank yapped, unrelenting, beside the feed troughs.

The peacocks rose up in a brouhaha of feathers. They flew onto the top rail of the yards and fought for position away from Frank.

The bulls bunched together, trying to escape the dog and birds, their huge torsos thwacking against one another. With several tonnes of bull banging against the steel fences, the yards shuddered.

Frank, seeing his success, came over to bark under their noses again. The peacocks screeched and flapped their big ungainly wings. The noise had the same effect as a dentist drill.

Evie ran around the side. She needed to open the yards up; let the bulls get away from the dog and the peacocks, into the pasture, where they'd be safe from one another.

Horace was jammed against the gate into the home paddock, the junior bulls piled up against him. He snorted in distress, and lowered his head. With a great shove, his head went through the gap between the rails. With a surprised bellow, he jerked his head up.

The gate moved off its hinges.

With a toss, Horace threw it away.

The gate, which had taken a tractor and three men to lower into place, lay on the ground.

The bulls burst into the home paddock which—fenced to keep animals out of it—was filled with the detritus of farm machinery (tractors, slashers, tools).

In Evie's mind, the scene became surreal, playing out in slow motion.

Frank's staccato bark still rent the air, and the peacocks shrieked and flapped.

Bea screamed as her pony bolted. Troy threw away the saddle he was putting on Jasper, and leapt onto his bare back, torn between rounding up the bulls and saving Bea.

Evie ran towards the ute, yelling at Dash, 'Can you shut that fucking dog up.'

The dog ran into a melee of three bulls. They kicked and trampled, he emitted a high-pitched howl, then whimpered as the bulls snorted over him, before he was finally silent.

Horace galumphed towards the cattle grid, eight hundred kilos of frenzy, saliva flying.

'Stop!' Evie yelled. She got to the ute and jumped in.

Horace lumbered onto the grid.

Halfway across, he fell.

Evie pulled up in the ute. Horace writhed and bellowed, pinned in the grid.

His hind leg was at a right angle to where it should have been. Blood spurted from a burst artery.

Evie stepped onto the grid holding her hand towards him, pleading. 'C'mon, beautiful boy. Be calm.'

Horace's eyes were wild, as he tried to thrash his way out. She couldn't touch him or he'd knock her over.

'There, there, my darling boy.'

The quad bike roared. Dash was coming.

She felt calm in the chaos, and knelt, balancing on her haunches, as what remained of Horace's life flailed before her.

Dash pulled up.

'You're going to have to do it,' said Evie.

Dash unlocked the metal box on the back of the ute, pulled out the rifle, loaded it, levelled it at her boy as he snorted in confusion and pain. A shot rang out.

Dash was a good shot. There was that.

On the other side of the home paddock, Bea wailed, 'Frank's dead.'

Bea and Troy got to the grid a few minutes later in Troy's ute. Bea had gravel rash and grass stains on her face and jeans. 'You all right?' Dash asked her. 'You come off?'

Bea stared at Horace limp on the grid, covered in blood and bubbles of snot, the wild look in his open eyes of fear and pain now frozen.

'Oh my God!' she cried.

Evie turned to Dash, pointing at Horace. 'We'll have to get him out of the grid, then figure out what we're going to do with him.'

Dash got on the quad to get the tractor.

A flurry of dust on the farm track, and a white BMW pulled up on the other side of Horace. Chandra emerged, her silver hair wild.

Bea must have texted her from the shed for her to be there so promptly.

'What did you do to Frank?' Chandra said, her voice a high pitch of distress. 'Is he all right?'

Rage engulfed Evie. 'I don't know, Chandra. Probably not. He was trampled by some bulls he spooked.'

'That dog cost me three thousand dollars.'

The silence hung between them, while Evie processed that.

'See that,' she said, pointing at Horace and his frightened dead eyes.

Chandra recoiled.

'That's Horace, my prize-winning bull. Until twenty minutes ago, he was worth about a hundred grand.

'You know why he was worth that much?' Evie continued. 'Because I chose his parents, I arranged for his conception, and since he was born two years ago, I have spent about a thousand hours with him. When we go on tour, I sleep with him, to keep him calm.'

She tried to quell her fury by walking away in the direction of her ute.

Chandra shouted after her, 'You bred him to exploit him. And kill him.'

Evie put her head down and kept going. There was no point engaging.

Chandra yelled out, 'If one harmless corgi can cause this kind of damage, it's not much of a farm, is it?'

That made Evie stop. She turned around and said, her voice hard as iron, 'If you can look at this scene and not understand the role you played in creating it with your half-baked notions about Frank's freedom and his fucking right to roam—' She didn't finish the sentence, but started another. 'We can only live together in the harmony you bang on about if we understand what impact we have on one another.'

She jumped into the driver's seat and drove back to the yards.

Evie didn't bother to get out of bed the next day. At ten, a car pulled up outside. The fucking BMW. Evie pulled the doona over her head. Dash could deal with her.

A murmur of voices. The BMW drove off.

Dash came in with an enormous bunch of pink roses, at least two dozen.

'She came to say sorry she lost her temper, love,' he said. He handed her a card.

Evie opened it reluctantly. *My dear Evie,* the note said in an elegant scrawl. *I'm so sorry I spoke like that to you. I know how much Horace meant to you, and I did not mean to cause you further distress. I truly hope that you can forgive me.*

Evie gave the note back.

'What should I do with the flowers?' Dash said.

'I don't care what you do with them.'

'She means well.'

'Does she?' said Evie. She put the doona back over her head. She might throw up.

A tear leaked out of an eye, and then they came in a sobbing gush. All gone: every member of her family, and now Horace, who was both family member and livelihood.

Even Dash could be whisked away by a hint of perfume.

Her vision for the whole farm was exemplified by one animal, and—bang.

At lunchtime, Dash came in with a glass of water and some Panadol. He held her hand. 'Maybe you should get away, love,' he said.

Maybe she should. Maybe things would be clearer if she had a break.

Maybe she wasn't cut out to be a farmer.

Evie stayed in bed, curtains closed, in the foetal position.

Dash brought in food and cups of tea. She drank the tea but picked at the food.

The marriage to Dash was looking less and less viable. It terrified her. What if they did have a child and he kept having affairs? How do you have a child and run a farm with no help? How do you divorce?

Harry Dunstan had said that, before divorce, the family should deal with succession first: transfer the property to the kid who was going to take it over, and then split up.

She turned her face into the pillow.

It came to her slowly.

Maybe she did have a way to deal with succession first.

It was mid-afternoon before she reached for her boots.

'I'm going out,' she said to Dash.

Evie drove to Rita's.

'I heard about your bull.' Rita gave her a hug. 'You can't win a trick.'

'My life sucks at the moment.'

'Sure does,' said Rita. She was folding the washing.

'Troy here?'

'Nuh.' Rita picked up two socks to unite. 'He's at work.'

Evie pulled out a book from the orange spines on the bookshelf and pretended to look at it.

'Rita?' said Evie. 'Can we tell Troy? That I'm his aunt.'

35

EVIE

June, a year before

MAYBE ONCE A YEAR, IN EACH OF THE SEVENTEEN YEARS SINCE JOOF'S death, Evie had startled when she thought she saw her brother in the street in Broughton or Sydney. She'd done a double-take, looked at the back of a figure who'd walked past her, and realised that it wasn't Joof. Because Joof was dead.

But then Dash had convinced Evie to go to a footy game. A kid—the winger for the Myddle team—flew down the side of the field. It was his gait and then his smile that reminded her of Joof.

This boy was obviously not Joof. He was golden brown, where Joof had been a wincingly white, freckly, fair-headed boy.

But Troy's hair had the unruly wave that had made Joof's hair stand out like straw. Troy's legs were the same as Joof's: wiry, strong and fast. And when he was with his mates, he had the same delight that fed Joof's magic smile.

She made some surreptitious inquiries of Patch, his teacher, then returned to the footy the following Sunday.

Evie and Rita had been in the same class in primary school but hadn't been friends. Evie remembered her in the school photos, eagerly sitting forward, a broad grin on her face, her eyes sparkling like she was hatching a plan which would be—in a cacklingly funny way—seditious.

Evie saw Rita in the crowd at the footy and made her way over to her. 'Hello, Rita,' she said.

'G'day, Evie,' said Rita, as if they had a conversation like this every week.

'Troy's playing well.'

'Yep. He's having a pretty good game.'

'Patch tells me he's doing well at school. Wants to go to uni.'

'Yeah. Well. We'll see how he goes.' Rita glowed as she looked at her son. 'He's a good boy,' she added.

'Pretty good footy player.'

Evie wanted to ask Rita how well she had known Joof. But it wasn't the right time or place so she left it.

The next day was Monday. Troy would be at school. Dash was in the shed, tinkering. Evie made a cake, drove into town, stopped outside Rita's house, hoping she was home. Rita had three kids. Troy was the eldest. The townspeople talked about how she had three kids by three different fathers. There were only two fathers. Evie knew that. The second one had shot through when the kids were little. Rita had been bringing up those kids on her own, although she had a lot of family in town. Of course.

If Evie thought it through, Rita's family had probably been on this country for tens of thousands of years.

Evie parked the car, got the cake tin out of the back seat and walked through the gate. Rita was looking down at her from the open front door at the top of the stairs. Evie had to squint into the sun.

'G'day,' Rita said. Her arms were crossed.

'I wondered if we could have a cuppa?' Evie said.

Rita looked at Evie for a long time, then stood aside to let her in.

The laminate table in the kitchen was clear and spotless, scrubbed so hard there were little scratch marks. Rita had filled the house with colour, a collection of bright retro things—a burnt orange chair, a purple cushion—which came together joyfully in the sunlight that streamed through the windows.

Rita boiled the water, dangled Lipton's teabags in two cups and poured in the milk. Each step was done with deliberate concentration as if she wanted to avoid the conversation she knew was coming. Evie kept up a patter, born of nerves, about her life, Dash, the footy. Rita said nothing but 'yep' when it was necessary.

Finally, Rita sat down opposite Evie, put her arms on the table and clasped her hands together. 'What can I do for you, Evie?'

'You're going to think I'm mad.'

'You're not mad. I'm surprised it took you this long.'

Evie tried to stop her eyes filling, but blinking made it worse. The tears were fat.

'How pregnant were you when he died?' she asked.

'Six weeks. Had only just found out.'

'Did Joof know?'

'Yep. I told him the day before.'

On the kitchen wall was a painting of a rosella, slashes of green and red.

'Did my parents know?'

'Yep. He'd told them that afternoon.'

'What did he tell them?'

'That Troy was on the way and that he and I were going to marry.'

Evie couldn't hold Rita's gaze. She looked down, broke off a piece of cake, put it in her mouth, looked at her cup of tea, took a slug of it. Finally, she looked up again. Rita hadn't moved. Her hands were clasped, still, in front of her.

'What did they say?'

'I wasn't there. Joof never got a chance to tell me.'

'The accident was at two in the morning,' said Evie.

'He'd gone to Azuri with his mates. He was drunk. So was Pete.' Joof's mate Pete had been driving. He died, too, that night.

'But after? What did my parents say?'

'They never spoke to me. Or to Troy. Ever. If I passed them on the street, they looked straight ahead.'

'They never helped out?'

Rita stood to take her cup to the sink.

'I get a cheque every year. On the thirtieth of June. I never cash them. They're in the cupboard behind the knives. You can have them back if you like.'

'Does Troy know?'

'No. I wasn't going to do that to him. I don't want you to tell him either.'

Evie folded into herself and studied her tea. Her parents had a grandchild in the town, living twelve kilometres from their house, and they never acknowledged him.

'I saw your mother a couple of times,' Rita said. 'Driving slowly past the school when the kids were coming out. She was looking at Troy.'

'Joof's death broke her.'

'It broke me, too,' said Rita. 'But I had to keep getting up in the mornings. I had a kid to look after.'

'She has dementia now,' said Evie. 'I can't ask her why she did it.' She tried to stop crying, but couldn't. 'I'm sorry. I'd better go. But I'm going to try to make it better.'

Rita's eyes narrowed.

'What was Joof going to do,' said Evie at the top of the stairs, 'if my parents said no?'

'He talked about us running away.' Rita leaned on the door frame. 'You'd better go now,' she said.

'Can I come back?'

'Not when Troy's here.'

Evie waited a week then made another cake. Returned and said sorry for the terrible things her parents had done.

'Your parents weren't the worst of it,' said Rita. 'You know that.'

'What do you mean?' said Evie.

'John Clive, your great-grandfather?'

Evie nodded. John Clive was the pioneer of the district, lauded for bringing cattle there.

'Your farmhouse has shutters that open inward. You know why?'

Evie squirmed. 'So they could be closed when they were attacked.'

'That's right. The evil attacking Blakfellas. Ever thought about it from their point of view?'

Evie shook her head. She tried not to think about it at all.

'So they are living their best life. Peaceful. Bringing up their kids. Then these white men move in with their animals and act like they own the place.

'If one of my people took a cow to eat—an animal on their land—your great-grandfather shot three of the men. As a lesson. Your great-grandfather called it stealing.'

Rita's laugh was caustic. 'Of course, moving in on the land wasn't stealing. That was progress.'

She kept going. 'They were short of women, so they raped the girls. You can see in the returns they sent to the government in Sydney. The number of kids they called "half-caste" went up every year. After a few years, not many—maybe thirteen or fourteen—they started with the word "quadroon". Think about what that means. About the age of the mother of that "quadroon".'

A hard heavy lump formed at Evie's centre.

Rita stirred her tea. 'You and I are probably second or third cousins.'

'And then John's son, what was his name? Robert?' Rita leaned forward over the table. 'He handed out flour laced with strychnine. Called the people in, friendly, gave them all some flour, slapped them on the back and sent them away.'

Evie recoiled.

'After a couple of kids died in horrible pain, my people fed some of the flour to a kangaroo and watched it die.'

Rita delivered this news, these tales of horror, without emotion, as if she was explaining nothing more remarkable than that the cackle they could hear outside was a kookaburra.

Evie felt sick. 'I'm so sorry,' she said, rising. 'I have to go.'

'Hard to hear, isn't it?' said Rita.

'Can I come back tomorrow?'

Rita nodded with a sceptical eyebrow. 'See ya then, cuz,' she said, sarcastic.

Back at the farm, Evie wandered around the old farmhouse, examining the shutters. She pulled out a book on the history of the district and reread the bits about her ancestors. It told a different story. There was passing mention of the people who had inhabited the land in the first two pages, covering she supposed sixty thousand years. Then John Clive arrived and history commenced. He suffered many hardships, mostly to do with the weather, which he had heroically overcome. The only real mention of the Aboriginal people was when they had kindly rescued the Clive family when the river was in flood, the book praising them for their magnanimity and local knowledge.

The next morning, Evie made another cake and returned.

'Jeez, if this keeps up we'll need a cherry picker to lift me out of the house,' Rita said.

'I've been thinking about what you said.' Before she came, Evie had written down what she would say, and practised until it sounded right. But even as the words came out, they felt hollow.

Rita crossed her arms. 'Cuz, you might be able to spare the time to deal with your white guilt over endless cups of tea, but I have three kids and a job. I'm in the middle of making dinner. And then I have to go to work.'

'I'm really sorry,' Evie pleaded. 'I was hoping we could talk about Joof . . . And I'm really good at cutting up meat,' she added.

Rita stood aside to let Evie through the door. 'You can help me with the stew for tonight.'

'When Joof was fifteen,' Evie said, as she sharpened the knife, 'he went onto the roof in a big thunderstorm and emptied the gutters because the water was coming through the ceiling. My mother was wringing her hands and Joof leaned over the gutter on the side of the house, which is three stories off the ground, singing.'

Rita laughed. She told Evie how Troy liked hanging out of trees upside down when he was small. Also, he liked reading.

'Well, Joof didn't,' said Evie.

'He read a bit,' Rita said. 'Detective novels. American.'

Evie realised that Rita had spent more time with Joof during the last year of his life than Evie had in his last five.

Their courtship had taken place in a secluded spot by the river, just below the Bluff, where the grass met the bank under the gum trees with the peeling silver trunks. Nobody could see them there.

Evie knew the spot. Dash had built his camping ground there. That's where the jet skis roared on weekends.

Troy was an accident, the news greeted with muted joy, but also dread. It would bring their relationship out into the open, and neither Rita nor Joof were sure what that would mean. 'They'll come round,' Joof had said to Rita. 'How could they not?'

Indeed. How could they not.

'Mum,' Evie said as she stroked her mother's gnarled and papery hand. Her mother was still at home, sitting in the recliner in the sitting room, her eyes ghost-like, seeing but not seeing.

'What about Troy?'

Her mother's eyes welled up.

'Joof's boy,' she said. 'Is he coming to see me?' She leaned towards Evie, conspiratorial. 'He's quick, like Joof.'

She leaned forward right up to Evie's ear. She smelt musty with a hint of urine. 'Don't tell Dad. He won't like it,' her mother whispered.

'Why not?' Evie asked.

'You know,' said her mother, drawing back.

'No, Mum. Why?'

'Well,' she said. 'He's—' she lowered her voice to a conspiratorial whisper '—Aboriginal.'

'But, Mum,' said Evie, 'he's your grandson.'

Mrs Clive pulled back. 'Dad won't have it.' She drew her cardigan together across her chest and pursed her lips. 'Give him a cheque. That'll shut him up.'

But they didn't have to shut anyone up. No words had been spoken, by Troy or by Rita. Her father was only suppressing the voice in his own head.

⯌

The next night, Evie waited until dinner, after she'd put her mother to bed and Dash'd had a couple of beers, but not too many. It would be best if he was relaxed but not belligerent. She cooked a steak, just how he liked it, not pink but not burnt: sort of grey.

'Troy is Joof's son,' she said when they sat down to eat.

Dash said, 'Yeah.'

He had left the TV on in the sitting room. An ad for shampoo blared out.

Evie and Dash had been together for more than a decade, and he'd never even hinted that he thought Troy was Evie's nephew. And here he was acknowledging it as if it was a banal and widely known truth.

'You knew?'

'Everyone knows.' He corrected himself. 'A few people know. Or suspect. Joof's friends knew he was hanging out with Rita. When she was pregnant, people put two and two together.'

The TV news was loud in the next room, intruding on her astonishment.

'You never told me.'

He shrugged. 'What good would it do, you knowing?'

What good would it do knowing that Joof had a child, and that he was living in the town?

He meant the shame of Joof having a child who was Aboriginal eclipsed her need to know.

Fat had congealed around her half-eaten steak.

It wasn't just her parents.

At her next meeting with Rita, she floated the idea of asking Troy to help with the farm work. She'd pay him, of course.

'Good idea,' said Rita. 'He'd like that.'

She rang Troy. 'Got some time to help on the farm?'

'Sure,' he said.

'Ridden a horse before?'

'Nuh. Not much anyway.'

'I'll pick you up on Saturday morning?'

She put him on Old Girl. He was a natural—relaxed, unafraid. Rode with his hips.

They spent the weekend together. She invented a task that involved the two of them on horses putting farm data into the tablet: number of cows, state of the paddocks, state of the Bluff.

'What are you going to do when you finish school?' she asked on the first afternoon, when they stopped near the confluence of the creek and the river. She pulled a thermos out of a saddlebag and served a cup of tea.

'Dunno,' he said.

'Any general idea?'

'Might go to uni. Law maybe.'

'What about farming?'

He looked at her under hooded eyes. That dispassionate look, like he was holding in a well of reason and judgement. He clearly didn't want her to know what he was thinking, but she could see the thoughts were accumulating fast.

'I'm not going to work for someone as a farm labourer for the rest of me life.' He picked up a stick to disrupt a trail of ants. 'Doesn't matter how nice they are,' he added.

He was ambitious. She wanted to cheer, but also nudge him in her direction.

'I meant ag. You know, as an ag scientist or something. Big future in that. And, you never know, you might get your own farm one day.'

'Maybe.'

'Farming is about preserving the land these days.'

He raised his eyebrows in amused doubt.

'It is for me, anyway,' she said. 'Come on, I'll show you the Bluff.'

They tethered the horses at the fence and climbed the Bluff on foot. He crossed his arms when he saw the view. People usually uttered voluble 'wows' and 'amazings', but he didn't say anything. She liked that.

She wanted to say, 'You were conceived by the river down there.'

Instead, she explained how the carbon credit system worked, and showed him where the trees were coming back, and how she wanted the rainforest to return. It would take decades.

They stood together, side by side. A pair of hawks hovered overhead.

They rode back to the yards where she introduced him to Horace. Troy knew to approach the bull from the side. He touched him on the withers and held out a hand with some milo seeds in it. Horace snuffled.

'You've bonded with him already,' she said. 'That was quick.'

'He's a huge bugger.'

When she dropped Troy home, Rita emerged and stood at the top of the front stairs. Evie waved from the car.

Troy reached for the door handle.

'Thanks for the help,' she said. 'I'll deposit your pay into your account. You can come out whenever you want. I don't get to ride Jasper as much as I should, so if you could take him out that would be great. And there'll be work. When we muster and stuff.'

She planned to find him work most weekends, if she could. She was going to teach him how to be a farmer.

Troy's eyes lit up. He gave her a smile. 'That'd be great.'

Evie asked Rita about the nursing home in Broughton where she worked. 'How would my mother go there?'

Rita stopped chopping carrots to look at her. 'She'd be fine.'

'Is it too much? Asking you to see her every working day?'

'How bad is she?'

'Sometimes she has no idea who I am. She remembers Joof but not me. And she's started wandering away from the house. Escaping. I can't handle it anymore.'

'We'll look after her,' said Rita.

36

EVIE

June, ten days before

NOW, A YEAR LATER—A YEAR OF KNOWING TROY, OF SEEING HOW GOOD he was on the farm—Evie was back in Rita's house. 'I want to tell him about his dad.'

'When we've figured out what we're going to say, we will,' said Rita.

'The longer we leave it, the worse it will be.'

'I know, sis. But it's a lot. It's like he has the whole history of colonisation to grapple with.' She paused. 'I just need to script it before we tell him. Plan for various reactions.'

Rita picked up a bedsheet and handed one end of it to Evie. 'Here, make yourself useful.'

Evie walked backward until the sheet was stretched between them.

'And you need to get your shit together,' said Rita. 'I'm not sure you've thought through the implications of telling him. You assume he'll be delighted, but Troy's a deep thinker. It's going to hurt. He'll be angry . . . at both of us.'

The sheet rippled between them as they shook it.

'I want to give him a chunk of Clive Downs,' said Evie. 'I want to give him the Bluff.'

Rita's end of the sheet dropped. 'You can't say that to him if you don't mean it.'

'I do mean it,' said Evie.

'I don't think you've thought it through,' said Rita. 'What about Dash?'

'Dash wants to turn it into a yoga resort with Chandra.'

'What about his jet skis and quad bikes?'

'Maybe he thinks he can keep them. I'm not sure he and Chandra speak the same language.'

They pulled the sheet taut, folded it over, shook it, folded it again. Rita walked towards Evie and took her end from her.

'Anyway,' said Evie, 'there's a chance we'll split up. And if I divorce him, he'll get a big part of the land. Maybe the Bluff. I need to keep it safe. For Troy.'

Rita folded the sheet and smoothed it down.

'Divorce. That's a big word.'

'No surprise, though.'

'No,' Rita agreed.

'So what do you think?'

Rita picked up another sheet and handed an end to Evie. 'Sounds like you want to do it to keep it away from Dash.'

Evie shook her head. 'That's not the reason. If Joof was still alive, Troy would be getting all of it. It's the right thing to do.'

'I think you're making this up as you go along.'

They shook the sheet.

Rita continued. 'What worries me is that you'll go away and think of reasons why he shouldn't have it. You might have children of your own, your income will reduce, Troy might want to do something different with it that pisses you off. And then I'll be left with a ball of fury and resentment. One with arms, legs, a mouth, testosterone and muscles.'

She added the sheet to the pile on the coffee table.

'So what are you saying?' said Evie.

'I need to see a plan with contracts and stuff before you talk to him.'

'Don't you trust me?'

'Jesus, Evie,' said Rita. 'That's a leap. I'm just saying that you need to get your shit together before you fire this thought bubble out into the world. Or, more specifically, into my son.'

37

RUTH

June, ten days before

IT WAS A CHILLY NIGHT. THE WOODEN FLOORS ECHOED WITH RUTH'S lonely footsteps. It was as if the rambling old house took umbrage at being empty of people; resented the absence of laughter and the thunder of small children running up the halls. She wished Charlie was there. He would have rubbed his hands together and lit the fire.

Ruth turned the lights off and sat back in a squatter's chair in the garden to gaze skyward. Dots of light shimmered through the immense matt black dome of sky. The bush rustled with night animals and the curlew sent out a wail of mourning. She felt small. Alone. Insignificant. She might vaporise, and nobody would notice.

She was drifting here in this town, becoming less corporeal as each day passed.

Charlie's visit had shown her that her life was filled with absence: the absence of Bill and Jack; the absence of work she understood; the absence of feeling competent and in control of some part of the world. Did she need someone with her to affirm that she existed?

Maybe this was what Chandra was for lonely people. If a person is energy, the potential for redirection of that energy becomes limitless.

Was Charlie a replacement for Bill? That seemed too neat: swapping out Bill for one of his best mates.

Buster snuffled up to her, wagging the back half of his body, and wedging his wet nose into her draping hand.

It was cold. 'You're right, Buster. I should stop feeling sorry for myself and go inside.'

She turned on the kitchen light. Harry and Marge's dining room table, capable of seating twelve, looked bereft on the worn wooden floors.

She turned on Beethoven's 'Piano Sonata No. 27' and drifted to her computer. She tried messaging Jack, but she knew he would be getting up to go to work in London.

Facebook was her last resort.

Dash had posted pictures of Horace. *RIP Horace,* the post said. *Our Horace passed away today in tragic circumstances.*

Oh no. Poor Evie. Ruth wondered what had happened.

She went to Chandra's Instagram page. It had a picture of her corgi. *Our dear Frank passed this afternoon. May he bring those in the afterlife as much joy as he brought his family.*

Were the deaths related? Last time she'd seen Frank, he was barking under the noses of those heifers. Surely Frank hadn't . . .

Her phone rang. Charlie.

'What's happening?' he said.

'Studying the mysteries of human nature in a cold, empty house.'

'Put on your new undies, that'll cheer you up.'

She chuckled as she pressed the red dot to hang up.

Before she put the phone down, it rang again.

Evie.

'Can I come to see you? Sorry, I know it's late, but it's probably better if I come to your house.'

Ruth looked at her watch. Eight pm. Bit late for a client meeting.

Did it have something to do with Horace and Frank?

She hoped Evie didn't want to sue Chandra for letting Frank wreak havoc. If that's what had happened. She'd have to say no. Conflict of interest. Tell her to find another lawyer.

Some people think that suing will solve all their problems with other people. It mostly just made the problems worse because it took up a lot of time, cost a lot of money and escalated hostilities.

She was still honing the little speech she would make when Evie's ute crunched on the gravel driveway.

'So sorry to hear about Horace,' said Ruth as she opened the door. She held up a bottle of wine with a question mark on her face.

'Thanks,' said Evie. She sat on the sofa beside Harry and Marge's cat, Cleopatra, which purred and put its face on her lap. Absent-mindedly, Evie scratched behind the cat's ears, which made it purr more loudly.

While she pulled the cork out of the bottle, Ruth asked what happened, and Evie told the horrible story in a few words.

'You poor thing,' said Ruth.

Evie shrugged.

'So how can I help?' Ruth handed over the glass of red.

Evie inhaled and compressed her lips. 'I need to know how to hive off a chunk of the farm.'

'Subdivide?' said Ruth. 'Sure, I can look into it for you. Which chunk?'

'The Bluff.'

'What do you want to do with it?'

'Not sure yet,' said Evie. 'Keeping my options open. But I need to subdivide, don't I, if I want to sell or lease it?'

'That's right,' said Ruth.

Why had Evie come over at eight pm to talk about something as banal as drawing a line down a property?

'There's a bit of urgency,' said Evie.

'Oh?' Ruth waited for an explanation.

Evie didn't offer one.

'How long have we got?' said Ruth.

'It would be nice to have it done in the next month or so.'

The cat stretched out a black paw. Evie was pale, and toying with her glass.

'You look exhausted,' said Ruth.

'Yeah, I don't feel great.'

'You've had a terrible time—with your mum, and now Horace. I know you went to Sydney recently, but maybe you need to take a longer break? Maybe a holiday at the beach?'

Evie nodded moodily and stared out the window into the darkness.

Ruth wanted to go to bed, but Evie was showing no signs of stirring. Perhaps she didn't want to go home.

'You can spend the night here if you like,' she said. 'That way you could have another glass of wine.'

'Thanks,' said Evie. 'I'd like that.'

Ruth showed her into a bedroom. 'It's Sam's,' she said, 'but the sheets are clean.'

Evie gave a half smile.

Patch had said they'd accidentally run into Sam in Sydney, but Ruth was still wondering how accidental the meeting was.

You can never tell what state someone else's marriage is in. People are usually pretty good at keeping up a facade, desperately holding on to the public face of marital tranquillity for fear a crack will cause the whole thing to collapse.

⸻

WhatsApp

Jack
Probably ought to tell you. Am seeing someone.

Ruth
Really? I would never have guessed.

Jack
[photo of Jack with extremely attractive girl]
Annabelle

Ruth
She looks lovely.
Have you enlightened her parents re Oz wine?

Jack
They're thawing

Ruth
I think Poms are affected by the miserable weather. Show them an old episode of *Home & Away* and they all want to move here.

Jack
What's happening in Myddle?

Ruth
Evie's prize bull was killed by a barking corgi

Jack
?

Ruth
Panicked. Ran onto a cattle grid.

Jack
[meme of man staring in wide-eyed horror]

38

EVIE

June, nine days before

IT WAS MID-MORNING BY THE TIME EVIE PULLED UP OUTSIDE THE SHED. She'd barely slept at Ruth's and sleeping in Sam's bed was a really bad idea. She couldn't get him out of her head.

Dash was tinkering inside. He emerged, spanner in hand. 'I was wondering where you were. You all right, love?'

'Yeah,' she said. 'I'm okay.'

'I was going to the footy this afternoon. But I can hang around if you like.'

'No, it's fine. I'm going to take Jasper for a ride. See you at dinner?'

'Sure.'

Evie wanted to keep away from him while she formulated what she would say.

Jasper was pleased to see her, and twitching for a gallop.

She rode him to the Bluff and sat on the summit for a long time.

Dash got home at five, unusually early for a footy day. He'd forgone the post-game beers. He went to the bathroom, wiped his hands and got a stubby from the fridge.

She chucked some sausages into the pan and peeled some potatoes for mash.

Dash opened the fridge to make a salad.

That done, he went into the living room and turned on the TV. A game show was on.

Potatoes boiled, she added the butter and milk and thumped the mixture with the masher.

Dash came back in to grab another stubby. 'Everything okay?'

'Yep.'

'You're just a bit quiet tonight.'

'I'm all right.'

He laid the table and sat at it, waiting for her to serve the meal. She lumped the mash on the plates and put the sausages on top.

They ate in silence. The plates were nearly clean.

Now or never.

'I've been thinking about the farm. I want to give some of it to Troy,' she said.

'Aren't you a bit young to be thinking about that now?' Dash took a swig. 'Thinking about your will. Who knows what will happen. There are our kids to think of, for a start.'

'I'm not talking about a will,' said Evie. 'I mean to give him some of the farm now.'

When Dash was confused, his mouth dropped open. 'Why would you do that?'

'Because that's the way it was supposed to go, from Dad to Joof to Joof's kid.'

She and Dash should count themselves lucky they had any of the farm: the luck of her brother dying.

'You can't do that,' Dash spluttered.

'Why not?'

'We're about to have kids.'

'We'd still have more than half of it. That's all I'm using for cattle now anyway.'

'Which bit are you going to give him?'

'The Bluff.'

Dash's beer was suspended in mid-air. From the TV, an ad for a bank promised longevity and bliss.

'What about our plans?' Dash said. 'For the eco-health resort?'

'They're not my plans. I don't want to operate a hotel.'

She put down her knife and fork and stood with her plate. As she walked past Dash, he grabbed her wrist.

'What's Troy going to do with it?' Dash asked. 'Turn it into a corroboree site?'

'I've no idea what he'll do with it. I haven't mentioned it to him. But a corroboree site would be good for a tourist venture, wouldn't it?'

Dash turned his head away, let go of her wrist, then stood and went to the fridge to get another beer.

He turned back. He hadn't retreated; he'd just withdrawn to gather reinforcements.

'Have you cooked this up with Rita?'

Now he was looking for a conspiracy.

'No.'

'How do you even know that Troy is definitely Joof's kid?'

'You said it was true.'

'Only because of what she's been saying around town. Probably lying. Seeing if she can screw something out of you. As if they don't get enough from the government. I bet she invented the story about Joof so she didn't have to explain which bastard of the many she'd been rooting was actually the kid's father.'

Evie knew from long experience that there was no point arguing with Dash when he was like this. He would become more belligerent and less rational as he downed more beers.

'I was watching Troy play footy and realised that it was like watching Joof,' she said. 'I guessed.'

Dash drained the beer and went to the fridge to get another. It was time to finish the conversation.

'It's the right thing to do. By Joof.'

'Or some wacky left-wing native title crusade.'

Evie rinsed the plates, packed the dishwasher and wiped down the kitchen benches.

Dash was only getting started. 'Because if that's what this is about, bear in mind that they'll wreck the land, bring in all their relations, and destroy what your family has built.'

'Troy is my family.'

'They just sponge off everyone else.'

If you want sponging, mate, take a look in the mirror.

'You'd take on a black family and deny me?'

'Does your whole identity depend on developing the campground into something bigger?' Evie asked. 'Just build the eco-health resort somewhere else. On the river, down near Roscoe's.'

'Everyone thinks I'm hopeless; that I married you for the money. This is my career, Evie. And it has to be the Bluff.'

He turned and threw the stubby at the wall. It hit the tiled splashback and the wall above it, leaving a hole in the gyprock.

'I'm going to bed.' She prayed he wouldn't follow her.

'I'm not the only one who's useless, though, am I?' Dash yelled after her. 'You're so useless you can't even produce a kid.'

39

EVIE

June, Sunday night, eight days before

DASH SLEPT IN THE SPARE ROOM.

Evie didn't sleep much.

In the morning, she felt very ordinary—the Australian euphemism for a hangover. Except she hadn't had any alcohol.

The day felt ordinary, too. The sky was grey, an oppressive drizzle that was enough to dampen the surface but not the earth beneath it.

So ordinary she was going to . . .

She gagged, ran to the loo and vomited.

Staring into the porcelain, fighting the nausea, she turned over the reasons she might be sick.

The pregnancy kits were in the bathroom cupboard. She was well-practised in the drill: take a plastic stick out of its package, pee on it, stare at the lines as one turns blue but the other doesn't. Bow head. Weep.

Ripping it open, she did the first bit, the peeing part.

She looked at the plastic stick with its two blue lines in disbelief. *Must be defective,* she thought.

She got another one out of the packet and peed on it. Waited. The first line went blue straight away and then, as she could see the wetness progress up the paper in the window, so did the second.

A baby. At last.

Delight and nausea rose within her. She wanted to laugh and vomit at the same time.

She did vomit.

She stared into the bowl as the water sloshed it away.

What now?

Dash would make a great dad. He'd be fun. He'd teach their child how to fix an engine and play footy.

Would it stop him sleeping around? She didn't want to think about that.

What about giving the land to Troy? It had seemed so clear last night; the perfect solution to her conundrum. But as soon as she told Dash about the baby, it would make him even more resolute that she should keep the farm intact.

She needed to think it through.

My God, she felt sick. Lucky she was still kneeling on the floor because it looked like the porcelain was going to be her friend for a while. She vomited again.

How long would this go on?

How pregnant was she?

When was her last period? She had to think about it. Count back by weekends. To the last time she'd spent a day in bed. Five weeks ago. If ovulation happened at the right time, this baby must have been conceived three weeks ago.

Where was she three weeks ago?

Oh.

Right.

Maybe Dash wasn't going to be a dad after all.

A soft knock on the bathroom door. 'You all right, love? I heard a noise. Are you sick?'

She wiped her mouth and opened the door.

'You are sick! Did you get pissed last night or something? Come on, I'll make you a coffee.'

Dash hugged her and guided her into the kitchen.

She still had the stick in her hand. She handed it to him. 'I barely drank last night,' she said.

He stared at it, uncomprehending.

She'd fantasised for years about his reaction when she told him: his delight. It was the thing she loved most about him—how he could brighten the darkest space whenever there was a reason to celebrate.

Instead, he frowned in confusion. 'How?' he said.

That was a strange response.

'What do you mean *how*?' she said.

'Whose is it?' Dash's voice was elevated. His chin was tight and his Adam's apple wobbled.

He was angry.

Why would he doubt that the baby was his?

He'd never doubted her. He'd not questioned if she'd seen anyone in Sydney.

She went back over their long history of infertility. He'd gone off to have tests. He'd told her they were okay. She'd believed him.

She'd never thought to ask to see the results.

'Are you sterile?' she said.

So much fell into place: his evasion whenever she pressed

him to start IVF; his protestations that they were too busy, that they'd get to it one day, when the time was right.

'You lied to me?' Her voice was rising in pitch.

'Whose kid is it?' he repeated.

'You let me go through all that pain every month just because you couldn't admit that you're sterile?'

'Whose kid is it?' He stepped towards her.

'It's not like you're innocent of fucking outside this marriage,' she said.

He moved forward, his fists clenched. 'It's Troy's, isn't it?' he said.

Her stomach turned in revulsion. She tensed.

He'd never hit her, ever. She'd never thought he might.

Until now.

But, instead, he stepped back, sat down in a chair at the kitchen table and put his head in his hands. He sat like that for a long time. Then he put his hands on the table, slowly, like he was conscious that he needed to control them.

'I'll be in the shed,' he said.

The screen door slammed behind him.

Evie sat and drank the coffee he'd put in front of her earlier, trying to quell the outrage churning inside. She needed to get out of the house. She changed into her riding gear and went out to Jasper. A gallop through the paddock would clear her head.

Jasper's mane was damp from the insipid rain. She leaned down close to his neck. She felt hollow inside, the same way she'd felt when she'd received that text message from Deirdre.

But she wasn't hollow, was she? There was life inside her.

Once she was riding, she rose out of the saddle to coax Jasper into a gallop, bending forward to give him the reins. She wanted to feel his energy and power, his joy and abandon; to hear the rhythmic beat of his hooves.

They headed, like they always did, to the Bluff. The river below was swathed in mist. She dismounted. Her riding boots made the damp rock too slippery to climb so she sat on a ledge at the bottom watching Dash's ute approach.

When he got out at the gate at the bottom of the hill, he looked up and gave a tentative wave. She didn't wave back.

'Hey,' he said, when he reached her.

'Hey,' she responded.

'Not going up there?' he said, a twist of his head gesturing towards the top of the Bluff.

'It'll be too slippery in these today,' she said, indicating her boots.

'Come on, I'll give you a hand.'

He pulled her up.

The mist softened the river and forest with hues of grey. Black cockatoos rose out of the eucalypts on the rise past the far bank, their caws echoing.

'Maybe it's for the best,' said Dash. 'Maybe it solves the problem.'

She raised her eyebrows at him.

'My sperm count. Zero. Nada.'

'We still have a problem, Dash.' She kept her voice soft and low.

'I'll accept the kid as mine.' He stepped towards her as if he was going to hug her. She stepped back.

'You didn't tell me the truth. The most consequential thing in our lives—well, my life anyway—and you lied to me.'

'I didn't lie.'

'You lied by omission, which is just as bad. You let me believe it was all my fault.' A sob escaped, and then she couldn't stop them coming. 'Why would you do that?' she asked.

'Ashamed, I guess.'

A faint smell of campfire rose from the trailers below.

'But what about Deirdre? She said she had an abortion.'

'She did, when she was eighteen. Way before me. Did she make out it was mine?'

'Why else would she say it?'

'Wow,' said Dash. 'What a bitch she was to you.'

Evie scoffed. Why had she never noticed his lack of insight before? Maybe she had and papered over it in her mind.

'I was going to tell you, Evie. We would have gone on IVF, when we were ready. I just had trouble facing the fact that my balls were going to be the focus of a lot of attention.' He was trying to wave it away, as a small matter.

'And needles,' he added. 'Didn't fancy my balls being a pin cushion.'

Now he was trying to make a joke out of it.

'I'm thirty-eight, Dash. I don't have any time.'

'Well, it's fixed now. We can make this work, love.'

She crossed her arms, not trusting herself to respond.

'Whose is it?' he said, still looking towards the horizon.

'Sam's.'

Dash frowned, puzzled. 'Do I know him?'

'Harry's son.'

He looked confused, then amazed. 'Harry the lawyer?'

She nodded.

'I coached that kid.'

'He's twenty-six now.'

Dash made a noise that was meant to be a derisory laugh. 'Did you do this when you went on that girl's weekend to Sydney?'

She nodded.

He turned away, squared his shoulders, then turned back. 'Well, anyway,' he said, 'at least that's an end to the discussion about giving away the Bluff.'

Was this the trade-off?

'If we have our own kid, I mean,' he said.

'Is that what you're worried about?' said Evie. 'You'd take on another man's child if it means you get to run a tourist venture?'

Dash shook his head and moved closer to her. 'I was probably always going to have to accept another man's kid, love. It may as well be Sam's. He's a good-looking fella. And smart.' His chuckle was genuine this time.

'Dash.' She had to say this gently. 'This pregnancy makes no difference to my decision about Troy.' It had solidified. She was going ahead with it.

Dash was uncomprehending. 'What do you mean? What about your own kid?'

'Troy is Joof's kid. I can't keep the land. It's not mine.'

'You can. You have to.'

'I don't, Dash. I really don't.'

A cockatoo squawked, long and mournful.

'You're doing this just to get at me, aren't you?'

'No, Dash. You haven't been listening. I'm doing it for my brother. And because it's the right thing to do.'

'Your brother's dead, Evie. It's not going to bring him back.'

Irritation crested within her, and something gave way in her head. 'You know the worst thing about this? I finally realise that the only thing you're interested in is my land. You're not interested in me. You're just a greedy fuck.'

An angry red bloomed on his lovely skin. 'You can't do this.'

'Why not?'

'The deal on the resort.'

'I'm not building a resort, Dash. I don't see my future catering to a bunch of tourists. I'm sick of it.'

It escalated quickly then. When Dash played poker, he doubled down, a see-you-and-raise-you man. He had an innate confidence that he would win. Sometimes he did, but mostly he didn't. The losses disappeared into a foggy marshland of failure, where his thoughts never ventured. He only focused on the wins.

'You selfish bitch,' he said. 'I'm just trying to improve our financial position and all you can think about is yourself. And giving away our biggest asset to some Blakfella.'

She ignored the jibe, as she always had. 'I don't think you realise how little we know about tourism, Dash. How risky it is.'

Dash never absorbed information he didn't want to hear. He just batted it back and blamed someone else—Evie, usually. 'You never support me. All you ever do is think about yourself. And complain. You never say how good I am. I'm the one who thought this all up.'

That was undeniable. His grandiose plans. His attempts to push against reality.

He stepped towards her. She recoiled.

The rock was smooth and wet. She slipped. When she reached out, there was only air.

40

EVIE

June, Sunday night, eight days before

EVIE LAY ON THE SOFA. HER HEAD HURT. A LOT.

Dash's phone rang. 'Hello?' he said. He sounded breathless, anxious.

'Oh hey, Chandra.'

Evie kept her eyes closed. She could only hear Dash's side of the conversation.

'No. Evie's had an accident.'

His voice was taut; a stretched-out wire.

'I think so. I just got her back to the house. She's lying on the sofa. I think she's okay.' He faltered. He wasn't sure. That never happened. Dash was always certain: often wrong, but never in doubt.

'I might need to take her to emergency in Broughton. Just to check her out. Do you think it'll be open?'

Evie didn't want to go to hospital. She just wanted to sleep.

'Thanks,' said Dash. 'That'd be great. Second opinion.'

Oh no. Chandra was coming over.

Evie drifted off. Dash was stroking her forehead when Chandra walked in.

'Hellooo,' she said softly. 'Is everything okay?'

'She has a headache,' said Dash. 'Just closed her eyes five minutes ago. I can't rouse her. I think she might have passed out. Can you help me get her to the car? I'm wondering if I should call an ambulance but that would take even longer.'

Evie hadn't passed out. She just didn't want to talk to him. Also, she was arguing with her stomach about its need to throw up, and that took a lot of concentration.

Dash paced away from the sofa and then back. 'Can you watch her? I'll get the car out of the shed and bring it round to the door.'

Chandra felt Evie's forehead. 'Evie?' she said. 'Can you hear me?'

Chandra reached for her wrist.

Evie opened her eyes. She leaned over the side of the sofa and vomited into the bucket Dash had put there.

Chandra put her hand on Evie's neck.

It was the touch that made her explode. 'Do you ever give up? This fucking eco-resort. Just fuck off and leave me alone.'

41

RUTH

June, Monday morning, a week before

RUTH'S PHONE PINGED.

A text from Evie.

I'm going to the beach for a while to think things through. Talk when I get back.

42

BEA

June, Monday morning, a week before

THE PHARMACY DOOR CREAKED OPEN.

'Hey, Bea.'

Dash Rogers leaned over the counter. 'How ya going?'

'Yeah, pretty good,' she said, feigning calm when her heart was thumping in her chest so loud she worried he could hear it.

'Just grabbing some Panadol,' he said.

She ran her fingers over the boxes on the wall behind the counter. 'Twenty-four or a hundred?'

'Biggest you've got. Haven't seen you out at the farm lately.'

She put the box in a paper packet.

'After Horace I didn't want to intrude.'

Evie had shouted at her. She'd been so angry—the way Bea's mum got, but it was worse because Evie never lost her temper.

Bea had vowed never to go back.

'Yeah, I get it,' Dash said. 'Evie was pretty upset. Sorry about that.' He waved his card over the pay thing. 'She's gone away for a bit. Needs the break.'

'That's good,' said Bea. 'She's had a lot to deal with lately—her mum and Horace and that.'

'Yeah.' Dash put his card in his back pocket. 'Got anything on after work?'

'Nah,' she said.

'How about a drink at mine?'

'Sure.' She tried to sound cool, as if an invitation to Dash's house was routine.

'Come in my car. I'll drop you back later.'

At five, he swung by and she jumped into his ute, still in her work gear.

She'd never had a conversation one on one with him before. Dash asked her about her work at the pharmacy. She asked how Jasper and Old Girl were going. Then they ran out of things to say.

'Don't worry,' he said as they pulled up at the house. 'There's no one else here.'

He got a couple of beers out of the fridge.

Their lounge room was lovely. A fireplace. Paintings of Evie's ancestors on the wall. A sofa that was so soft she sank into it.

He was distracted: his fingernails rubbing against the nape of the velvet on a cushion. 'Can I ask you something?' he said at last. 'You can't tell anyone. I just need to talk to someone.'

A dog jumped onto the sofa and snuggled into the other side of Bea.

'We've been having a few issues,' he said. 'Evie has . . . She hasn't been coping lately.'

'Jeez,' said Bea. 'That's no good. Makes sense but.'

He stared at his stubby, rubbing at the condensation around the label. 'It's been pretty stressful.'

Bea couldn't think of anything to say, so she reached out and touched his leg.

He gripped her hand. 'It's good to be able to talk about it with someone I trust. It's been pretty hard on both of us.'

He stroked her arm, absent-minded, his thoughts still on his distressed wife.

'Is she depressed?' Bea asked.

'I think she is, yeah.'

'My mum's a bit crazy,' said Bea. 'It's hard to live with sometimes. Never know when she might go off. Sometimes I just have to get out of the house to escape it. People don't realise how bad it can be when you're living with someone who has mental health problems.'

'Yeah. Still, someone's got to keep things moving on the farm. And with the campsite and everything.'

They were still holding hands while they sipped on their beers. It felt nice, like they were helping each other.

'So great to be able to talk to someone about it. Someone who understands,' he said, and put his arm around her shoulder. 'Thanks, Bea.' Dash rubbed her shoulder as he said it.

He leaned his head against hers, then turned, aiming to kiss her on the cheek. She twisted her head at the wrong moment and the kiss landed on her mouth.

'Poor Dash,' she said. She moved her kisses down his chest, to his crotch. His hand was gently pressing the back of her head.

Poor Dash, she thought again as her mouth connected with his penis. She wanted to provide him some comfort, assuage his anguish. There could be no harm in it. Evie was away and he was having a hard time.

And, wow, if their marriage was bad, maybe there'd be a future for Bea. Did she love Dash? Was that what this was? Maybe he loved her.

There was the age thing. But lots of older men got with young women. Movie stars did.

Afterwards, they were still on the sofa. He held her in his arms, her head against his chest. 'I feel so guilty about Evie,' he said.

'No one will ever know. You can trust me,' said Bea.

He laughed. 'We're two damaged people. The sane people in our families.'

'We can look after each other.' *Maybe forever,* she thought. It felt like the beginning of something incredible. Inside her, there was a gushing fountain of excitement. And joy.

'You're a good person, Bea,' he said. 'I'm so glad we found each other.'

43

RUTH

June, Monday morning, a week before

RUTH GOT IN EARLY SO THAT SHE COULD WORK OUT WHAT EVIE NEEDED to subdivide the farm.

She had a vague idea that you had to get approval from the council. For that, you'd need a survey and a report from a consultant about how the farm would function in two parts.

Evie had already subdivided off a couple of hectares for Roscoe. That would be a good place to start—see how Harry did it—but she needed Evie's file for that. And Evie had made some application for the carbon credit scheme at the Bluff. She'd need that, too.

At the office, Ruth checked in Harry's filing cabinet. No file of Evie's.

She checked Troy's neat piles of files in the file room.

Checked R for Rogers, then C for Clive. Not there.

She rang Harry. The call went to voicemail.

She needed Harry to explain what he'd already done, and to point her in the right direction, but he seemed to be incommunicado.

'Fuck,' she said to nobody in particular.

Ruth had to drive up to Brisbane that night for a meeting first thing in the morning. She needed an action list for when she got back.

She put her fingers on the keyboard, thought for a few seconds and typed in a search term: 'farm subdivision'.

Troy arrived at work before Deb and sat at the reception desk.

The bell on the door jangled.

From her office, Ruth heard Dash's voice. 'What are you doing here?'

'Work experience,' said Troy.

Work experience sounded demeaning to Ruth. He should call himself a clerk. She made a mental note to speak to him about it.

Then the door clanged again.

She went out. 'Was that Dash Rogers?' she asked Troy, who was dabbling about on the screen with the mouse.

'Yep.'

'Where's he gone?'

'Dunno. He just left.'

'Is he coming back?'

'Didn't say.'

Ruth looked at the closed door, puzzled.

Then Troy said, 'Mate.' His voice was uncharacteristically tentative, as if he had to tell her something she wouldn't want to hear.

'I can't believe I'm responding to being called mate by someone even younger than my son.'

'There are people in town who don't like that I'm working here.'

'Well, fuck them,' said Ruth. 'You can stay on reception permanently if that's what they think.'

'I'd rather stay out the back.'

'Really?'

'Uses up less energy that way. Best to pick the battles you really want to fight.'

'Whatever you want.'

She stomped back into her office but was soon back out again. 'Did you see any file of Evie Rogers' when you tidied the back office?'

'Nuh.'

She frowned. Where was it?

When Deb arrived at work an hour later, Ruth went out to reception. 'Any idea where Evie Rogers' file is?'

'It'll be in the back office if it's not in Harry's cabinet.'

'I can't find it in either of those places.'

Deb frowned, stood and disappeared into the back office.

After twenty minutes, she found Ruth in her office. 'You're right,' she said, as if that was a surprise. 'I'll call Harry and ask him. Why do you need it?'

'Just a few things,' said Ruth vaguely.

Deb turned tail and walked out.

She returned after a few minutes. 'Left a message on Harry's voicemail,' she said.

Things were looking up in one respect: that was the most help Deb had ever been. By four pm, Ruth had a list of things she needed for a subdivision. Top of the list was Evie Rogers' file.

As she passed through reception, jangling her car keys, she said to Deb and Troy, 'Off to Brisbane, see you Wednesday.'

'Oh, by the way—' Deb paused while her eyes lingered on her computer screen.

'Yes?' said Ruth.

'You just missed Harry.'

'You're kidding,' said Ruth. 'He rang?'

She turned to go into her office to call him back.

'You might have trouble reaching him,' Deb yelled after her. 'His phone went flat while we were talking.'

'Did you ask him where Evie Rogers' file is?'

'He said it's at home but he'll talk to you about it.'

'I'm off to Brisbane now,' said Ruth. 'He can call me on the mobile.'

'Sure.' Deb turned back to her computer screen, somehow managing to exude dismissive sarcasm. If she was a teenage girl, Deb would have been diagnosed with oppositional defiance disorder, but she was in her mid-forties.

On Ruth's way out of town, the rain started, more torrent than sprinkle. It soon turned to a deluge, the windscreen wipers ineffectual.

She rang Charlie for a chat. 'What's that din?' he said.

'Rain on the car roof.'

He checked the weather radar. 'It's orange and red all the way to Brisbane. You shouldn't drive in that. Can't you go in the morning?'

He was right. Brisbane could wait. She rang to tell the person she was meeting that she might come the next day, weather permitting.

She drove home. Rang Harry, but it went to voicemail.

Ruth stood in Harry and Marge's kitchen and looked around. Where would Harry store a file? The room that passed as the study—the floor covered in piles of books—had an old wardrobe. She opened it and was nearly buried under a pile of paper and dust. No files, though. Just electricity bills going back to 1983. She gave up. Harry would call back soon. Surely.

Ruth immersed herself in her book, then made herself a poached egg on toast and took her book to bed.

◆

Ruth startled awake. There was a noise. A rattle. Was it the wind? No. The rain had stopped. Someone or something was jiggling the front door. She lay in bed, frozen with indecision.

Why wasn't Buster barking?

That's right. She had taken him to Patch's because she was supposed to be in Brisbane.

It was probably a possum or something.

Now there were footsteps, a crunch of gravel. Unmistakable. A person was walking around the house, looking for a way in.

Thank God she'd locked the front door.

It was dark, the thick black night of the country under a new moon. She couldn't see the ceiling, the walls or the door.

In Harry's house the lack of locks, plus the cornucopia of doors and windows, meant that the separation between outdoor and indoor was only a matter of semantics. The house was designed to keep the weather out, not whoever the fuck was walking around out there now. Who were they? Murderer? Rapist? Robber?

As if on cue, there was a scrape and a bang as a double-hung window went up, followed by some rustling as an intruder came through it.

He or she was inside now. Ruth could hear footsteps, faint but unmistakable. A refracted, dancing light—a torch—flashed on the wall outside her bedroom door. The dining room light came on. They made no attempt to be unobtrusive and seemed unconcerned about waking her up. As if they knew she wasn't going to be home.

They were looking for something. Drawers were opened and the contents clattered out. First the kitchen, then the dining room.

The footsteps got louder, the dancing light more constant. The person was coming down the hall towards her bedroom.

Ruth wasn't going to confront this person. Not from her bed anyway. She got up and quickly felt her way to the built-in wardrobe, stepped inside and closed the door.

Damn. She should have picked up her phone. The footsteps were in the bedroom now. The dancing light was visible through the slit at the bottom of the wardrobe door.

What would she use her phone for anyway? If she rang the police she'd get Gazza. And she'd have to talk, which would reveal she was there. Could you text the emergency number? That seemed like something it was important to know. How could she not know that?

What should she do? Cowering in the wardrobe seemed like a bad idea. She was a sitting duck if the person decided to look in there as well. But what was the alternative?

The person worked through the chest of drawers beside her bed. Was it a him? Or a her? She couldn't tell.

Boots on the wooden floors approached the wardrobe. She wedged some socks under the door, to jam it.

A hand was on the wardrobe door, turning the handle, shaking it.

She was going to have to speak. What should she say? *Hey, fucker, get out of my fucking bedroom?*

The jiggling was getting more urgent, more irritated, more violent.

Then there was a thud, a grunt—*'Ooph'*—and a groan.

Another sound, more of a whack.

A heavy object sliding down the door.

Then nothing. Silence.

What to do now? She stayed inside the cupboard for what seemed like an hour. Still nothing.

She opened the wardrobe door a crack. Peered out. The door was jammed against something. She pushed harder.

'Is that you, Ruth? Are you here?'

'Troy?'

What was he doing here?

'I'll pull him out of the way.'

She emerged from the wardrobe. The light was already on. A body lay prone on the floor. Troy turned it over.

Dash.

Ruth checked. He was breathing, but Troy had given him a monumental whack.

Troy got some rope and tied the unconscious Dash's hands and ankles together.

'Why are you here?' Ruth asked him.

Troy looked up. 'I overheard Deb telling someone on the phone that you were asking about Evie's file, that it was at Harry's house, and you weren't going to be at home tonight.'

'Was Deb talking to Dash?'

'I couldn't tell who she was talking to but I assume so,' said Troy. 'Anyway I thought I'd come to make sure everything was okay. He was already here, trying the doors and that. Then I saw he got in the house.'

He paused. He was distressed, not, it seemed, because he had just clocked someone over the head, but because he was worried about how it looked to her.

'So I came in, too. Sorry, I didn't realise you were here.'

Dash came to, eyes slowly focusing. He was on the floor, trussed up, his head facing the chest of drawers. His hands tested their constraints, then his feet. He didn't seem surprised to find himself there. He didn't struggle. He was calculating. Ruth and Troy said nothing, didn't move, just watched to see what Dash would do while he couldn't see them.

Dash twisted his head. That didn't expand his view much, so he convulsed his body to turn it over. Dash was strong, his stomach able to execute the move without any help from his arms or legs. He could see Ruth then.

'G'day, Dash,' Ruth said.

'Ruth!' He spoke warmly. Dash could charm even while trussed up on the floor of her bedroom. 'Sorry, I thought you'd gone out of town.' As if that explained why he had entered her house at one am.

'Looking for something?' Ruth asked.

'Yeah, mate, sorry. Couldn't sleep. Harry has some things I need. Thought they might be here. Funny time of day to be looking for it I know.' He smiled.

It was only then that Ruth realised Troy had moved out of Dash's view. He was standing in the hall, in the shadow, behind Dash.

'Where did you learn to tie a rope like this?' Dash asked.

'I was brought up on a farm,' said Ruth. That at least was true. 'Learnt some things.'

'You sure did. I've got pins and needles in me feet.' He laughed, exuding that Dash charm, waiting for her to take the hint and untie him.

'Look, Ruth, I understand you might be a bit upset about me being here. Seriously, I thought you were out. I would never . . .' He let the rest of the sentence hang. 'If you're worried, why don't you just ring Constable Parker and we'll get him to sort it out.'

Ruth smiled at him. 'What were you looking for? Specifically?'

Dash watched her from behind a mask of insouciance. 'Just looking for those papers Harry had of mine.' He paused. 'Of Evie's,' he corrected himself.

'What papers?'

'About the carbon credit scheme. We have some issues with the deal on the resort. Evie's away at the moment so I just thought I'd grab them.'

Ruth nodded, trying to seem as relaxed and uncaring as Dash. He was talking about the resort as if a deal was about to be signed.

'I'm so sorry, Ruth,' he said. 'I know this looks bad, but I'd never hurt you.'

She picked up her phone and called triple zero.

A very nice and concerned woman said a police car was on its way. Then she patched Ruth through to Gazza, who had the bleary voice of a man who had just woken up. Not surprising. It was now close to two am.

'Constable Parker,' she said.

Troy lurked in the darkness of the hall. He shook his head.

Ruth nodded. She wasn't going to tell Gazza that Troy was there. Not after the interaction she'd seen on the main street weeks ago. Despite the fact that Troy had broken into her house as well.

'You've got someone tied up on the floor,' said Gazza.

'Dash Rogers.'

'Put him on,' said Parker.

'He can't hold the phone. I'll put him on speaker,' Ruth said.

'Mate,' said Dash, 'I feel pretty stupid.'

'What have you done, mate?'

'Couldn't sleep. Was looking for some documents of ours that Harry has. Didn't realise Ruth was at home. I've said sorry.

Gave her a bit of a fright. Feel like a dill.' Dash flashed his most charismatic smile. It was starting to annoy her.

Laboured breathing at the end of the phone until Gazza said, 'You broke in.'

'Yeah,' said Dash. 'Well, not really. A window was open.'

More gusty breathing.

'I'm coming over,' said Gazza. 'Be there in fifteen.'

Gazza arrived as promised.

He untied Dash's feet. 'I'll take a statement from you in the morning,' Gazza said to Ruth.

'Sure,' she said. She'd type it up herself. At least that way she'd have control over what it said.

'You can work out if you want to press charges.'

Ruth nodded. Gazza's view, clearly, was that pressing charges was a waste of time.

Still, she wanted to go to bed.

Just as he was leaving, Dash said, 'Sorry again, Ruth. Can't apologise enough.'

'How did you know I was going away?' Ruth asked.

'Small towns, eh?' said Dash. 'Everyone knows everyone's business. Thought I heard someone mention it. Can't remember where. Might have been the pub.'

Ruth said nothing. Closed the door. Locked it. Went into the kitchen.

'Glass of wine?' she yelled.

Troy re-emerged. 'Thanks,' he said and sat at the kitchen table. 'Sorry for scaring you like that,' Troy said.

Ruth stroked her wine glass. 'Thanks for looking out for me.'

Troy dropped his eyes, embarrassed. 'Yeah,' he said. 'Well . . .' His voice drifted off.

Ruth smiled at him, reached over and put her hand over his. 'I mean it,' she said.

The eighteen-year-old man-child clearly yearned for the moment to end. 'No worries,' he said. As soon as he decently could, he withdrew his hand to scratch his nose.

'Why would Deb tell Dash the file was at Harry's house?' Ruth said, thinking aloud.

Troy shrugged. 'She *is* his cousin,' Troy said, emphasising the 'is' because, in Troy's mind, everyone would know that.

Of course, thought Ruth. It's a small town. Everyone is related to everyone else. It wouldn't occur to Deb to tell Ruth that. It's so embedded in the consciousness of the local population, they assume universal knowledge.

There were lots of things Ruth wanted to ask Troy. But her eyes were heavy, and it was cold. She had an urgent need to be horizontal under the doona. She could ask him in the morning.

'Well, thanks anyway. There are plenty of beds here if you want to stay.' She showed him a bedroom and disappeared.

There were no noises after that, except the squawking of the flying foxes and the drip of the trees after rain.

In the morning, the bed was neat as a pin and Troy was gone.

WhatsApp

Ruth
Had a break-in last night

Jack
You all right?

Ruth
I'm fine

Jack
What happened?

Ruth
Dash Rogers looking for a file

Jack
Fucking weird

Ruth
Evie's file

Jack
What does it say?

Ruth
Don't know yet

Jack
Why was he at your house?

Ruth
Harry hid the file here somewhere

Jack
Is Dash in gaol?

Ruth
Doubt it. Gazza would have let him go.

Ruth's phone rang.

Jack, concerned. It was comforting to go through it with him. He sounded like a young Bill.

44

GAZZA

June, early Tuesday morning, six days before

'MATE, IF YOU'RE GOING TO DO A BREAK AND ENTER, WHY DO YOU HAVE to pick a fucking lawyer?'

'Yeah, sorry, mate. I thought she was away. And I know it's never locked. Whose house is in Myddle? She would never have known.'

'You scared the shit out of her,' said Gazza. 'We'll never hear the end of it. A woman and a lawyer. Worse combination you could think of. Fuck.'

'Yeah. Not great.'

'What were you looking for anyway?'

'Harry's got a file of Evie's. I just wanted to know what they were doing with it. Where it's up to. She's talking about giving a chunk of land to Troy Matheson.'

'Why would she do that?'

'Well, you know,' said Dash. 'She's got it into her head that Troy's her nephew.'

'Fuck,' said Gazza. 'Is he?'

As if it's not enough the black kids get all the free stuff, and pretty much immunity from prosecution. Well, not immunity exactly but its fucking difficult to take them in for questioning now. They get a friend and shit. And now this lucky bastard gets gifted the best land in town. Typical.

'Yeah,' said Dash. 'Her brother put a bun in Rita's oven before he got himself killed.'

'Fuck me,' said Gazza.

'Nope, don't think I'll do that. Tempting as the offer is.'

'Anyway,' Gazza said, 'probably best I don't take your statement. Sounds like it would be nothing but an admission. I'm going to leave it and hope the lawyer lady gets distracted by something else.'

'Thanks, mate.'

'Where's your car?'

'At Harry's. On the road.'

Gazza did a U-turn and dropped Dash at his ute. 'You stupid bastard.'

'Too right I am,' said Dash. 'Really appreciate it, mate. Why don't you come over to mine for State of Origin tomorrow night?'

'Yeah, mate. That'd be great. Thanks.'

45

BEA

June, Tuesday, six days before

DASH PICKED BEA UP FROM WORK THE NEXT DAY, AND DROVE HER OUT to the farm.

He undid his belt as soon as they got through the door.

After, he sat on the sofa in front of the TV.

'Is Evie okay?'

Bea wanted him to say she was fine and had realised that the marriage was over.

'Yeah. Much better. Much happier.' He smiled. Dash was a good smiler. His face opened up like he was inviting you to share his joy.

Dash feeling joy when he thought about Evie wasn't what Bea hoped for. Maybe she needed to remind him how bad it had been. 'Jeez it musta been rough for you. When she was home. Depressed.' She paused, wondering if she could download her own experience of people with mental problems to show that she understood. 'You know how I said my mum has a few issues?'

'Yeah.' Dash picked up his phone.

'Sometimes she's like a full-on nut job.'

'That's no good,' said Dash, eyes on his phone.

Bea ventured on. 'She makes me sleep outside sometimes.'

Dash looked up from his phone and smiled. 'What, like in a tent?'

'No. Like at the park.'

'Jeez,' said Dash. 'The whole night?'

'Just till her boyfriend leaves.'

She waited for him to ask who the boyfriend was, but he was looking at his phone again.

He looked up as if he'd just realised that she hadn't said anything for a while. 'That's not so bad then, I s'pose. Maybe she wants a bit of privacy.'

She wanted to impress on him how bad the situation with her mum was.

'She chucks tantrums all the time. At Christmas she chucked one at the chemist shop. Broke the makeup bar.'

Dash laughed. 'I bet Chris was pissed. What did you do to make her do that?'

'Nothing,' said Bea.

That was the trouble with telling people about her mum. They tried to explain it away; make it seem insignificant or Bea's fault. Or both.

'Jeez,' said Dash, reaching out to touch her leg. 'Sounds bad.' With his other hand, he put down his phone, picked up the remote and turned on the TV.

Dash's hand moved up her leg. Like he expected sex when he wasn't even listening to what she said.

She got up, to let him know she was a bit pissed off. She went into the kitchen. There was a computer in the corner. She sat at it and jiggled the mouse.

The screen lit up on Facebook: a picture of Dash with a fish.

The highlights of the footy were on the TV.

She tried swapping to Evie's page. It popped up easily.

A couple of DMs. *Hey Evie, call me.' 'Are you all right? I wish you'd answer your phone.*

That was weird. Why would Evie not answer her phone? She flicked out of it and opened Google so he wouldn't think she was spying on him.

She returned to the sitting room.

'Evie's all right, isn't she?' Bea asked.

'What?' said Dash.

'Evie. She's all right?'

'Yeah. What makes you think she isn't?'

'Just wondering,' said Bea.

'She bumped her head, but she's okay.' He took a slug of beer and continued to watch the footy. Bea was bored, and still upset that he hadn't engaged with her about her mum, and was paying more attention to the TV than he was to her.

'Can you take me home?'

'Could you take the ute? Come back in the morning?'

'I don't have my licence. Mum hasn't got round to doing the hours with me.'

'You can still drive, can't ya?'

'What if I get caught?' said Bea. 'Anyway, I'm pretty shit at driving. Only done it a few times.'

'I'll take ya when this is finished.' Dash's eyes were still on the footy. 'If you're heading to the kitchen, mind getting me another beer?'

Bea got his drink and handed it to him.

Dash grabbed her hand and pulled her down onto the sofa. 'You're so beautiful, Bea,' he said, as his hand moved to her boobs.

She smiled. Everything was okay after all.

46

RUTH

June, Tuesday, six days before

RUTH SLEPT IN, UNSURPRISINGLY. SHE DIDN'T FEEL UP TO A DRIVE TO Brisbane, and postponed the meeting. It was ten thirty by the time she left for the ten-minute commute to the office.

On the way, she composed sentences to deliver to Deb, about betrayal, breach of confidence and being a general fuckwit. It took the whole trip to come up with a script that didn't include any swear words.

When she arrived, Deb wasn't there.

Maybe Dash had warned her that Ruth would be very unhappy.

She sent Deb a text. *Are you coming in?*

No response.

Her phone rang. Harry.

'Mate,' said Ruth.

'Problem?' said Harry.

'Where have you been?'

'Sorry. Out of range a lot here. We're in the Kimberley. What's the problem?'

Where to start?

Ruth recounted the events of the previous night.

Harry listened in silence, his breathing heavy. 'Oh, that's awful,' he said. 'I'm sorry. I have my reservations about Dash but I didn't think he'd do that.'

'Deb told him I was in Brisbane for the night. Did you know Dash and Deb are cousins?'

'Yeah,' he said. 'That's why I have Evie's file at home.'

'So Evie wouldn't want Dash to see it?'

'I talked with Evie about what happens to properties in the event of divorce. Best to keep it away from him.'

Evie was thinking about a divorce. Not a complete surprise.

Ruth told him about Evie's request for subdivision.

'Wonder why she wants to do that?' said Harry.

'To keep her options open, she told me. I wonder if she's decided to go ahead with the resort.'

'Huh. Maybe. We subdivided Roscoe's land from the farm. It's a bit of a rigmarole. And it will take a while.'

'Where did you put her file exactly?'

'Same place Marge stores the photos.'

Of course. The big chest in the sitting room that doubled as a coffee table.

'Back to the cousin thing,' Ruth said. 'I can't work with Deb. Telling Dash I wasn't home so he could break in was pretty bad, but she's also lazy. If it was up to me, I'd sack her.'

Harry stalled before answering that, deep breathing down the phone.

Eventually, he said, 'If I try to sack her, she'll fight it. She's been on the phone to me complaining about you.'

What the fuck. Ruth counted to five, so that her response could be calm with a touch of irony. 'Ah, the pre-emptive strike by the disgruntled employee. She has the technique honed.'

'Deb's an acquired taste,' said Harry. 'Bit of an expert in passive aggression.'

'Why do you keep her on?'

'Bit hard to sack her in Myddle,' said Harry. 'She knows everyone. And she's not as bad to me as she is to you.'

He paused. Ruth didn't say anything.

'Look, she's part of the furniture and I can't bring myself to do it.'

'I'm sorry that I'm punting that particular problem back to you, Harry.'

'Thanks,' said Harry. 'I'll talk to her.'

Ruth rang Charlie. Tried to sound casual. 'Had a break-in last night.'

'What? While you were there?'

'It was one am. I was in bed.'

'Who was it?'

'Dash.'

'What was he doing?'

'He thought I was in Brisbane. He was looking for Evie's file.'

Pause.

'I'll come to stay for a few days,' said Charlie.

'Really, there's no need. I'll be okay.'

He clacked at his keyboard. 'There's a flight that gets into Broughton at six pm. Can you pick me up?'

'Don't you have work to do?'

'I'm writing papers. I can do it from anywhere.'

She felt a little teary. Someone cared for her safety enough to drop everything to come to her.

'Thanks,' she said.

Ruth pressed the red dot on her phone, put it on the desk and stared at it. She had to tell Evie what had happened, but she wasn't sure what to say or how to communicate with her. She couldn't put '*Your husband broke into my house looking for your file*' in a text message, or an email. She'd have to do it in a conversation.

She rang. Evie's phone was turned off. Ruth left a message: 'Can you call me,' she said. 'Not urgent.' Because it wasn't, was it? She didn't want to add to the list of troubles Evie was working through.

Last, she rang Roscoe.

'Do you need to come and stay with us?' asked Roscoe.

'I'm all right. Anyway, Charlie is coming on his white horse to save me.'

'Pleased to hear that.'

'I owe you a few meals. Why don't you and Chandra come over for dinner tomorrow night? I'll ask Patch and Shane and the Wildlings. Nothing fancy.'

Ruth hauled open Harry's big sea chest in the sitting room. Under some framed photos, magazines and a pile of electricity and phone bills were six fat manila folders, each tied up with a pink cloth ribbon.

She piled them up on the dining room table, got herself a pot of tea, reached for the most recent file and dove in.

Evie's only discussion in the months before Harry left was concerned with one subject: divorce.

Harry had told her that Dash was entitled to a big chunk of the farm. She was worried what he would do with it; that he's not interested in farming and might want to develop some sort of tourist venture—expand the campsite.

Dash will want the Bluff, said Harry's diary note. *Evie says over her dead body. I told her if they can't resolve it, a court will decide. She needs a good alternative—money or a different parcel of land—and a convincing argument.*

She suggested land adjacent to Roscoe's.

Then Harry's note said, *I told her that these days it's no-fault divorce so Dash's infidelity will be irrelevant.*

None of this explained why Evie wanted to subdivide. To sell the property so Dash couldn't have it? If so, that was next-level spite.

Or maybe the death of Horace was existential and she'd decided to go ahead with the eco-health resort.

Ruth got to the tortuously complicated procedure to get the approval to subdivide the land Evie sold to Roscoe. It was going to take months of consultants' reports and government departments. One thing was for sure: whatever Evie had in mind was no quick fix.

47

RUTH

June, Wednesday, five days before

DEB WAS ALREADY AT HER DESK WHEN RUTH GOT IN ON WEDNESDAY morning.

She gave Ruth a grunt and a grimace. 'Sorry,' said Deb, 'about telling Dash to go to Harry's. I didn't think about the consequences.'

'What happens in this office is confidential, Deb. You can't tell anyone about it, not even your cousin.'

'Sorry,' Deb repeated.

At least it was an apology.

Ruth said, 'Sure.'

Relations with Deb during the day were cordial. They had reached détente. That was good enough, Ruth supposed, to tide her over until Harry returned and she'd never have to speak to Deb again.

Chandra handed over a couple of bottles of homemade kombucha as she and Roscoe walked through the door.

'Patch and Shane not here?' she asked.

'They had something on,' said Ruth.

'They'll be watching the football,' said Roscoe.

The State of Origin rugby league game: a match between Queensland and New South Wales. The utes of Myddle had been driving around all day with blue flags fluttering from the windows.

Ruth accepted a glass from Charlie who had poured the drinks. 'Glad we're missing that.'

'You all right after the break-in?' said Roscoe.

'I'm fine,' said Ruth. 'Bit weirded out by seeing Dash in my bedroom at one am, but no harm done.'

'I'm glad you're here, Charlie,' said Roscoe. 'To look after the old bird.'

'Don't call me an old bird.'

'Wouldn't want to leave the old duck on her own,' said Charlie.

'Hilarious,' said Ruth.

'We're all just fourteen-year-olds in pensioners' bodies,' said Charlie.

They shared a collective chuckle.

'Dash was never going to hurt me,' said Ruth. 'He was as surprised as I was when he saw I was there.'

'Very strange. What was he looking for?' said Chandra.

'Evie's file, I think.'

'What's in it?' said Chandra.

'She can't say, darling,' said Roscoe. 'Confidential.'

Chandra sighed.

'Did you know that Deb is Dash's cousin?' Ruth asked Roscoe.

He shook his head in genuine surprise. 'Everyone in this town is related to everyone else and nobody bothers to tell you.'

'It's a nightmare managing conflicts in a legal practice,' said Ruth.

'Harry's all over it, I'm sure,' said Roscoe.

Ruth harrumphed in agreement.

Chandra's phone buzzed. She peered at it, picked it up and went into another room.

She was away for half an hour, during which Roscoe and Charlie engaged in an escalating competition in exotic and obscure places they'd visited: Charlie, a vanilla and cacao plantation in Belize that belonged to a mate of his; Roscoe, Tibet in his quest for spiritual enlightenment.

Chandra returned to the table frowning.

'Everything all right, darling?' said Roscoe.

'Yes, yes. Fine.' She was distracted after that. Kept checking her phone.

Finally, she gathered up Roscoe and they left.

'Wonder what that was about,' said Charlie.

'Maybe one of her flock is in trouble.'

'Mind if I watch the game?' Charlie asked after they had cleaned up the kitchen.

'Of course not,' said Ruth. 'I'm off to bed with a book.'

Nice of him to be with her in Myddle entertaining her friends, when he just wanted to sit in front of the telly with a beer. She kissed the hollow in his cheek. 'Thanks for coming,' she said.

Without moving his eyes from the screen, he rubbed her shoulder and kissed her nose.

WhatsApp

Jack
You all right, Ruthie?

Ruth
Yes.
Charlie is here.

Jack
Right

Ruth
I'm telling you because you need to know. That you know . . .

Jack
[online]
Good that someone is there

Ruth
I would have been fine. But it's nice to have him.

Jack
Any developments in the great home invasion?

Ruth
I've delivered a statement to Gazza. He couldn't
have been less interested, even though I saved
him a few hours work by doing it for him.

Jack
You took it out of his control. He wouldn't like that.

Ruth
I told him I wouldn't press charges.
He was pleased about that.

Jack
Is that a good idea?

Ruth
I don't know

48

BEA

June, Wednesday night, five days before

ON WEDNESDAY, DASH PICKED BEA UP FROM WORK AGAIN. SHE'D brought something to change into this time: her lucky T-shirt—the Rolling Stones lips.

It was the same routine as Tuesday night. Get through the front door. Jeans down. Jeans up.

Then Dash grabbed a beer and turned on the TV. The footy was about to start. State of Origin. She'd forgotten that it was on tonight. He wouldn't drive her home until it was over, and by then he'd be drunk.

How would she get home?

A car pulled up outside. She looked out the window. 'It's a police car,' she said.

'That'll just be Gazza. He'll want a beer.'

Bea alone with Dash and Gazza. A lump of foreboding formed in Bea's throat. What would her mum say if she found out?

'What's he here for?'

'He's just over to watch the footy with me.'

Gazza walked through the door without knocking, and walked straight into the lounge room.

'G'day, mate,' said Dash. 'Do you know Bea?'

'How are ya, love?' said Gazza. His face and chin were exploding over his footy jersey like a boil about to burst.

Bea went into the kitchen. Opened the fridge. It was stocked with beer. Not much food. A block of cheddar. Bit of mould on it but she could cut that off. There was a packet of Jatz in the pantry. And a lot of two-minute noodles.

A box of party pies in the freezer.

'Mind getting us a couple of beers while you're there?' Dash yelled from the other room.

There were a couple of different types of beer, and Gazza was going to drive home so he might only want a light. She walked down the hall back to the lounge room to ask him. Just before she reached the open door she heard Gazza say, 'What's that all about then, mate?'

And Dash said, 'Mate, what can I say? She gives great head.'

Gazza laughed. 'Lucky bastard. Wouldn't mind a bit of that meself.'

'I'll see what I can do. She's pretty obliging.'

'Swallows?' said Gazza.

'Sure does.'

Gazza cackled.

Bea felt sick.

It was night, it was cold, they were fifteen k out of town, and Dash had driven her there. There was no way she could get back. Unless she walked.

She went back to the kitchen, spread her hands out to lean on the kitchen bench and tried to think through her options. Tried to be calm.

Dash yelled, 'Where're those beers?'

'Just putting together a snack,' she said.

'Good, love. Bring us the beers first, eh.'

She opened the fridge. It would be best if Gazza was drunk. Best if they were both drunk. Legless. She opened two stubbies, poured a bit out of each, found some vodka in the pantry and poured some into each of them. Took them in.

'Thanks, love,' said Dash. 'Hey, come here.' He patted the space on the couch between him and Gazza.

Gazza leered at her, right at her chest. His gut had escaped from his footy jersey and was rolling over the top of his track pants. She could see black hairs amid a great curve of pasty white.

'Yeah, come here and sit with us,' he said.

'I'll just finish getting some cheese and bickies together.'

'Righto, love,' said Dash.

As she disappeared down the hall Gazza yelled, 'Don't be long. We're missing you.' And they both sniggered.

'I'm just putting some of those party pies in the oven,' she yelled. 'Where's the sauce?' She opened and shut the oven door.

How was she going to get away? She'd have to walk. Then she remembered. She'd seen some mountain bikes hanging from hooks in the shed.

Dash came into the kitchen. 'Whatcha doin'?'

'I told you. Making some food.'

She was worried he'd ask where it was. But he was more interested in getting her back to the lounge room. 'C'mon. Leave that. Gazza wants to talk to you.'

He took her by the hand and dragged her down the hall.

In the sitting room Gazza had his dacks off already. 'Suck on that would you, love,' said Dash, pushing her onto the couch beside his mate.

She froze. If she was completely still, maybe they'd realise she wanted no part of it.

'C'mon. Do it for Gazza,' he said and pushed her head down into Gazza's crotch.

'No,' she said. 'Please.'

'Won't take a moment. You know how to do it. Just do that thing with your tongue. Be over in a sec. Look at him. He's nearly off just thinking about it.'

Dash and Gazza both laughed.

If she did it, they might leave her alone.

While she was down there, Dash pawed at her, taking off her jeans.

'What are you doing?' she asked.

'You keep doing what you're doing, love,' said Gazza. 'Don't stop.' He pushed her head back down. He groaned, then laughed as Dash got her jeans over her feet. She could hear Dash unzipping his fly. Gazza laughed again. 'What's it called, mate? A spit roast?'

'Always wanted to do it,' said Dash.

She was crying now. She tried to lift her head but a hand, Gazza's, was holding it down. 'C'mon, half-time will be over soon,' said Dash.

Gazza's groans built to a crescendo. 'Maaaate, maaaaate,' he yelled.

She went limp, wanting it to be over. She tried to empty her mind.

When he was finished, Dash said, 'That was great, love. Wanna do it again after full-time?' he added. The question wasn't directed at her.

'Swap places,' said Gazza.

Gazza's stuff was on her face, and in her hair. She ran into the toilet and leaned over the bowl. Gagged.

The State of Origin was loud in the living room. The Maroons scored a try. Gazza and Dash shouted at the TV that it was a joke.

She had to get out of there. Who would help her?

Not her mum, obviously. She would only make it worse. Whatever she did would involve shouting and blame, most likely directed at Bea.

She tried Troy. No answer. He was probably watching the game.

Who then?

She couldn't call the cops obviously. The only one in town was in the lounge room watching the footy.

Chandra lived a few k down the road.

Bea pulled out her phone. She pressed the green phone button to ring Chandra's number. It rang and rang, until finally Chandra answered, 'Bea?'

Bea couldn't speak. She tried to but the words wouldn't come out. Just sobs.

'Just breathe, Bea. With me. In for one, two, three. Out for—' And she counted to six. Slow. That deep voice.

They did that for a while. Probably only a minute or two, but Bea felt a bit better.

'What's happened, Bea?'

'Dash and Gazza.' She choked on the words.

'Where are you?'

'At Dash's house.'

'Did they rape you, Bea?'

Was that what it was? She wasn't sure. It had happened so quickly. And rape was such a big word. But what else could it be?

'I think so. It must have been.'

Chandra didn't say anything for a while, but just having her on the other end of the phone helped.

'Did you say they could have sex with you?'

'No.' The word came out with a sob.

'Did they ask you?'

Did they? She couldn't remember.

'Did you say no at all?'

'Yes. I think so.' It felt like she did. Her whole body was screaming no. Did she say it? She couldn't remember.

'Did you keep saying no?'

'I couldn't.'

'Why not?'

'My mouth. Gazza.'

Chandra groaned. 'Where was Dash?'

'He was at my other end.'

'At the same time?'

'Yes.' A picture jumped into her mind. The helplessness.

'Bea, I'm sorry, darling. I'm not home so I can't pick you up. But I'm going to ring Troy and ask him if he can. It will take half an hour. Can you get away to the front gate? What's his number?'

'I think I can get to the farm gate,' said Bea.

'And there's something I want you to try to do first. It will be hard, but if you do it now, it leaves your options open.'

49

RUTH

June, Monday afternoon

RUTH HUNG UP FROM ROSCOE, PROCESSING THE SHOCKING NEWS THAT Dash was dead. She put her phone in her backpack and closed down her computer.

She needed to talk to Victoria about her lack of success trying to get Gazza to look for Bea, then pick up Charlie to go to dinner at Roscoe's.

But first, she had to break the sad news to Deb, that her cousin had died.

She walked past Troy on the way to reception. He was chewing on a pencil as he frowned at his computer screen.

'Everything all right?' Ruth asked.

He looked up and smiled. 'Just working out what an easement is.'

'A reason for neighbours to fight,' said Ruth. 'Usually about garbage bins.'

'Thanks. So helpful.' Troy turned back to his screen.

There was no evidence of anxiety. He'd obviously not heard about Dash, and she'd just told him Bea was missing and he wasn't giving it another thought.

She stuck her nose out to reception. Deb wasn't at her desk. 'Deb not here?' she said to Troy.

'Nah, she got a phone call and ran out.'

'Troy, you ought to know—Dash Rogers has been killed.'

His mouth dropped open in shock.

'Looks like he was shot.'

Disbelief on Troy's face. 'Who did it?'

'Don't know.'

His fingers reached for his phone beside his keyboard.

'What about Evie? Is she okay?'

'She's been away. No one's heard from her. They're looking for her.'

He picked up the phone and then his keys. 'I'd better tell Mum.'

She watched him go, then left herself, locking the office door behind her.

Victoria lived a couple of blocks back from the main street.

A dry cold westerly blew Ruth's hair to shards. She longed to be inside, but approached Victoria's front gate with trepidation. The house was encased by a verandah which had been fibroed and louvred in. In its heyday, a century ago, the house would have been grand, but the palm trees sagged under dead fronds and the garden was laden with weeds. Ruth waded through the short, overgrown path from sagging front gate to peeling front door.

Victoria answered the door by opening it an inch and peering through the crack. A dog barked behind her. She was a tiny woman, her face set in a scowl of combative defence.

'Hi, Victoria. It's me, Ruth. The solicitor.'

The door opened a little wider. 'The house is in a terrible mess,' said Victoria. The muscles in her throat were so constricted with stress that her voice was a squeak.

'I'm not here to inspect your house,' said Ruth without thinking. It was supposed to be a little joke but it came out all wrong. A blue cattle dog, straining to be released from Victoria's grip on his collar, barked at her.

'I'll just close the door so I can let him go,' Victoria said. 'The neighbours don't like it when he barks.'

That seemed to be an invitation to enter the house. Would the mad woman's lair be full of hoarded rubbish?

Ruth was surprised to discover it was actually more like an antique shop, cluttered with rugs and cedar furniture, tapestry cushions of Victorian flowers, chintz sofas with down cushions, and every horizontal surface piled with books.

The chair covers were worn, the outline of the springs showing: Miss Havisham without the cobwebs. It would have been faintly oppressive except that the northern sun streamed in, warming the room, and the closed louvres were protecting them from the wind.

The dog enjoyed its freedom by nudging Ruth's hand for a pat, before wandering off and, with a sigh, stretching out in the dappled light.

Victoria stood beside Ruth, shifting from foot to foot as if seeing her sitting room for the first time. 'Can I get you a cup of tea? Where would you like to sit? I'll just move these things.'

She lifted a pile of books from a chair and looked around the room before depositing them on the floor.

Not a lot of visitors, Ruth guessed.

When Victoria left to go into the kitchen, Ruth examined the books. They all seemed to be biographies of members of the European royal families.

Ruth flicked through one, a tome about Princess Diana, featuring a lot of lovely frocks, and a tale of a disastrous marriage. She'd skimmed through most of it when Victoria returned with a pot of tea, matching cups and saucers that were Royal Crown Derby circa 1920, pink roses, silver teaspoons.

'Lovely,' said Ruth. 'Thank you.'

Victoria's right index finger was wearing a hole in her left palm.

Time to dive in.

'I spoke with Constable Parker,' Ruth said. 'About Bea.'

Victoria looked up quickly. Her eyes focused on something to the left of Ruth's ear.

'You're right,' said Ruth. 'He's not going to do anything.'

The dog sighed and shuffled into a more comfortable position.

'I'm sorry,' Ruth said. 'This must be very distressing.'

Victoria closed her eyes. Her lips thinned as she bit them from within. She inhaled. Her mouth opened and out came her constricted voice. 'He's not a nice man, Constable Parker.' The pitch of her voice rose into grievance and anger, driven by a kind of powerlessness, as if the only weapon she had against a hostile world was unbridled rage.

'What makes you say that?' said Ruth.

'He's hiding something.'

'What would he be hiding?'

'I don't know. Bea met a man the afternoon she went missing.'

'Who?'

'I saw a text. On her phone.'

The westerly gusted, making the palm fronds squeal across the roof.

'What did it say?'

'*Meet me after work*. Sort of demanding. Threatening.'

How could words in an isolated text have emotion attached to them? 'What made you think there was a threat?'

Victoria didn't answer. The muscles in her cheeks moved as she ground her teeth.

Ruth threw suggestions at her. 'Was there an emoji? Or capital letters or something? Did you see any other texts from him?'

'No,' said Victoria. 'I don't have her password. I don't spy on my daughter.' This was said with self-righteous anger; a response to an accusation Ruth hadn't made.

'Could you see who the text was from?' Ruth asked.

'There was no name. The contact said *Him*.'

'Who do you think it was?'

'I don't know. She was seeing a bad crowd.'

'Who?'

'A group of Aboriginals,' Victoria said, her mouth curling as if she'd inserted a quarter of a lemon in her mouth.

Ruth froze, her cup suspended in mid-air. There was a lot of hate in this woman. It oozed out of her. 'I think you mean the young Koori people. Any in particular?' she said.

'A boy called Troy.'

Ruth made herself count to ten. Don't react, she told herself. Change the subject.

She said what she'd come to say. 'I've had a look at your options. You can file a missing persons report yourself online. But maybe you should drive over to Broughton and talk to the police there. Tell them what you told me.'

'I'll try that. Thank you,' said Victoria.

Ruth stood to go. 'You heard about Dash Rogers?' she said.

'No?' said Victoria.

'He's dead.'

Another gust of wind, another drawn-out squeak on the corrugated-iron roof.

'How?' Victoria asked.

'Looks like he was shot.'

Victoria's eyes widened and fixed on Ruth's while she stroked the side of her teacup.

'A rifle?'

'Apparently,' said Ruth.

'Where did it happen?'

'On the road near the entrance to Dash and Evie's property.'

Victoria put her teacup down on its saucer. 'That's sad,' she said. The word came out as 'sed', spoken from high up in her nose. She was so tight with stress, her voice had no cavity in which to reverberate. 'Bea talked about them all the time. Liked riding the horses. She'll be upset when she hears.'

The dog grunted, sighed and rolled over.

Victoria looked up. 'Who did it?'

'Don't know,' said Ruth. 'I'm so sorry, Victoria, about all this. I hope you find Bea soon and the police over at Broughton can help. If you think I can do anything, give me a call. Let me know how you go?'

She couldn't bring herself to offer to drive Victoria to the police station in Broughton. Was that bad? She just couldn't listen to her accuse Troy.

She was incensed on Troy's behalf, but full of foreboding. Victoria was determined to put him in the firing line for Bea's disappearance. Should she warn him? Or would it only succeed in making him feel like shit? No wonder Troy had smoke-bombed when Victoria had turned up at the office.

But Victoria was right. Bea and Troy were friends. And he seemed unconcerned by his friend's disappearance.

'Hello, darling,' Ruth said, kissing Roscoe in the gaunt hollow of his cheek.

Roscoe pushed a glass of wine into Ruth's hand.

'Beer?' Roscoe asked Charlie.

Charlie held his six pack of beer aloft. 'Mind if I put these in the fridge?'

Roscoe picked up a glass half full of chardonnay. 'You drinking?' Ruth asked him, finding it hard to conceal her surprise.

'I can't unsee what I saw today,' said Roscoe. 'Hoping this will help.'

Chandra wafted out. 'Hello, Ruth. Hello, Charlie,' she said. 'Come on, let's sit on the deck.'

Even she had a glass of wine. This had clearly rocked both of them.

'Bad?' Ruth said to Roscoe.

Roscoe shook his head. 'He'd been there awhile. In the sun. I smelt him before I saw him.'

'You said he'd been shot in the shoulder?'

'I think he must have bled out. Looked like he'd been hit by something huge and hard. Maybe a ute.'

'A ute with a ding in it. That'll be hard to find in this town.' Ruth rolled her eyes.

Chandra nodded. 'True.'

'Might not even have a ding, if they hit him with the roo bar,' said Charlie.

They sat in silence, each sipping on the wine. What a horrible way to die: bleeding out alone on the side of a road.

'Has anyone spoken to Evie?' Ruth asked.

'Patch is trying to contact her,' said Roscoe.

'Evie still hasn't rung me back since Dash broke into my house,' said Ruth. 'I hope she's all right.'

Roscoe rose and went inside to pour himself another glass of wine.

'You know that girl Bea?' said Ruth when he returned. 'Works at the chemist?'

'She's been coming to Chandra's yoga meetings. Hasn't she, darling?'

Chandra nodded.

'Her mother says she's missing.'

Roscoe jerked his head up. 'How long?'

'Last saw her five days ago.'

'The mother came to me as well,' Chandra said, 'asking if I'd seen her.'

'Terrible,' said Roscoe. He put the wine bottle down on the coffee table. 'Surely they couldn't be connected. Bea missing and Dash's death?'

Ruth shrugged. 'Gazza thinks Bea would have run off because her mother is a bit'—Ruth waved her hands about to help find the right word—'weird.'

'She's not very nice to Bea,' said Chandra. 'It would make sense.'

'Huh,' said Roscoe. 'You know she's Gary Baulderstone's daughter.'

'The judge?' Ruth said. 'Ballsy?' He was a blustery county court judge known for his bombastic pomposity, and his firm views on the appropriate ways to deal with people he described as dole bludgers and rent seekers. He had regularly made the newspapers for the sound bites he delivered from the safety of the bench, until he retired amid a swirl of controversy about his racist sentencing remarks in a car theft case and some judgments that had been outstanding for two years.

It did explain Victoria's accent. Ballsy was born with a silver spoon wedged in his palate.

'What's she doing in Myddle?'

'Don't know,' said Roscoe. 'Maybe she's hiding from her father.'

They slumped in their deep cane chairs.

The river seemed calm but, when you looked hard, it was full of movement. The pink light of sunset played with the ink blue of evening; eddies and ripples, forming and dispersing.

'Gazza was pretty upset at the scene. He wasn't thinking straight. Picked up the gun when he found it in the grass and had a look at it. He would have put his fingerprints all over it. He had to call in homicide from Broughton, and leave the body where it was. It was pretty grim. The crows had got to him.'

The last vestiges of light were fading. Curlews wailed out the last of the day.

Roscoe stood. 'I think the pumpkin is ready.'

'Satisfaction', Ruth's ringtone.

She picked it up.

Evie.

50

RUTH

June, Monday night

'HELLO, RUTH,' EVIE SAID, HER VOICE SOFT AND WAN.

'Evie, you poor darling. I'm so sorry about Dash. Are you okay?'

'I'm at home with the police now. Actually, could you come over?'

'Of course.'

The entrance to Evie and Dash's farm was lit like a night-time footy match.

A uniformed policeman stopped Ruth on the road before she got to the turn-off.

'I'm Evie Rogers' lawyer,' she said.

'You'll have to leave your car here and climb through the fence. We'll drive you to the house in a police vehicle.'

A big stretch of road, the gate and the cattle grid were taped off as a crime scene. Three people in white plastic moon suits were crouched on their haunches examining the ground and the grid.

A young constable escorted Ruth into the house.

The kitchen was a mess: empty beer bottles, pizza boxes, dirty plates.

Evie was sitting at the dining room table with Sharon Messer.

'Ms Dawson,' said Sharon.

'Detective Messer,' said Ruth. 'Homicide squad been called in?'

Sharon nodded.

'That was quick.'

'You know each other?' said Evie.

'We met on a case a year or two ago,' said Ruth. She put her hand on Evie's shoulder. 'You okay?'

Evie nodded, her hair lank, great dark shadows under her eyes. She looked like she hadn't slept for a week.

'I'm going to have a chat with my client,' Ruth told Messer, and without waiting for a response, led Evie down the hall. Forensics were even in the main bedroom. Ruth led Evie into a spare room and they sat side by side on the bed.

'You poor thing,' she said. 'How did you find out?'

'I heard on the news that a body had been discovered in Myddle. Turned on my phone and saw all the messages. I rang Patch to find out who it was.'

'When did you speak to Patch?'

'About an hour ago. I only just got here.'

'So you weren't far away?'

'Azuri. Only forty minutes.'

'The police want to ask you some questions?'

Evie nodded.

'You don't have to speak to them.'

'Won't that make me look bad?'

'You'll look a whole lot worse if you tell them something now that is different to what you tell them in a week.'

Evie ran her long fingers over the patchwork quilt. 'I can't think straight anyway.'

'I'm going to tell the police you're tired,' said Ruth. 'You need to sleep. We'll reconsider our position in the next few days. You can't stay here. There's that spare bed at Harry's if you want to come with me.'

Evie shook her head. 'Patch asked me to stay with her. I think she'd be offended if I didn't.'

'Okay,' said Ruth. 'Where's your car?'

Ruth was keen for Evie to drive that car to Patch's. Get it out of the way of the police.

'On the road,' said Evie. 'Near the grid at the front gate.'

Bugger. The police would already have taken photographs of its every ding and scratch.

Ruth went to the dining room to chat with Sharon Messer.

'Just one thing, Evie,' said Ruth when she returned. 'Detective Messer wants to know if that's your backpack?'

Messer was holding aloft an emerald green backpack, worn and grubby on the corners.

'Not mine,' said Evie.

Sharon emptied it out and sifted through the contents: a camera, a couple of pens, some random bits of tatty paper, tampons, and a small wallet. She opened it up and held up a driver's licence, a learner's. 'Beatrice Baulderstone.'

Oh no. Bea was tied up in Dash's death. 'Her mother thinks she's been missing since last Wednesday. She tried to report it yesterday to Constable Parker but he wasn't interested.'

Messer frowned.

'Any idea why her backpack would be in your living room?' Sharon asked Evie.

Evie shook her head. 'None.'

'Come on, Evie,' Ruth said. 'Let's go. Detective Messer, can we have a lift to the road?'

⸻

WhatsApp

Jack
Update?

Ruth
Evie's back

Jack
That's good. Where was she?

Ruth
Azuri

Jack
Isn't that only 40 mins away?

Ruth
Yes

Jack
[online]

Ruth
Bea's backpack was in Dash's sitting room

Jack
?

Ruth
😱 And Bea's mum is pointing the finger at Troy

Jack
How?

Ruth

She saw a text from a man Bea was seeing that Wednesday night saying he'd meet her after work. She thinks it might have been Troy.

Jack

What a clusterfuck

51

RUTH

June, Tuesday, the day after

RUTH PARKED IN HER SPOT BEHIND THE OFFICE AND PICKED UP A takeaway coffee from the local caff. On the main street she saw that Gazza Parker had ensnared Troy ten metres from the office door.

Ruth strode up.

'Everything all right?' she said. The question was addressed to Troy, who leaned against a post, studying his feet.

Gazza stood close to Troy, almost on top of him, making six-foot, wiry Troy look almost puny.

'I'm just asking him a few questions,' said Gazza.

'About?'

'Do you want her here?' said Gazza to Troy. 'To hear this?'

Troy shrugged.

'You want her to know what you've been up to?'

Troy remained impassive.

After a beat, Gazza turned his face, but not his body, to Ruth. 'I'm just asking young Troy here about his relationship with Bea Baulderstone.' He turned back to Troy. 'Aren't I?'

Troy examined his feet scuffing the footpath.

'Suggestions have been made that you were one of the last people to see her before she disappeared.'

Troy's head jerked up. He looked Gazza in the eye for a moment longer than a truly submissive person would. Then he slowly moved his chin down to resume his study of the concrete.

'I'm onto you,' said Gazza. 'You watch it. And make sure you don't stray far from town. Because if you do I'll be onto you before you can say Jacky Jacky.'

Urgh. Another racist slur.

Ruth touched Troy's forearm. 'Troy,' she said, 'I need you in the office. Got some urgent work to do.'

Troy kept his head down. She felt the electricity in him, the anger.

He moved his arm to repel her touch. She wasn't his mother, and she wasn't his protector.

Gazza swaggered off, jumped into his white police LandCruiser and roared down the street. The interview had attracted some attention. People whispered to one another and studied Troy. If Gazza's intention had been to alienate Troy from the Myddle community, to openly accuse him, it had worked.

Was this how it rolled in Myddle? The copper picking on a local Aboriginal kid and making a public display of pinning an unsolved mystery on him? Or did Gazza have some evidence? Also, Gazza now seemed interested in Bea's disappearance. He'd said nothing about Dash.

'Coming back to the office, Troy?' Ruth asked.

'Nah, not at the moment,' he said quietly.

Ruth drove over to Patch's to talk to Evie. The wooden farmhouse was surrounded by a lush garden: dripping ferns; bright pink impatiens. Roscoe was there, too. 'I'm the babysitter,' he said. Patch was at work.

'Roof!' Milly yelled and cocked her elbows so that she could be picked up for a cuddle. Ruth obliged and inhaled the sweet smell of a recent bubble bath. Ruth set her down and she trotted off.

Ruth had never registered how thin Evie was before. Her collarbone was prominent and very white. 'How are you feeling?' said Ruth as she sat down at Patch's dining room table, in the middle of a room filled with the detritus that comes with small children: toys, a washing basket of clean clothes waiting to be folded, cereal bowls draining on the sink.

'Not great.'

Outside, Milly squealed and Roscoe chuckled.

'So, as I said last night,' said Ruth, 'you don't have to talk to the police. You don't have to tell them anything. We can use the interview to work out the direction they're taking the investigation.'

Evie fiddled with a placemat which had been left on the table.

'So you have your alibi,' Ruth said. 'They know that already. Is there anything you need to run by me?'

'Nope,' said Evie. 'I've been thinking about it. I can't tell them anything. I was in Azuri for a week before . . .'

'They'll ask about your marriage,' said Ruth. 'It could get very personal.'

Evie traced her fingers around the edge of the placemat.

'I can't tell them about your wish to subdivide off the Bluff. They can't ask me questions about you because I'm your lawyer,' said Ruth. 'But if they find out that's what you intended, they might fix on it.'

Evie nodded but didn't volunteer any information.

'Any idea how Bea's backpack got in your house?' Ruth said. 'The police will ask.'

Evie shook her head. 'No idea.'

Another squeal from outside. Evie got up and went to the window. 'Milly, what are you doing?'

From outside Roscoe said, 'It's all right, we're playing a game.'

Evie sat back at the table. 'Kids are a lot of work, aren't they?'

'Sure are,' said Ruth. 'I don't know how Patch and Shane wrangle four of them.'

Evie said nothing.

Ruth tried again. 'Looks like Bea visited Dash then?'

'I don't know what he did when I was away,' said Evie. 'Troy brought Bea over a few times to ride the horses. So maybe she left the backpack there then.'

Ruth decided to leave that line of questioning.

'The police are going to ask you what you were doing on Sunday.'

'Had a swim in the morning. Read. Had a snooze.'

'Anyone see you?'

Evie put her head on one side. 'I'm pretty sure I went to Coles on Sunday afternoon.'

Out the window, Roscoe was flapping his arms like a bird and Milly was squealing in delight.

Evie clacked the placemat against the table.

'There is something you should know,' she said. 'I spent the Sunday night before last in hospital because I hit my head at the Bluff when I was with Dash. I slipped in the rain. I'm fine. They kept me in for observation. I went from there to Azuri.'

Alarm coursed through Ruth. 'Dash didn't hit you, did he?' It slipped out before she could temper it for tone.

Evie greeted the suggestion without emotion.

'No,' she said. 'Dash didn't touch me.'

Ruth longed for a diversion from the next subject she had to address.

'I'm sorry to ask this,' said Ruth, 'but I think the police will ask you, and it's best you're prepared for it. Was Dash sleeping with Bea?'

A guttural song sounded from the roof; a kookaburra warming its throat as a precursor for the resonant laugh.

'Kookaburra,' yelled Milly outside.

'I don't know,' said Evie. 'Dash and I promised to look after one another. And we did. But he felt like he was entitled to more. He thought he was special.' Evie turned her head to look Ruth in the eye. 'So to answer your question, it's possible that Dash was sleeping with Bea. Very possible. But I don't know.'

By the time Ruth drove back to the office, it was three pm.

'Troy not been back?' she said to Deb.

'Nup.'

'Just going out again,' said Ruth.

She pulled up at the house on stilts. It was a little square of worn weatherboards, paint peeling off, louvred-in verandahs, long steps down to a yard lush with bougainvillea.

'Just mopping the floors,' Rita said. 'Then I've got to get to work.'

The orange spines of Penguin classics lined the walls of the verandah under the louvres. A child had set up a wooden train track which wound beneath the cane chairs.

'I'm a bit worried about Troy,' Ruth said.

Rita moved the mop back and forth.

Ruth pressed on. 'He didn't come in the office this morning. I saw him speaking with the local constable, but I haven't seen him since.'

'He's gone away.'

'Do you know when he'll be back?'

Rita dumped the mop in the bucket and pressed the pedal to squeeze it out. 'He'll be back when he's ready,' she said.

'Is Constable Parker harassing him?'

'Probably,' said Rita. 'That's the way it works.'

'Parker wants to speak to Troy,' Ruth said. 'About Bea Baulderstone.'

'It could be about anything,' said Rita. 'It could be about what he's wearing. His vocabulary.'

After seeing Gazza's encounter with Troy and his friend when she first arrived in town, Ruth didn't doubt it.

'He has an impressive vocabulary,' said Ruth, searching for some warmth, some connection with Rita. 'He told me he gets it from you.'

Rita leaned on the mop. Ruth had the feeling she was being measured. For levels of trust.

When Rita spoke, she was terse. 'He'll come back when he's ready.'

It was a non-answer, the straight bat.

The missing persons report came up on the New South Wales police Facebook page that evening. Ruth pulled it up and phoned Sharon Messer.

'You've put Bea on the missing persons page.'

'I didn't. Your local constable put his hand up to take on that part of the investigation.'

Gazza.

'Have a look at the report,' said Ruth.

She could hear clicking down the phone. Sharon didn't bother with the niceties of sustaining conversation. There was something very utilitarian about Detective Messer. She engaged with people to the extent necessary and not an iota more. Ruth found it endearing. There was no artifice, no pretence.

'Yep. Here she is. Jesus! I thought you said the kid was Instagram glamorous. She looks like the devil in this photo.'

'Exactly,' said Ruth.

The photo was confronting. Bea was dressed as a Goth, with a blank oppositional stare.

'Why did Gazza choose this photo?' Ruth said. 'For a missing teenager?'

'Dunno,' Sharon said. Ruth could almost hear the cogs turning on the other end of the phone.

Ruth filled the gap. 'It's hardly likely to capture the attention of the press, is it? It doesn't scream human interest story on a slow news day.'

This was the kind of photo you used when putting a kid on the missing persons register was a performative gesture to signal that you'd noted she was missing.

'Check out what he says about her,' said Ruth.

It said, *Missing woman. Beatrice Baulderstone. Issues with drugs and alcohol. Last seen a week ago after argument at home with parent.*

'And?' said Sharon.

'Gazza has called her a woman even though she's only seventeen. Then mentioned issues with drugs and alcohol and a fiery relationship with her parent. If I were a copper and I saw that, I wouldn't bother looking for her. I'd figure she probably wanted to get away from the parent she fought with so she could get high.'

Still nothing from Sharon. It was like she was talking into a hollow log.

'It may as well have said, "Don't bother looking for her, but if you stumble across her give us a call at the Myddle police station." And don't believe a word she says. And there's no mention of a connection with a suspected murder.'

Sharon finally spoke. 'You'd make quite a good copper, you know that?'

'As I recall it, you should have formed that view a year ago,' said Ruth.

'I did actually,' said Sharon. 'But you're a bit stuck-up for us.'

'Thanks very much.'

'I take your point. I'll have a chat to Constable Parker,' said Sharon.

'If you want a better photo of Bea, there are a few on her Instagram feed. She mostly took photos of landscapes. Good ones. But there are some nice ones of her.'

'Thanks,' said Sharon. 'Your client Evie ready to talk to us yet?'

'Nope.'

The hanging-up process was perfunctory, as was usual with Sharon Messer.

But Ruth smiled. Operation Plant Seed of Doubt about Gazza in the mind of Detective Messer had commenced. Hopefully, it would work. The wider the investigation, the longer it would take Detective Messer to swing back around to Evie. It would buy Ruth some time.

Ruth rang Harry to fill him in.

'Marge thinks we should come home,' Harry told her.

Sounded to Ruth like Harry was attributing to Marge a worry he held himself.

'You don't need to come home for the practice,' said Ruth.

Myddle was in crisis. Harry was a mainstay in the town. She understood why he felt he should be there. And he had lived here since birth. He might see things she couldn't.

'I'll talk it over with Marge. Might have to fly. Would take a week to drive the rig over the Nullarbor.'

'Up to you,' said Ruth.

'I understand why you'd want to be here, but it's a long way for you to come. I think I can handle it.'

Did she think that? Not really. She said it with a confidence she didn't feel.

WhatsApp

Jack
Update?

Ruth
Troy's gone AWOL

Jack
?

Ruth
Gazza roughed him up in the street. Verbally. He scooted.

Jack
What are you going to do?

Ruth
His mum knows where he is but won't say

Jack
[online]

Ruth
I don't understand this town. I'm worried ignorance is going to make me stick my foot in it.

Jack
You'll be right. You always are.

Ruth
I'm not so sure

52

RUTH

June, Wednesday morning, two days after

DEB WAS AT HER DESK WHEN RUTH GOT IN THE NEXT MORNING. 'I WAS so sorry to hear about Dash,' said Ruth.

Deb shook her head. 'Tough on Diane,' she said. 'He was the apple of her eye.'

'Very tough.'

Deb pulled out a Coles bag and unloaded a framed photo of Dash. She positioned it beside her computer. That flashing smile.

'Saw a couple of police cars outside Troy's place on the way to work,' she said. 'Wonder what that's about.' She raised an eyebrow as if she knew exactly what that was about. Justice was about to be served.

Ruth picked up her keys.

'When will you be back?' said Deb.

'Not sure,' said Ruth. 'Got to see a client.'

There were two police cars outside Rita's house.

A police officer was taking photos of Troy's ute.

The front door was open. Ruth bounded up the front steps and entered the house uninvited. Rita was in the hall, a wet tea towel in her hands.

Gazza's large frame dominated the doorway.

'Sorry, for just walking in,' Ruth said. 'I wanted to check that everything is okay.'

'Depends what you mean by okay,' Gazza said. 'We've just found Bea Baulderstone's phone in Troy's room.' He held up a snap-lock bag with two fingers so that the mobile phone in it swung in space.

'How do you know it's Bea's?' asked Ruth.

He held it out and turned it over. *Bea's phone Hands off* was scratched into the crimson case, with a love heart.

'It was hidden in the ceiling, wasn't it, Rita? We're just asking her where Troy is.'

Rita looked up at Ruth. Anguish. Fury.

'Do you have a search warrant, Constable?' said Ruth.

Parker pulled out a piece of paper and threw it on the table.

'When you're ready to assist police with our inquiries,' he said to Rita, 'we'll be down at the station organising a search for your son. It's going to be easier for everyone if he turns himself in.'

Parker nodded to the three other policemen and walked out.

'How did they know it was there?' said Rita.

'They probably contacted the phone company after they found Bea's backpack at Dash's house. They're serious about this, Rita. And now there's a connection between Troy and Dash's death.'

Rita was standing at the sink, her hands either side of the soapy water.

'Do you know where he is, Rita?' Ruth asked. 'He must know what happened to Bea.'

Rita examined her hands.

'It would be best if I talk to Troy soon,' Ruth said. 'If we leave Gazza Parker in charge of an operation to find him, it could get ugly. Manhunt. Explosive tempers. We need to exercise some control over this. Get Troy's side of the story before Gazza extracts it from him.'

And Messer. That's what Ruth was most worried about. She'd seen Messer's incisive questioning firsthand when Messer was investigating her and Roscoe's big law firm. Messer got to the nub of a mystery while everyone else was catching up.

Rita turned. 'It'll be ugly all right. I don't think you get how much it's stacked against him.'

'I'm going back to the office,' Ruth said. She wrote her mobile number on a receipt from her handbag. 'It might be best if we talk here rather than at my office.'

Deb was at the office. Always listening. Why had she agreed to let her back in, even a little bit? Harry was so insistent.

'Anything Troy tells me is confidential. I won't tell the police, Rita. I'm not allowed to. You can trust me.'

Ruth wasn't sure whether Rita's slow nod indicated agreement or doubt.

Ruth left.

Half an hour later her phone rang.

Rita.

It was a clear afternoon, cold, the eucalypt leaves sharply delineated in the crisp light.

Rita led Ruth along an overgrown track in the national park. After an hour, the track faded. They were on the banks of a creek, part track, part lichen-encrusted blocks of granite. They trudged in the opposite direction to the flow of water, which skittered over rocks, then as it got steeper, dropped first in rapids, then a series of short waterfalls between pools.

The track on the bank of the creek disappeared and Ruth and Rita climbed up the creek bed. They pulled themselves up the rock face by grasping the vegetation—ferns, baby saplings, bushes—which had thin purchase there.

A loud mournful caw. Ruth looked up to see a large bird high in a eucalypt, scratching at the trunk. It was jet black, yellow dot on each cheek, a little punk crest over the centre of its head.

Black cockatoo. As they approached, the bird flew off, swooping gracefully away in undulating flight through the trees. It was joined by another, and another. Nine of them, their tails spread out to display an arc of bright yellow, cawed as they glided away. It was as if they were suspended in the air, so slow and graceful was their flight.

Rita and Ruth paused to watch.

'Sign of a strengthening spirit,' said Rita.

The birds settled in some branches further up the slope. As Ruth and Rita approached, they swooped off again, their mournful call heralding flight.

'Do you think they are leading us to him?' Ruth asked.

Rita smiled at Ruth, mouth closed, a softening of her eyes, amused. It was a smile that said, *Steady on. Don't get too carried away.*

Another hour. They were back on a path, still climbing. Ruth was exhausted. She stopped for another gulp of water.

'Nearly there,' said Rita.

The hill flattened at the crest, and the forest thinned. It must be the crag above the Bluff, an even more expansive view over forest and farms; the sea a hint of glistening dark blue out on the horizon.

'G'day.'

Troy.

Rita and Ruth had each brought a backpack of food. There was a broken-down hut on top of the mountain, which provided rudimentary shelter. Troy sat on the grass, and Rita and Ruth sat, too.

'All right, bub?' Rita asked Troy.

'Yeah. Okay.' He looked at Ruth. 'Sorry I haven't been at work.'

She didn't say 'no worries' because she'd done nothing but worry since she last saw him. Instead, she nodded. 'Let's see if we can sort this out,' she said.

Rita laid out the food on a cloth she pulled out of her backpack.

They ate first. Ruth was thinking about her knees, niggling in complaint, and wondering how they would cope with the descent.

Troy was calm, even amused, as he wolfed down the sandwiches and bananas. They may as well have been sitting in the office puzzling over a form to complete a sale of land.

They heard it first, the *chobba chobba chobba* of a helicopter. It was loud, flying low. Then it invaded their line of vision, flying low over the crest of the hill, so big, so close above them it consumed the landscape. There was a flattening wind, a deafening noise.

It was blue and white.

'Police,' Troy said as he rose to his feet.

The trees groaned in the gale the helicopter made. The air itself was desperate, filled with stress and panic.

Two policemen emerged from the bush on foot, armed like paramilitary, black vests, guns pointed at them.

They were shouting something. It was hard to hear over the noise from the chopper but Ruth thought it was, 'Arms up, weapons down.'

'Fuck,' said Ruth.

Troy was sizing up the surroundings. There was no panic in him, not visible anyway. He was still, tensed up and ready for action; his eyes assessing, his mind processing.

Was he thinking about running? The bush was thick twenty metres away.

Ruth forced herself to be calm. 'I think we should do as the police officer says. Put our hands up,' Ruth yelled over the noise.

Troy was calculating.

Ruth shook her head. *Don't do it Troy,* she willed. *They have guns.*

Eyes narrowed, he looked at Ruth and his mother. That's when she realised he was working out how to protect them.

He nodded, just like he had the first time she'd met him by the campfire with Bea, and his arms went into the air. A right angle at the elbow, but unmistakably a sign of surrender.

Ruth raised her arms as well. So did Rita.

The police advanced and cuffed Troy.

Gazza Parker emerged from the bush too late for the arrest.

'Where is she?' he asked Troy. 'Is she alive? Is she here?'

One of the policemen had been searching the hut. Now he yelled and held up a small T-shirt, pink with large red lips on it. The Rolling Stones T-shirt Ruth had seen Bea wearing on her Instagram page.

Sharon Messer appeared from the chopper. She walked over to Troy. 'I'm arresting you on suspicion of the abduction of Beatrice Baulderstone and the murder of Wayne Rogers,' she said.

What the fuck? Ruth stepped forward. 'Based on what?' she shouted. Sharon ignored Ruth and addressed Troy again, 'And because an arrest is reasonably necessary to stop you fleeing from a police officer.'

Ruth knew Sharon didn't have to say why she had a suspicion that Troy had committed those offences. Sharon wouldn't have put on this kind of show, spent this much police money on a helicopter and a tactical response unit, unless she had some pretty good information implicating Troy.

Next step would be an attempt to get Troy to confess. In a police interview room.

Ruth told herself to calm down. Think through it.

'Where are you taking him?'

'Myddle police station.'

'Well, you've got six hours to question him. It'll take me half that time to get there if I have to go by foot.'

Sharon smiled and gestured for Ruth to get into the chopper. They both knew the time would be extended if Ruth couldn't get there. But why have the argument?

'And his mum,' said Ruth. 'She's his support person.'

'She can't be his support person,' said Sharon. 'She's a potential witness. But she can come, too.'

Ruth couldn't communicate with Troy in the chopper: they had Troy in cuffs down the back, and anyway the noise was all consuming.

Sharon put Troy in the lockup at Myddle police station.

A sign stuck on the glass barrier on the bench said, in capital letters, bold font, PLEASE RESPECT OUR STAFF. ABUSE WILL NOT BE TOLERATED.

Gazza took Ruth through a door to a corridor: cramped, concrete, stinking of stale urine.

Troy was sitting on a bunk with a skimpy grey blanket, head in his hands.

'I'm so sorry,' said Ruth.

The police must have tracked someone, a car or a phone. It could have been Ruth's, it could have been Rita's. Either way, Ruth felt responsible.

'Are you all right?' she asked.

'I'm fine,' Troy said. 'Pissed off. But fine.'

'They've arrested you but haven't charged you,' Ruth said. 'They want to talk about Bea's phone.'

Troy's eyebrows went up. 'So that's why they suddenly care about Bea.'

'Do you know where Bea is? Do you know whether she's alive?' Ruth whispered.

He shook his head.

'Troy, if you tell me anything, anything at all, I have to keep it a secret. Unless you tell me not to.'

No response. His eyes narrowed. He was sizing her up.

'It's called legal professional privilege. It's your privilege. Not mine. You decide.'

She had a notepad in her hand and a pen. He reached out and took them.

He wrote on the pad.

Do they get to see this notepad?

She shook her head, and mouthed no.

He must have thought there was a listening device in the cell. Police listening to a conversation between a prisoner and their lawyer. Sharon Messer would never condone that, but the cell was controlled by Gazza, so it was possible. Ruth said breezily out loud, 'Your mum is very worried about you, too.'

Troy wrote, *I need to get out of here.*

She wanted to put her hand over his but resisted the urge. Instead, she nodded and said out loud, 'They can only hold you for six hours unless they get the permission of a magistrate. So, unless they've got some significant information, or they charge you, you'll be out later tonight. They can get a magistrate to extend it, but they need a good reason to do it.'

Troy had the pen poised over the notebook. He wrote, *Let's get this over with. I'm not saying anything.*

Ruth nodded and said out loud, for the sake of the microphone Troy thought was there, 'Let's go to the interview room, shall we? In general it's wise to not answer questions. Hopefully, the questions will indicate where they are with the investigation. If there's one you want to answer or you're not sure of just signal to me.'

She asked him if he wanted a support person. He shook his head.

Sharon and Gazza took them to an interview room. Gazza turned on the tape. Sharon went through the preliminaries: date, time, who was there and why, Troy's right to remain silent.

She leaned forward. 'Where's Bea?' she said. 'You must know. We found her phone in your ceiling. Telstra got the last ping at ten am on Thursday morning. Must have been turned off then. You were the last person to see her.'

Troy's face did not move. He sat very straight, every muscle tensed, concentrating on letting no information out.

'You and your mother.'

That was a threat. Against Rita. Of course they would question her.

'Is Bea dead, Troy?'

Ruth reappraised Troy. He must have a mind of steel to sit there silent while she insinuated he was involved in the death of a girl.

Ruth felt sick, made herself relax and exhale.

Gazza moved in his chair, his breathing audible.

Sharon Messer asked about the dings on the bumper bar of Troy's ute. Troy said nothing. If that was the best they could do, it wasn't much. Troy's ute was twelve years old. It was a cornucopia of dings and scratches.

Sharon moved the papers in front of her, and pulled up a list so Ruth couldn't see it. The next few questions came in rapid fire.

The bicycle had traces of blood on it. They were doing DNA tests. Would it be Bea's blood? How did it get there?

Ruth was glad her eyes were directed at her notepad and pen. She could hide her alarm. What bicycle? Where was it found? She knew it would be pointless to ask. Detective Messer was under no obligation to tell her.

Troy said nothing.

Sharon Messer fired off the next question. 'Where were you on Sunday afternoon?' So that must be when Dash died. He'd been dead twenty-four hours when Roscoe found him.

'Why were you driving along Clive River Road at approximately three thirty pm on Sunday afternoon?'

Troy's head jerked up. He wasn't expecting that question, and now everyone in the room knew it. Sharon smiled and made a small note. She'd broken through.

'You were at the gate to Dash's farm, weren't you? What were you wearing on your feet?'

Why would she ask that? Were there footprints at the murder scene?

Sharon leaned back in the chair and crossed her arms. 'Was Bea pregnant, Troy?'

Woah. Where did that come from?

Troy's surprise cracked his silence. 'How would I know?'

Sharon leaned into a box she had at her feet and picked up an evidence bag with a pregnancy test kit inside it. 'This hers?'

'How would I know?'

'Where's Bea?' said Sharon again.

Nothing.

'Why was Bea at Dash's house that Wednesday night? Why did she leave her backpack there? Did she have to leave in a hurry? Did Dash realise why she was there?'

Nothing.

'Was she the honeypot, Troy?'

Ruth looked up at Sharon in disbelief. They're accusing him of being Bea's pimp?

'Is she dead? Did something happen to her? An accident?'

He said nothing.

'Or are you trying to protect her? Because it's looking very bad for you, Troy.'

Looking bad? That was an understatement.

Sharon wouldn't be asking these very specific questions unless she had information from someone. And, in her quiet way, Sharon oozed confidence about the information's veracity. She could have saved up the specific question about Troy driving along Clive River Road to trap him after he made an inconsistent statement. But she was trying to spook him with her detailed knowledge. It meant she might be saving up even more damning evidence.

They might have enough to charge him, at least with Bea's abduction. Ruth swallowed in dread. He'd said he needed to get out of there. Was it a perfectly normal aversion to being locked up, or was there something more?

Gazza stared at Troy with sneering contempt. His hands were red, and rough. Would he be violent to a prisoner in a lockup? A picture flashed in Ruth's head of Gazza leaning over Troy in the street. Dominating.

'We need your phone, Troy. And the password,' said Sharon.

She gathered together her pens and paper, preparing to leave. It was then that she casually dropped the zinger, as if it was an afterthought. 'And we need to know what conversations you've had with your aunt. In the last two weeks.'

Troy did respond to that. Surprise and confusion loosened his tongue.

'My aunty?'

'Evie Rogers,' said Sharon.

Ruth's head whipped around. *What?*

Troy's eyebrows widened, then narrowed into a frown. His head drooped.

Did Troy know this?

Sharon crossed her arms and waited. The stench of musty grey concrete.

Nothing from Troy.

'Got your eye on that property of hers?' said Sharon.

One thing you could say about Troy: he'd had a lifetime of practice in controlling how to display emotion. He'd let the surprise escape, and now, a few seconds later, he locked it down. Under the table, he slowly put one hand on his knee. It was shaking.

53

RUTH

June, Wednesday afternoon, two days after

BACK IN THE CELL, TROY LOOKED AS SHOCKED AS RUTH FELT ABOUT THE revelation that Evie was his aunt.

Ruth decided to leave it and save her questions for Evie and Rita. Instead, she wrote on the pad, *You need to prepare yourself. They might charge you. I'm sorry.*

She said loudly, for the benefit of the microphone, if there was one, 'I need to tell you all about legal professional privilege.'

The smell of piss and hopelessness in that grey airless room, harshly lit by a fluorescent tube.

I've got to get out of here, wrote Troy.

She put a question mark on the paper.

His head moved back in the direction of the corridor.

Gazza? she wrote.

Nod.

He's threatened you?

Troy gave her the 'der' look. Of course he has.

Troy wrote, *Better for him if I don't say anything. So better for me.*

Ruth: *I'll talk to Messer.*

Troy scrawled another message. *Ask Messer about Bea's phone.*

Sharon Messer was behind the reception desk of the police station as Ruth was leaving, pretending to make a note on a pad. She wanted a chat. Ruth obliged.

'Your six hours are nearly up,' Ruth said to Messer. 'You've got less than an hour. Why not release him now?'

Messer scoffed. 'No way I'm releasing him. We've already gone to the magistrate. Got an extra twenty-four hours.'

'Are you going to charge him?'

'We're close.'

'He's worried about his safety. Constable Parker threatened him.'

Messer shook her head. 'Constable Parker's a country cop doing his job. He might be a bit rough around the edges. Doesn't mean he's bad. Of course your guy's going to say that. Fancy city lawyer like you—you'd believe anything that fits the narrative. You've got to accept, Ruth, that all the evidence screams that he's got that girl. I'm trying to work out if she's still alive. Seems to me you've closed your mind to saving that girl's life. If she has any life left in her.'

'I'll put it in writing,' said Ruth. 'That he feels threatened.'

'You do that,' said Messer. 'But I need his phone first.'

'What about Bea's phone?'

'What about it?'

'You didn't ask any questions about that? Surely you've looked at it.'

'Your boy wiped it, Ruth. It's dead as a doornail. He drowned it.'

The sign urging visitors to be courteous was peeling at the corners.

'That doesn't make any sense, though, does it?' said Ruth. 'Why would Troy have kept a phone he deliberately trashed? Why wouldn't he just chuck it in the river?'

Messer shrugged. 'Maybe he was worried we'd find it. Maybe he hadn't got around to getting rid of it. Maybe he's not too smart.'

'The phone was in Gazza's possession,' said Ruth. 'Has it occurred to you that it was he who drowned it?'

Messer shook her head. 'You never give up, do you? Get me Troy's phone. And I'd like all of his shoes as well.'

Rita was outside the police station, the tip of her cigarette orange in the dark.

'Didn't peg you as a smoker,' said Ruth.

'I gave up twelve years ago,' said Rita, and rolled her eyes.

'They'll question you about Bea,' said Ruth.

'They already have. I know the drill. I said nothing.'

'Questions about the phone in your ceiling?' said Ruth.

'Yep.'

'Nothing else?'

'Troy's movements from Wednesday to Sunday. How much he was at home.'

Behind Rita, a breeze disturbed the surface of the river, streetlight reflected on the ripples.

'Is Evie Troy's aunt?'

Rita startled. 'Why do you say that?'

'Messer said.'

Rita paled. 'Not to Troy?'

Ruth nodded.

'Oh, fuck,' said Rita. She took a drag on her cigarette and turned to look at the river.

'Is it true?'

'Yep,' said Rita. 'But he didn't know. I've never told him.'

'How would the police know?' said Ruth. 'Who would have told them?'

Rita shook her head. 'No idea. What a mess.'

A splat from the river. Sounded like the clumsy landing of a leaping fish or a bird.

'Who else knows?' said Ruth.

'Well, I don't go spreading it around. I haven't told Troy so I'm hardly likely to talk about it with anyone else. Evie guessed when she saw Troy playing footy last year. Nobody had told her. But I suppose there would be people in town who figured it out when Joof died. Small town. Everyone knows stuff about everyone else.' She paused and kicked a tuft of grass. 'Harry Dunstan knew. He used to send me a cheque for two thousand dollars every year on 30 June. From Evie's father.'

Ruth and Rita stood side by side, both watching the black river.

'I've still got them. Never cashed them. Nasty old bugger he was. Evie's dad, I mean.'

'What about Evie's mum?'

Rita took another drag on her smoke. 'His faithful, nasty wife.'

It occurred to Ruth then. 'She was in your nursing home. You were looking after her?'

Rita didn't respond.

'That was a lot for Evie to ask of you,' said Ruth.

'She was demented, so she had no idea who I was.'

'Still. To do that. You must be some kind of saint,' said Ruth.

Rita rolled her eyes. 'You get all sorts in a nursing home, ranging from nice to bloody awful. Someone's got to look after them.'

Didn't make her any less of a saint, but it was clear that Rita considered that particular line of inquiry at an end. Back to the topic at hand.

'Troy said nothing to the police. Stayed silent. That's a good thing.'

Rita nodded. 'Yeah. Silence is his default state. Or grunting.'

'Teenage boy,' said Ruth.

'They want his phone,' said Ruth. 'Can I come over and pick it up in an hour or so? I'll deliver it to the police after I've backed up the contents. We have to give the police the password. Can't avoid it.'

Rita stubbed out her cigarette with her foot, then bent over to pick up the stub.

'Why didn't you tell him who his dad was?' Ruth said.

'I was waiting for the right time,' said Rita. 'But as he grew up, it got harder.'

A flying fox, black against the moonlit sky, flew overhead.

'I'm worried about his reaction,' said Rita. 'His anger. And now I'm worried that Evie will renege.'

'On what?'

'She's talking about transferring the Bluff to Troy.'

Ruth was glad that she and Rita were both looking at the river. Rita couldn't see Ruth's face as the information shuffled into place.

'First I heard of it was a couple of weeks ago. Just after her bull was killed,' said Rita. 'I reckon it was a brain fart. Spur of the moment thing.'

Another fish flew and landed with a crack on the water.

'She might revert to type after she has a think about it. Screwing us over is a Clive thing. Gives their lives purpose and meaning.' Rita paused. 'Which are just two whitefella words for land and wealth.'

'Didn't Troy think it was weird? That this woman from the town starts talking to him and welcoming him into her life?'

'No,' Rita said. 'It's Myddle. Our lives all flow together.'

Did Troy figure out that something was afoot? Money and the promise of it did weird things to humans.

'Will they let me talk to him?' Rita asked.

'I'll talk to Sharon Messer,' said Ruth. 'But be careful. Troy thinks there's a listening device in the cell.'

Ruth rang Charlie. He'd got Roscoe to drive him out to the national park and had retrieved her car. He came to pick her up.

She was reminded again what it was like to have someone who asked no questions but enveloped her in a moment of crisis.

She came out of the shower feeling a bit less tainted.

'I'm making a risotto,' said Charlie. He poured her a glass of red.

WhatsApp

Jack
Update?

Ruth
This is getting weirder and weirder. Police hunt up the mountain today. Helicopter. Guns.

Jack
OMFG

Ruth
They arrested Troy. Seem to have a witness who saw him on Clive Road when Dash was murdered.

Jack
!

Ruth
And I've discovered one of the Myddle Unknowns.
Unknowns I was worried about.

Jack
?

Ruth
Evie is Troy's aunt

Jack
WTF

Ruth
Indeed

Jack
So he did do it then? Kill Dash?

Ruth
😱

54

RUTH

June, Thursday, three days after

FIRST THING AFTER BREAKFAST, RUTH DROVE TO PATCH'S. AT THE CATTLE grid a flock of rosellas squawked in the huge wattle in vivid yellow flower.

Sharon Messer wanted to interview Evie that afternoon.

'Sorry I've been out of action,' said Ruth, gripping the mug Evie pushed into her hand.

'You've been busy I hear,' said Evie. 'Saving Troy.'

'Not doing much saving.'

'Will he be charged?'

'Hope not,' said Ruth. 'We've got to get him out.' She stroked the side of her mug. 'The police know that Troy is your nephew.'

Evie stiffened. 'Oh,' she whispered. 'Has anyone told Troy?'

'He heard it from Detective Messer.'

Evie slumped over her mug and wiped her eyes.

Her T-shirt was pink. Ruth had never seen her wearing pink before. There was a stain on the rear, as if a child had regurgitated milk down her back. A mother's T-shirt. Must be Patch's. She was borrowing clothes because she couldn't get into her house.

'Is that why you wanted to subdivide the Bluff? Something to do with Troy?'

'I wanted to give it to him. So Dash couldn't get it, and wreck it.'

'No need now,' said Ruth. It came out before she could stop it.

Evie looked Ruth straight in the eye. 'That's right,' she said. 'No need.'

Ruth met her gaze. 'Someone saw Troy on Clive River Road on Sunday afternoon.'

Evie's head went back as if she'd been pushed. 'Who?'

'Don't know.'

'He wouldn't,' said Evie. 'Surely.' It didn't look like disbelief. It looked more like a question; an expression of doubt about Troy's innocence.

'There's worse news,' said Ruth. 'The police found a pregnancy test kit in your house. It was positive. They think Bea was pregnant.'

Evie emitted a snort of laughter.

Was it funny? A girl missing, possibly dead, who might have been pregnant. And had done a pregnancy test in Evie's house. Perhaps Evie's laughter was gallows humour: a consequence of the accumulation of terrible news.

'Sorry,' said Evie. 'I shouldn't laugh. It's just that, if they found that in our bathroom, it's mine.'

Ruth concentrated on closing her mouth.

'I'm pregnant,' said Evie.

A lawyer thought jumped straight into Ruth's head. That was good. A wife pregnant with a longed-for baby, and then the husband dies suddenly. Couldn't pin that on the wife.

Then the human thoughts subsumed the lawyer thoughts. Poor Evie. She finally gets the thing she wants most and, straight away, is engulfed by yet another tragedy.

Assuming the baby was Dash's. Should Ruth ask the question? She decided not to. Instead, she reached out her hand. 'Wonderful news. And so sad. I'm sorry.'

Evie nodded.

'Who knew?' said Ruth. 'That you're pregnant.'

'Dash,' said Evie.

'When did you tell him?'

'Before I went to Azuri.'

'He must have been worried about you, when you fell,' said Ruth.

'Yes,' said Evie. 'He rang Chandra. I was vomiting so I told her as well. She took me to hospital.'

Chandra hadn't mentioned that. Was that odd?

Ruth looked at her watch and stood. 'We'd better go to the interview. You don't have to answer the questions. But if they're going to find out anyway, and there's no harm, you might consider answering.'

Evie nodded again.

'Let's go,' said Ruth. 'I'll drive.'

Same depressing grey musty interview room. Ruth realised what the smell was. Mice.

Sharon. On her own with a tape recorder. No Gazza.

The questions focused on Evie's alibi: the trip to Coles on Sunday afternoon. Evie was answering questions.

'I needed to pick up something for dinner.'

'And before that?'

'I was asleep.'

Sharon knew about Evie's trip to hospital. Wanted permission to access her hospital records. They'd get them, whether Evie agreed to it or not. She agreed.

'I fell over and hit my head,' said Evie. 'And I'm six weeks pregnant.' Volunteered it. No point in hiding it. Sharon was going to find out anyway.

Sharon said, 'Thanks for being candid.'

'Did you leave a pregnancy test stick in your bathroom bin?'

'Yes,' said Evie.

Sharon's movements slowed when Evie said she was pregnant. That was as close as Sharon would get to showing some empathy. She felt for Evie: pregnant at last and the father was dead.

'What shoe size are you?' said Sharon.

'Eight.'

Why ask Evie that question? Were there two sets of footprints at the murder scene?

'Sorry I have to ask,' said Sharon, 'but is Dash the father?'

Evie frowned. 'What are you insinuating?'

'I'm just asking if your husband is the father of the child.'

Evie bit her lip. 'I can't believe you would ask me that question.'

'So he is?' said Sharon.

'Who else would it be?'

Sharon made a note. 'And Troy Matheson is your nephew?'

Evie leaned back in the chair. 'Yes. He's my brother's child. My brother died when Rita was pregnant.'

Sharon concluded the interview. She had no more questions. No questions about the plan to gift Troy the Bluff.

Sharon mustn't know.

Ruth did the driving. It's easier to have a conversation when you are both looking out a window: Ruth out the windscreen; Evie—chin in her hand—out the side.

Evie had avoided Sharon Messer's questions about the father of the baby. Sam Dunstan's presence at the girl's weekend in Sydney looked like it might be a relevant fact.

'Sharon Messer can ask for DNA tests,' said Ruth.

Evie startled, and turned to look at Ruth. 'Not of the baby?' she said.

'Of the baby.'

'But if they do that now, they could destroy the pregnancy.'

'Then they can wait,' said Ruth. 'And medical records. Dash's medical records. Yours. They'll get access to all of them, including old ones.'

Evie didn't say anything. Just looked out the side window.

Ruth dropped in at Roscoe's on the way home.

'How did Evie's interview go?' said Roscoe.

Ruth didn't respond. She addressed Chandra. 'You took Evie to hospital the week before Dash died.'

She didn't pose it as a question.

Roscoe looked at Chandra. 'You didn't tell me that.'

'How do you know?' said Chandra.

'Did you?' said Ruth.

Chandra nodded.

'Why?'

'Looked like she had concussion.'

'Why didn't you tell me?' said Roscoe.

Chandra didn't answer.

'Why were you there?' Ruth asked.

'Dash rang me. She'd had a fall and he needed help. She was vomiting. I was worried.'

'Did it look like he'd hit her?' said Ruth.

'You can never tell, can you? What other people's relationships are like.'

'Did you ask her?'

'She was sick. I took her straight to hospital.'

When she got home, Charlie opened a bottle of red. He'd lit the fire already. The house was warm and safe.

'Evie's pregnant,' said Ruth.

'To Dash?'

'Sharon asked the same question.'

'What did Evie say?'

'She didn't really answer.'

Charlie nodded slowly at the crackling fire. 'That's not good.'

'I think Sharon Messer is still focusing on Troy,' said Ruth.

That's as much as Ruth could say to Charlie without breaching Evie's confidence. But she was wondering what she would do if Sharon found out that Evie was going to gift the Bluff to Troy. Because the baby complicated that decision of Evie's. Considerably.

Should Ruth organise separate legal representation for Evie? Troy's defence would have to include pointing the finger at Evie. And even the father of the baby, if it turned out not to be Dash. Was Sam Dunstan the father? He would have a motive as well.

If Ruth stopped acting for Evie, she'd also have to refer Troy to different lawyers. If Troy was charged and it looked like Evie was a suspect, Ruth couldn't act for either of them. Probably couldn't act for anyone in Myddle.

If that's the way it went—Troy charged—Ruth's professional obligation was to shut up, and butt out.

She wasn't at that point yet, but it didn't look good.

A car crunched on the gravel outside.

Rita came to the door. She had Troy's phone.

'What's the password?' said Ruth.

'It's on the yellow sticky note.'

'Fancy a glass of red?' said Ruth.

'Nah. I've left the kids at home. Gotta go.'

Ruth unlocked Troy's phone.

Opened the call log.

Nothing. Good.

Opened WhatsApp.

On Wednesday night, the night she went missing, a missed call from Bea.

A call from Chandra to Troy. At eight thirty-three. This time he picked up. Three minutes twelve seconds.

That was during the State of Origin game, when Chandra was at Ruth's.

On the night Bea disappeared, she'd tried to contact Troy.

Fuck.

Ruth's own phone beeped.

A WhatsApp message. Someone called Schnootster123. *Dongo pub 9 pm. Tonight. About Troy.*

Ruth googled it. Dongo was a tiny town on the tablelands an hour west of Myddle: pub, general store, a few dejected houses. She was exhausted and needed a night-time drive up a mountain road like a hole in the head. And Schnootster123 could be anyone.

She returned to Charlie by the fire. 'Fancy a drive in the country?'

Lucky she'd only had two sips of her wine.

55

RUTH

June, Thursday, three days after

A DRIVE THROUGH THE AUSTRALIAN BUSH AT NIGHT HAS A MILLION witnesses, their eyes reflected in the headlights, low on either side of the road. *Please don't jump in front of us,* Ruth prayed. The bodies of those that had tried to cross lined the bitumen: kangaroos, bandicoots, a wombat.

'Who is this person we're meeting?' Charlie asked.

'Don't know.'

'Gender?'

'Sorry, don't know.'

'Hostile?'

'Hopefully not.'

'Associated with crime?'

'Not inconceivable.'

'Good to know. Glad I did taekwondo when I was eight.'

After that, they drove in silence.

The Dongo pub had an undulating floor with an ancient sticky carpet, an antechamber behind the bar filled with pokies, and four men with a three-day growth and flannelette shirts holding up the bar. The barmaid was Ruth's age, give or take. Actually, more give than take.

'What are ya having, luv?' the barmaid asked Charlie.

'Two schooners.'

'We'll bring 'em out to ya.' That was a level of service Ruth wasn't expecting.

They sat at a table in a dark corner and waited.

A young woman, little more than a girl, with bright crimson hair approached with their beers and a tall glass of Coke. In keeping with the sartorial requirements of the Dongo pub, she was dressed in jeans, clumpy Blundstone boots and a singlet.

'Ruth?' the girl said.

'Yes?' said Ruth.

'It's me.'

Of course. It was Bea. Pale, washed out, hair a bright distraction to her face.

Ruth lurched out of the booth to hug her. 'I'm so glad you're okay. You've no idea what a ruckus there's been about you. We've been so worried.'

She squeezed Bea then broke away.

'This is Charlie,' Ruth added. 'My . . .' What was he?

'Boyfriend,' said Charlie, holding out his hand.

Bea was obviously unused to people shaking her hand. She held his hand limply and smiled, embarrassed.

Bea sat in the booth beside Ruth, with the Coke.

'Why did you disappear?' Ruth asked. 'Why did you contact me like this?'

'Because I'm scared, and I don't know what to do.'

'Scared of whom?'

'It's a bad story,' said Bea. 'You might not believe me.'

A Harley Davidson motorbike approached, a guttural roar. Ruth waited until the din subsided.

'Tell me, Bea. Start at the beginning.'

Bea faltered her way through her story, of Dash, and Gazza and her mum, and the terrible events on State of Origin night.

Her head was silhouetted against the garish reds and greens from the slot machines next door and Ruth had to lean in to hear her over the pings and zaps. As Bea recounted it, a scene of two middle-aged men enjoying the footy and a beer became a horror flick.

'Oh Bea,' said Ruth. 'I'm so sorry.'

'I couldn't go to the police. I couldn't tell my mum. She'd lose it,' Bea said. 'I needed to get out of town for a bit. Troy took me to his house and let me stay the night there. We went up to the national park for a few days. Then he and his mum arranged for me to stay with their rellos here in Dongo.

'You know about Dash?' said Ruth.

Bea nodded, tearing up. 'Troy told me. It's so awful.'

What a gentle soul Bea was. After what Dash had done, she still felt sorry for him.

Ruth had resisted touching Bea, worried about encroaching, but couldn't help herself.

'You poor darling girl,' she whispered into Bea's head.

Across the table, Charlie was slack-jawed in dismay.

The lawyer cogs creaked into action in Ruth's head. Troy was talking to her after Dash was found dead? That hadn't shown up on Troy's phone. She hoped that Rita hadn't deleted the conversations because that would be uncovered by the police forensic people and would go very badly for Rita.

Ruth pulled back to watch Bea's face as she asked, 'Troy rang you?'

'No. We speak through comments on random TikTok accounts we both follow.'

'Cryptic comments?'

'What?' said Bea.

'Were the comments in some sort of code?'

'Oh, yeah. We've worked out a kind of language.'

Clever.

'Anyway, I never meant for Troy to be arrested.'

'Not your fault,' said Ruth.

Bea ran her finger down the drops of moisture on the outside of her glass. 'Who killed Dash?'

'I don't know,' said Ruth.

'I hope it wasn't Evie. I hope she didn't find out what happened with me, and killed him.'

You and me both, thought Ruth.

Reasons to kill Dash were proliferating, as were the suspects. Finding Bea wasn't the panacea to Troy's problems that Ruth had hoped for.

'You said you stayed at the national park for a few days,' said Ruth. 'What day did you move from there to Dongo?'

She considered it. 'Sunday.'

The day Dash died.

'And how did you get to Dongo?'

'Troy drove me.'

Ruth's gut sank.

'What time did he drop you off?' said Charlie.

Bea considered it. 'I dunno. Lunchtime.'

'And then he drove back to Myddle?'

She nodded.

'Someone told the police they saw Troy on Clive River Road at about three thirty on Sunday afternoon. That's possible, isn't it? The turn-off to Dongo is on Clive River Road.'

'I s'pose,' said Bea. 'But why would Troy hurt Dash?'

'The police will say it was because Dash hurt you,' said Charlie.

Or because Dash could prevent Troy from getting the Bluff, Ruth thought.

Bea slumped over her Coke. 'Troy wouldn't do that.'

Not much of a defence, though, is it? thought Ruth. The 'But he's a good bloke, Your Honour' defence is as old as time and not very successful.

Ruth hadn't intended to touch the beer, but she took a big slurp.

So did Charlie.

She turned back to Bea and reached for her hand.

'So what do you want, Bea?'

'To get Troy out of gaol. And I'd really like it if Gazza was—I dunno—punished or something, for what they did to me.'

Ruth blanched. These cases were really hard to prove. The men would say she was at Dash's house to have sex. Then, when his mate came over, that she was up for it. That she agreed she'd do the same for him. They'd pull her apart in the witness box. It'd be brutal.

'Is there a problem?' Bea's neck was rising pink.

Ruth was gentle. 'To convict someone with rape, Bea, we need to prove two things. First that there was sexual activity.'

'Yeah,' said Bea. 'I kept my undies and the stuff on my face. You know, his—like—um—you know—jizz. I kept it on pads that were in the bathroom.'

Ruth nodded slowly. 'Amazing you thought to do that.'

'And I took photos. Of my face and body after.'

'Where are they?'

'On my phone.'

Only problem was Bea's phone had been drowned. Ruth decided to park that thought for now.

'That's great, Bea. Really great.'

Ruth stroked Bea's hand.

'The second thing is a bit more tricky,' said Ruth. 'We would have to prove in court that you didn't consent.'

'I didn't,' said Bea.

'I know. But the question isn't what you think. It's what they thought. Did they think you agreed to have sex with them? They didn't have to hear you say yes. They just had to think you agreed to it.'

'So they just have to say they thought I was up for it?' said Bea.

Ruth nodded.

'I have to prove that I told them no?'

'Yes. In words or actions.'

'Well, obviously I said no. Who would agree to that? It was disgusting. And I couldn't keep saying no because my mouth was full of that creep and my head was pushed down.'

Ruth squirmed in her seat and leaned forward to soften the blow she knew her words would deliver. 'They'll say you'd just done it with Dash.'

Bea flipped a cardboard coaster around and around in her hand, banging an edge on the table with each flip.

'I didn't agree to it. Not two of them at once. And who'd have sex with Gazza? Apart from my mum,' she added. 'But she's desperate.'

Charlie raised an eyebrow at Ruth. Gazza had the mother, then the daughter. It was grotesque.

The coaster flipped and banged. A dog wriggled up to their table to put its snout on Bea's leg, poking her for a pat. In a reflex action, her hand went down to the dog's head.

'What if I asked Dash about it?' Bea said. 'And I recorded it?'

'It's too late to do that, Bea,' said Ruth gently.

'No, I mean I've already done it.'

Stunning news. A girl who had just been raped had had the presence of mind to record an admission from one of the perpetrators.

It's a lawyer's dream to have a client who has packaged together the evidence you need to prove their case.

'Where's your phone?' Charlie asked.

'Gazza took it from Troy,' said Ruth. 'And then destroyed it.'

'It's okay,' said Bea. 'I backed it up to the cloud.'

'I can't watch it,' said Bea after she downloaded the video to Ruth's phone.

'Charlie and I will go out to my car. You stay here.'

In the car, Ruth pressed play, the phone lighting up her face in the dark.

The opening shot. A close-up of Bea's face studying her phone: running mascara; hair messed. The light was fluorescent, a ball of harsh glare in the mirror above her. What was that liquid on her face?

Ruth recoiled. Semen. In her hair.

Charlie put his arm over Ruth's shoulders.

Bea's face disappeared off camera, and the shot jogged up and down a skirting board as she walked from a tiled floor to hardwood floor. It moved again, a static shot of a white ceiling and downlights. The State of Origin half-time show blared in the background, the distinctive rich Australian accents of rugby league commentators.

Bea's voice off camera, a hoarse whisper. 'Dash. Can I talk to you? I can't find . . .'

Dash's chin, mouth and nostrils came into the frame, filmed from underneath. She must have put the phone on the kitchen bench.

'You all right, love?' he said. 'You look terrible. Why don't you go and wash yourself up. You'll be right. You've just got a bit of . . .' His hand gestured at her face.

'Why did you do that to me, Dash?'

'Love?'

'Made me give Gazza a blow job? You know I don't like him. You know I didn't want to do it.'

'Sorry, love. It's just, you know, Gazza's lonely. We needed to do him a favour. He's a good bloke, Gazza. He means well.'

'Why did you do that to me?' she sobbed.

'Oh, love,' said Dash. 'Don't be upset.'

'Spit roast.'

'People do it all the time. You'll be okay.'

'I was stuck between you. I couldn't get out.'

'C'mon, don't be like that. You're usually such a good sport. I didn't think you'd mind.'

'You didn't even ask.'

'Yeah, well . . .' Dash's voice faded with uncertainty.

'Gazza pushed my head down and next thing I know you're doing that. While I couldn't move.'

Dash's eyes darted sideways.

'It was like you think I'm nothing. Just a body with holes.'

'Sorry, love. I'll ask next time.'

Footsteps approached. Dash turned towards them.

Bea picked up the phone. It jerked around as it focused on the skirting boards again, going back to the bathroom, first wood floor then tiles.

'Watcha doing, mate?' That was Gazza's voice, off camera.

'She's just a bit upset.'

'What were you talking about?'

'Just. You know,' said Dash.

Bea went through what looked like the bathroom door. Closed it behind her. Locked it.

The phone focused on her reflection in the mirror, racoon eyes from running mascara.

She filmed her hand taking a box of pads out from under the sink, each in their own little pink bag. She took one out, wiped the semen off her face. Put the pad back in the pink plastic packet. Put it in her pocket.

A knock on the door. Dash's voice. 'You all right, love? Gazza says you should maybe have a shower.'

She watched herself in the mirror.

Another knock, soft. Dash's voice. 'I'll leave some of Evie's clothes here. You can change into them.'

Charlie said to Ruth, 'Why would they want her to do that?'

'Gazza wants her clothes,' Ruth whispered. 'So he can destroy the evidence.'

Bea turned on the taps in the shower. The view went white. She must have put the phone against the door so the viewer could hear over the shower.

'You all right, Bea?' Dash said. 'Open up and I'll give you Evie's clothes.'

'Leave them there. I'll get them when I finish in the shower,' Bea said.

Murmuring on the other side of the door. Over the shower it was hard to hear. Ruth turned it up. Gazza remonstrating. Dash urging. 'She's good. Don't worry. She wouldn't know anything about that stuff. She's pretty dumb.'

More murmuring.

Gazza's voice, raised. 'Did she have her phone with her?'

'Yeah, she had it in her hand, like she always does.'

Then, 'No, I'm not going in there.'

More murmuring. A thud against the door.

Bea's face again. Bea's index finger descended to the screen. The recording stopped.

'Wow. That was absolutely . . .' Charlie's voice petered out.

Ruth pressed replay and watched it again.

Dash's first responses to Bea's questions were in his customary empathetic bonhomie, the smile in his voice, the certainty that he could make any situation better by emitting his golden glow.

The distress in Bea's tone intensified, her questions were more insistent.

There came a moment, viewed from under Dash's chin, when he registered that she was complaining that he hadn't asked her whether she consented. His voice faded. He swallowed. His lower lip was limp, his mouth gaped.

But even with that, at the end of the conversation, he did not twig that he might be accused of a serious criminal offence. In his mind, Dash had just been doing a favour for a mate, because Dash was blessed and could do anything.

And it was just sex: a laugh, a bit of fun, something to do on a Wednesday night while watching the footy with a mate.

The girl would be fine with it, too, because, after all, she'd do anything he asked. She worshipped him.

Now he knew she was a bit upset. He'd ask next time, and they could do it again, and it would be more fun for everyone. It was a minor misunderstanding, a glitch that the Dash charm would soon overcome.

If she would just clean herself up, she would feel better about the whole thing.

Then Gazza's voice.

Gazza was worried that Bea was chatting with Dash.

He knew what damage a video could do, how powerful it could be, in evidence, or uploaded to the internet. He was urging Dash to get the phone.

Ruth sat back.

'That poor girl,' said Charlie. 'I've never seen anything so raw.'

'But how did she know to record it?' said Ruth. 'To do a pretext conversation?'

'A what?'

'When a rape victim tries to get the perpetrator to admit they didn't seek her consent. Police do it.'

'Maybe she thought to do it herself.'

'I'd be surprised if she could think that straight. It's so targeted. Almost scripted. Someone told her to do it. Question is who. And when.'

Back in the pub, Ruth hugged Bea, her nose in Bea's crimson hair. 'I'm so sorry, Bea. It's traumatic even to watch it. You're very brave.'

They sat back down in the booth.

'How did you get out?' Ruth asked.

'Climbed out the bathroom window while the shower was on. Got a bike from the shed and rode down to the gate. Troy picked me up. Just missed Gazza in his LandCruiser with the spotlights.'

Charlie shook his head, with a smile of admiration.

Back in lawyer mode, Ruth addressed the good news first. 'The video might help Troy.'

'How?'

'Gazza won't have told Detective Messer he was one of the last people to see you before you went missing. She'll have to take him off the case. It's pretty bad. He'll be suspended. Might lose his job.'

'Should lose his job,' said Charlie.

'The only problem with the video is that it's evidence that you had a reason to kill Dash,' said Ruth. 'Might make you a suspect.'

'Will it help with getting Gazza charged with rape?'

The pokies dinged in the back room, a haze of coloured light giving the room a psychedelic hue in the gloom.

There was no way to break it to the girl gently.

'It probably can't be used against Gazza. Not in relation to consent anyway. You didn't talk to him. You asked Dash.'

Ruth pictured the shot of Dash's chin and nostrils. Dash's mouth was open, his Adam's apple prominent. It was the moment he realised that Bea hadn't said yes, that he hadn't asked her. That uncomfortable silence.

'All it does is place Gazza at the scene. So if he denies being there, the court will use it. But otherwise, I don't know. Maybe the parts where you are distressed.'

Ruth didn't mention her other concern: that a defence barrister might seize on it to say she can't have been that upset, or scared, or threatened, if she had the time and opportunity to make a video with the people she says just raped her.

'What if I just upload the video to YouTube or TikTok or something? Without saying who did it.'

'Anonymously? Yes, you could do that. Even that would help Troy with Gazza.'

'Will it stop Troy being charged?'

'No,' said Ruth.

'How do I stop that?'

'To stop him being charged with your abduction? Show them you're alive and weren't abducted.'

'What about him being charged with Dash's murder?'

'I can't see how it would help with that,' said Ruth. 'Might make it worse.'

'So what should I do?' said Bea.

'You've got three choices,' said Ruth. 'First is come back to Myddle and give the video to the police. Second is come back to Myddle and keep the video to yourself. Third: stay hidden.'

'But what is Bea supposed to do for the rest of her life if she stays away?' said Charlie. 'She'd have to go off-grid, change her identity, or operate for the rest of her life with no bank account and no health care. And when they do find her, it's going to look really bad for her that she stayed away.'

Ruth nodded. 'It's a shit sandwich.'

'Troy might be charged whether or not Bea goes back,' Charlie added. 'And Bea would have to find a job that pays cash.' He grimaced at Ruth. 'If anyone should be banished from the kingdom, it shouldn't be Bea. It should be Gazza.'

Bea hit the edge of her coaster on the table, flipped it, slid her fingers down and banged it again.

'Your mum's very worried about you,' said Ruth. 'It's hard on her, too.'

'Poor Mum.' Bea's voice gravelled over the words. 'She gets lonely. I'm the only person she's got.'

The pokies pinged out a tinny tune, their garish lights reflected on the ceiling.

'Fuck it,' said Bea. 'I'm going home. Can I come with youse?'

'Of course,' said Ruth. 'Do you want me to send the video to Detective Messer?'

⸻

During the drive back to Myddle, Ruth got a call from Sharon Messer.

'Have you seen the video?' asked Ruth.

Sharon was perfunctory. 'Yep. Can you come in? We want to talk to Troy.'

'You have to release him.'

'We were going to charge him. But now this. We need to understand what it means. Can you promise he'll stay in Myddle if we let him go?'

'I'm not promising anything.'

'Thought you'd say that.'

'Detective Messer,' said Bea from the back seat.

'Who's that?'

'Bea Baulderstone.'

'Can you confirm that, Ruth?'

'I can,' said Ruth. 'I'm ringing Troy's mum now to tell her to go and pick him up. Because you have to release him. Right now.'

Ruth hung up and rang Rita.

⸻

'One thing I was wondering,' said Ruth, as she drove into the thick dark.

'Yeah?' said Bea.

'Who did you talk to? About doing the video.'

A long silence.

'Chandra?'

Pins of light shining on the side of the road. Eyes. Watching.

Then, very quiet: 'Yeah.'

Chandra had her fingers in every part of this story. Dressed in her wafty white shift, she manifested like a spirit being at every crisis: Evie falling off a cliff, Bea being sexually assaulted.

'You rang her from the house?'

'Yeah.'

'But she didn't pick you up?'

'No. She wasn't home.'

Charlie's head swivelled to look at Ruth. They both knew where Chandra was on State of Origin night. She'd been at Ruth's; she'd disappeared to take a call. And then she'd rung Troy.

Troy was ten minutes closer to Dash's house than Chandra was that night.

'Can I ask,' said Ruth. 'Your shoe size?'

'Eight.'

Same size as Evie's.

It was past midnight when they arrived back in Myddle.

From the darkness in the back seat, Bea's voice was tired. 'Mum's going to be really pissed with me. Waking her up and then telling her about Gazza.'

'You can stay with us tonight if you like,' said Ruth. 'I'll drop you at your mum's in the morning.'

WhatsApp

Ruth
We've found Bea

Jack
Good

Ruth
Gazza and Dash raped her on State of Origin night. She ran away.

Jack
[meme of man looking stunned and horrified]

Ruth
Troy helped her

Jack
The good guy

Ruth
He was on Clive Rd at 3.30 pm on
Sunday after he dropped her off

Jack
Alibi?

Ruth
No. It puts him very near the scene of the
crime with two motives to kill Dash: money
and revenge. The opposite of an alibi.

56

EVIE

June, Friday, four days after

EVIE PULLED UP OUTSIDE RITA'S HOUSE, WALKED UP THE FRONT STAIRS AND through the open door. Rita was in the front room. She hugged her. 'Where is he?' Rita nodded in the direction of the kitchen.

Troy was eating a bowl of cereal. He stood: gangly, awkward.

Evie held out her arms.

'He was the best brother. He would have been the best dad.'

He submitted to the hug, and stiffly squeezed her back. She handed him the framed photograph of Joof from her mother's room in the aged care facility, standing by a horse, grinning. 'This is for you,' she said.

Rita came in. Troy showed her the photo.

'Wasn't that the photo in your mum's room?' said Rita. Her tone was asking, *Is that it, the sum total of your giving, after all that talk?*

Evie shrugged. 'It's all I've got. I had it in my ute. The house is still taped off.'

Rita slowly nodded.

'When we get through all this and the dust settles, we'll sit down and work out what the future looks like.'

Rita's eyes narrowed.

Now wasn't the time to tell them about the baby. Evie was still working out what it meant herself.

57

RUTH

June, Friday, four days after

BEA DAWDLED OVER BREAKFAST. BENEATH HER GLORIOUSLY CRIMSON hair, she was pale and small and vulnerable, her thin white legs ending in a bulky pair of Blundstone boots.

'You okay?' Ruth said.

'Yep.'

'We need to take you to see Sharon Messer.'

Hunched down, Bea was tiny in the front seat of Ruth's car.

Sharon came out to reception and took Ruth and Bea into the malodorous interview room.

'Are you okay, Bea?' asked Sharon. 'Thanks for that video. It looks like you had an awful time.'

'I'm okay, thanks.'

'Do you want to press charges?'

'I don't know.'

'Well, I'm here if you want to have a chat about it. When you're ready.'

Sharon stood. That seemed to be the end of the interview. Nothing about alibis in Dongo. Nothing about Troy. No word of caution or encouragement in relation to the rape charges.

Sharon beckoned to Ruth. 'Can I have a word?'

'You go to the car,' said Ruth to Bea. 'I'll be out in a minute.'

Sharon sat again. That smell: a marriage of mould, mice, damp cement, cheap disinfectant and urine.

'After we got Bea's video, we did a search of Constable Parker's police vehicle. There was blood on the driver's seat. And on the floor mat. He tried to clean it off. It's being tested, but it's less than a week old.

'Looks like the older footprints near the body were his. And his fingerprints were all over the gun, under Dash's prints. Which would explain why he picked it up when he was called out to Dash's body.'

Wow, Ruth thought but did not say. Instead, she said, 'Have you arrested him?'

'No. He admits to being at the site on Sunday but denies killing Dash. Even gave a statement.'

Ruth's eyebrows went up.

'I know,' said Sharon. 'He ignored his legal advice, obviously.'

'What's he saying?'

'That he found Dash like that. Dead. And sat with him, crying. Says he was drunk so he didn't call us in.'

'What about the prints on the gun?'

'Dash found it and Gazza held it, he says.'

'So he was there when Dash was alive, as well as finding him dead?'

'Exactly. Not a very convincing story, is it? He's our prime suspect at the moment. We're waiting on bloods.'

'Why are you telling me this?'

'Because you were right. Again.'

Was she, though? Ruth had never asserted that Gazza killed Dash, only that he was trying to frame Troy.

Why would Gazza kill his only friend in Myddle?

WhatsApp

Ruth
Troy's in the clear. For now.

Jack
?

Ruth
Gazza is going to be arrested for Dash's murder

Jack
You're a legend

Ruth
🤔

Jack
What?

Ruth
Gazza and Dash had just consummated their relationship. They'd literally just celebrated their bromance by having sex together. Why would Gazza murder him?

Jack
1 Not sure I should be talking to my mum about this
2 Jealousy?

Ruth
🤔

Jack
Shouldn't you just be punching the air because your clients won't be investigated anymore?

Ruth
Yes that's exactly what I should do

Jack
But?

Ruth
We need to find out who did it. Or I'll never sleep again.

58

GAZZA

June, Friday, four days after

THERE WAS NO AGGRO IN SHARON MESSER'S QUESTION. BUT COPS WITH no aggro are sometimes the ones you have to worry about.

The blood on the driver's seat of the LandCruiser. Fuck. His plan was to torch it if he had to, and blame the local kids. But he assumed that he would be the first to know if Bea turned up; that he'd have time.

Now the opportunity was gone. And he was in deep shit.

Dash with his fucking Pollyanna view of the world—where nothing bad ever happened—was always going to get Gazza into trouble. It was inevitable.

He should have realised State of Origin night was too good to be true.

Bea seemed to be up for it. She didn't argue. Or object.

Although now that he thought about it, he realised it had been Dash who was up for it.

And she wasn't all that keen at first.

But what was he supposed to do when it got started?

Fucking fantastic while it lasted.

But it didn't, did it?

The crying.

And the conversation he'd heard Bea having with Dash sounded suspiciously like a pretext conversation. He'd never been involved in one himself but he'd been made to go to a course on sexual assault where they talked about it—the girl rings up the perpetrator in the presence of a police officer and a recording device and tries to get the guy to admit she didn't consent.

Dash was so clueless he didn't realise what she was doing.

It was beyond Dash's comprehension that a woman would say no to something he proposed.

But if Gazza was right about it: what a way to end a career. A rape trial and possibly even gaol.

Humiliating. And gaol for a copper would be bad; very bad.

Oh Christ.

And then Bea just fucked off. Not easy to do when you're a quarter-hour drive from town and you don't have a car.

Dash didn't seem overly worried about it when Gazza came back from looking for her.

'She must have rung a mate to pick her up,' he said. 'She'll be right once she sleeps it off.'

Gazza wondered who Bea's mate was. She was usually out the times he'd gone over to Victoria's place for dinner, so she must have lots of friends.

He waited until the end of the game, but it was shithouse. The Blues lost. Again.

He saw no sign of her on the way home. Dash was probably right. It would blow over.

The Sunday after the State of Origin, Victoria rang to complain that Bea hadn't been home. She rang the police station landline and it diverted to his mobile.

Gazza told her Bea had left because of her, which probably had an element of truth.

Victoria let fly a torrent of abuse, so he hung up on her. He didn't have to listen to that shit.

He rang Dash.

'Victoria's looking for Bea.'

'What's her problem?' said Dash.

'Bea hasn't been home.'

The bottle of vodka on Gazza's coffee table was only half full. He'd have to go to the bottle-o.

'Since Wednesday night?' said Dash.

'Yep.'

'Fuck,' said Dash. 'I hope she's okay.'

'Was Bea videoing you when you had that chat. After . . . you know.'

Pause.

'Dunno. She might have been, I s'pose.'

'She was in the bathroom before that. Did she call anyone?'

'How would I know?'

'But she was crying, wasn't she?'

'Yeah, she was a bit upset.'

'She might try to allege a rape.'

'Nah, Bea wouldn't do that. She's a good sport.'

'They're all good sports until you break up with them,' said Gazza.

'I didn't break up with her.'

'Don't give me that, mate. You're not going to leave Evie. If you haven't broken up with Bea yet, you're about to.'

There was a pause. Then Dash said, 'Evie might leave me.' His voice cracked up. 'She's pregnant. To Sam Dunstan.'

That news surprised Gazza. He didn't think Evie had it in her. You could never tell with women.

Dash added, 'She's very pissed off.'

'Shouldn't you be the one who's pissed off?'

'Put it this way, mate, I didn't play it very well when she was trying to get pregnant.'

It was Gazza's turn to say fuck.

'So yeah,' said Dash. 'She's gone away for a bit. Won't take my calls. Not looking good.' He made a noise. Sounded like a sob he was trying to contain.

Gazza held the phone away from his ear.

'What a mess,' said Dash. 'Fuck, I hope Bea's okay. I might see if I can find where she went when she left here. I'll call you back.'

Five minutes later, he called. 'Mate,' said Dash, 'she took the rifle.'

'Who? Evie?'

'No, I'm assuming Bea. We keep it in the lock box on the tray of the ute, and it's gone.'

'Fuck,' said Gazza. 'I'm coming out.'

He was in jeans and a hoodie. It was Sunday, his day off.

Dash had the ute on the other side of the grid at the farm gate. He was scrabbling about in the long grass in the ditch by the road.

'She took one of the bikes,' said Dash. 'Was wondering how she got away so quick.'

'Where is it?' said Gazza.

'In the back of the ute.'

'Where did you find it?'

'Here. In the grass by the gate.'

'Found it,' said Dash, holding the rifle aloft. Gazza held out his hand for it and Dash passed it to him.

Gazza checked the rifle. It had a bullet in the chamber. 'Do you keep this thing loaded?'

'Nuh.'

'She must have loaded it. If she slung it over her shoulder while she rode the bike she's lucky she didn't shoot herself. The trigger lock's bent. You should have that looked at.'

'Glad she doesn't have the rifle with her. That's one thing anyway.'

'Yep.'

Dash pulled his phone from his back pocket. 'What's Victoria's number?'

'You're not going to ring her?'

'Course I'm going to ring her. She must be beside herself.'

'She's always beside herself,' said Gazza. 'What're you going to tell her?'

'That Bea left here on Wednesday night. Musta got picked up by someone.'

'How are you going to explain why she was at your place?'

'I'm going to have to suck that one up.' Dash shifted his body so that his feet were apart. He stood strong, centred, steady. 'Because I am concerned about her safety. Aren't you?'

'We're not ringing anyone, mate.'

Dash smiled in disbelief. 'Mate. Be real.'

'I am being real. If she makes an allegation, I'll lose my job.'

'But what about poor Victoria?'

'She's nuts, mate. Don't engage with her.'

Dash stood there in the ditch with his phone in his hand.

Gazza stood on the road above. He was still holding the rifle. 'Don't do it, mate,' said Gazza. 'I'm warning you. Don't do it.'

Dash flashed his million-dollar smile. 'C'mon, mate. Let's do the right thing. I can't do it here anyway. There's no phone coverage. I'll do it later, in the house.'

'I'm not giving you her number.'

That's how Gazza remembered him. Dash below him in the green ditch, smiling.

Gazza put the rifle down by the bitumen and drove home. He swilled a bit of vodka. He only meant to have a mouthful or two to take the edge off. He tried to watch some footy. Stewed. Took a few more mouthfuls of vodka. Couldn't stop thinking about Dash. How being a good bloke would get them both into trouble.

He decided to go back to Dash's and reinforce what he'd told him. Make sure he didn't do anything stupid.

He passed Troy Matheson just outside Myddle on Clive River Road. Troy was driving into town. Smartarse black bastard. Where had he been?

Dash's ute was in the same place on the other side of the grid. But no Dash.

Gazza stopped the LandCruiser. Got out. Stumbled. He was a bit pissed actually. Lucky nobody was watching.

The dogs were there so Dash must be somewhere around, too.

Then he found him. In the long grass in the ditch, his dead eyes staring upward in fear. Frozen.

There was a lot of blood. A bullet wound in his shoulder.

Looked like he'd been hit, too. Something big and hard. A car.

He found the gun in the grass nearby. Didn't touch it. His fingerprints would be on it from earlier. And Dash's. Over the top of his.

He sat beside Dash. 'What happened, mate?' he said.

He cried. First a bit, and then in great sobs. First time he'd cried for a long time. Seven years. When Barb left.

Dash was his best mate. His only mate.

He wasn't sure how long he sat there.

Then he went through what he had to do. And what he couldn't do.

He couldn't ring for help of any kind because he was drunk. Very, very drunk.

Also, how would he explain his presence, the gun, his fingerprints, what Dash was doing?

He needed to go home to think straight.

There was no way he could wait until he was sober, go up there and 'find' Dash's body then alert the authorities. Too risky. Anyway, he wouldn't be sober until morning.

He had to leave Dash outside on his own, dead.

The kelpies would keep an eye out; keep the scavengers at bay.

And someone would find the poor bastard.

In the morning, he remembered Troy driving the other way down Clive River Road. Troy killed Dash. Gazza was sure of that. And Gazza was going to make it his life's work to ensure the black bastard went to gaol.

The last thing he could do for his mate was make sure his murderer was punished.

The bell on the door jangled.

The lawyer lady was standing in front of him, trying to look friendly.

Victoria was trying to pull out the big guns in her search for Bea.

59

BEA

June, Friday, four days after

RUTH JOINED BEA IN THE CAR OUTSIDE THE POLICE STATION. 'TIME TO go to your mum's,' she said.

Bea shrank down in the front seat. Had to do it, she supposed.

The car pulled up outside Victoria's house.

Bea put a reluctant hand on the door handle. It felt like there was a lump of dry cake stuck in her throat.

'You can stay with me if things are awkward,' Ruth said.

She was such a nice lady. Imagine if she'd been Bea's mum.

'Thanks,' said Bea. 'I'll see how it goes.'

Bea walked up the overgrown, cracked concrete path. Ruth followed.

'It's me,' Bea yelled as she walked through the door. She said it loud, trying to sound confident. Unassailable. Cheerful. Like nothing was amiss.

Rufus, the cattle dog, nearly wagged his bottom off, and stuck his nose on her leg.

Victoria rushed out of the kitchen and flung herself onto Bea. 'Where have you been? I've been so worried.'

'Sorry, Mum.'

Victoria saw Ruth and frowned; her mouth compacted into a faded strawberry.

Bea had to get it out. 'Mum, Gazza raped me.'

It came out a bit loud. And how do you say something like that without being blunt?

Victoria stepped back. 'He what?'

Her mother's mouth quivered. That always happened when she was about to blow her top.

Bea wanted to run out the door and back to Ruth's place. But she was here now. She had to stick it out.

'He raped me, Mum. Him and Dash Rogers. That's why I left.'

'No.' Victoria's voice was rising in pitch.

'Yes,' said Bea.

'Oh God. Was he the one you were meeting? Gazza?'

'No,' said Bea. 'Dash. I didn't know Gazza was going to be there.'

'Why didn't you tell me?' Victoria pointed at Ruth. 'Why did you tell her, and not me?'

Ruth stepped forward as if about to engage. That would only make it worse. Bea needed to fend her off; take the brunt of Victoria's hysteria herself.

'This is why I didn't tell you.'

'What have you done?' Victoria's voice rose into a scream.

'I didn't do anything,' said Bea. 'It wasn't my fault.'

Victoria turned on Ruth. 'What are you doing here?' Spit flew out of her mouth.

Rufus stood to attention, eyes on Victoria.

'Bea, you go back to the car,' said Ruth. 'I'll be out in a sec.'

Bea hesitated. Her mum was her responsibility.

'Off you go,' said Ruth. 'There's something I need to talk to your mum about.'

She was firm, gently demanding compliance.

Rufus followed Bea, his snout nudging her hand. Bea hovered at the bottom of the steps. She wanted to hear what Ruth said. And make sure she was okay.

'What are you doing?' Victoria screeched. 'She's *my* daughter!'

Ruth walked to the door. Backward. 'Bea is going to stay with me,' she said. 'When you're ready to have a calm conversation, she and I will come back.'

Victoria advanced. Screaming. Incoherent.

At the door, Ruth said, 'Victoria, you need medical help. This isn't normal.'

Nobody had ever said that to Bea's mum before. People normally tiptoed away and then avoided her.

'Don't you tell me what's normal.'

Ruth moved through the lattice door and closed it. 'You can't do this to Bea.' She walked down the cracked concrete path.

Victoria was on the other side of the lattice. The paint on the crossed slats was blistering.

'When you're ready, Victoria,' Ruth yelled from the car door on the street, 'Bea and I will come back. But if you do this again, we will leave.'

'Jesus, Bea,' Ruth said when the car was at the end of the street. 'Have you been dealing with that on your own?'

Bea huddled in the front seat. It had gone worse than she hoped but pretty much how she expected. The only surprise was another person telling her it wasn't okay.

'It's not normal, Bea. She needs help. And so do you. To deal with it.'

'No one's ever said that to me before,' said Bea. 'That she's not normal.'

'You poor thing,' said Ruth.

As they drove past the pub, Bea put her elbow out the open window. Twister was sweeping the footpath. He looked up and waved in delight when he saw Bea.

The main street petered out to a straggle of houses. They passed the big blue gums by the river.

Ruth's thoughts dribbled out over the ten-minute drive. 'It's abuse. She has a psychiatric condition. I don't know what it is, but she needs treatment. I'm sorry you've had to live with it on your own for so long.'

Ruth's house had a gazillion bedrooms. Charlie was there, working on his computer. He came out to see how it had gone and Ruth shook her head at him.

'You can stay here as long as you need to,' said Ruth.

She poured Bea a lime juice cordial. The three of them sat together at the kitchen table. With a sigh, Buster the labrador settled on Bea's feet.

Maybe Bea's world could be different.

60

RUTH

June, Friday, four days after

AFTER SHE'D SETTLED BEA IN, RUTH SAID, 'WILL YOU BE OKAY HERE? There's something I have to do. You'll be on your own. Charlie's going out, too.' Ruth widened her eyes at him so he took the hint. She didn't want to leave Bea with a man she barely knew.

Charlie twigged. 'Can you drop me at the bank on your way through town?'

'Watch some TV or something. Chill for a bit,' said Ruth to Bea. 'I'll come back as soon as I can.'

After dropping Charlie in town, Ruth drove to Roscoe's, parked the car, and walked in the door past him.

'Can I have a word, Chandra?'

She glowered at Roscoe, daring him to stay in the room. He got it. 'I've got to chop some wood,' he said.

Ruth launched straight into it. 'On State of Origin night, you told Bea that you couldn't pick her up. But you were at my place. Half an hour from her. Tops.'

Chandra nodded.

'Why didn't you pick her up?'

'I asked Troy to pick her up. He was closer.'

Ruth crossed her arms. That couldn't be the only reason. Chandra—a survivor of rape—had received a call for help from a girl who had just been raped. If it had been Ruth she would have been in the car before she hung up.

From outside, Ruth heard a clap of the axe as Roscoe cracked a log.

'I don't want to offend you,' said Chandra.

'I'm unoffendable.'

'I was in a house with two lawyers and a doctor. You'd have contacted the police. Bea would have been in the criminal justice mincer, being ground to a pulp.'

'You underestimate me,' said Ruth.

And more importantly, Chandra underestimated Roscoe. Ruth knew he'd be very hurt when he found out. He would have been in that car with Chandra to stage a rescue mission. So would Charlie.

'I thought at the time it would be better for Bea if her friend picked her up. You lawyers and doctor were Plan B.'

Roscoe brought the axe down again.

Chandra stood and moved to the huge picture window. 'My life was ruined because I made a complaint about a rape,' she said. 'I wanted her to have some control. I wanted her to have the space to make an informed decision. Knowing what it would be like.'

Ruth said, 'I'm sorry the legal system let you down so badly, Chandra.'

The noises from Roscoe were softer now as he stacked the wood. Chandra leaned against the window frame, watching him, her arms crossed.

'I told Bea to record a conversation with Dash, so that she'd have the evidence if she needed it. It would buy her time to decide what she wanted to do next.'

'That was clever,' said Ruth. 'It would've helped a lot if Dash hadn't . . .' She trailed off.

Chandra scoffed. 'I'm sure the defence lawyers would have twisted it against her. Said she planned it, set him up, or something.'

Roscoe was banging his boots on the mat at the door.

'Bea showed me the video the next morning. Dash's admission didn't really go far enough, did it?' said Chandra. 'He would have got off.'

Ruth agreed with that analysis. Dash's surprise on the video about Bea's accusation would have worked for Dash rather than against him. 'You could be right,' she said.

Chandra was in profile against the window, gazing out at the river.

If Chandra had no faith that the legal system would deliver, was she capable of seeking retribution herself?

Chandra's bare feet were long and thin, toes in silver toe rings. Ruth looked at her own feet, size seven. Chandra's were more than an inch longer.

'What's your shoe size Chandra?'

Chandra moved her right foot around as if seeing it for the first time. 'Nine and a half.'

'Are they Evie's footprints where Dash was killed? Or Bea's? Were you there with one of them?'

No answer. Chandra was like a heron in the reeds: alert but completely still.

'Was Evie at the farm on Sunday afternoon when Dash was killed?'

No answer.

'She would have had to drive past your house.'

Nothing. The light reflected on the silver in Chandra's hair.

'What happened after you took Evie to the hospital the week before Dash died?'

Right behind Ruth, Roscoe cleared his throat. She startled. She'd been so absorbed in Chandra, she wasn't aware that he was in the room, listening. 'Is this conversation privileged?' he said.

No. It wasn't. If Chandra made some admission that she'd committed a crime—helped Evie kill Dash, say—Ruth could be called to give evidence about it in a court.

Roscoe wasn't going to let Chandra say anything more.

Ruth picked up her keys.

She needed to know what Evie had done.

Ruth pulled up outside Patch's house, stomped over the verandah and through the open front door.

Milly squealed in delight. 'Roof,' she said.

Ruth gave her a pat on the head. 'I need to speak to Evie.'

Milly trotted off down the hall. 'Evie!'

Evie emerged: pale, thin.

Ruth walked back out to the verandah, down the stairs into the garden. Evie followed.

Ruth kept up the mantra to herself, 'Steady on, sister.' She had Sharon Messer's voice in her head, that raspy sound telling her to hold it, to wait and see where the facts took her, don't jump ahead, let it pan out. But her heart was thumping, loud, in her chest.

Ruth had become fond of Evie in the short time she'd known her—her lanky body, her discomfort in dealing with campers, her love for Horace, her skill with the cattle, her easy tolerance of Gazza. But the facts were looming up against her.

'The police found bloody footprints near Dash's body. Women's size eight and men's. The women's prints are either yours or Bea's. I think they're yours.'

Evie picked up a stick and poked at the ground.

61

EVIE

June, the week before

THE NIGHT AFTER EVIE FELL AT THE BLUFF, AND EVIE TOLD CHANDRA TO fuck off, there was a thick silence filled with Chandra's dismay. Evie looked up from the bucket into which she had vomited.

'I really am sorry about Horace,' said Chandra. 'I feel awful about the distress I've caused.'

'I just want you to stop harassing me about the fucking eco-resort,' said Evie.

'I'm sorry. It's just that it's a special place. I didn't mean—'

'I fucking know that, Chandra. My dead family lives on the Bluff, my dead brother. Troy's dead ancestors live there. A building there would contaminate it. Destroy it. I can't do it.'

Chandra had that look on her face people have when they finally understand how to solve a problem that has been troubling them. Revelation.

'It means a lot to you,' said Chandra.

Evie shook her head. Of course it fucking did. There was a chasm in understanding between them.

Chandra reached out for Evie's hand. It had vomit on it.

'Oh yuck,' said Evie. 'Sorry about that.'

Chandra gripped Evie's hand. 'I'm sorry. I didn't realise what the land meant to you.'

'That's because you've made a whole lot of assumptions about me. Which are not just wrong, they're fucking offensive.'

'I think you should go to hospital,' Chandra said. 'You might be concussed.'

It came out before she could censor it. 'If you're worried about the vomiting, don't be. I'm pregnant.'

Evie realised then, when looking at the shape of Chandra's mouth, the rapture in her face, that the pregnancy of a person who has been waiting for years for a baby was cause for public joy. If it ever came out, the origin of the sperm would be a very complicated news story. For the whole town.

Chandra hugged her. 'That's amazing.'

Evie inhaled. 'It is amazing.'

'Dash knows?'

'We just found out. This morning.'

'So you're just pregnant?'

'Five weeks or so.'

Chandra stroked Evie's forehead.

'It's so wonderful,' said Chandra. 'After all this time. A miracle.'

Evie kept her eyes closed.

'Dash must be so happy.'

Evie opened one eye to gauge why Chandra's voice rose slightly at the end of the sentence, as if she was asking a question.

Chandra's green cat eyes were staring down at her with empathetic concern.

Evie closed her eyes again.

'What happened at the Bluff?' Chandra asked.

'I slipped.'

'Why were you up there?'

Evie didn't answer.

'Did Dash push you?'

'No.' Was that true? Evie couldn't recall him touching her.

Why was Chandra expressing doubt about Dash's reaction to the baby? It was as if she knew about Sam.

Evie leaned over the bucket and vomited again.

'I think you should go to hospital,' said Chandra firmly. 'Get checked out. I'll drive you.'

Chandra went outside to tell Dash. Evie didn't hear what Dash said, but Chandra convinced him to stay at the farm while she took Evie.

Chandra asked no questions during the drive. By the time they arrived at Broughton emergency, Evie wondered if she was wrong about Chandra. Maybe Chandra was okay, even if she was a vegan.

Evie was admitted to hospital for the night for observation.

Chandra slept in the chair beside her bed. Keeping guard?

The next morning, Chandra drove Evie to an Airbnb she'd organised at Azuri. That afternoon, she delivered Evie's ute to Azuri.

'I told Dash you needed it,' she said, without embellishment.

'Does he know where I am?'

'I told him you're at Azuri. He doesn't know where.'

'Is he angry?'

Chandra shrugged. As if it wasn't relevant.

Maybe it wasn't.

Once Evie was settled, Chandra caught the bus back to Myddle.

While Evie was at Azuri, Dash called her three or four times a day. She didn't want to speak to him. What was the point? Recriminations. Shouting. It was unresolvable. The baby. The farm.

She couldn't see how he could be a part of her future.

Divorce was inevitable, but it might take a month for him to realise. Or five years. But at some point, if he hadn't already, he was going to go to a lawyer and work out he was entitled to a chunk of the farm. And once he had that land, he could do what he liked with it: campsite, five-star hotel, space station. The only people who were going to limit him were the planning authorities.

Evie had a block in mind, near Roscoe. Whatever Dash did with it, wouldn't affect her. Nice land, on the river. Hotel, subdivision for house blocks. He could make a fortune out of it, if he did it right.

But she knew he wouldn't want it. Dash wanted the Bluff. To defile it; conquer it. And when he realised how much she wanted it, he would want it even more.

She turned her phone off.

She spent days in the Airbnb in Azuri, in turns vomiting, and puzzling through her options to be rid of Dash. The sicker she was, she told herself, the stronger the pregnancy, the more healthy the baby.

The only certain way to preserve the Bluff was to gift it to Troy: give it to someone to whom it meant even more than it meant to her. She had to hope that the transfer to Troy would go through before Dash brought divorce proceedings.

Evie and the baby would get half of what was left. Would it be viable? It would have to be. She'd get the herd, surely. Dash had no interest in breeding cows.

She went for a swim, which made her feel better. It wasn't such a shit sandwich really—she'd have the baby, and a bit less land and income.

Every morning when Evie woke up, she turned her phone on and deleted Dash's messages without reading them. Then she did the Wordle.

On Saturday, Chandra turned up in Azuri with a bottle of homemade Rosella cordial.

'I would have brought kombucha but pregnant women can't drink it. Don't know why.'

'I've been reading up,' said Evie. 'There are all these rules with pregnancy, which effectively mean I can't eat or drink anything with flavour: blue cheese, ham.'

Chandra fiddled with a beach house coaster at the kitchen table. 'I don't know what to do,' she said.

'About what?'

'Dash. I know you're thinking through your future with him. I know something that may be relevant to your decision. It's kind of awful. Do I tell you?'

'You have to now,' said Evie.

Chandra pulled out her phone and played her Bea's video.

Evie recoiled as she watched it, then watched it again through her fingers. 'He raped her?'

'He doesn't think so,' said Chandra.

'It would be beyond his comprehension that anyone would say no to him,' said Evie.

'That's the legal test,' said Chandra. 'Did he think she agreed to it.'

'Is he going to be charged with rape?'

'Bea's gone away to think about whether she goes to the police.'

Chandra reached for Evie's hand. 'I have two women who've gone AWOL to think through their future because of Dash.'

'Jesus,' said Evie.

She couldn't live with him now.

She had to tell him to move out of the house.

But if she did that, she wouldn't have time to transfer the land to Troy before the divorce proceedings got under way.

Evie barely slept.

Sunday. As good a day as any to tell Dash to move out. And she needed some clean warm clothes.

She'd deliver an ultimatum today.

She left her phone in Azuri, on the charger.

When she got to the cattle grid at the gate, Dash was poking around in the grass near the road, looking for something.

She stopped in the drive before the cattle grid and got out.

The kelpies leapt up against her. She put her hand out to hold them at bay. 'Hello, Bryan. Hello, Rachel,' she said to the dogs. 'I'm pleased to see you, too.'

'G'day, love.' Dash tried to hug her. She stiffened. 'How're you feeling?'

'Not great,' she said. 'We need to talk.'

He straightened and stepped back.

'At the house,' she added.

'Can I see you at the house in twenty?' said Dash. 'I've just got to clean up here.'

He didn't say what he was doing and she was beyond caring.

'I'll see you there,' she said.

Dash's ute was on the other side of the grid blocking the drive, so she jumped in it and drove to the house. It was a mess—dirty plates, empty bottles—and smelt of sausages and stale beer.

There was a small backpack in the sitting room. Bright green. She opened it up. Bea's learner's licence and debit card. She left it there. Maybe he hadn't noticed it in the mess.

She packed some clothes in an overnight bag. And some toiletries.

She heard a crack, like a gunshot. It had come from the direction of the farm gate. She drove tentatively back there.

Where was Dash? She stopped the ute and walked over the grid. Then she saw him, lying in the grass in the ditch, on his side.

He had a graze on his chin, more weeping than bleeding. It had bits of dirt stuck in it.

'What happened?' she said.

'Don't know,' said Dash. His eyes were dancing around, looking for something to focus on.

'Are you hurt?' said Evie.

'I think my arm's broken.'

She looked at his arm, limp by his side. It was broken all right. Bent. He must be in shock and couldn't feel it yet. She saw it then, under the grass. Blood was pumping out of his shoulder.

A surge of adrenaline inside her.

'What happened?' she said again.

His brows knitted in confusion. He was in shock.

She knelt beside him, felt his forehead.

'I'll call an ambulance,' she said. 'Don't move.'

Phone coverage at the gate was patchy. She might have to go back to the house.

But of course, she'd left her phone in Azuri.

She checked Dash's pocket for his phone. Not there. Not in his ute. It might have been in the grass. Maybe it flew away when he was hit.

He was losing a lot of blood, fading out of consciousness.

He needed an ambulance. She needed help.

'Back in a sec, Dash,' she said. She jumped in her own ute this time and drove fast to Roscoe's. He wasn't there but Chandra came out to greet her.

'Dash is injured,' she told Chandra.

'What happened?'

'I don't know, but he's losing a lot of blood.'

Chandra's eyes widened.

'I don't have my phone. Can you call an ambulance?'

'Wait there.' Chandra ran into the house and came back with a big bag and white running shoes. 'I've got something for the pain,' she said, jumping into the passenger seat.

Evie drove fast up the road but slowed as the ute neared their farm gate. She approached Dash at a crawl. His eyes were closed. It had been twelve minutes, tops. She'd driven very fast.

Chandra got her bag and jumped out of the car.

'Can you call the dogs onto the tray of the ute? Maybe you should turn around down there,' Chandra said, pointing down the hill.

It was only a couple of minutes or so. Evie backed down the hill to where there was a bit of shoulder, turned and reversed back to Chandra, who jumped into the passenger seat.

'How long will it take for the ambulance to get here?' Evie asked.

'There is no ambulance,' said Chandra.

'What do you mean?' said Evie.

Chandra shook her head and reached out to touch Evie's leg. 'He's dead, Evie.'

Time slowed.

That black foam around her again; the protective barrier against a big stormy trauma. The day was dolorous calm, green hills rolling away down to Myddle. A crow in the eucalypt above them let out a long caw, which rose up into the blue sky and dispersed as a fading note.

'It's okay,' said Chandra. Her mellifluous voice was soothing.

'Oh,' said Evie. It squeaked out.

'What you have to do now, Evie,' said Chandra, 'after you've dropped me at home, is drive back to Azuri. Take the back road, at the speed limit. When you get there, drive to Coles from your Airbnb. Go in with a shopping bag and pick up some groceries. Make sure you're on the CCTV. Nobody comes up this road. We've got at least a day I reckon before anyone twigs that Dash is missing.

'Because if they know you were here, and find out what state your marriage is in, you might be charged with murder.'

'But I didn't kill him,' said Evie. 'I found him like this.'

'Best if you weren't here,' said Chandra.

Bryan and Rachel, the kelpies, sat at Evie's feet. 'What about the dogs? Who'll feed them?'

'Nobody will feed them, Evie. Because nobody is here. Let them out.'

The kelpies jumped out of the ute, and lay against Dash. 'There's no record we've been here. Your phone isn't here. Nor is mine. Your ute doesn't have a computer. My car, which does, is safe in the garage. Now all we have to do is create a record of you in Azuri.'

Chandra's voice was so calm, that lyrical tone she had when weaving mystic escape.

Evie couldn't look at Dash again.

She took her foot off the brake and the ute rolled down the hill.

62

RUTH

June, Friday, four days after

EVIE'S STORY CAME OUT HALTINGLY AT FIRST, THEN IN A TORRENT.

'So Dash was mortally injured by someone who drove up to your farm gate while you were in the house?'

Evie nodded.

'You didn't see the car?'

She shook her head.

Telling that story to Sharon Messer would have been a challenge before she discovered the blood in Gazza's LandCruiser. Now it fitted neatly in.

But was it true? Ruth couldn't overcome her doubt that Gazza would kill his best mate.

Evie could be lying.

Who else could have driven up there? Troy? Chandra?

Ruth drove to Roscoe and Chandra's house.

They came out to the car.

Ruth was beyond skirting around the issue now. 'Did you drive up there, Chandra?'

'Don't answer that, Chandra,' said Roscoe.

'I thought it was Evie,' said Chandra. 'But if it wasn't Evie . . .'

Ruth waited.

'The only other person I spoke to that morning was Victoria. She rang me demanding to know where Bea was, accusing me of hiding her away. You know what she's like. Shouting. Accusations.'

'Did she know about the rape?'

'No. She rang me because she knew Bea spent time here. She said she was coming out to the house to see for herself if Bea was with me.'

'Did she?'

'She never turned up.'

Ruth drove to Victoria's.

Rufus, the cattle dog, knew her now and came to the lattice door to wag his tail and put his wet nose through to her hand.

'Victoria!' Ruth shouted through the door. 'It's Ruth Dawson again. Can I have a quick word?'

A scowling Victoria unlocked the lattice door without enthusiasm, avoiding Ruth's eyes. There was no greeting.

Ruth stood near the door, in case she had to leave quickly.

In the car on the way over, she'd formulated the best way to extract information from Victoria.

'I'm worried Bea's in the firing line to be charged with Dash Rogers' murder,' said Ruth. It wasn't a complete fabrication. Ruth *was* worried about that. Not very, now that Sharon Messer's attention was on Gazza, but Bea would certainly be a suspect.

Victoria didn't move.

'She had a motive. The only alibi she has is Troy, who is implicated as well.'

Victoria turned away and walked down the hall to the kitchen. Ruth followed. Victoria filled the electric jug with water, put it on the base, pressed down the switch.

At least she was listening. But her anger was pent up in that small body, those hunched shoulders. She was like unexploded ordnance. It was hard to tell when it would go off.

Victoria opened the cupboard and pulled out two teacups. Floral design. Royal Doulton. And saucers.

'If Bea's arrested for murder, she goes to prison straight away. Remand. It will take a couple of years for it to get to trial. She won't get bail. Not for a murder charge. So, even if she's acquitted, that's maybe two years in prison. She'll be twenty when she gets out. And that's if she gets off.'

Water makes a noise as the molecules move around more with the heat; a soft roar, louder and louder as the pressure builds.

'Is that what you want for her?' said Ruth. 'And you. You'll be alone.'

Victoria opened the fridge and removed the milk. She opened the cupboard again and retrieved a milk jug, also floral.

Ruth wanted to shake her, wanted to shout, 'Stop with the fucking tea set!'

'You drove out to Clive Downs to talk to Dash, didn't you?' said Ruth.

The water bubbled. The jug whistled. Victoria swallowed. Her gaze fixed on the wall above the jug, and she embarked on her response as if on a journey.

'I just went to ask him if he knew where she was. People were saying she'd gone away. Where would she go? She was always talking about Dash and his wife and their horses. I thought they might know where she'd gone. Or maybe that she was staying there.'

'When was that?'

'Sunday. Bea had been gone a few days.'

'So after you spoke to Gazza?'

'I realised I was going to have to look myself. He wasn't going to help.'

'So you drove out to talk to Dash?'

'He was near the cattle grid at the entrance to their property. Looking for something in the grass by the road.'

Ruth nodded.

'You spoke to Dash?'

Victoria nodded.

'I stopped and asked him if Bea was there.'

'From the car? Your engine was still running?'

Victoria's hands were shaking. She clasped them together.

'What did Dash say?'

'He said, no.'

Rufus grunted and rolled over in the sun.

'I said because she went out there a lot.'

Victoria glanced at Ruth. 'He was worried, wasn't he, that I knew he'd raped her? I didn't know.'

Ruth shrugged. 'Perhaps. What did he say?'

'He said, "She's not here. You don't think she's just left town to take a break?"'

Victoria's eyes locked onto Ruth's. 'He tried to say she'd run away from me.'

But he didn't say that. He was asking whether that was a possibility, as if he wanted to make sure there wasn't a simple explanation for her absence. Ruth saw no point in challenging Victoria about her interpretation. It would only make her more angry.

Victoria had a note of triumph in her voice when she said, 'I told him what I thought of that idea.' She nodded as if she was expecting Ruth to congratulate her.

Ruth said, 'And what happened next?'

'Then he said, "I think you should calm down, and we can talk about it."'

Victoria sneered. 'Patronising me, saying I can't control myself.'

'And?'

'I drove off.'

Dash was inviting her to talk, and instead she'd driven away, because she distorted everything said to her, fed it through a prism of fear that people would abandon her or criticise her. Poor Bea, living with this.

'Where was Dash at that point?'

'Still by the road.'

Her right index finger scratched away at her left palm.

'So you turned around?'

'There isn't much room there. A ute was parked in their driveway. So I went up the road quite a way, and turned around. It took a little while. I had to do a five-point turn. I was coming down the hill, had built up some speed. He had a gun in his hand.'

'What? He picked it up?'

'Must have. I didn't notice it until then.'

'He pointed it at you?'

She faltered. 'He was holding it.'

'So not actually pointing it at you.'

'He could have been. And then he jumped in front of the car.'

Ruth couldn't believe it. Who would jump in front of a car going that fast? Not Dash.

'He must have,' said Victoria.

'Because you hit him.'

Victoria nodded. 'He had a gun,' she repeated.

Ruth waited.

'It was just a tap,' said Victoria. 'But he fell.'

'Under the car?'

'I stopped when I heard the gun go off.'

She was going to wear a hole in her palm.

'I didn't mean to,' said Victoria. 'It was a mistake. He was standing on the road. He had a gun. He stepped in front of me.'

It made no sense, a jumble of inconsistent actions and justifications.

'What did you do next?'

She turned back to the jug. 'I drove home.'

'You left him there.'

'I thought his wife would find him. He wasn't dead. I didn't kill him.'

She fidgeted with the jug.

'How do you know? That he was still alive,' said Ruth. 'You got out of the car to check on him?'

'No. He was making a noise.'

'Talking?'

She put her head to one side to consider that, to remember it.

'Sort of. Making a noise. The gun had gone off.'

'And then you just drove off.'

'I panicked.'

The dog sighed and rolled over.

'You left him there to die.'

'No. His wife should have found him. Or someone driving past. Why wasn't his wife there?'

Ruth didn't answer that. Human beings were capable of absolving themselves of responsibility by blaming someone else; explaining away the most terrible things by identifying what other people 'should' have done.

'The way he spoke to me. It was so'—she searched for a word—'disparaging.' Victoria looked up, looked Ruth in the eye. 'I get so angry.'

Ruth pulled out her phone.

'What are you doing?' she asked.

'I'm ringing the police. You need to tell them this.'

Victoria shook her head, as if shaking off a bee that was stinging her.

'If you don't do this, Victoria, Bea could be arrested. She's seventeen. It will destroy her life. Is that what you want?'

Victoria shook her head again.

Sharon Messer picked up the call on the first ring. 'Yep.'

'Can you come to two Woodland Street.'

'Be there in five,' said Messer. 'Is that soon enough? You in danger?'

Ruth looked at Victoria with her hand on the jug of boiling water.

'No,' she said.

Ruth pressed the red dot on her phone, stepped forward, took Victoria's arm, led her gently to the kitchen table and guided her into a seat.

'I'll make us a cup of tea,' said Ruth. 'While we wait for the police.'

WhatsApp

Ruth
Victoria confessed

Jack
Who?

Ruth
Bea's mum. Unbridled rage. Got out of hand.

Jack
I wouldn't have picked that

Ruth
None of us did

Jack
You solved it

Ruth
Yes

Jack
Wow
[online]
I'm coming home in September

Ruth
♥

Jack
Might bring Annabelle for a bit

Ruth
I'd like that

63

BEA

June, Friday, four days after

SHE AND TROY WERE BY THE CREEK AGAIN. THE LIGHT WAS CRISP, THE crows cawing. The horses stood under a eucalypt. It was funny how they always stood with one of their back hooves tipped up at right angles.

'So is it true?' she said. 'That Evie's your aunt?'

'Yep,' he said.

'You had no idea?'

'I thought it was a bit weird that she wanted to spend time with me. And mum was always very cagey about my dad, but not hostile, so I never got the sense he was a bad person; just that it was sad that he died. So when Evie started sniffing around and talking to me about being a farmer, I wondered.'

'Aren't you pissed?'

'Nah. My mum does her best. And Evie was always sad and lonely, even when Dash was alive.'

Troy stepped out onto a granite boulder in the creek and examined the surface of the water.

'Hey, Bea.' He held out his hand. She took it and stepped on the boulder. There wasn't much room. They had to stand hip to hip.

Platypus. Two of them, passing one another.

'See how each of them pretends they're the only platypus in the creek?' said Troy. 'They never acknowledge one another's presence.'

'Huh.' Bea left her hand resting lightly in his.

'You're lucky. I wish I knew who my dad was.'

'Sucks,' said Troy.

'I never said thanks,' said Bea. 'For coming to get me that night.'

Troy squeezed her hand. 'No worries.'

The platypus ducked under the water, leaving concentric rings.

'You all right?' he said.

'Yeah. I'm okay,' she said. 'A lot going on but. Not sure what'll happen with my mum. She might have to sell the house to pay for a lawyer.'

He squeezed again.

'And I have to work out whether I press charges against Gazza.'

'It is a lot,' Troy agreed.

He put his arm over her shoulders. She leaned against him.

He turned and kissed her.

'You're brave, Bea,' he said.

She kissed him back. Her knees felt soft and limp.

Harry and Marge flew home for Dash's funeral, leaving the camper in Western Australia.

'Charlie and I can move into Evie's farmhouse for a week or two,' said Ruth.

Bea stood on the edge of the room feeling like an intruder. She didn't want to live in her mum's house on her own. Ruth had let her bring Rufus with her while her mum was in remand.

It was like Marge could read her thoughts. 'What are you going to do, Bea?' She said it in a nice way, smiling. 'There's plenty of room here, if you want to stay for a while.'

'Would that be okay?' said Bea.

'It would be great. The house has been very empty since the kids moved out.' Marge gave Rufus a pat. 'Rufus gets on well with Buster. He can stay, too.'

64

EVIE

Ten days after

EVIE WANTED PEOPLE TO REMEMBER GOOD DASH. SHE ARRANGED THE funeral Diane wanted for him: one that involved the whole town and a festival of beers at Clive Downs.

She wanted to tell Diane that 'Tears in Heaven' was about a four-year-old child who fell out a window. Not a thirty-seven-year-old man. But why walk over the woman's grief? What would that achieve? Diane's grief was normal. Evie's numb indifference felt like she was committing a crime.

And she missed him. She missed his smile; his capacity to light up a room. But she was also relieved that he was gone; that she was saved the stress and complexity of a big fight in the courts. Two big fights in the courts, if Bea pursued the rape charge.

Dash's death had saved her farm. And that made her feel guilty.

There were even more people at Dash's funeral than had come to her mother's. The footy community from all over the state was there, young muscled men with tight shirts, square jaws and crossed arms.

After, while the men caroused, she wandered down to the paddock to whisper in Jasper's ear about their future together.

She didn't hear Sam approach until he said, 'Hello, Evie.'

She kept her hand on Jasper's neck as she turned. 'Hello, Sam.'

'How're you going? I'm sorry about Dash.'

'I'm okay,' said Evie. 'Just feeling a bit sick.'

She wasn't going to tell him about the baby. Not until she'd had time to think it through. She'd lined up reasons in her mind like soldiers on parade. She certainly didn't want a relationship, much less the entire Dunstan family.

But it just came out. 'I'm pregnant.'

'Aww,' said Sam. 'That's—' He halted. 'Is that great? Is that what you wanted? But sad. With Dash, you know . . .' He trailed off.

'I'm seven weeks pregnant, Sam.'

'Right,' said Sam.

'Which means conception happened five weeks ago.'

Sam nodded. She could tell he was wondering why she was confiding this level of detail to him.

'In Sydney, Sam. Conception happened in Sydney.'

His eyes stilled as comprehension settled over him.

'You mean?'

She nodded.

'Oh, Christ,' he said.

Jasper stamped his back foot to dislodge a march fly.

'What are we going to do?' asked Sam. His arms were jerking. He wanted to hug her.

She stepped forward and wrapped her arms around him. 'I can do it on my own, Sam,' she said in his ear.

'You can't do it on your own. A baby. And you've got the farm.'

'I can. We're going to have to give it time to work out how we handle it. It's very complicated. A lot of people will be affected.'

He sniffed. She checked his face. He was crying. She was, too.

'But you know, it takes a village to raise a child and all that. So I guess it's a good thing that you know. Even though I hadn't intended to tell you yet.'

'I'm glad you told me.'

Jasper shifted on his feet and flicked his tail. The pungent gassy smell of horse wafted over them.

'We'll figure it out. We'll do it together. Somehow or other.'

And he enveloped her again, for a long time.

They returned to the crowd around the campfire. Dusk was falling.

'Eagle Rock' roared out and the blokes gathered around in a group hug and dropped their dacks.

Evie positioned herself beside Rita. 'We need to have a family meeting.'

'Who were you planning to invite?' said Rita.

'The three of us,' said Evie. 'And there's a fourth.' She pointed at her tummy. 'Turns out Dash had a zero sperm count and had failed to tell me. So I wasn't worried when Sam's condom broke.'

Rita stared.

'Are you . . .?'

Evie nodded.

The delight on Rita's face. The joy.

'Sis,' said Rita, as she held out her arms. 'A baby.'

It was a rocking hug that went for a long time.

'Bring Troy over tomorrow night?'

'We'll bring a bottle of red,' said Rita.

'You'll be the only one drinking it.'

'Even better.'

Evie made smashed potatoes and barbecued some eye fillet. The barbecue was Dash's domain, but she was going to have to get used to it.

'I've changed my mind, Rita,' she said when they sat at the dinner table. 'I'm not going to transfer the Bluff to Troy.'

Rita stilled. Her eyes narrowed.

'Troy might want to go to university. There's another child to consider.'

Troy put down his knife and fork. Rita waited.

'I'm thinking something bigger. More inclusive. Futureproof. A family trust. For Troy, the baby and me. It means Troy's options are open, but he'll own a portion of the whole thing. And we can manage the land together.'

Rita lifted her glass and took a slug of wine.

Troy frowned at Evie.

'What do you think, Troy? Can we do this together?'

'Yeah,' he said. 'I reckon we can.'

'And I was thinking that you could move into the farmhouse, if you want it. All of you: Rita, Troy, the kids.'

'Can we take the shutters off?' said Rita.

'No, it's heritage listed.'

It was Rita who started to laugh, and it infected them all.

'That's very generous,' Harry said when she raised it. Everybody would say so.

Generous? Not really.

She would have a partner in the farm. She wanted Troy to go to university. Come back during the holidays and help her. They'd make decisions together.

Joofy decisions. She'd have her brother back.

The Bluff would be protected from the encroachment of the new age.

Forever. Or as long as forever was.

65

RUTH

A few weeks later

SHARON RANG RUTH. 'HEADS UP. OFF THE RECORD. WE'VE INTERVIEWED Gazza. He's not saying much. The prosecutor is lukewarm about the prospects of Gazza being convicted. She's prepared to run it, argue consent was obtained by force when he pushed her head down. It's just that conviction is a long way from certain.'

'Bugger,' said Ruth.

'The cross-examination will be really tough.'

The poor kid. There was a reason why Ruth had stuck with corporate law. To avoid cases like this, feeling the rage about the injustice of it, feeling responsible for a person's life being ruined.

'The video doesn't help?' said Ruth.

'No. He admits that they had sex so the judge probably won't let the jury see it. The prosecutor reckons he won't even give evidence. Leave it to us to prove.'

'What's Gazza doing with himself?' said Ruth.

'Drowning his demons in booze between police counselling sessions,' said Sharon.

Ruth convened a meeting with Bea and Chandra. They sat in the caff on Myddle's main street, at a formica table on plastic chairs, on a bright crisp morning, the rosellas having a high-pitched squawky argument in the silver gums.

Ruth went into lawyer mode, explaining that Gazza might not be convicted if Bea pressed charges.

'So we need to think about your options,' said Chandra.

'You mean he'll get away with it?' said Bea.

'He might,' said Ruth. 'We're more worried about the impact that will have on you: standing up before a jury, going through the details, being cross-examined, and then perhaps having a jury not believe you and letting him go.'

'It can stuff you up,' said Chandra. 'I wouldn't recommend that anyone go through it.'

A green Ford Falcon V8, lovingly restored, chugged past, a tattooed arm cocked out the window.

'Gazza and Dash treated me like I was a thing,' said Bea.

'I know.' Ruth reached out across the table to take her hand.

They sat in silence while the coffees were served, with Bea's lemonade. Half a dozen rosellas flew past in vivid colour to a different gum, where they continued their argument.

Ruth took a sip and leaned forward. 'What would you like to happen Bea? The outcome, I mean.'

'I want him to go to gaol,' said Bea.

'What is it about him being in gaol that would make you feel better?'

Bea stroked the side of her lemonade, and watched the condensed water run down the side. 'He'd be banished from the kingdom. And everyone would know.'

The green Falcon chugged past again on another performative lap of the main street. Half a dozen black cockatoos flew into the gum, to the consternation of the rosellas.

'We might be able to achieve that, without you giving evidence.'

66

GAZZA

A few weeks later

GAZZA WATCHED DASH'S FUNERAL ON ZOOM.

Watching online meant he could cry without embarrassment. And he did: loud, wet sobs pouring out.

'See ya, mate,' he said, raising his stubby. 'Enjoy the footy in the underworld.'

Although, knowing Dash, he would have charmed his way into heaven.

After the funeral, it was the uncertainty that he needed to drown in booze. His whole life was in the hands of a seventeen-year-old girl.

He recalled that night again and again, even when he was drunk. Should he ring her? Say sorry; that Dash assumed; that he assumed.

Nah. Bad idea. He'd say something stupid and the chances of him being convicted would just go up.

Prison. He shuddered as his stomach contracted in fear. He knew what would happen to an ex-copper in there.

His phone didn't ring much these days, so he jumped when it went off a month after Dash's funeral.

Messer.

'What can I do for ya?'

'Bad news, sorry, Gary.'

'What's that?'

'Bea Baulderstone wants to press charges. Sexual assault.'

Gazza's breathing slowed. His mind clicked over, going through what he needed to do.

'You know the drill,' said Messer. 'Can you come in?'

She was offering that as a courtesy, to spare him the surprise raid, the handcuffs and the walk of shame.

'When?'

'You work out a time that suits you and your lawyer. Give us a call.'

'I'll call you back, but can we aim for Tuesday?'

'Sure.'

Gazza pressed the red dot on his phone. It was Wednesday. He had nearly a week.

He got the keys to the shed and opened the roller door. There it was: his rig, the twelve-year-old 4WD ute, with fake territory plates and the roof tent which would be his home from now on.

He'd heard they pay cash on prawn trawlers.

By the time they came looking for him, he'd be lost in the Territory. Forever.

67

RUTH

A few weeks later

THE EUCALYPT BETWEEN THE HOUSE AND THE RIVER RUSTLED AGAINST the picture window in Roscoe's vast living area. The mandala was gone, replaced by the vast pink and blue Emily Kame Kngwarreye, which Roscoe had bought thirty years ago, before its value sky-rocketed.

'Chandra's moving out on the weekend,' said Roscoe.

'I'm sorry,' said Ruth.

'The thing I can't get my head around,' said Roscoe, 'is that we were sitting at the dinner table when she got a call from a girl who'd just been raped, and she didn't ask us to help.'

'I know,' said Ruth. 'That's hard.'

'Because we're men?' said Charlie.

'No,' Ruth said, 'because Roscoe and I are lawyers. She doesn't trust us.'

Roscoe shook his head.

'Not a big surprise,' said Ruth. 'She's still traumatised over the treatment she received from the legal system.'

Roscoe reached for the bottle and filled Charlie and Ruth's glasses.

A car pulled up outside, and four red-headed kids tumbled out of it. 'Patch is happy about it,' said Roscoe.

'Roof!' Milly yelled.

Ruth held out her arms.

Patch organised a debrief at Rita's. They chose Rita's so Rita didn't have to get someone to watch her kids.

It involved wine.

For once, Rita sat down while she had guests. Left the housework alone.

Ruth was early. Got there before Evie and Patch. Rita's little kids were in the backyard playing a complicated game.

Troy appeared, with Bea.

'G'day,' he said.

'Hey,' said Bea.

'You've heard that Gazza was charged but can't be found?' said Ruth. 'Looks like he absconded.'

'Banished?' asked Bea.

'Self-exile,' said Ruth.

Bea smiled.

'I was thinking,' said Ruth, 'if any of you come to Sydney to study or whatever, I've got a big house, if you need somewhere to stay. While you get your bearings.'

She turned to Bea. 'I'll get you a job. In a law firm, if you want. Secretarial, then we'll work from there. Get you into the marketing department. Or uni.'

Ruth hoped she didn't sound desperate. Or bossy. She wanted to make it all better.

'Maybe next year for me,' said Troy. 'Got a bit on.'

He and Rita exchanged a smile.

'I'll come with you to Sydney,' Bea said to Ruth.

She looked at Troy. 'I'll come home on weekends.'

'Rita,' Ruth said.

'Ruth,' said Rita.

'You can do uni remotely you know,' said Ruth. 'On the internet. Come to Sydney for intensive weekends.'

Rita's eyes brightened.

'And you could stay with me,' Ruth continued, 'when you come down. I'd help. With the assignments . . .' She paused and added, 'I'm quite smart.' She rolled her eyes. 'Some people think so anyway.'

Ruth went to Brisbane for a week because Charlie needed to be there to finish his paper.

They hung out in an easy daily rhythm: coffee first thing, then breakfast, then Charlie did some writing or went to a meeting while Ruth had lunch with pals, then reunion at dinner, then bed. A lot of bed.

'Haven't had this much sex since I was on my honeymoon,' observed Ruth over the morning coffee.

'I thought you didn't have a honeymoon,' said Charlie. 'You keep saying you and Bill never married.'

'True. If you want to be technical about it. We did go on a holiday to Fiji after we decided to move in together.'

Ruth was absorbed back into her book. Charlie crossed his arms and stood to look at the view of the river from the sliding glass door. From there, Charlie said, 'What are you going to do now?'

Ruth looked at her watch. She wasn't going to do anything, except read a book.

'Next?' he said.

Oh. He was looking for some sort of plan for the future. 'I'm going back to Sydney to get a real job.'

There was a hiatus while Ruth turned a page of her book.

Charlie remained at the sliding glass door, studying the view.

'I think I'll go back to Sydney, too,' he said.

'Good,' said Ruth, still reading.

'Let's move in together,' said Charlie.

Unexpected. Was that some kind of proposal of not-marriage?

His brow was furrowed. His attempt at a grin was shaky. He swallowed.

He was nervous.

She smiled. Actually, as an idea, it felt good. Quite good.

And if it turned to shit, it was reversible.

'Okay,' said Ruth. 'Let's.'

Charlie moved towards her. She put the bookmark in the book and closed it.

'The only thing is,' she said, 'full disclosure—I've promised half of Myddle a bed when they're in Sydney, so it might be a bit crowded.'

'Oh, well,' said Charlie, 'we'll have to get a big house.'

68

EVIE

Three months later

TWO AM. HORACE'S MUM WAS CALVING, WITH TWO MIDWIVES: A BOVINE one who stood guard, and Evie.

A low moo, and Horace's full brother spurted out, wet and slimy.

Horace's mum licked the white gunk off him. On unsteady legs, he stood and hobbled over to search for a nipple.

Evie gave the mum some grain and molasses, and walked back to the house in the moonlight. She'd put Horace's mum in the home paddock a week ago, in anticipation of tonight.

Evie was too excited to sleep. She made a cup of tea, and sat on the deck in the squatter's chair, the Milky Way suspended above her. The baby kicked and rolled. With her hand she traced the outline of something hard on her tummy: was it a tiny bum? A knee? An elbow? She couldn't tell.

The house was empty without Dash. She felt his absence: his ebullient enthusiasm when the footy was on the TV; his insistence that people come over for beers. If he was here, he'd get up, crack a beer, and join her out there. 'Is he a good one?' he'd ask.

'I think he is a good one. I think he might be better than Horace.'

How could she know, though, a calf half an hour old, on rickety legs? It was wishful thinking.

She'd have two babies. Canute, the new calf, and this one inside her.

She would coach Troy while he trained a prize bull.

Good job, Evie. Good job.

'Sorry things didn't work out with Roscoe,' said Evie.

Chandra shrugged. 'He's such a lawyer. It was probably never going to work. Good while it lasted, I guess. You need to hold your core and breathe while you lift your legs.'

'How're the plans for the retreat in Azuri?'

'Getting there. I'm talking to the guesthouse on the hill. They're keen. Gently. Don't want to put your pelvic floor under too much strain.'

'I'm more worried that my pelvic floor is so well developed it won't let this baby out.'

'Nah,' said Chandra. 'You'll be fine.'

Evie's belly undulated as the baby turned.

'Woah, little fella,' said Chandra, putting her hand on Evie's tummy.

'Two things I've been wondering,' said Evie.

'What's that?'

'When you got out of my ute that day at the farm gate. With Dash.'

'Hmm,' said Chandra.

'How did you keep your running shoes so white? Why was there no blood on them?'

'I was very careful where I put my feet,' said Chandra. 'That's a strange thing to wonder about.'

'Was he dead when you got to him?'

Chandra put her hand on Evie's knee.

'What are you asking?'

'I'm asking if you killed him while I turned the car around.'

'How would I have done that?' Chandra asked.

'I'm thinking suffocation.'

Chandra smiled. 'For the next movement,' she said, 'I want you to lift your arms above your head.'

Evie never went back to Chandra.

Yoga wasn't her thing.

ACKNOWLEDGEMENTS

I GREW UP ON A FARM NEAR A SMALL TOWN, BUT IT WAS A VERY LONG time ago, and had to refresh and verify my recollections. Thank you to the farmers I spoke to, particularly Kylie Schooley and James Davy, who chats to his cows, all of whom are named Gertrude, and always wears blunnies on the farm, even on hot days.

For several decades I was what one of my editors described as a 'fancy city lawyer', which basically means I don't know any exciting law. (It turns out bending development contracts into a tension-filled plot was beyond my skills as a writer. Strange: it was so full of drama when I did it every day.)

Thank you to the lawyers who filled in the substantial gaps in my understanding of criminal and family law: Anne Rees, Peter Callaghan, Cathy Muir, Terry Fisher. It was all illuminating and some of it was gobsmacking.

I should say in relation to all of the expert advice I received, none of them have read the manuscript. Any errors are my own.

To the people who read early drafts—Michael Watts, Russell Lake, Elizabeth Musgrave, Susan Bryant, Jacinta Koch, Judy Davis (no, not that one)—you were very patient with me. It's not easy being a beta reader, and you accomplished it with skill and tact. Russell sat opposite me at my kitchen table saying in tones of incredulity, 'And then she's in the shower unconscious with a bone sticking out of her leg and he doesn't call an ambulance.' (When you put it like that . . . I placed the bone back in the leg.)

A big shout out to Poppy Gee, a legend of the Brisbane writing community, who selflessly provided detailed and encouraging feedback.

Thanks to Jeff Sneddon, for his understanding of what happens to mobile phone records and what records are kept of, if any, wi-fi calls. And to Graham Davis for his expertise on spotting platypus during the day while wading up a river.

Editors are mind-bogglingly talented people. Thank you to Jane Palfreyman for having the faith that the manuscript she acquired would morph into something better; to Deonie Fiford for the terrific copy edit; to Rebecca Starford whose editorial report caused me to change both victim and perpetrator; to Dannielle Viera for picking up the continuity issues in the proofread; and to Myra Tyne for the lovely and helpful sensitivity read.

To Gaby Naher my agent, thanks for backing me.

Getting a book into the world is a team effort, and the writer is just one member of it. Thank you to the team I've been privileged to be a part of, particularly Jane Palfreyman, Annette Barlow, Christa Munns and Jenn Thurgate. To Isabelle, Odette and Deb who were instrumental in birthing my first book, thank you for your assistance with this one.

And thanks to Christa Moffitt for the cover.

Thanks to all the people I grew up with in the country town in Queensland, my myriad rural relations, and all the wonderful blokes I know who were the inspiration for Troy.

Thank you to the Catherines (Kenny and Millar) for a number of reasons, but mostly for being fabulous.

Thank you to the Freeburn men: Paul, Douglas, Max and Jim. You sustain me, and your jokes are unfailingly hilarious.

One advantage to starting a writing career late is that there is a lot of life experience to unpack. So lastly, thank you to my sister Judith, with me the only one left from that family on the farm; to my mother Jennifer and brother Andrew; and the gentle soul, my father, who every night studied the stars which, in the country, are bright in the heavens.